MOMENTARY PLEASURES

Short Stories

(2014–22)

Phillip Derone

Published by Hybrid Publishers

Melbourne Victoria Australia

© Phillip Derone 2022

This publication is copyright. Apart from any use as permitted under the Copyright Act 1968, no part may be reproduced by any process without prior written permission from the publisher. Requests and enquiries concerning reproduction should be addressed to the Publisher, Hybrid Publishers, PO Box 52, Ormond VIC Australia 3204.

www.hybridpublishers.com.au

First published 2022

Cover design, typesetting and layout: Bruce Welch

ISBN 978-1-922768-10-0

for John Cleverley

CONTENTS

One Dab at a Time

I looked at the grass passing below me. A scruffy affair, parched by the droughty summer, struggling manfully in its inhospitable home, half gravel, half dust, yet surviving on this tenacious verge of life's interminable bustle, an endless ribbon of hope.

Life sucks, I thought as I trudged. Like a lemon, it needs a dash of vodka to make it palatable. You want to dive into it but all you achieve is a belly buster. It's like a big new jar of Vegemite. You bring it home all shiny and pristine, open it up with a placental pop and marvel at its smooth, glossy virginal surface, pure coal-black.

I took a deep breath. Partly to brace myself for the shock I could hear approaching, and partly to get some fresh air before the onslaught of exhaust fumes that would inevitably follow. I scrambled down the embankment to escape the worst. Nobody would stop for me here. Even if they felt guilt-ridden by their callousness, or felt charitable, or felt like some company, stopping and getting going again was not worth the gain, whatever that might turn out to be, if any. And it required a decision to be made quickly when decisions were the last thing on the mind of someone in various states of forced meditation or chosen distractions.

When you push your knife tentatively into that silken black sheen for the first time you never wonder just how it might end.

That defloration leaves its pitted mark and makes it easy for the next assault, and the one that follows even more so, and so it goes. Such petty picking at the initial layer leads eventually to depths where chipping away becomes inconsequential and mindless. Each day just a smidgeon more, each day a taste of what life has to offer, just much of the same. All those breakfasts, lunches and dinners. But like any icon it is really a fraud, a crutch, a diversion. Something to get us through. They had to add the vitamins to Vegemite, the ones they claimed were there naturally, once it was discovered they weren't in it at all. Life needs its additives too, to stay bearable.

Then one day your knife suddenly is scraping the glass at the bottom. You see light coming through all those commingled pigments which make up the blackness that has been sucking out your life for so long. It's the first glimmer of the end, the realisation that the Vegemite will not last forever. And so you begin to scrape, and scrape. What had been so abundant and without any hint of running out, though on reflection that should have seemed inevitable being as it was contained in a solid glass jar, was now clearly coming to an end. More and more light appears, knife tinkles on glass. A last swipe with your finger, an apron of smudge as legacy of what once was, and it's over.

The onslaught passed, I regained my composure and my footing, scrambled back up the embankment, prepared for the next one, and continued to push the world back behind me as I plodded, one step at a time.

Birthday Buoys

Warning: Brush up your Shakespeare!

Henry Kingsman could not recall exactly when he had first realised that his birthday was the same as William Shakespeare's, though it was definitely when he was still a mere boy. He had certainly been introduced to Shakespeare, the author, well before that and had already been won over as an incipient devotee. So, when he did make the connection between a private passion and sharing something very intimate and unique with the most brilliant exponent of the English language who had ever scribbled on a scroll, he was thoroughly and immediately bedazzled. This appreciation of genius grew into an adulation over the years and formed the underpinning of Henry Kingsman's whole existence.

He had very fuzzy first memories of participating in an end-of-year school play, at age around nine he thought. It was Romeo and Juliet, appropriately expurgated he imagined, looking back from the perspective of his adult insights into its steamy sexual allusions, and he may have even been cast as Romeo. He remembered feeling totally silly in his period thespian outfit and being in a constant state of fear of having to deal with those strange human creatures known as girls. They were so unlike his own kind, especially as his background was as an only-child, and hence lacking female siblings. Nevertheless, there was a strange excitement involved in it all: the make-believe aspects, some powerful mystique in the uttering and re-uttering of those magical sounds called words, and the fact that certain of those girl creatures looked and acted in such a way that aroused anxious but pleasant feelings in him, feelings that he was quite unfamiliar with till then.

Once into secondary school, and with Shakespeare on the syllabus, Henry found he was more in his element. Unlike for most in his cohort, the plays and the poetry struck some special chord with him and he threw himself into the rapture of their world. English became his favourite subject and his favourite class, and he became their star student as he gradually comprehended and memorised more and more of the wondrous ideas and lines he was discovering. He found the library to be an especially agreeable ambience and enjoyed spending time there amongst a universe of words. He suffered some bullying for his behaviour and beliefs, being what these days would be referred to as a nerd, but he was always capable of defending himself above the punching weight of his puny physical form, using those very same words he had come to cherish, to devastating effect. While he remained the object of much derision through the years, the power of those words he commanded continued to ensure he was always treated with respectful caution by enemies, real and potential.

One day in his youth, perhaps when he was around 14, after lengthy consideration of the financial burden it would entail, he purchased a second-hand copy of the *Complete Works* which he had been sizing up in a second-hand bookshop, another one of his favourite milieu. After he had nervously handed over the hard-won and laboriously accumulated cash, all in the smallest denomination note of the time so it looked impressively bulky, and with the thick one-volume hardcover held tightly in his grasp, he raced home filled with excitement over simply possessing such a treasure, and for the endless hours of pleasure it promised. He shut himself up in his bedroom, sat at his little desk, pricked his finger tips one by one with a needle and, dipping a nib into the droplets of blood, scrawled his name and his *ex libris* painstakingly onto the front flyleaf, letter by letter, finger by finger. He learnt from this exercise that self-sacrifice for one's passion was paradoxically highly satisfying, but also that there were more suitable, and less debilitating, places to prick on the body in order to extract one's own blood.

This ardent identification early on with his hero deepened even further in a very personal way through his reading of that *Complete Works* once Henry discovered that a large number of the plays actually bore his name; seven in fact, out of the thirty-seven or so that constituted the oeuvre. It became such a close and special bonding that he felt at times that he might well be William Shakespeare reincarnated. At school, at that certain age and being boys, he enjoyed the kudos that came his way from his fellows when he explained the lewd pieces: the "die" and "nothing" metaphors, or heads-in-laps moments, and puns about essential bodily functions. Later, as he grew into adulthood, he took every chance to go and see productions of any of the plays, he read as much as he could about Shakespeare and his work by the legion of critics and academics that had already amassed and was still proliferating as time went by, loved reciting the sonnets to himself and learnt most of the best lines off by heart.

On his first trip overseas, to England naturally, he made sure he tracked down all the landmarks from the vicarious explorations of his youth. In London, following, he hoped, the footsteps of the Master through the city, he floated from Blackfriars to Bishopsgate Street to Cripplegate and by ferry across the Thames to Southbank, entranced all the while by the ambience and what his imagination was doing with it. The Globe not as yet having been reconstructed, he took in as many of the revered dramatist's plays he could find, wherever he could find them, feeling that seeing them there in that authentic setting was as close as he could get to the real thing.

He ensured that a visit to Stratford-upon-Avon was a highlight, making the journey through what he considered an unsettlingly unnatural spring countryside on the day the Bard's, and of course his own, birthday was celebrated. A journalist from *The Times*, there to report on the festivities, interviewed him by sheer coincidence - or perhaps not, as it later occurred to him when in a more spiritual frame of mind - and asked for his favourite play. He answered firmly and without hesitation *Macbeth*, although he knew it was not the popular choice, quoting from it some lines he had long roted, the most despairing words ever penned about life and the unmitigated pointlessness of it. "It may appear in tomorrow's edition," she told him, and he had chuckled at the irony, but did not bother to try to explain it to her. Nor was it in there on the morrow.

At an early stage it seemed obvious to him and to others, especially his long-time friends who knew and understood his obsession, both indulging him and ribbing him for it, that he would choose something like librarianship as his career path, and he did. The profession provided him with everything he needed in a working life to suit his personality and interests: its surroundings, security, serenity, income, steady progression in seniority and status, access to increasingly sophisticated technology for researching and enjoying his favourite author, not to mention that most of his colleagues were women and there was a regular progression of often starry-eyed female clients seeking intellectual awakening, which Henry was always more than willing to help provide. He augmented what he considered to be his innate appeal by beginning to take on some of Shakespeare's assumed looks and manners. He adopted a slightly foppish style, an affected accent, grew his hair long and pulled back in an effort to simulate William's frontal dome and for a time tried a trimmed goatee with moustache. Fortunately this period did not last long, partly because he was not balding and partly because he realised he was making a bit of an idiot of himself. In any case he decided the important connections were internal and naturally endowed so there was no need to pursue the superficial.

He did often consider taking up acting so that he would have the opportunity to declaim those wonderful words publicly and be applauded for it, but he was not an extrovert and was never able to make the commitment, even as an amateur. On the other hand, he made sure he acquired any new film versions of the plays and built up a considerable library of, first videotapes, and then DVD copies - there were hundreds of them to seek out. He loved popular adaptations of them as well, especially musicals like *West Side Story* and Cole Porter's *Kiss Me Kate*, and the songs they produced - *Brush Up Your Shakespeare* stood out, as bawdy and ingenious as the Bard's own work. And who could not be tickled by the contortioned rhyming of 'Cleopatra' with 'flatter 'er'. He immediately recognised the Shakespearian association with *My Private Idaho* when he first saw it. Being based as it was on the *Henrys,* Henry especially identified with it and though he was not quite so keen on how the director had handled the main character, whose sexual proclivity he certainly could not identify with, this did not undermine its appeal as a further example of due homage.

There was one particular film, however, that he detested and would not watch, let alone have in his collection. *Anonymous* it was and in anonymity, or in ignominy, he believed is where it should ever have remained, or something along those lines. The contention that the works of Shakespeare had been authored by others, or another, was anathema to him, an abomination, and he would brook no discussion on the subject. Friends in his salad days of university would taunt him about it. They compared the authorship of the canon to Henry's well-known views on the nature of God. He believed that it did not really matter to define what God was, that God could simply be an amalgam of all and any of the concepts available to explain the mystery; the main thing was what followed. He was vaguely disturbed by a certain logical process in the argument that connected Shakespeare and such a composite God, but nevertheless found comfort in the comparison.

The main contender in this charade of spin and fable was the wastrel Edward de Vere, an Earl of Oxford and arch-villain, whose name he refused to even speak and which he made every effort to expunge from his memory. It seemed to him to be just so much a product of the fashionable tall-poppy syndrome that pervaded contemporary life, the fascination of shallow minds with conspiracy theories which had burgeoned in the fertile soil of the ten-second grab and equally superficial social media, and the fraudulent nature of popular culture generally that had usurped a much more solid and stable world. He was, after all, like Will, a Taurean.

Almost nothing would shake the unwavering loyalty he had to his co-mate. Even when he learnt about Baret's *Alvearie* and the allegations of a minor plagiarism by his idol - no more than a mere dipping into the lexical honeypot - he remained faithful. Why would a writer not resort to any available resource to achieve their artistic goals, and in this case such glorious ones, just as they do today with infinitely greater means? Still, Henry's image of the poet sitting by candlelight dashing off with his quill pen all those extraordinary lines of native wit straight from his head was smudged a smidgen. Even then, though, it managed to bring him closer to William by giving him a human profile, with flaws along with all that emotion, behaviour and ability, just like every mortal, including him, Henry.

He had begun writing just for his own amusement quite early on, and often tried to parrot the master's style. He signed some of his lesser, whimsical works as 'Will-I-Am', with perhaps an undercurrent of Freudian slippage. When he experienced his first serious adolescent romantic murmuring of the heart he presented to the object of his fond desire an example of his early sonnet insinuations, this one being a reply to the questionable acuity of the inner eyesight of both Romeo and Juliet. He was very proud of it. It is preserved as part of his opus which he, eventually, placed on the internet for all to freely access, and reproduced here from that source. It was titled 'To a Noble Brow' and went:

No, love's not blind
Yet others cannot see
What lovers' eyes behold: each other.
Sweet lips, bright eyes,
What features come to mind
When you're not near? None!
Still, a silent face may smile
And I see you once again
Through love's eyes.
Lovers hear,
But hear beyond the senses of the ear;
Sweet words, heard with the heart
Felt by every bone and nerve
Then sent back, in imitation, with love's voice.

While its meter was reasonably sound, and it included a tenable conceit and some acceptable if overblown poetic devices, his mastery of the sonnet form was still critically lacking. But, ever more sadly for Henry, it did not have the effect he had hoped for, though it did have a very Elizabethan one: that of the unrequited, courtly-love variety. He relied on more conventional and urbane methods of allurement henceforth, including genuine poetic references, with greater success. When he finally married it was with some mixed feelings, as she was not an Anne, nor pregnant, nor considerably older, though his dedication to his birthdaysake was not so compelling as to overwhelm him in all regards, not at that stage anyway.

He was pleased when each of his girls came along and he was able to sneak naming them Katherina, Beatrice and Miranda past his wife's defences, or so she let him believe. These were the female characters he admired most for their undaunted mettle and hot-blooded intelligence and whose names he hoped might transfer those qualities to his own progeny. He preferred this to calling them after Will's two daughters, Susanna and Judith, on the grounds that they were a little mundane, little was known of them as people and, well, this copycat business could perhaps be taken too far. He was, nonetheless, disappointed not to manage a Cordelia or Portia, two more of his favourites, or have a pretext to be father to a Hamnet, despite its poor prognosis, and so the latter probably for the best.

Over time he extended his writing from poems and theatrical drama pieces, a mix of comedies and tragedies, often based on historical figures - he had many more tragic subjects to draw upon than Shakespeare had - into rap and hip-hop music and scripts for television series and full-length films. He considered that, had Shakespeare lived in the present day, any and all these might be the style of work he could well have been creating, along with serious theatre, and would be the way for him to make his mark and his fortune in the modern world.

Though he tentatively circulated some of his work, mainly but not only amongst friends, nothing of Henry's efforts was ever picked up by producers or publishers. The truth was in reality he lacked any vaulting ambition and was a little loath to expose his output for fear of rejection. This would in turn have ruined the notion he had of the tenuous association, given Shakespeare's unbridled contemporary success. Not that this analysis of his reluctance crossed his mind. However, he wasn't so backward in his various private circles, and at any opportunity, especially around the annual time of his birthday, he would loudly and widely proclaim the significance of the date. Though this never seemed to make much impact on his friends in the way of flattering comparisons, which was a disappointment to him, it continued to provide great sustenance for his otherwise rather inconsequential existence.

At one point he plunged into studying astrology and numerology and was always keen to unearth which characteristics of Taurus he might share with his fellow bull. This proved to be not at all difficult. If he had searched further he would just as assuredly have found similarities in most astrological directions, it being of infinite flexibility, not unlike the heavens themselves. So he was well satisfied with what he found. He was mildly chuffed when the contemporary Prince of Denmark married an Australian. There was both affinity and affirmation in that for him.

His love of language had caused him to study Latin at school which later devolved into an affection for Spanish. Through this he found to his amazement that the illustrious Spanish writer, Miguel de Cervantes, had also died on the very same date as Shakespeare had died. When that day, April the 23rd, was promoted, first by the Spanish and then by UNESCO, as World Book Day, he felt he owned some complicity in its conception. Curious it was though that the British did not follow suit, they believing that the Easter holiday period might clash with it. Such a pedestrian approach to what was their true glory, he thought. No such slight however could blight his vision of this global and spiritual poetic harmony to which he believed he was in many ways central.

One day, when he was well past his middle age and life had moved into the internet and iPhone era, he was doing some casual surfing on the web as a diversion from his workaday world and came across a brief reference to calendars, Julian and Gregorian. There were vague echoes channelling down his recollection tunnel of the words, probably no more than a conflation with famous names, past and present, or with chanting. In any case he was always easily seduced by history and science of all types, so he dallied. And while the basics of the story were clear enough to him, they only lodged in his memory bank as seeds in hibernation ready to burst forth at some later propitious, or possibly inopportune, occasion, and did not germinate then. As he newly understood the position, calendars were not rigid things, but errant and constructed to purpose, whereas he had always assumed they were born of some natural law. The original flawed calendar, which had operated since Roman times, since Julius Caesar in fact hence the name Julian, had turned slowly awry, placing the seasons out of joint with the dates. These were slipping behind, or more accurately, linguistically speaking, leaping backwards, since the cause of it was those leap years. Easter was sliding towards winter, heatwaves might strike during northern Christmas. It was creeping artificial climate change, medieval style. The Church could not allow it. So the Church, as Pope Gregory, set it right, as a Pope could, hence the name Gregorian, more than just a chant. Leaping years were reined in, still restricted to one in four, but with the proviso and exception of any round centuries, like 1700, unless it could be divided by four hundred, a proviso and exception to the exception. The year 1600, for example, and then again 2000, both of which took the great leap forward. It meant re-setting the calendar when the change was implemented, just as with the summer time change each year when we lose, or gain, an hour. In the Gregorian case at that time, however, it was a loss of a full ten days, never to be regained. The new date was dubbed 'New Style', or 'N.S.', as opposed to 'Old Style', or 'O.S.', but these tags faded out of common use quite quickly as the distinction was lost in the steamy haze of evaporating months and years.

These were all concepts that Henry had difficulty digesting fully, but there was also an element of denial in his reaction. It seemed that this restructuring was taking place manifestly during Shakespeare's lifetime so there may have been implications in his case, but the matter was never pursued, either by Henry nor apparently by anyone else. In truth it was even more complicated than Henry realised. The reforms were brought in piecemeal, indeed during William's lifetime, first in Catholic Europe, and therefore applying to Cervantes in Spain, but not in Protestant Elizabethan England. That had to wait another one hundred and seventy years, by which time it required eleven days to plug the gap, there being no stopping the inexorable march of time.

The years continued to turn over at their petty, though seemingly quickening, pace. One birthday followed another until Henry found himself increasingly confronted by his mortality as an inevitability, rather than as a youthful speculation, or as a middle-aged elusion. His lifelong affiliation with Shakespeare's life and the presumed parallelism with his own led him to at first suspect, then fear, then desire, then crave that he, Henry, too might die on the same day as he was born, as he knew William had, and likewise on the same date as William had. As each year rolled around with that looming date these emotions became more and more entangled in his mind so that his anxiety over his actions on the day, as each one approached, became increasingly intense.

His original thinking that he would simply be struck down by natural causes as a fitting finale, though highly unlikely unless there were truly some cosmic connection, shifted into more manipulable territory whereby he would arrange and therefore ensure his correct departure. Of course he had no need to research the possibilities: his knowledge of Shakespearean drama was by then as complete as necessary. This was straightforward statistics. He typically knew such key facts as how many words William had used, how many he had used only once, which ones he had concocted, the longest play, the dates of first productions, the dramatis personae, even trivia like his not using any words beginning with an 'x'.

So Henry certainly was aware that there had been seventy-four scripted deaths, mostly stabbings, and including suicides. He became progressively obsessed by this notion, contemplating whether he would be capable of stabbing himself to death - could he take such a hell of pain? Or of swallowing poison - one without too much agony associated with it. Or hanging, or drowning himself. He shuddered at the thought of being bitten by a snake, though there were more than sufficient numbers of them in his homeland to do that job sublimely well, and beheading was quite obviously out. So too was one sure-fire method, that of gunshot. He would never contemplate such an un-Shakespearean practice. Though it had become a common technique in the modernised adaptations of so many of the plays, and he admired the imaginative creativity otherwise involved in them, he frowned upon its deviation from authenticity. Likewise, arranging to have himself murdered, though murder or assassination might seem to be very appropriate given its involvement in so many of the plays, would unfairly involve another otherwise innocent party in a seriously illegal act.

He did, however, warm to the idea that the hubris which was gradually enveloping him in this planning might be the cause of his death, along the lines of Enorbarbus dying of shame in *Antony and Cleopatra,* or King Lear from grief. But what of the crucial timing? That was the rub. In a similar manner, attempting to sleep-no-more yourself to death, the curse of Macbeth and his Lady, might prove a relatively painless method if successful, at least physically, but it would be drawn-out and might miss the all-important birthday cue. In any respect, its direction and consequences were too uncertain. No, any planned final exit would have to be exceptionally disciplined and carefully programmed.

The four-hundredth anniversary of the renowned wordsmith's death was approaching, as was Henry's sixty-sixth birthday. He concluded that this should be the occasion of his grand conclusion. He secretly made the necessary preparations and put all his affairs in order. He left more than sufficient funds to provide against what he considered the inherent frailty of his four dearest, and to set up a scholarship for budding young playwrights. In a moment of quirky sentimentality he considered specifically bequeathing the conjugal bed to his wife, as William had done, but given the eccentricity of such a deed and the mysterious nature of the original act, he did not go through with it.

He finalised uploading his own complete works to an internet site. He sent out invitations to all his friends and to a select few of his relatives, booked a large room at the nearby Tudor Hotel, and ordered the catering for a banquet. He carefully planned the affair, and particularly his finale. Everything went smoothly: the night was boisterous, with lots of cheer, and was well fuelled and lubricated by beer and wine. As the large birthday cake, adorned with its centrepiece of four mock-quill rockets spinning a catherine wheel surrounded by sixty-six candles each encircled by six sparklers, was trundled in to much singing, stomping and best-wishing, Henry, fairly tipsy, leapt up, reversed his chair, stepped up onto its seat and put one foot upon its back in oratorical style. Waving his arms around above his head he launched into the great Hamlet soliloquy.

Almost immediately, just as the "not" issued from his mouth and became an elongated "ahhhh", the chair teetered and he toppled forward, kicking the bucket of ice and champagne off the end of the table with his splaying legs as he splattered face-first into the birthday cake, the carving knife which was resting next to it and tilted upwards on the plate somehow piercing him straight through the heart, killing him instantly. It was not as he had planned, but it was effective, and dramatic, and as everyone repeated over and over, so tragic, while all were privately unable to resist a guilty giggle at its histrionic, comedic touch.

So, alas, a few days later, poor Henry joined Yorick in silent subterranean rest, with a headstone marked as he always dreamt it would be: 'Born 23rd April - Died 23rd April'. The famous inscription followed: 'Blessed be those that spare these stones, And cursed be any that move my bones'.

But what Henry did not live long enough to shockingly reveal to himself, had he delved further, was that while Miguel de

Cervantes did indeed die on his birthday and now deathday, the twenty-third day of well-apparelled April, Catholic Spain having converted by then, William Shakespeare did not. He died eleven days later, on the fourth day of the merry month of May, England having maintained the Julian faith. Nor was it the same day as the day he had been born on. He died in 1616, and 1600 had been a special leap year adding another day to the hypothetical switchover. So his official birthday in 1564 was our third day of that same month of pride and pomp, May, these days and dates floating around at the mercy of some tide of time, like buoys, tethered to a solid foundation, but still permitted a certain fluid freedom.

The best that could be claimed by Henry is that they shared an astrological home. But most happily for Henry, surely the bardolater without peer, what he never discovered was that when he, Henry Kingsman, was opening his eyes to the light of an early day for the first time that twenty-third of April N.S. in the wandering antipodes, at the very same moment, though late at night the previous day, north of London on the other side of a slowly rotating world, Edward de Vere, seventeenth Earl of Oxford, clandestine pretender to the Shakespearean domain, was also just coming into the same world, exactly four hundred years before: the very span of time the new-fangled Gregorian calendar had instigated as its o'erleaping exception to its exceptional proviso.

Whether dead Henry will ever find such historically disturbing cause to turn in that antipodean grave beneath the headstone of local Triassic Yellowblock, with its neat verbal and numeric bookends and intimidating Shakespearian inscriptions, and thereby move his own bones, must forever remain a matter for conjecture, or of time to tell.

A Christmas White-Out

Jingle bells, jingle bloody bells, jingle all bloody day everywhere you go. Or everywhere you pay. Sophie clutched her store bags and rushed to the exit, bumping her way through the madding throng to escape the incessant musical battering from Christmas carols and cheery seasonal pop songs. Christmas was still weeks away but the celebrations had already been going for weeks. Celebration of what? Celebration of a bumper crop of sales figures, she answered herself.

So much for snow and sleighs, she thought, stepping out into the sizzling heat of a southern summer. She headed for home trying to avoid clicking her heels on the pavement to the rhythm of that damnable tune she was carrying in her head. She focused elsewhere. At home she would kick off the heels, pour herself a cold glass of Prosecco, flop onto the sofa and pull out all those delights she'd bought for herself. She'd have herself a merry little pre-Christmas. Retail therapy followed by a consumption massage would chase all her troubles out of sight.

She waited in the oppressive hot heaviness of the underground station and then hustled her way onto the train, clinging to a handrail, unable to sit anywhere in the carriage crowded with commuters and tourists and day-trippers and aged pensioners using their cheap travel entitlements to go somewhere, anywhere. There were no conversations to overhear and understand and possibly be amused by as nobody was speaking English. Conversations as there were were one-sided in any case, animated and oblivious of others around them, though most of her fellow travellers were silent and head-down, glued to their little glowing screens, or blank-faced, eyes staring into space, earbuds in place, thin umbilical cords connecting them to some virtual world somewhere where only they existed. She wanted to scream at them. "Come back, get real, talk nonsense if that's all you can manage, watch the scenery even if it is industrial carnage, smell the roses even if it is only diesel fumes or body odour".

Sophie bustled herself off the train at her station then dodged the oncoming mob of workers heading home and clicked through the mall and along the footpath to her door. She got herself inside, dumped her load, dropped onto the sofa, pulled off her shoes and thought about getting up again to pour that bubbly revival she'd promised herself but couldn't raise the effort. She felt relieved enough just to be out of the mess.

A buzz came from the front door. With a resigned sigh she pulled herself up and went to answer. It was a mail courier holding a box. A signature and a thank you and she shut the door and carried the box back to the sofa. Inside was another box, wrapped in fancy paper and with a ribbon and bow neatly tied around it. She tugged on the bow, released the ribbon, unfolded the wrapping and lifted the lid. She peered in to find a posy of dark-green holly and red berries.

In the middle was a card that read: 'Have a wonderful Christmas, Mum. We miss you'.

She broke down and sobbed.

The Bottomless Graveyard

Peter felt the clunk of the hookup, clicked a few keys and heard the hiss of decompression. Another couple of nifty finger taps, more clinks and clanks and whirrs and the trademarked 'coffsule' rolled through the opening double doors, just like through dangly curtain strips into a cremation chamber, or through pearly gates into a bright, misty, empty landscape.

The rich paid squillions for this privilege of what was dubbed a space burial. Peter often wondered whether it was possible to be buried in a void. Or entombed by nothing, interred in a vacuum. 'Take the journey of your everlasting life' was the promotional line. With his experience in the industry, his good health and psychological profile he'd landed the lucrative job and, after specialised training, was doing his six-month stint at the station. They were only allowed such short periods due to the mental stresses involved, mostly boredom and depression. The others on the station were all specialist scientists involved in highly technical work. They were polite to him, but he felt their condescension. He could take that for the six months, given the remuneration. And if anyone did happen to die while aboard they were offered a free space burial à-la-coffsule, and he would get to do the honours. Unless, of course, it was him.

Peter tapped some more keys, and screens came to life: a diverse crowd of what he confidently assumed were family, friends and a celebrant gathered to remotely wave off their dearly beloved. These groups all looked very much the same to him. On another screen was an image of the coffsule resting nearby, the high-tech kevlar-carbon-fibre hermetic model prescribed for the task, capable of withstanding most extremes of the odyssey: temperature, pressure, time, radiation, maybe the odd minor collision. But then, Peter thought, who would know, who would care? Plus a little reinforced window onto the face of the departed so, Peter assumed, the congregation could see it for one last time, and be sure it was their loved one being launched. Or perhaps so the deceased could look out if they by some miracle returned to life.

The congregation stared up at their giant screen. The celebrant intoned.

"In the name of the Father, the Son …"

Peter chuckled, the Sun, more likely.

"Thy will be done …"

Whatever a 'thy' might be. Peter had carried this mystery over from his childhood naivety.

He looked out the porthole. Earth was coming into view, floating, of sorts, under him in the blackness. There was no real distinction between Heaven and Earth from up here. Was not Earth just a part of the whole, held in some universal clutch?

Unseen by the cameras Peter went through the necessary checks of the coffsule together with the documents supplied. The ceremony on Earth came to a conclusion with a hymn, Grace with her infinite vision and sublime voice leading them all home. To an eternal grave of amazing emptiness apparently.

Peter sent the coffsule off on its way with a slight shove and a few deft finger flicks on his keyboard, its copper shingle inscribed with the passenger's name and basic personal information, some banal half-true poetic thought, like 'Forever Remembered', plus the official registry reference number -

PMDUR#23041947121120 52/0725, the latter a combination of his birthdate and death-time by the Christian era calendar, the letters standing for 'Permanent Mortal Disposal Universe Registration' - just in case it turned up one day on somebody's doorstep and needed identifying, Peter sneered each time he sent one off. Then, with a few more taps he cut the connection to Earth.

He watched out a porthole as the coffsule silently whirled without end into the un-ness, carrying its human-remains cargo, both quick and dead, towards its personal Judgment Day.

Bet Your Bottom Dollar

Dying was the last thing Howard Grading wanted to do. Yet he was beginning to accept, reluctantly but ineluctably, that in this non-endeavour he would ultimately succeed. He wasn't actually ill with anything terminal, and his life had reached a stage which could best be described as, well, acceptable, satisfying in a dull, consummated way. But it was clearly dawning on him that he was definitely dying, or more accurately, going to die.

He had certainly reached, or rather attained, the age of aches and fading faculties. He found he was still quite adept at focusing on one subject, but holding two in mind at once was a capacity which increasingly deserted him. He would even admit to an occasional, very occasional, doddery moment. He liked to refer humorously to what he called his growing pains, and his 20/20 inner vision. He boasted that as he had continued to improve with age he had less and less need for his long beauty sleep each night, so central to his good looks over the years. Friends would no doubt say he had become set in his ways, but from his viewpoint it was all about what he knew he was, and was not, comfortable with. What purpose could be served by testing new ways, or repeating actions and agreeing to do things which he knew were not to his liking, he would assert. His memory, that key signpost to potential senescent decay, was as good as ever, better even, since there was so much more to remember.

He was essentially of a cheerful disposition. He thought of himself as a happy pessimist: in imagining the worst, things always turning out better than expected. Still, he had grudgingly come to the conclusion that yes, he was going to die. Sometime. He just didn't know when. But it was still inevitable. Everyone who had ever lived had, so far. Thus, Howard deduced, it was pretty much an undeniable certitude, an existential truth.

A school old-boys reunion had not only underscored the disconcertingly accurate definition of old in that once-jocular expression, but had brought the point home bluntly through those prominent for their mournful absence. The roundness of life had presented itself to him finally, as a finality. After all, there is no life without birth and death, not anything that he could think of anyway. Jellyfish, he had heard tell, while there was water at least. Trees on mountain tops whose roots could pop out here and there and start a whole new tree which was still the same tree. Some virus in the vacuum of space? God, or gods perhaps? His god wasn't technically alive, it was just an infinite and timeless, time-curling energy. More of a concept than a living, recognisable being. All other so-called gods were false, then, mere metaphors, conjured up for the purpose by and for the puny and needy intelligence of human beings. And, surely, every journey must have its terminus. Life, a time journey, without a beginning and an end would simply be existence, not life; it would be immortality. And that, it was clear, would mean he had not been mortal, and he wanted to be mortal, was mortal.

Nevertheless, he did not want to die yet. Howard knew in his heart he was rationalising, that it was really all about looming deathness and eternal non-consciousness and how he had to face the fear of such an emptiness. Even giving it a name like emptiness or nothingness was a feeble understatement of its true void. He had read somewhere that the after-death stage would be much the same as the pre-birth stage, that in both stages there was simply non-awareness. Yet he didn't feel they were the same. He knew so much about the times before he lived: the history, the pre-history, even the primal, Jung's winding evolutionary memory lane, that he did feel some awareness of it. Not to mention the memories of his own life and lifetime. Of that future stage, however, he knew nothing, and never would. He would be like one of those old, terminated computers he had seen photos of, piled in junk yards, functionless and unfunctioning, defunct. In fact, even they survived partially more so than he would, given their less destructible casing and various immortal elemental innards. He did not want to contemplate in any way whatsoever the fate of his own fleshy and flaccid support platform. He did feel a faint comfort from the knowledge that his basic components could not be ultimately destroyed and would waft around the universe in their various guises forever. Faint indeed. But why not rationalise if it helped. Wasn't that what religious belief did for people? Help them pass, or at least limp, through the valley of death by supplying a crutch. Why shouldn't he have his own, personal, distinctive survival crutch if he could create one?

So he decided he should plan for it.

For starters he thought he had better see a lawyer, take some advice and draft a will, and a financial adviser too. He found both nearby to his home from a quick web browse and made appointments. In the meantime he did some thinking. On a whim, and after hearing about it from friends who had done it, he also had his DNA analysed by GENoMEnate.com. He'd heard rumours of some tar-brush touches - as his father put it - in his mother's past and he was interested to know whether it was true or not. It was, but it had never had any significant impact on his life and would not now either. Afterwards GENoMEnate.com would occasionally contact him about link-ups with others who had had their DNA analysed and whose results indicated some relationship to him. 'Hey, Howard! You have new family: so-and-so is estimated to be your 3rd to 5th cousin with 1.2% of your DNA matching. You can make contact through this link … ' etc. But Howard was no longer interested in these connections. He could see no use in seeking out people with whom he shared a few centimorgans of similar genetic material. As far as he understood the matter he shared more than that with monkeys, or perhaps it was rats. Anyway he was only interested in his ancestry, not some artificially contrived super-extended family. That part of it was now all done and dusted to his satisfaction: he was a proud custodian of convict blood, with a mildly mixed racial make-up plus a welcome dollop of Ashkenazi, and that was the end of it.

Howard had lived what he considered had been a balanced life of neither over-regulated order nor unfettered disorder. There had been no great dramas along the way, either in the general nature of war or economic depression or political upheavals, nor in personal matters such as medical close-calls, horrific accidents, financial ruin, felonious disgrace, or abysses of alcoholism or drug addiction. He had certainly achieved satisfactory academic success through applied effort when he was younger though this had not led him into any long-term career path. He had become lazy once he ventured into such journeys, not being able to find any area that truly excited him or that he particularly excelled in. On the other hand curiosity did drive him, so knowledge and challenge were indispensable conduits for his intellect. He became a vocational butterfly flitting between jobs and experiences. He had lived a frugal life, and had saved regularly so that he had a small nest egg for retirement. He had bought and sold several homes. This would normally have resulted in financial comfort were it not for the breakdown in his final relationship which had cost him dearly, both emotionally and materially.

He had been a little sickly and weedy during his childhood but had enjoyed it and the quality state schooling that went with it. After he had finished university - further benevolence on the part of the state - he had worked for a couple of years and saved enough to travel at a time when young thoughts and aspirations turn temporarily to carefree adventure. Towards the end of this period of footlooseness he had found himself in Thailand teaching English and had met and soon after had married Boonsri. He had brought her home to live and they remained together for several years, but it had eventually foundered on the twin rocky headlands of cultural differences and diverging personal development. They had never had children. They saw each other occasionally afterwards but this dwindled away to nothing as their lives continued to diverge. His next relationship, the final one that had ended disastrously, had been with Carlie. Not long after their marriage they both agreed it was a little late to comfortably start a family and not too long after that it became biologically unlikely, then impossible anyway. It was just as well they hadn't because suddenly, at least so it appeared to Howard, she had met another man and left precipitately with him to live overseas. When the divorce process had turned nasty over the finances she and Howard had become estranged, eventually having no further contact whatsoever. Before these two marriages, and on a couple of occasions in between, he had toyed with other possibilities with several women but nothing had ever come of them, though they were exciting enough in their brief unfolding. But all that sort of thing was over now and had been for quite a while.

Older women, his age or older, or even a little younger, quite simply did not attract him. They were, he thought, frankly unattractive. Lost their bloom, as he remembered his mother used to declare in her usual direct manner. He was not so crass as to not realise that the same might be said about him and older men in general, but that didn't help. It remained the case that an affair or intimate relationship with an older woman was just not going to happen; he couldn't bring himself to be interested enough. He understood why men took on younger women: they were simply physically, and sexually, appealing. And if younger women found features in older men that suited them in some way, then so be it. If one came his way he would not hesitate, with conditions, but in the meantime his still-very-active libido remained a difficulty for him.

It would simply have to be handled in other ways. If he were going to be honest with himself he would have to admit that women, and especially older women, frightened him somewhat. They seemed to have reached a stage in life where they were very confident in themselves, self-assured, were thoroughly fulfilled, particularly, so Howard surmised, if through childbearing and child-rearing, and most germanely, self-sufficient to the point where they had no need of a man.

He was, whatever the case, alone, and old, and though he missed companionship and the carnal benefits that accompanied it when it went well, or even to some extent when it didn't, his single life was not without a certain satisfaction for him. He had hobbies and interests and his friends, and there were always new acquaintances coming onto the scene, though the number of these opportunities seemed to be diminishing as he aged and he spent more time at home alone.

The meetings with the lawyer and financial adviser went as most do: rational, factual, down-to-earth and in the lawyer's case, with the hour-glass in front of him on the desk remorselessly leaking its sands-of-time from one globular zone to the other at an alarming rate, expensive. Yet not at all boring, as this was *mise-en-scene* with its focus entirely on himself. A little like the narcissistic pleasure he felt when visiting his doctor, though on those occasions unmarred by its cost thanks to Medicaid. More like visiting his dentist, in fact, which he always enjoyed, unlike most others, since it gave him the feeling of being cared for and pampered. The endings to these meetings were inconclusive, but educative, and further work and appointments would be required. This again alarmed Howard for the potential cost involved but which, on the other hand therefore, paradoxically suited his plan as it was now beginning to form in his mind.

With what he had learnt from the lawyer, and going through

his financial situation so he could understand it all, everything gradually fell into place and became reasonably clear to him. He had a steady income and it was stable and government-guaranteed for as long as he lived, and would adjust for inflation or whatever other economic fluctuations came along. If in fact anything went askew with it, it would mean there were far more serious matters to be concerned about: a nuclear or meteorological holocaust, or complete economic collapse, for example. This income would sustain him but certainly would not accumulate, and one key aspect to it with his planning was that it would not last forever, it would cease with his surcease. He also had some more income from his private annuities. This was also reasonably guaranteed and reliable but unlike the other income would gradually run out at a fixed time in the foreseeable future. Combined then, this income was adequate, but hardly one to fund living the highlife. That left his assets, and here was the crux of the matter. The liquid part was accessible, spendable, expendable and exhaustible. The house was none of those and would have to be sold to release its value. So, taken together, these funds he could then use up, or leave behind.

The first part of the conundrum was that, without anyone related, blood or conjugal, to leave his wealth to, what would he do with it. There were plenty of causes and organisations with which he sympathised, people in his past who had helped him or towards whom he simply felt kindly, people who were in sore need of some financial salvage; young people with talent or potential who would benefit from early underpinning of their situations. Any of these were deserving of assistance. But in truth none of his current and past friends or distant relatives were in any real need of extra funds. Additionally, he wondered about how dependable and, quite frankly, honest, organisations were in this regard. After all, there would be no way of checking on it once enacted. The way he began to look at it was to question why anybody but himself should have the benefit of any of the money he had worked for and saved and gone without for over his lifetime in order to acquire and put aside for those times when it would be needed, such as from now on. This wealth represented his time, his effort, his life, and he felt that only he should be the one to enjoy what it had to offer in exercising its capacity to bring gratification, to the one who had created it. He did not feel he was being a niggard since what he would be doing would be sharing it all around in a generous manner while he could, which just happened to include a measure of self-largesse.

The second challenge involved timing, getting the pacing right. Once having decided to be the sole beneficiary of his own wealth how was he to ensure that it would last, or to put it in another way, be used up quickly enough. He had concluded by this time that what he wanted was to spend his last dollar as his dying deed. He wanted, in other words, to die dead broke. He could see how hard it was going to be. In any case what was the alternative: build the house of his dreams and then live in it in splendid isolation and poverty? Get himself to an old folks' home and shuffle his boring way to the ultimate exit?

After giving it further thought he felt it would be useful to devise a mathematical formula to optimise his spending so that on the day he died he would spend that last penny. This was going to prove very difficult to achieve. Isn't it what actuaries and superannuation insurance companies spent much of their time on formulating? The challenge he had presented himself with proved insurmountable, as in fact his friend Boris had informed him when he had asked him if he could provide such a formula. So he tried to come up with the next best: work out how much he could spend given the balance of his accounts and his expected guaranteed income and given that each day he lived was one less day he had to finance, as the total of days remaining was diminishing accordingly. When he put this revised approach to Boris, the econometrician just shook his head and refused to co-operate.

"Howard, such ridiculous idea," Boris said scornfully, "is not worth effort or even thought of moment."

"But Boris, my intuition tells me that each day or year I live I should be able to spend more and more given I haven't got as much time left to spend what funds I've got left in, if you know what I mean."

"Your intuition may tell you that or this but it is still silly and requires you to focus on the thoughts that are not conducive to getting on with living the life happily."

"But that is the very point: I would be happier if I could spend more each day, and I could do this if I knew what that amount might be."

Boris grimaced, and shrugged, and said: "Well, good luck then, I cannot give you answer nor necessary algorithm. Or just spend up big and kill yourself next Friday." Boris had a dry, fatalistic attitude to life.

Howard gave up with Boris on that note but continued to try to work out his formula for how much more he could spend each day as each day passed. Of course it would be a vastly simpler calculation if he knew when he would die, and such a certainty did lie in everyone's power to exercise if they had sufficient courage and resolute desire to take that course, as Boris had forthrightly intimated. Unless nature or fate intervened beforehand. Yet he knew himself well enough to be certain he would not have the fortitude to go down that road, at least as the situation was at the moment. When he thought about it he had to admit though that it could change to a level where courage might be necessarily summoned up, or not even enter the picture if dire need had taken command and the e-word, or eu-word to make it more phonically identifiable, might be invoked. He resolved he would not think about such possibilities for the time being and keep it perhaps as some sort of default position if all else went wrong. Yes, just leave aside that cheating siren, who might in this context be delicately referred to as 'Sue', to wait in the wings until any impending unprogrammed final curtain should require her untimely entrance.

The amended formula proved to be just as elusive for Howard. Every time he thought he was within reach of grasping the problem it slipped away again. The theory was solid, he believed - to divide all his available money by how many days he had left to live and then spend that amount each day - but how to work it out, not quite so. There was something Boris had said about life insurance and actuarial stuff that rang true though he hadn't really taken it in. He also envisaged a Plan B, something he imagined was based on differential calculus, whereby the longer he lived thriftily the more and more he could splurge as the years went by. He had not, however, been able to grasp calculus much at all at school and therefore was less than confident about it. And as for algorithms, that was well and truly beyond his concept zone. The problem with this plan was the risk that it would come a complete cropper, a tragic waste, in the case of premature demise. Foresight is indeed vain. While we might not be able to see into the future, we can't resist guessing at it, and consequently fearing it. And who knows when some black swan might swoop quite out of the blue.

But Howard resolved not to be frustrated. He would follow his instincts, draw on his intuition and go for it. Perhaps, he propounded to himself, take a bet each way on both the plans. Start cautiously but build up towards the full package as death, by definition, got closer. One thing was clear: the frugality of his life should change. It was time to adapt to his changed circumstances, to recognise the reality of diminished time left but to concomitantly explore the advantages which that oddly brought. He began to get down to details. He would sell his expensive late-model car, buy an old cheap one for those trips where only a car would do, and otherwise take taxis. The house would go on the market, in no great hurry in order to achieve the best price, and he would move into more salubrious rental accommodation with long-term security. And just as satisfying would be to pay others to do all those chores and responsibilities he hated attending to: he would pay to have his housekeeping all looked after; nor any more lawns to mow, gutters to clean; no more catching buses and trains with all their inconvenience.

He would eat out more often and at more upmarket restaurants; no more cooking, washing up or shopping for it all. Top-class wines after years of suffering the house reds. Nor would this not mean taking a healthy approach to life: he would join a gym, choose organic foods, pay exorbitant prices at health food stores for supposed quality. He would get all his dental work out of the way. Start going to theatre and opera and musical extravaganzas in vineyards. He would tip people generously, something he had pointedly avoided in the past on the basis that it undermined the imperative for workers to act collectively. Such notions had been of no interest to him for some time anyway. He would research travel possibilities, though this might wait a little until the later stages as it was one big way to unload large amounts of cash. In any case he thought travelling somewhat overrated, being as it could be stressful, uncomfortable, disruptive and often simply disappointing, and it could wait therefore until he would do it in style. Or perhaps combine it with some purpose like his dental work. He had heard about such exploits. That might in fact give him some motivation, some material reason to travel despite his general aversion, somewhere safe and not too demanding of course.

Importantly also, there would be no more purchases of valuable items like artworks that would basically add to his asset worth and defeat the purpose. Quite the opposite in fact, these would be sold off. He would visit galleries as compensation. Expensive clothes, though, yes, he could venture into that field too. Personal grooming generally, spend more on himself purely to feel good. Ah yes, age may be wearying and daunting but its effects could be leavened with luxuries.

As he worked on his plan and became increasingly

preoccupied by the whole project he branched out into other areas where he would want to have his lifestyle more honed to suit his circumstances, even though it may not involve any increased spending.

He decided that he would sleep less. He calculated that two hours less each night would give him an extra day of conscious life every nine days. A full forty days a year. His year would then contain more than thirteen months not just twelve. If he could continue that for the rest of his life he would gain, well, two, three maybe four more years. What a windfall! And it wouldn't just come as a bonus at the end either when the probability was that he would not be in the best shape to make the most of it. No, he could tap into the dividend straight away. What would the price be though? Tiredness, less energy to enjoy the extra time, those two delicious hours of snooze? Still it was a potentially excellent idea and he set about instigating the new regimen that very day, or night. Going to bed at the end of each day and again getting up in the mornings had always been difficult for him so he recognised it would be best to choose just one end of his sleep to concentrate on reducing. He would rise each morning two hours earlier.

Nor could he see much point in daily ablution. In summer when it might be most needed the effect didn't last long and quickly required a replay; in winter it was hardly needed. He would treat taking a bath as an indulgent luxury and cut down on showering.

So then he would use these extra hours to attend classes and learn new skills or have fun, on top of all the extra entertainment he would be treating himself to. He had always wanted to dance and sing, paint and make fine furniture, so he would be devoting whatever time and effort it required to learn such skills. And getting out into the bush a little, and onto the water for some sailing or fishing. And sex. His once-lively sex life had almost unnoticeably faded into solitary affairs of momentary deliverance from basic libidinal urge. Despite his efforts with internet dating he seemed to have lost the knack of hitting it off with women. He had never been with a prostitute, but now that his activities were to be very much financially driven why not sex as well? This was an area where he could definitely create some excitement and find satisfaction, even solace perhaps, while using funds as befitting his purpose.

His mind in its imaginative planning mode wandered to indulging in some cheeky fun as well. He determined therefore that even if he failed to spend his last dollar at his last breath he did not want to just blandly leave it to somebody or some purpose. He would make it difficult, or at least meaningful and challenging. He hit upon an idea for something akin to a piece of conceptualism, an art movement that had been rather chic ages ago and had caught his interest then and lodged somewhere in his mind since. He converted a solid amount of his cash assets into small gold ingots and coins. He then went out on excursions into the countryside seeking suitable out-of-the-way places where he would bury them. He chose a secluded public wooded area, protected from any future development. He dug small holes, not very deep as that wasn't at all necessary, and carefully made a note with a rough map of their location. He wrote all this down then and put it in a sealed envelope where it could be found by others, if the occasion arose before the second stage of his plan arrived. He had visions of crowds of people swarming around the forest searching for their little pots of gold once the word got out. This private little joke that Howard added to his project as an adjunct had the further benefit of allowing him later to access funds in the event that he was running low otherwise. He bought himself a metal detector as an extra means of ensuring the recovery of his little caches when or if the time came, and then realised he had always liked the idea of prospecting for gold too, so added it to his list of new pursuits to consider.

His mind wandered briefly into darker places as well.

Impending death presented an opportunity to impose some wild justice without fear of overwhelming consequences. At his age, or more advantageously closer to the threshold of passing, what punishment could be imposed that would be at all effective. Indeed, a comfortable incarceration along with the glory of recognition as a hero may well prove to be the perfect default ending. There were certainly many he could easily think of who deserved to be terminated, people who had committed unspeakable acts against humanity or animals or even the planet itself, people who were still committing such acts. The offensively super-rich. Despots. He harboured no such feelings about anyone he knew personally, and in any event that would be a misplaced objective. Realistically all this was not in his nature to carry through, but he enjoyed the fantasy.

Thus things were rollicking along splendidly and Howard was having the time of his revitalised life, despite feeling a little sluggish at times. Oh, promised joy! The house sold and he had settled into a new, classy and very central apartment. His lifestyle was heading towards the standard he had dreamed of with yet more advancement to come. Still, the thought nagged him of how it would all end, how he might somehow control that end. In particular when it might be made to occur. He could not shake off the feeling that he might suffer a sudden, premature and haphazard demise and all his prudence be for nought. Or worse, that he would persist well beyond the plenitude of his resources and experience a lingering misery. Living high on the hog was all very well while you could but what about when decrepitude set in and not all the money in the world would ease the burden of life. Look at Steve Jobs or George Harrison.

Then, one day, he was checking his emails as he always did now first thing in his earlier mornings as he prepared to go out into his new shiny world of pleasure and delights. He had noted a few days before an advertisement fixed on the noticeboard of a local supermarket for 'mature adult services' and had decided that day would be the time to venture down that track. There were a couple of emails from friends to read and reply to, the usual culprits to delete without reading - offers of penis enlargement which in his case he had never felt was required and in any case was now totally irrelevant, notifications of huge amounts won in some fanciful lottery, bizarre offers of enormous wealth from family of a fictional third-world tyrant - plus another with an attachment from someone whose name he didn't recognise. He deleted it without opening as he always did with attachments in the cautious fashion which had guided his life.

There was yet another from GENoMEnate.com similar to so many he had already received and deleted in the last few months. He skimmed it hurriedly: 'Hi Howard, good news,' it said in its breezy over-familiar way, as if by supplying it with some of his DNA it now considered itself to be one of his close family. 'We've discovered new DNA matches for you: - *33.1%* - shared DNA suggests you have the following estimated relationship with: - *Elspeth Johansson* - who is - *18* - and lives in - *Canada* - it looks like - *Howard Grading* - you have a - *grand-daughter* - ' it announced in all its formulaic jollity and innocent high-mindedness.

Then, as the import of this revelation slowly sank in, penetrating his resistant consciousness, Howard's mind commenced alternatively to swirl in boggling confusion then freeze in numbing shock. It seemed he had very briefly and recently come across that name before, and realised suddenly that 'for evermore' had meaning after all.

Getting Over It

The medicine was doing its job. It was fixing you. Giving it the name medicine made it sound so benign, so kind, so helpful, but it wasn't. The side effects were far from friendly. Apart from the nausea, the vomiting, the peripheral loss of feeling and tingling sensations, and the depression, your hair fell out. So what if it was fashionable now to shave your head. You still wouldn't choose to do so. Now you had no choice. You were chemically clean-shaven, chrome-domed and grieving for lost locks.

Eventually you would need to show yourself. To the world, to friends, to family. You would have to gird your loins, or your pate, and face up to it. You would walk down the street past neighbours, past strangers. You would sit on a train with other strangers directly across from you. Would they notice, would they stare, would they titter, would they point, would they look away embarrassed? How were you going to cope with that? You were a naturally shy person anyway, an introvert, not anti-social, but quite private.

You could not put it off much longer. The milk had run out. You could manage with black tea and coffee and perhaps just hot water over your cornflakes. But the bread was almost finished, and now the cigarettes. You couldn't go without toast for breakfast, and as for cigarettes, well.

The supermarket wasn't far, but far enough. Hell, you wished you'd have planned for it better. If only you had bought that wig on eBay a month ago and not left it to last Sunday so that it would have been delivered by now. You didn't even possess a beanie. You could buy one of course at the cheap Chinese on the way to the supermarket. It wouldn't help much, you would still need to take that first giant step outside into the spotlight. A scarf? A woman could get away with a scarf. You felt you would be just as self-conscious and way out-of-character with some sort of towel wrapped around your skull as you would be if it were totally exposed.

Exposed, that was it. You couldn't bare feeling exposed like that. You'd rather disembowel yourself, let your innards spill out for everyone to see and puke over than have this egg-like form that is your head encasing your brain exposed so that people could laugh at it.

But the craving for a cup of tea with milk was overwhelming, and you knew tomorrow would be ruined without your cornflakes and milk and toast to kick it off. In any case it had to happen sometime.

You went scouring through your drawers and cupboards and travel bags looking for a cigarette or better still a packet of them. You checked in your coat and then your trouser pockets in your wardrobe. Perhaps if you could have a smoke you could take it a bit longer. No luck there, it was game up.

You changed shirts. It was too hot to wear a jacket so you wouldn't be able to turn a collar up and pull your head down into its protective wrap. You found your chunky wrap-around dark glasses and put them on. You went to the mirror and looked in it. With the dark glasses on you couldn't see yourself very well but what you could make out resembled some sort of a gangster type. There was some comfort in the feeling that if you couldn't see things very well then people possibly may not see you very well.

You felt nauseous. You stumbled to the toilet and vomited.

You cleaned yourself up, put your glasses on again, grabbed your keys and wallet and walked down the hallway to the front door. You put your hand out onto the knob, turned it and pulled the door back. You were shaking. You stepped out onto the street and into the sun. You could feel the warmth on the skin on the top of your head like you never had before. It was a constant unwelcome reminder until you reached some shade. Then you felt the cooling effect of the airflow as you walked without the heat of the sun on it. There seemed no escape from the non-stop torment.

You continued on, scurrying to the supermarket, scampering up and down the aisles, enduring the crawl of the queue at checkout and then suffering the agony of becalment and close attention at the register, the whole time your expression grim and your whole body tense, expecting at any moment to be humiliated and wanting to slink away and bury yourself in some dark burrow.

You sidled along the footpath homeward. Nobody looked twice at you. Nobody noticed you. Nobody cared. You opened your front door and stepped out of the glare, slammed it behind you, dashed to the bathroom, knelt down, and vomited. You were glad it was over.

In Treachery We Trust

"Hey, Jude! Join us, pull up a pew."

"Thanks, I will, just for a while."

He sat down at the long table on the bench opposite.

"Have some of this wine, it's memorable. And try this, it's delicious."

"It does smell good; a little hot for me yet."

There was a momentary pause.

"So, are you with us?"

He looked him straight in the eyes.

"If I were, what would it mean exactly?"

"It would mean, my brother, that you'd be committed to follow us, and those who follow us, to the very end."

"That would require a great deal of trust, of trust in you, and in the cause."

"Why would you not trust me? I am, after all, your brother."

"And the cause? Is your cause the same as my cause, your truth, my truth? Is our fervour for truth worthy of such actions as we are undertaking? Is this the way, the only way?"

"You must know by now that our actions are justified by truth and therefore we are bound to succeed."

"But absolute trust?"

"It is a beautiful and terrible thing, and should therefore be treated with great caution."

"As I am doing."

"As you should do."

He hesitated, then spoke again in a more modulated tone.

"Trust is the silver stream that threads its way through our lives. We can drink from that stream and bathe in it and take its waters for our crops whenever the need arises, and it sustains us, but it will never reverse the direction of its flow. Beware, however, the duplicitous for they are the snake hidden in the tall grass near the stream. Duplicity is like dividing that stream into two streams, taking one secretly for ourselves while maintaining the happy illusion of the other. Yet it is the traitor who is the ultimate destroyer, revealing their true selves when it is too late to counter, masking their real emotions with a deceptive kiss. Treachery is like an explosion that breaches the walls of the dam we have built for our mutual benefit across our stream, releasing a flood of fortune or gratification in a single perfidious burst for one, but leaving the ruins and aftermath never possible to repair, for both."

"You have such unflinching confidence in your beliefs. There seems to be no room for compromise."

"As I have explained to you we will be acting for the good of humanity. It is never an easy mission to overturn the natural order, to bring light to the darkness. But Peter is with us and he will be rock-steady."

"He's never done anything like this before."

"Neither have we!"

"Are we then not like innocents to the slaughter?"

"There is formidable truth in innocence which gives it a power not so easily reckoned with."

"You always make it sound so simple, so obvious, so ... truthful."

They both raised their cups and drank from them.

"It's late and the light beckons. You should leave, you have important work to do."

"You sound like you want to be rid of me."

"Whatever you do, it will be for the good."

"So, in the name of goodness, good-bye."

He twisted himself around on the bench, stood up and walked away.

"What's it going to be then, eh, Jude?" Jesus called after him. "Bathe in the same stream, or breach the dam? Betrayal of the weakest by the most powerful? Trust, or treachery?"

Judas continued on his way.

Ripples

Veronica walked out from the house only half-dazed, still thinking clearly enough to realise what she had just done and what to do next, yet incredulous that she had finally carried it through, that she could have done what she did.

She was not sure if her shivering was because of the cold or her emotions; perhaps it was both. She took the front steps of what once had been a happy home one at a time, stopping two-footed on each. She trod tentatively along the path they had made many years ago from flat rocks they had quarried from wherever they could find them, right up to the edge of the lake now bathed in the cool light of a gibbous moon, arms hanging limp by her sides.

She and Lucas had spent many happy hours there once. She stopped at the spot where there was a little pebbly beach. They used to sit here together glasses in hand, with some nibbles and a bottle of cold white wine scrunched into a bucket of ice, and watch as the children splashed and frolicked and screamed with delight on hot summer days.

She could hear them now, but their screams had become mixed with her screams, screams she had lived with for too long, and they were no longer screams of joy.

She looked down at her right hand, smeared with the blood that had fuelled his brutality all those years, swung her arm backwards and then threw the carving knife out into the lake in a high arc as hard and as far as she could. Why, she wasn't sure. It would make no difference. They would search and find it. She would probably even tell them where to look. She would still go to jail.

It came down with a loud plop in the silence of the night. The ripples, as they spread out, caused the moon's reflection to career wildly across the lake's surface every which way. After a while as she stared off into nothingness the ripples reached her little beach and tiny waves touched her toes as they swished over the pebbles ever so slightly.

There was no escaping life's actions. Life would catch up with you. It had caught up with Lucas. A knife could be thrown away but the ripples would seek out the perpetrator relentlessly, flow over then dissipate, their work done.

A cloud passed across the moon and the lake went dark; dark as grief, as guilt, as revenge, dark as her future. She stared out through the darkness to the far shore and saw a wall of total blackness. She could not see where the lake ended and the forest began.

There was a wisp of a breeze carrying the damp smells of a lakeside night and she could hear the sighing of the casuarinas coming across the water from over there on the other side. It brought with it a brushing of cold and a renewed shivering ran through her body.

The cloud moved away and she could just make out the line of the shore and see the jagged edge of the treetops against the night sky. The lake was again as smooth as a mirror and now reflected a near-perfect shimmering moon. What she had done would follow her to her death, but she knew that those ripples would also reach the far side of the lake, that they would make tiny waves there too, and soon they would be gone, then replaced by others made by whatever fate had in store.

As she stood and listened to the sounds of the night, the insects on all sides, the call of a boobook in the distance, the frog nearby, she felt the peace and the understanding, and knew that those ripples were not ripples of a lingering regret.

Saving Kai

Rodney jostled his way off the train and joined the stream of impassive faces all hurrying to get home after work. He pressed his travel card on the exit reader, hesitated fleetingly to listen for the ping, then raced to catch the green pedestrian light and cross the road to the mall. As he separated from the main throng to go his own way a tall, thin young man stepped out from his lair in the shadows.

"How was your day, sir?" the young man disingenuously enquired in an attempt at disarming engagement. He had a carefully cultivated stubble on his face and his hair up in a man-bun with long, fractious wisps floating around it. His dress code was definitive hipster: skinny jeans, a pair of classic Raben high-top gym boots in bright green, and a tee-shirt showing a lumberjack clubbing a seal pup with 'IRONIC?' scrawled underneath it, dripping blood, all in bright red. Scribbly tentacles of a tattoo that looked suspiciously like the root system of a tree curled their way out from under the right sleeve of the tee-shirt and encircled his arm.

Rodney wondered whether the rear side of the tee-shirt would give the answer to the Delphian question, and what other horrors of tattoo art might be lurking beneath it. Rodney knew what this poser wanted. Rodney despised him, while not disagreeing with what he stood for. If he stood for it, that was.

"In a hurry," he spat out as he brushed past. He wasn't going to be "sorry" about it either. It was late. The rush hour, and getting home after work, just seemed to be growing later and later, year by year.

"Oh, well, you enjoy the rest of your day then, sir."

Rodney walked on but this hunter had more lures in his tackle box and he pulled one out, loaded and lobbed it with a professional's precision.

"But I was just wondering," the young man called after him, his tone rising as his quarry slipped further away from his grasp, "if you care about the planet?"

Rodney stopped in his stride. He knew the tactic. And he knew he was succumbing to its stratagem and his own baser instincts, but the utterly annoying crassness of the question simply arrested him. A few extra minutes before he could slump onto the sofa with Becky and a decent drink wouldn't kill him, he decided. He spun around and snapped back.

"Stupid bloody question that is." And a piss-poor retort too, he chastised himself.

The young man smiled broadly, his eyes gleamed as he took a few bouncy steps towards Rodney, holding out a pamphlet for him, sensing he had hooked his prey and would now reel him in.

"Well, not if you want to help the planet. How do you think you might be able to contribute somehow?" He had sashayed up to Rodney and was now capering exuberantly right in front of him.

Rodney ignored the pamphlet being shoved his way, leaving the young man floundering somewhat.

"I would probably think about some way of removing you from the equation for a start, that would help," Rodney let fly, pleased that he had managed something a touch smarter and more barbed than the previous blunt instrument.

The young man gave a genuine laugh and Rodney softened

a little. "Well, I'm here to help," he said. "Name's Kai."

"Help what, Kai? Help yourself?" Rodney wanted to use the name so he could show his contempt for it with some deprecating emphasis, making a point of not offering his own.

"Help the planet, with your help too," Kai said straight-faced. He resolved that he wasn't going to be needled. The aim after all was to extract money by virtue of a certain cordial affinity.

"Oh, and how would you propose we *do* save the planet this evening?"

"I'm representing an organisation called Noah's Arc – that's A-R-Cee," Kai stressed the last letter. "We want to change the trajectory, get it, of humanity's impact on the planet, especially to protect the animals that are our fellow inhabitants."

"So you want a donation for the planet and the animals," Rodney said deadpan, holding his fire.

"Look at it as an investment in the planet's and your children's future."

Rodney was clearly of an age where children could matter for him. The organisers had given Kai a rudimentary crash course in marketing techniques which had lasted about ten minutes.

In fact Rodney didn't have children, but it gave Rodney an idea. He could extract some entertainment from the situation as compensation for the delay in his homecoming benefits.

"OK, then, let's make it interesting," he said with an enticing tonal smirk.

"Yeah, how?" Kai asked, his excitement encouraged by noticing Rodney pull out his wallet and open it.

Rodney unzipped a compartment, checked for notes and pulled out two fifties, holding them up seductively before Kai.

"Let's see how well you know just how *you* might be able best to contribute to our planet's welfare."

Kai's eyes lit up at the prospect of a bonanza for the day's effort and he waited spellbound.

"If you can tell me the one most important action or activity, or non-action or non-activity, to do or not do, or desist from doing, or reduce doing, whatever, that you can personally bring into your life to save the planet, I'll donate one hundred dollars to your cause."

Kai's heart raced as he smelt blood, but which soon became tainted with rat, as he realised it may not be quite so straightforward.

"Cool. Yeah, sounds good, but how will I know the answer is the right one; how can I know you'll be honest about it?"

"Here, giv's that pamphlet and I'll write the answer down as a record." Rodney pulled out a pen from inside his coat, took the pamphlet from Kai, found a clear space and scribbled something. He put his pen back, folded the pamphlet over and popped it in the top pocket of his jacket.

"There you go," he proffered and patted his left breast.

"But how can we tell if what you consider the most important thing is actually the most important?"

"Well, I think when *you* consider it you will actually agree, but apart from that it's me who's paying the piper, isn't it?"

"Yeah, sweet then, call the tune."

"OK, go!"

Kai jumped straight in, performing something approaching a jig as he poured forth. "Well, to give up owning or driving a car, switching to riding a bike or a skateboard or scooter, taking public transport, and walking, would both reduce fuel pollution, save natural resources, improve health, lessen congestion and eliminate the effects of the mining and manufacturing process into the bargain." Kai beamed, totally oblivious to the fact that he had gone well beyond the two points of his claimed outcome as his imagination briefly pictured a world full of happy pedestrians scurrying along broad pathways with ecstatic commuters whizzing around them on skateboards, scooters and bikes in a sparkling smogless atmosphere with not a sign of chaos or hostility.

"A worthy intention," Rodney shot back with a self-satisfied shake of his head, "and it would certainly help, and it is high on the list, for all its impracticalities. But even if everyone gave up their vehicles, which is hardly likely or possible, or even if all vehicles switched to clean fuel it would still leave plenty more stuff - planes and ships and armies and airforces come quickly to mind - for us to keep on polluting with and destroying. No, that's not the answer. Want another stab for fifty dollars?" He smiled, not just a little relieved at saving his hard-earned, as he put one of the fifties back into his wallet.

Kai was disappointed in himself at having rushed it, so he considered for a minute.

"OK then, become a vegetarian, or even better, a vegan." He pulled himself up straight with pride at his own already-achieved status as a lacto-ovo-pescatarian and gave Rodney a confident nod of his head as he said it. "A simultaneous double whammy for the planet and its animals. And it's healthier." He thought to himself as he spoke that perhaps it might be time for him to take his eating commitments a little further up the virtuous ladder towards veganism.

"Another fine sentiment, and indeed if everyone became vegans, which is highly unlikely, though perhaps less so than giving up motor vehicles, many, many animals would be saved from death and suffering, and even more would never be born. It would certainly reduce the wasteful input into feeding animals, the waste from animals themselves, like all the farting and the consequences of that, but there will be plenty of crap still left to do damage. And though it may or may not be a healthier option, human health is not at issue here. Healthier humans won't save the planet, perhaps the opposite. It's not so high on the list. Laudable, but nup."

Rodney stuffed the second fifty back into his wallet further relieved, and pulled out a twenty. "'Nuther go?"

Kai was now feeling quite disheartened, down to a mere twenty dollars, all those hopes for a windfall slipping away. But he also felt he had less to lose, a dexterous piece of rationalisation to cushion his loss. The ebullient look had gone from his face, and his frenetic jigging had become more of a soft-shoe shuffle. He answered with less certainty, ending his sentence with a giveaway upward inflection.

"Work for world peace to avoid a nuclear holocaust?" Kai pictured newsreel scenes of atomic mushroom clouds being run backwards so that the earth sucked their malevolence into its pacifying embrace.

"Ah, now you're talking."

Kai's eyes sparkled, but only temporarily as he realised there was an impending "but" on the way, that once again he had struck out.

"Nuclear war would definitely wreak havoc on all the planet's living things, no doubt, and certainly comes near top of the list for something to avoid. But I don't think your personal efforts to avert it would get far given the reality of international power play and the world political situation, and we're talking personal action here. A truly noble aim, and maybe one day we can look forward to peace in the world becoming the norm, but nope."

Rodney put the twenty back and pulled out a ten, waving it tantalisingly in front of Kai. "Go again?"

Kai felt stymied by his continuing failures but was more intent on winning than ever, despite the diminishing haul. "Trees. Stop cutting down trees or causing them to be cut down. Use renewable timbers from plantations. No palm oil, stop land clearing. And plant, go out and plant as many trees as you can during your life." Kai was animated again and pleased with himself with the answer this time. He smiled with an air of vindication and did a little dance, something along the lines of a *gavotte*. He had an image of himself skipping across fields enthusiastically scattering the promise of future old-growth forests as he went, like a latter-day Johnny Appleseed.

"Good work, Kai. That would be a very effective effort, and if everyone did the same no doubt there would be significant progress in saving the planet – yes, high on the list and something all of us could do, but it's still not the answer. It's still not enough. All the other problems, and one in particular, would overwhelm any effort in that regard. Tell you what: how much have you taken today?"

Kai looked at him warily, and answered with reluctance. "Maybe $35, $40. Not sure." Kai knew it was more like $20 but he didn't want to appear to be a fiscal failure.

"OK. Then what say double that or nothing: I'll put up the original $100 against your takings for one more answer. And I'll give you a clue: looking at you my guess is you're still in the running to do your bit in this regard, and given your answers so far I'd say you are still a risk. And as a matter of fact I am to, although that could be slightly misleading as it would require a reversal of my circumstances. And Bill Gates and his wife would know the answer for sure, or come close anyway, given their track record. So you want one last crack?"

Rodney was half-hoping he might get it quickly this time, despite the cost. He had had enough and wanted to go home. He needed that drink, and a hug. It had been a long day. These days they were all long days it seemed.

Kai was now totally exhausted and exasperated but he couldn't stop, he had to know. He looked at this man in front of him in his expensive suit and tie and business shoes, his briefcase and neatly trimmed hair with his confident, near arrogant stance and wondered what on earth could he have done to help save the planet. And what the hell would he want to reverse out of all that? He knew Bill Gates was the richest man in the world and supported lots of causes like finding a cure for cancer and that he was giving his money away but he couldn't see what that might have to do with it. Unless he was saying that you should give all your money to Noah's Arc, and that would be highly improbable. He decided to let fly with a scattergun approach, envisioning as he did a perfect eco-pure world.

"Do everything I can to reduce my waste: turn off lights and appliances, wear warm clothes in unheated houses, ride a bike, walk, grow my own vegies, buy local, recycle, stop buying unnecessary things, reject plastic shopping bags, bring my own coffee cup ... um ... go solar, mend my clothes, don't wash, install a dry sewage system, feed my dog only my leftovers, compost the rest, invest in ethical industries only ... " He ran out of ideas and stumbled; he knew he was simply rolling out the party line.

"Oh, Kai, good try, but you're really grasping at straws I'm afraid, and you're well short of the mark. Still, I'm impressed by your knowledge of all the standard measures that we're made to feel guilty about while we dodge the major one. Guess you owe me then."

He displayed just the faintest smirk as he slipped the folded pamphlet out of his jacket pocket deftly with two fingers and handed it with a flourish to Kai.

Kai took it and looked quickly at what was written there, and then back up at Rodney.

"'Curb your cock!' Hell, what's that supposed to mean, man?"

"It means, simply, don't procreate, Kai, don't add any more people to this over-peopled planet. That's the one best thing you can do personally to save it forever into the future. Reducing the number of humans is the only thing that can save the planet from the ravages of humanity. Have you ever considered that the best thing for this planet would be to be rid of humans? Remember that all those little Kais and Kailies will produce more little Kais and Kailies, ad infinitum. When we talk about saving the planet we're not talking generations, we're talking forever. Your offspring could eventually number in the thousands, millions. Now that may well appeal to a primordial you, spreading your DNA and all that, but that is in fact our one great problem: the natural drive to proliferate ourselves seething away in our lower sanctum as it does with all life. But think of the implications of that, the resources they would use, the combined impact they would all have. So it's not just all about you, Kai, it's about the accumulation of all those part-yous that follow."

Kai was dumb-struck and looked totally despondent, though it wasn't clear whether that was because he had uber-zilched with the money or he had completely overlooked the obvious.

"Next to early suicide that is. That's for jihadists, to exit this planet for a better world rather than save this one. I wouldn't expect that of an eco-warrior." Rodney thought he needed to throw Kai something positive as encouragement given his crushed demeanour. "You have important work to do. Any single-minded defender of the planet should be developing a sterility virus and letting it loose on humankind."

"But that'll take too long, we need to do something now. I'm not paying up for that."

"It's not about now, it's about forever. If we'd thought about the future decades ago the now would be looking after itself." Rodney shrugged and turned to go on his way.

"Keep it then. Use it to buy some condoms for yourself and your mates while yous're waiting for the vasectomies," he tossed back over his shoulder as he walked off.

"Hey!" Kai barked at Rodney's back. "So what have you done to save the planet, dude?"

Rodney stopped, swivelled around and shouted right back.

"Well apart from being a vegetarian, catching public transport or walking, doing my utmost not to provoke an outbreak of nuclear war, planting lots of trees over my lifetime, letting you off the hook and all the rest, I castrated myself while I was still a virgin. I'm sure you know how it's done, every farm boy does. Now that's real commitment to the planet's future. And it's been responsible fun, fun, fun ever since. I recommend it. It wasn't at all painful, in fact had a certain pleasurable side to it. Have a nice day, *dude*."

And with a heavy emphasis on the last word he sauntered off, legs first straddled over an imaginary horse, then crossed over each other as a waddle in mock discomfort.

"Smug prick," Kai muttered to himself, but he could not shake off the feeling complacent assumptions about his life's future course had been dealt a mortal blow.

Guard Duty

What the …!

He jumped up and stared hard into the pitch black towards where he thought the sound had come from. It was all-senses-alert time, but with the pitch darkness and the air soaked in smoke, the stench of burnt timber overwhelming any other smells, only his pricked ears were in full operation. Touch and taste would have to wait till things got close, though hopefully it would not come to that.

He had heard that sound before. A crunch of a foot on dry leaves, then repeated. Tonight it was on cinders and parched rocky ground but still unmistakably recognisable. It was slow and stealthy, the most suspicious type, someone taking care to try not to be heard, hunting, or searching for one reason or another. Enough to be wary. Very wary. He remembered those previous times and felt the same thrill as then: adrenaline saturating tissues, muscles tense, heart thumping, the prospect of action. He found it hard to keep still with the excitement. This was life, purpose: to guard, to warn, to protect and defend.

The cautious crunching of footsteps continued and now narrow beams of light threw meaningless shadows and golden spots around the scene. What should he do? He flexed his whole body and took some steps backwards. He would sit it out, take what comes. He waited, ready. He would never forsake. To the death. He was not a warrior but he knew the meaning of loyalty and would do what had to be done.

The crunching steps came closer. There were voices. He didn't understand, but he sensed the tone. They were not threatening. Even so, he could feel his lips pulling back and quivering to show his teeth, and a slight uncontrollable gurgle start up in his throat.

"Over there! There's something … "

Lights flashed at him picking up the glossy reflection of his eyes. He was blinded by it, more so even than the darkness had managed to achieve, and more confusing, and he sat dazzled by them, resigned to his fate. But he had done his duty, he had stood his ground, maintained his faith.

The lights and whatever was behind them were right on him now and he whimpered, licking the air for taste, his tail lowered in capitulation and camaraderie.

"Bloody hell!" said the voice in words he didn't understand but in a tone he knew was sympathetic.

"It's Ken, that grey gum's come down and crushed him right and proper."

"That's his dog, Congo, the bluey-kelpie bitsa been with him forever, i'n't?"

Congo recognised the sounds that referred to him and indicated familiarity, and his fear subsided.

The back of a leathery hand appeared from the emptiness beyond the light and held itself in front of his nose, turned downwards.

"Hello, Congo, old fella. You wouldn't leave him, eh?"

He sniffed and knew there was no danger here. He turned and lay down next to Ken and gave a long sigh, chin on paw, eyes turned up, whites showing in calm acceptance.

The men were speaking, but it wasn't for him to care now. Job done.

Distracting Anthony

It was Anthony at the door. Janet, surprised, smiled.

"Hello."

She drew that single word out giving it a welcoming warmth.

"Hi, you're back."

He was gazing at his feet. Not unusual, Anthony always had a self-deprecating look about him. A touch of the clown. But only a touch. Otherwise, he was very serious. Sometimes his small mouth would curl upwards sheepishly a little at each side, and his eyes twinkle, even when he was plumbing his depths. He was built solidly, but neither muscular nor pudgy. Less a wombat or bear, more a badger. His auburn hair was longish, a little over his ears, wiry, crinkly, his neck short. He'd grown a wispy goatee chin beard since she'd last seen him and had a silver stud in one earlobe; just a little showiness, a whisper of rebellion, but no more than an insinuation. His clothes were casual but always smart and well-fitting, proclaiming good taste, and healthy finances. A classy brown leather shoulder bag topped off his style. He looked like the young architect going places that he was.

"Yes, a few days now."

"I'm a bit depressed," he went on.

Then looking up: "Can I come in?" His mouth curled up a

little at each end.

"Yes, of course. Come in, come in."

Janet opened the door wide and stood back allowing him past. She shut it quickly, swung around and gave him a big hug.

"Poor Anthony," as she squeezed him tightly, stretching up on her toes. She was in just a loose tee-shirt, shorts and bare feet with the toe-nails painted deep red. It was warm inside her house.

He let her linger. She let go and leant back to look at him. Holding by his shoulders.

"What is it? Come and sit down. Give me your coat."

She helped him off with his coat and bag, hung them on a hook behind the door, then found his hand and led him into the loungeroom to a sofa and they sat down one at each end. She turned fully sideways to face him, tucked one long, shapely, suntanned leg underneath the other and leant forward to him.

"Tell me."

"I've just had a long email from Jennifer. She's in Melbourne doing her internship, you know. I wanted to go and see her. She said it would be better if I didn't."

He looked to the side, downcast, no sign now of comic relief.

"Perhaps she just wants to concentrate on her work there for a bit," Janet attempted, but she could read the signs: a long email.

"It's made me very depressed. I got a bit teary after the email."

His voice cracked a little.

"You'd think I'd take the hint, wouldn't you?"

"Oh, Anthony, don't be so negative. Sometimes women just have some second thoughts, that's all. She'll probably be on the phone tomorrow having changed her mind again."

Janet knew she was clutching at straws for Anthony. Perhaps

she shouldn't be even giving him hope. She knew Jennifer was never going to work out for him. Jennifer was strong and determined and had plans for her career. Anthony was only going to drag her back with constant emotional turmoil. She also knew something else about Jennifer but thought best not to mention that with Anthony as he was now. He needed distracting, not deflating.

"I've been reading some philosophy, about what we all should know about ourselves, what we all should want in our lives. I know I want a nice lady to love, and love me. Preferably Jennifer."

His mouth gave a little sheepish grin.

Janet felt just slightly irritated now by his self-indulgence.

"Anthony, you can't just wish for something to fill a hole for you when that involves another person's wishes that may not fit into yours."

"It's just been such a bad year you know. I'll be glad when it's over. Jennifer's email hasn't helped. It's made me depressed again. You can probably tell. I'm just sitting in my room trying to work and listening to music like I used to do. Do you remember the Pointer Sisters? It's quite funny really. Or pathetic I mean."

"Well, it's better that you do keep on working."

She could see that this would be going nowhere no matter what she said. What could she say? It wouldn't do to try to distract him yet.

"I feel totally lost. I really think I should go to Melbourne and talk it out with her. Emails are hopeless. I really think you need to talk these things out person-to-person."

He was talking to nobody now, trying to convince himself of something he didn't believe would happen.

"It might not be the best thing to go down there if she says not to. Why don't you try to do something here that needs doing. You have your work, why not get stuck into that for the time being."

She spoke slowly, her tone a little deeper.

"So you can see I'm a bit depressed right now, can't you?"

He paused.

"I went and saw a couple of movies. Cohen Brothers. Perhaps I could just ring her, that might do."

Janet untucked her leg and shuffled a little towards him.

"Yes, I know you're not feeling your best, and perhaps you could call her, but it might also work if you were to simply get on with what you could be doing here."

It was going to take more than a hint before Anthony would get it. Her eyes ran over his face and down to his hands, good strong hands, nails trimmed, skin smooth and clear. Not yet.

"I'm sorry to be such a sad sack, but I think it's over with Jennifer. Shit, shit. I think I still love her, that's what it is."

He was gazing down again with no sign on his mouth of a smile, forced or otherwise.

Janet, moved a little closer and reached out to touch his hair with her fingers, tucking some behind his ear, and put her other hand on his knee.

Now might be just the right time, she thought, to distract him.

End Game

"What'll we do now?" Sh'vaughn got up and walked idly over to the kitchen bench.

Aznia looked up at her from beneath her long fringe, her mouth twisting into a wry smile, took a sip of her wine and got up from the table.

She walked around the bench into the kitchen.

"Hm, let's see. First, a candle." Aznia looked at Sh'vaughn and waited a moment.

"Should I go on?"

Sh'vaughn bent forward a little to lean on the bench. "Yes, please do, I'm intrigued. And I want more."

Aznia reached out, pulled open the drawer on her side of the bench, peered in and picked out a long, golden brown beeswax candle, one end pinched into a point with a curly white wick leaking out.

She held it up in front of Sh'vaughn.

"One candle."

She put it down on the bench.

"OK, now find me a sharp knife, something like a paring knife."

Sh'vaughn walked around and pulled open a drawer and took out a small knife with a yellow handle.

"That'll do the trick," Aznia said grabbing it.

She took the knife and drew it along the edge of her palm. A thin line of red appeared as if by magic.

"Oh!" Sh'vaughn looked at it and her with some dismay.

"Perfect," she said, and licked the blood off her hand.

She picked up the candle again and held it in her left hand, the wick end pointing towards her.

She placed the blade of the knife about an inch from the other end pointing away from her.

She looked up at Sh'vaughn.

"Like this." She thrust the knife forward suddenly, slicing off the end a neat, triangular piece of wax which flew into the air and landed on the floor at their feet.

Sh'vaughn winced slightly. "Ooh!"

Aznia looked at her and smiled. "There's more."

She rotated the candle, placed the knife again one inch from the end and repeated the process, this time with more of a flourish.

Another sliver of beeswax flew into the air and across the room.

Sh'vaughn took a step back with just a slight mousy squeal.

Aznia turned the candle right around so its unsullied side was uppermost and she rapidly stripped three more shavings of beeswax off, rotating the candle slightly each time, to achieve a point, very much like sharpening a pencil.

Sh'vaughn gave a little laugh in admiration at Aznia's dexterity and watched in great expectation for the next move.

Aznia looked up at Sh'vaughn and smiled. "Now for some finessing," she purred.

In a series of small cuts, in what amounted to not much more than scratching the surface, she pared the end of the candle bit by bit, exposed the wick, a little at first, round and round, until more and more of it showed and then she stopped.

She put the knife down on the bench and held up the sharpened candle proudly.

"Let the games begin," she triumphed. "Matches!"

Sh'vaughn opened a cupboard door and found a box of matches, brought them out and handed them to Aznia.

"Hold this," Aznia said offering the candle to Sh'vaughn, "horizontally, in the middle."

Sh'vaughn did as she was instructed, with a thumb and forefinger.

Aznia took a match from the box, struck it on the side of the box and lit the long wick.

She looked up at Sh'vaughan.

She leant forward and kissed her.

She moved her hand slowly to the other end and lit the newly exposed wick.

"Now we are going to burn our candle at both ends," she smouldered.

Eggs and Egos

It was another Dungeons-&-Dragons night at the Choudharys. Elise and Dilip were the designated hosts for this week and they took their role very seriously. Both were spruced up and looking the part. Dilip had downloaded a random musical playlist he thought would fit the flavour of the evening as it unfolded, and which he had dubbed 'Rock & Roll the Dice' for his own amusement.

A buzzing came from the front door. Someone was early. Elise fussed in a last-minute rush with the dips and glasses and plates in the kitchen while Dilip left his fiddling with the game table set-up in the adjoining open-plan living area and went to answer, turning up Beyonce a little on the way. Tristan and Yvonne were there waiting in ebullient though what seemed to Dilip an indeterminably tense mood. There was something about their body language that suggested a problem, a slight leaning away from each other, a little too much distance between them, and he thought he had detected an abrupt change of expressions as he opened the door and they had turned to greet him.

Dilip and Tristan, for their part, manifested the mutual ease of relating that comes from long friendship, their hands quickly outstretching and clasping, their smiles and delight genuine. Aside from that though the two were very different. Dilip's combination of Bollywood good looks, with his floppy, shiny blue-black hair, slim, lithe body and warm coppery skin, plus gentle, sociable nature contrasted with Tristan's pasty complexion, spreading waistline and short fuse. Yvonne looked serene and dazzling as always, an anomaly that never ceased to amaze Dilip whenever he considered her partnering with Tristan.

He led them back inside and there were greetings and hugs and pleasantries to get things underway, though he could still sense some undefinable tension. Leaving them together with Elise he went to answer the second buzz at the door. Coming from the kitchen Dilip could hear Tristan begin to spout forth his latest views on the political state of play. He sounded like he was in a combative mood. They had both been strongly involved in political action for various causes when younger, but action had dwindled into attitude as life had worn down the idealism. Tristan was Dungeon Master for the night and was building up a head of steam for the task, while at the same time being overly anxious about his responsibilities, or so it seemed. At the door Sean and Caitlin were in the forefront of the second brigade, smiling and holding up bottles of white wine in a cooler, with Carl and Azar coming up the stairs just behind them calling out their hellos.

"Be there dragons here in such lofty environs?" Sean said in a silly pirate voice as he reached the top and peered in with mock inquisitiveness.

"Let's just say, if there be, they could well be in high dudgeon in such a high dungeon," Dilip shot back in what was more Scottish with Hindi-Oz overtones than anything else specifically recognisable. They laughed and Dilip stepped back a little to let them through.

"Kids all tucked up?" Dilip asked as Azar handed him a bunch of pink and red trumpet lilies wrapped in purple cellophane.

"Yes, we found a terrific young Spanish woman, here studying English. Though they're reaching the stage where beautiful young female babysitters may no longer be the most suitable choice, especially for Ethan."

"You know they call a babysitter a 'kangaroo' in Spain? It's the pouch connection I gather," Sean said.

"And their currency is named after an Australian macropod, too: 'euro'. They're a weird lot," Carl bantered.

"A consolation prize, delusions of grandeur, past glories of empire; had designs on *Terra Australis* y'know," Sean turned and tossed back. Sean had spent time in South America and was no fan of the conquistadors.

Laughing, Azar and Carl paraded in past Dilip and down the hall lined with impressive artwork. Dilip shut the door and followed them. Azar and Caitlin had gone through university with Elise and then all had travelled and generally mucked around together in Europe and Asia for quite a while before coming back, each settling into their comfortable professional lifestyles. Along the way Elise had met Dilip in Bangalore and they had both taken the double plunge: to get married, and to live in Australia. All of them were somewhere along the third decade spectrum, Tristan the first in line to spill over into the fourth very soon.

"Pizzas ordered for 7.30 all round, yeah?" Dilip called out to check as he joined the throng in the kitchen.

A chorus of voices came back. The tone was boisterous.

"One large gluten-saturated vegetarian delight is our contribution," Caitlin cried out.

"One family-size Vivaldi's gift to gluttonous humanity from us," Tristan added.

"One large rotting-flesh lovers' orgiastic pleasure, hold the anchovies," Azar quickly piled on.

Tristan's diatribe against back-pedalling, back flipping, backstabbing, backsliding politicians was then further interrupted by another round of greetings and hugs and some necessary social updating along with the filling of wine glasses and the uncapping of craft beers. In the case of Elise it was apple cider, an ostensible concession to Dilip's cultural abstinence. She made a point of never revealing whether it was alcoholic or otherwise, though this subterfuge took quite a lot of planning and obfuscation.

Bouquet from the beverages was overwhelmed by savoury food aromas and, blended with the women's perfumes, along with perhaps a little men's aftershave, it provided a further subliminal sensory lift to add to the commotion. Any aftershave would have had to be coming from Dilip since Tristan was making the most of his fiery red bristles with a full Ned Kelly, Sean sported a designer stubble and Carl was taking the lazy option with a scissor-trimmed approach. Elise's expression indicated she had become irritated by whatever opinions Tristan had been expounding while they had been left alone together. Yvonne had wandered off to freshen up or possibly escape the situation, but Tristan was not going to be put off his ranting momentum and soon had the conversation back onto a polemical track of his choosing.

"Just look at the issue of same-sex marriage," he spouted anew.

"Which thankfully was decisively won," Elise said.

"They didn't have the balls to lead, they had to put it to a plebiscite: 'Let the people decide'."

"And just what might be wrong with that, apart from the testicular deficiency?" Azar proffered. She didn't know Tristan well and seemed to be proceeding cautiously. Then, before Tristan gathered his thoughts, she appended abruptly with specific emphasis: "And even that's not considered a problem by most people."

This had the effect of provoking him and provided an opportunity for him to head in a direction his state of mind was inevitably leading him.

"I'm speaking figuratively. But now that you've brought it up…"

"You brought it up…"

"OK, but it's interesting that that expression, you know, like someone is ballsy, is so widely used, and even applied to women, especially in these times."

"That's right," Sean entered the fray. "And there's no equivalent expression for women and their, um, equipment, nor can I see there could be one."

"She's got eggs?" Carl chanced, and received several glares for his effort.

"It's a relic from less enlightened times surely and should be pensioned off," Azar sighed.

"Executed!" Elise bought in.

"Castrated!" Azar one-upped.

They laughed together.

The group was spreading itself out now around the open area, taking their drinks with them, settling into favoured positions and occasionally making moves to dip a cracker into Elise's homemade humus, which she proudly proclaimed was based on Yotam Ottolenghi's recipe, or grab one of her canapés placed around on coffee and side tables and mantel. Sean had slumped into the armchair next to the sideboard and Azar had draped herself along one end of the grey-toned modular lounge displaying a shapely body that showed no signs of deterioration from the tribulations of child-bearing. Dilip privately admired what he saw on the lounge as he sipped on his special shikanji lemonade he made from ripe limes and always kept in full supply. Tristan remained standing in declamatory pose surveying the scene. Yvonne had returned after her absence and taken a place standing quietly in the kitchen. Carl had gone to the door of the balcony and was standing half in, half out in the shifty, conspiratorial manner that remnant modern smokers develop as semi-outcasts.

"After all," rejoined Tristan, unperturbed and sensing again the potential for a new direction to run in, one which more suited his purpose, "men are the only ones who need equipment in top working order without which it's a fizzer. It's why men can't truly be raped by women."

"Oh come on, that's got nothing to do with equipment, Tristan, it's power and attitude and ethos and personal politics, and cultural." Caitlin looked at him briefly and turned away again.

"And alcohol, Cait," Sean interposed with conscious provocation, as if it were needed at this point.

"Would women be rapists if they were somehow able to be?"

"No, Tristan!" Caitlin shot back without looking around. "And you're not listening."

"The pressure is on men to perform at sex because they are the only side of the equation who in truth can perform. And unlike women, may have sub-standard, or superior, equipment to boot." Tristan cast his gaze defiantly around the room as he spoke. "In fact, with women it's the very opposite."

Caitlin spun around and stared at him, the wine almost spilling from her glass as she did. "What the hell do you mean by that?"

"Well, I'm suggesting it's a sort of clitoral monologue, more akin to a lecture really, with pretensions to becoming a dialogue." He hesitated, revelling smugly in his newly discovered assumed clever insight.

Azar was mesmerised by revulsion. "Oh, please, don't stop there, tell us more." She had decided she didn't like Tristan at all and was torn between wanting to see him dig himself into an even greater hole than he had already managed, and cutting him into little pieces with her razor-sharp riposte.

Tristan made the most of his opportunity.

"Men have no real interest in the clitoris, it's more of a long-term investment really, rather than something offering immediate returns. I'm not saying that women don't do anything; they just don't have to, well, lead in the dance. And there's an interesting and persistent allegory for you. As Wilde, or Shaw, pointed out, vertical and horizontal whatnot."

"Now you're just turning the whole thing into a performance."

"Well, how to put it? Men are quite frankly easily satisfied in sex, they really only want to get in and get it, though that doesn't mean they don't want to, ahem, draw it out a bit and enjoy the expedition occasionally. And I'm not talking here about those adventurous preliminary reconnaissance missions. I'm talking more about daily commuting. But in the final analysis the pleasure is pretty straightforward for men."

"And just whose final analysis would that be then, Tristan?" Elise spat out.

"Whereas women," he ignored her and continued, "have a much greater range of pleasure and a far longer journey to indulge in. Men can enhance that journey for a woman, make it a memorable one, not that they feel like doing that too often, generally speaking. Hence the expression: he's good in the sack."

The three other men stared at him, generally stunned and in intense anticipation both of what he might say next and of how the women were going to react. Dilip inwardly winced and wondered what the hell was going on, where it was leading and what he could do to dampen it down.

"Women can't do the same for men. For men the most exciting thing is that they are willing. Hence the expression: 'easy'."

"Oh my God! I'm dumbstruck," and Elise confirmed it with her expression and subsequent muteness.

Tristan thought about it briefly while silence reigned. Dilip was becoming very uneasy, allegiance to his abiding friendship feeling strained.

"Men just want to poke; anything that will take their penis really."

Carl had finished his puffing session, committed himself to the indoors and taken a seat on the lounge along from Azar. He shifted uneasily. "True, to some extent I suppose."

"Though most prefer it to be a woman's vagina, most of the time." Tristan threw him a lifeline.

"Well I certainly do," Sean insisted, perhaps too readily. "And there are certain fringe benefits go with it."

Caitlin cast him a withering look and he knew that that comment would cost him dearly soon enough, perhaps on an ongoing basis.

"Women on the other hand just want to be filled up, and a man's penis fits the bill."

"Thank God for small mercies," chimed in Dilip, spying an opening for some much-needed levity.

"Speak for your own," Sean scoffed. Everyone laughed and Dilip pulled a face as he took the blow but felt some relief for the breather, however short-lived.

"For women this craving to be entered comes from their desire and need to be implanted with seed and have it germinate and grow inside her. That's why it's called impregnating, and then she's ... 'pregnant' ... " and he made appropriate air quotes with his fingers to go with it. "You might say women are pregnable, and men are impregnable ... or think they are."

Azar and Elise looked at Tristan aghast, apparently struck speechless by shock. Yvonne maintained her separate silence.

"Homosexual men want both, and can get it. That's why they should be thought of as ambisexual ..."

"Oh, come on, you can't be 'homo' and 'ambi' at the same time." Sean warmed to the attack, feeling he should boldly counter this dangerous course Tristan was taking but was somehow otherwise spellbound by the purely intellectual challenge.

"From the practical point of view, rather than the biological one."

"Spin," Sean retorted.

"Lesbians however only want to - and can only be - filled up, but have trouble achieving that with any great natural success, in fact at times, excess."

"Oh really, Tristan," Azar finally interrupted. "That's all very crude."

"And specious," Elise added.

"Hence bysexual - as in bee-wye not bee-i, meaning nearabouts - would be the most accurate description of them."

Tristan was not to be put off and his voice rose against the protests and laughter. It was deep and mellifluous and he could make it boom with authority if need be with an orator's sense of pace and rhythm and tone, a little like Richard Burton without the looks. He had a touch of that actor's hubris as well. Dilip had often noted this and thought it perhaps went towards why he had won over Yvonne.

"They may be sexually gratified but are continually unsatisfied and therefore perpetually grouchy."

Tristan was almost shouting now above the hubbub.

"I know one or two who are quite happy," Elise claimed with a certain conviction.

Tristan looked around for Yvonne and his gaze dwelt on her for a hesitating moment.

"Exceptions. Or frauds. 'Gay' was hijacked and applied to homosexual men for good reason, but 'crabby' could well be conscripted as the lesbian equivalent."

Tristan sat back, grinning though his intent was deadly serious. All around him there was noisy merriment and angry dissent.

Yvonne's voice emerged clearly, though calmly, from the pack. "Many more women enjoy homosexual experiences than men do. That negates your argument of frustrated fulfilment."

Tristan gazed steadily at Yvonne again and then shifted it briefly to Elise and back to Yvonne. Elise looked at Yvonne.

"Ah, but that's not sexual, you see. It's intimacy, beyond sex. It's standing naked in front of one another, physically and metaphorically, without shame or pride. Women find intimacy more easily with other women than men do with men."

"It does come hard for men." Dilip smirked while still smarting from his earlier humiliation, trying to cloak his embarrassment by counterattack and at the same time working on defusing what he could see had become a primed powder keg.

Tristan shot him a dagger-glance but maintained his pace. "To understand men you have to understand that, and that men have intractable egos. At least, they have much bigger egos than women."

"Fuck their egos," Azar shot out.

"But that is like a man saying fuck women's hormonal swings." Tristan turned on her. "Neither egg nor ego is a dirty word. You have to take men as they are, as men, with powerful egos. A man will never forget, perhaps not even forgive, a humiliation, having his ego crushed, more than any other hurt. Look at the way old soldiers get over their hatred of an often brutal enemy, and forgive. But never a slight to their ego. Women know this intuitively, yet, or and, still use their verbal dexterity to crush men's egos. Next to a scorned woman's fury, neither hell nor dungeon has ferocity like a man with a wounded ego. It's all a product of that distinctive libidinous drive: men act, women react, sexually-speaking. And that's why when relationships go off the rails men might turn to violence and women to vindictiveness … the two furies … the v-words … the gender venges."

The orator in Tristan made the most of those last words.

"Are you seriously suggesting, no, asserting that rape is justified because of men's overpowering egos?"

Azar had long abandoned her slouch on the lounge and now jumped up and stormed around the room, one shoulder pointing at Tristan, her head turned to face him, circling him like a matador, rapier ready. Dilip was now immediately concerned he might have to physically intervene.

"Oh, and when did you stop brow-beating your husband, Azar? Of course I am not, but I am saying that egos have to be acknowledged and accepted …" A cheeky grin took hold of his face and he adopted a sing-song tone. "Kept in good shape, exercised daily and put down on tape …"

Suddenly, and as if on cue, Tristan's phone began to ring, or rather vibrate and play Wagner's *Ride Of The Valkyries*. He immediately froze and fumbled in his pockets completely overcome by the demanding sound. As he did so both Caitlin's phone also started to chime with the standard Nokia ring tone. Caitlin made a beeline towards the source on the nearby sideboard where she had left it with her keys and bag. Elise made her way over to the bookshelf where she made a point of always putting it so she'd know where it was. She picked it up to check it though it remained silent. Sean's phone had now also started to play, in this case the Star Wars theme, and then Azar's set itself off with some current pop tune. All four together presented a discordant minor concert in the room, with Nokia providing a strong melodic underpinning. With some disappointment Yvonne looked at hers which had also remained silent. Carl now found, much to his horror, that he had left his phone in the car, and Dilip's battery had run out and in his excitement over preparing for the evening had forgotten to plug it in. But they were sidelined anyway by the insistent call of the others, and the consequent focussing elsewhere.

Right at that moment came a buzzing from the front door and then an importunate knocking, a percussive backing to the general symphonic cacophony.

The cavalry, in the form of pizza delivery, as ordered, and piercingly announced, had arrived. The bugle call of retreat could not be ignored. Tristan's relief.

But somebody was going to have to pay, for everything.

Tristan put his hand up and made a dash for the door,

wallet held out in front like a drawn sabre, over-eagerly leading the counter charge.

Caitlin, standing next to Azar, both of their phones now silent and held out in front of them like unexpected gifts, turned, looked at her and murmured: "Poor Yvonne." They had not noticed Elise, on her way around the kitchen bench to get to her phone, brush the back of her hand against Yvonne's cheek as she passed, and Yvonne's cheek welcoming the touch in return.

Tristan reappeared looking sheepish and holding out in front three stacked boxes of baked, if not burnt, offerings. But he was still going to need earnest recourse to some major fantasy role-playing for the rest of that night to survive. They all were. In the meantime the beguiling and commanding call of digital devices had done its usual job of distraction, though in this case for the general good.

Dealing with Delilah

Delilah.

What kind of parent would visit on a child the name Delilah with all its connotations? Well, in the case of this Delilah, it came about as a compromise between her Tom Jones-loving gentile mother and her tenacious Jewish father.

My, my, how they bickered over it. For three weeks the little one remained nameless. From Aabagail to Zuzuana they racked their brains and trawled the internet. He insisted it be Ashkenazic to reflect his heritage and give her connection, though technically she would still be not-Jewish. Her mother was determined it be distinctive, contemporary, neutral, pleasant to the ear, and certainly not have silly spelling. They pushed and shoved; they pulled their great-great-grandmothers and their great-great-grandaunts into the fray by historical proxy. They rejected rational arguments at the same time as they appealed to reason. They threatened dire consequences. They both knew they were mutually stymied.

And then, just as mental exhaustion and terminal frustration placed the newborn at risk of being orphaned while still nameless, Radio Greytone, 'playing all your golden oldies and smoulderin' mouldies', beamed out the Tom Jones classic. It was lay-down *misere*. There was no question of why, why; it just was.

But this story is not about them, it's about that Delilah. Delilah Diamond.

It was not just the name that Delilah would have to wear like cheap ostentatious jewellery all her life. It was also what she would refer to as her liminality, a living limbic suspension. Betwixt and between. That original tussle over her name left as its symbolic legacy a feeling in her of hovering between two worlds, of being caught in the middle, sitting on a very uncomfortable paling fence with legs dangling either side, feet seeking to find ground, first one side then the other; of an unachievable longing to settle in one or the other, of a life-long exile to marginality. How she would have happily settled for being beyond the pale, or within it for that matter.

With her gentile mother she could simply be deemed Anglican, but she would have had to convert to attain Jewishness. From her Jewish father she acquired no standing, yet felt she should at least be accorded a certain Jew-*ish*-ness even if she took an Anglican path. Nor did she find any relief as she grew up and learnt the background of her name. While it was Hebrew there was no certainty that that meant it was Jewish. There was no joy for her in the Bible either, whether it was her mother's King James Christian version or her father's. The original Delilah may have been Jewish or may not have been. Either way she was a temptress and a betrayer. The Tom Jones song didn't help any. *Oy vey*, where should a poor girl turn for comfort and certitude? It could have been worse, Delilah often mused. It could have been Caroline, sweet Caroline.

———

So then, imagine you had been seeing this Delilah Diamond off and on for six months, like I had. You had come across her profile on an internet dating site you had delved into occasionally with the usual disappointments. Hers was a stand-out. Looking good in an all-black outfit, wine glass in hand jauntily at an angle, a confident stance and steely gaze, she was as sexy as they come. A touch of Juliette Binoche in the face, with long jet-black hair framing that alabaster high-domed brow, serious dark eyes, determined mouth and high cheek bones, on the body of a Demi Moore, a very agreeable combination. The self-description was literate and appealing: a professional artist, she was into fine foods - no place for vegetarians, or worse, in your life, you'd learnt that, too confining and challenging for domestic arrangements, and she drank, thank God, any god - communing with nature, arthouse movies, communicating with and connecting to the world, whatever that may mean; live music, jazz and rock, reading serious stuff and, good heavens, the *New Yorker* and *Economist*. You had both of them on your coffee table. She also thankfully did not claim to have a 'GSH' - for you the kiss of death rather than the professed laugh of love-of-life - and although swimming was mentioned as her sporting hobby, you chose not to let that spoil the effect. Your best pool memories and aspirations extended only to those ones with a slate, rather than a tiled, bottom. Nor did you let her very ordinary site nickname, 'Enigmatic1', put you off. It would surely have some deep significance. And this profile, which she had written herself without any doubt in your mind, was not sullied by even the most minor spelling or grammatical error, a welcome contrast to the norm.

You included her in your next round of flirt messages to various women you scatter-gunned off – the ones that the site conveniently, and at no charge, composed for you about how their profiles caught your eye or made you smile. And how true that was in her case. Your routine method was to send off ten at a time, keeping the standard as high as you could from among the dross, and without serious regard to any chances of success. You'd generally get rejected by half, ignored by two or three more and score with one or two, an acceptable result. And to your amazement this time, Delilah, or Enigmatic1 as she still was, gave you a tick response.

Before you paid up and sent her an introductory email you showed her profile to a couple of friends on one of your regular nights together. Norma took one look at the photo.

"She'll have you for breakfast," she immediately spat out, and tossed the profile back to you. In your star-gazed state you shrugged this off as base envy, unworthy of consideration. Norma obviously harboured feelings for you and was subconsciously acting that out.

Judith, herself an artist, and therefore with some interest in a positive outcome, took a different line:

"She looks interesting," she said, considering the details more thoroughly than Norma had bothered to.

Neither of them could have been moved by the image of her as you were.

"That's right," you said, giving Norma a dirty look. "She seems to be very impressive and I'll take my chances." Of course you would, that is what it was all about, surely? This dating game, this rolling of dice based on two-dimensional, carefully selected images and one-dimensional carefully edited information. And wasn't romance in any form about taking a chance anyway.

Norma scoffed.

Next came the hard part: you had to formulate an impressive opening response - expand on whatever it may have been in your profile that she liked, express your connection to her own avowed interests and possibly add some intrigue, or some flirtatiousness, though that was a fine line and dangerous territory. You didn't want to come across as either sleazy or desperate. You would be open and honest too, though this could be a risk in another way. You had learnt from experience that being open and honest could very easily lead to exposure and hurt. You felt though that you had this woman's measure, and you were confident you could trust her. This on the basis of very little, mainly hope and more probably, delusion.

And so you called upon any morsel of evidence from your life that you could associate with what seemed to be her major concerns: art, travel, serious cultural interest. Of course you showed modesty while at the same time indicating that your life was full and meaningful, though not so much as to have no potential for something extra to be worked into it. You were just a little revealing of your private self, allowing for some vulnerability, and displayed your self-confidence by giving her your phone number and name. After all, you can't stalk a phone number, and names can hardly give too much away about their owners, can they? Can they?

The response from the enigmatic one took three days. A manageable time lapse, just making the wait uneasily long enough without appearing to be over-anxious with a premature follow-up. She was now, for the first time for you, Delilah, and the face, the body, had nominal substance. You were surprised by such a name and wondered briefly whether it might be a put-on. But she also gave you her phone number so you assumed it to be real. She would reassure you soon enough with the story of its origins. The email was as literate and open as her date-site profile, validating your assessment of her intellectual powers. It confirmed her main focus was her artwork – you'd got that right – and she had obviously thought about your profile statement too, in much the same way as you had hers, by alluding to some of your interests and concerns. And she revealed some vulnerability by telling you her father, that Ashkenazi force in her life, had developed Alzheimer's, and how that was affecting her, a risky disclosure if true. She was also forthright enough to jump straight to arranging a meeting for real conversation without further to-do, expressing her curiosity to know more.

Well, it couldn't have gone better, you concluded.

There was much still to work on there and several more emails were exchanged. With her full name at your disposal you googled her and found out as much as you could, though you never told her that of course. You found images of her art and were genuinely impressed just as you were with some of her academic writing, which also explained her literary precision. You really had to strut your stuff now: knock her dead with your prodigious literary skills, empathise with her pain and give support, forge deeper connections to her central concerns, make some philosophical observations, show a solid practical side, boast a little but not too much, venture a safe political stance, one that was somehow neutral and non-committal while still showing a caring attitude and desire to be involved.

It wasn't overly difficult with such an accomplished accomplice and she gave as good as she got in emails again as literate as her profile. And very serious. Your humorous asides, something you were particularly proud of and considered to be fine examples of the form, did go without any acknowledged response, you noticed. And though she was exhibiting interest in you and was being open and apparently honest there was a caution, a holding back of anything that could be considered flirtatious; and no humour, but at least no GSH either. No problem there: she was being sensibly cautious. She seemed a little forlorn, but that was good: vulnerability in a woman can evoke very strong protective instincts in a man, which it did on this occasion. In any case, there was her father's condition to keep in mind.

Her commitment to her art came through clearly, including the fact that, what with her teaching responsibilities and the preparation for a new exhibition to be held in Israel coming up, she was very busy. Israel? And Delilah Diamond, hmm. Nevertheless she rose eagerly to your suggestion of meeting at the City Art Museum sometime soon, a well-targeted venue you chose carefully. She agreed and said she would like to take in the annual portrait competition hangings and then meet in the museum's café afterwards, with the proviso that you might recognise each other and meet beforehand in one of the galleries.

And indeed you did. As you wandered around checking the entries, most of them portraying well-known people in artistic and political circles, you noticed the back of a Demi Moore body dressed all in black standing assuredly and staring at one of the larger entries. You had already done the rounds and this one was one of your favourites. You walked up and stood beside her, just turning your head slightly to check the profile to be sure it was indeed Delilah.

"One of my favourites," Mr Cool said casually, looking straight at it.

"I love the sense of immediacy it gives, and how it conveys the confidence of the artist in herself and in her work." She spoke, with only the slightest turn of her head, as if you and your presence had been assumed. It was like her writing: calculated, literate, serious and without error.

"Delilah, Peter, nice to meet," you said holding out a hand which she took as she smiled and said:

"You found me." The smile was just a little forced but you appreciated the accuracy of the allegation.

You walked around the exhibition together and exchanged views on the works. Her ability to give intelligent comments on each of the artworks impressed you and certainly left your appraisals in the shade. You continued to get along well, spending several hours on that first date, going downstairs to the museum's café for a drink, then another, then segueing into dinner, right up to the time of closing. You talked art, family, relationships, your experience with the internet dating, a touch of general political inclinations, warily, and light, bantering chit-chat, cautious proto-flirtational style. She insisted on dropping you home as she had her car in the museum's underground parking station, so you stumbled along a garden path in darkness to get there and then had some fun finding the way out through the concrete maze. She stopped to let you off at a convenient spot near your home and you leant towards her and gave her a light kiss on her cheek as you opened the door to get out. It had gone very well. You agreed to see each other again.

And you did, although it was limited to only one date a week by Delilah's schedule, if you were lucky. She was always "so busy". She went to your place two or three times, just as a practical meet-up spot before dinner or a movie as she always came by car, much to your delight. But she never invited you to hers, nor to her art studio where she was working on her next exhibition, to be held in Safed, a place which you quickly did some internet research on. It was a topic you talked about a great deal, and you helped her with travel arrangements, something you were more experienced with than she was, and about which you were more than happy to display your superior knowledge and ability since there seemed precious little room for you to manoeuvre otherwise in this regard.

A routine had established itself. That first kiss on the cheek became standardised at the end of an evening after a movie or an art exhibition and a meal. The lively conversation and intellectual discussion that always marked any outings were followed by one or two emails where points were expanded upon and daily concerns explored. Whenever the topic entered her realm of art she was particularly incisive. She was not one to take prisoners in an argument. On one occasion when you ventured a flippant remark on young people and their fresh ideas she put you in your artistic place right down there with the young people. Self-expression was of little use in itself, she wrote. It required pairing with visual knowledge and intelligence to achieve its potential, and that was her aim. Nevertheless, she was consistently warm towards you and expressed her enthusiasm for the next meeting each time, even to the point of suggesting to do it more often.

However, after a month or so of this you noticed she had not taken her profile down off the internet dating site. You had. More often did not eventuate and frustration led you finally to express itself to her as your confusion. Her response was to express her reluctance to be in a relationship due to her heavy commitment to work, meaning her art. Yes, she said, this seemed to be a cop-out, a skirting the issue, especially since she did feel somewhat lonesome. For this reason she enjoyed your social life together. "I do like you," she claimed, "and want to continue our friendship."

Friendship! Oh dear, the death of a thousand cuts in one deft swipe. You winced and minced out of it with a declaration of "understanding completely" and being able to "handle it." Well, after that you really only had yourself to blame if it all stalled at friendship level.

After another month of this unconsummated arrangement it fizzled, and there was a hiatus. No doubt she was busy. Then you unexpectedly ran into her in an elevator at the college where she was teaching an art class and you were doing some language classes. Again you talked animatedly and she showed no sign of wanting to leave during the single hour she had off between her classes. She suggested you have dinner after classes one night and once again you were going out periodically, though it generally took a lot of arranging. You generally saw each other every week at the college but she was so busy: her daughter was getting married. There were always occasional emails in between meetings, hers were always perfectly formed, grammatically faultless, but with never a trace of flirtatiousness, much like her behaviour in person.

The college break for the summer period was upon you and an invitation came again for a night out. To see a movie, though you don't like going to the cinema at all, but it would be followed by dinner which you do like. You shared a passion for duck, like Billie Holiday, and she was a good eater. Arrangements for another meeting before Christmas followed, during an extra-busy time. You planned to use the silly season, a dead period for you, to concentrate on your writing.

You went to see a movie on the 23rd, then had dinner

afterwards. You weren't as keen on the film as she was, but she gave it a lively and formidable critique and analysis over the meal that followed which left your viewpoint floundering. She told you she was having dinner with a girlfriend the following night, then Christmas dinner with her daughter's new family. You emailed her a thank-you greeting the next day with wishes for the season and an invitation to a Boxing Day party.

Late that night, Christmas Eve, you got an unexpected reply to say that she had had a serious car accident, had written off the car, and questioned whether she could make the Boxing Day party. She was obviously in a distressed state by the expression of her email, though it was still immaculately written. You wrote her a comforting reply. On the afternoon of the 25th she rang, unusual in itself. You learnt more details about the accident and you did your best to reassure her about some of the catastrophising she was doing, a common reaction in post-traumatic situations, you had learnt. She said she was still not sure about Boxing Day but you told her to relax, not to make any important decisions, and to give you a ring whenever she wanted. You were concerned about her welfare as well as touched by the fact she had turned to you in these circumstances.

And she did. She rang the next day from Clovelly, a long way from her Glebe home, saying she wanted to come and see you. You readily agreed of course, highly surprised at this new turn, and waited for her to arrive, telling her not to rush as you had to prepare, which in reality meant have a scrub and wash your hair. She arrived in the early afternoon, having taken public transport, she told you, not an easy trip. She was agitated, though in a typically controlled way, and you calmed her down, offered her a drink, sat and listened.

What unfolded was a story of considerable long-standing duplicity, made more remarkable by the fact that she seemed to have no appreciation she was confessing her dishonest behaviour directly and forthrightly to the one she had deceived.

The Christmas Eve dinner had been not only with a girlfriend but also with Will, a boyfriend, or ex-boyfriend, or "non-relationship" as she insisted on calling it, a tradesman of some sort, now unemployed, something and someone she had not mentioned to you once in all that time. She was driving Will home where she was apparently going to stay the night, although that detail was muddied somewhat, when the accident occurred. You suspected this happened partly because she was in strange territory and partly because of the tension between them in the vehicle. She suffered no injury but Will had a head gash for which he had to be taken to hospital for checking and stitches. She went with him and later took him home.

She stayed the night there. She now had a dilemma. Should she continue to stay with him to look after him or go as planned to have Christmas lunch with her adult daughter, someone she had mentioned to you while emphasising the absence of any father. She wanted unarguably to spend Christmas with her daughter, but felt some responsibility to Will, who in reality was not particularly hurt. She discussed it with Will, probably with some acrimony as the tension developed. He said go, and eventually she did, but with the compromise that she would come back and cook a dinner for him and stay again to look after him. This she did, but the tension increased over what to do next and their general situation.

They slept that night on opposite sides of the bed, stiff, and not touching or even getting close to each other, at least from her point of view or so she told you, though you were imagining otherwise. She became outraged when he said he was going to go as planned to have lunch with some mates anyway. She felt that he was being ungrateful to her when she was offering to look after him. They had arguments. She said she felt like he was treating her as a doormat. He said she didn't prioritise him, something which resonated with you as she said it. She felt she had to be rid of this relationship, that it had to end. Did you agree? Well, yes you did, as a matter of fact, though clearly with completely different motivation. She packed up what few things she had there and stormed out. As she did she noticed a present she had once given to him. She grabbed it in revenge and threw it in her bag, feeling he did not deserve her kindnesses.

As the emotions of anger, guilt, remorse, vindictiveness, fear swirled around in her agitated state she developed added worry that he might sue her for the injury and that he would take all her money, not a great deal it seems and only just inherited from some relative, along with the car she had also just wiped out. It had certainly not been a good year for her.

She came to you.

After she'd told you all this over a period of a couple of hours you realised that it was getting late to go to the party, if indeed you wanted to. You had thought it would be a good opportunity for her to meet new people, people with money and appreciation for art, and now there was the added attraction of it being an opportunity to distract her from her woes.

The full implications of what she had told you had still not sunk in. They were probably in fact being repressed by a heavy bout of cowardice and denial. You discussed how to get there and decided to go. She pulled out a dress from the backpack - one of the things she'd had at Will's - and asked if it would be more suitable than the jeans she had on. You said put it on and let's see, which she did using your bedroom, not for the first time for that purpose, though never for any other.

She stepped out back into your view and said, "How do I look?"

She looked great of course. It was something of a minor

shock for you to see her in a dress for the first time. Generally her fashion sense was not good, running mostly to black as an easy default as well as being the accepted artistic uniform. The transformation provided her with an extra dimension of attraction for you, a softening, an extension of her already considerable attributes, almost a blossoming, at least from your point of view. Still, she wasn't coquettish, she didn't sashay before you, she didn't, in a nutshell, flirt or entice. You should have had your antennae out, or rather had them tuned in. You assured her it looked better, downplaying what you really thought. This when you should have pounced on her, with her in her weakened state, sent all inhibitions and fear of failure and rational explanations and possibility of remorse on their way. Yet you didn't, you couldn't. In reality it was you who was skirting the issue of any serious relationship, not her. You simply were unable to bite the bullet. She seemed to be surrounded by some impenetrable force field, perhaps generated by that liminality seething within her.

You decided to go. She said she needed to put on make-up, which she then did in the bathroom, stopping on her way back to ask you as she passed whether it looked good. It did, and you said so. All this attention to her appearance, right in the heart of your domain, was unsettling for you, but seemed to have no impact on Delilah. It was as though she found herself caught in another one of her liminal situations, both protected and isolated by such unseen and undetected barriers that she had built around her. And again you should have detected the signs of disattachment, but you were in effect befuddled.

You went to the party, waving goodbye to most of the people as they left and you arrived. You caught up with the few old friends who remained, but she made no attempt at any sort of pitch to them of her work, understandable given the circumstances. You came back and went and had dinner, duck, nearby. She ate heartily as usual and you drove her home quite late. The farewell was friendly but reserved; she was controlled while still giving the feeling she was operating in an emotional fog. You weren't invited in.

You didn't hear from her the next day though you sent her a couple of emails reassuring her about some matters to do with the accident, but on the Monday you got another phone call. You were still acting like a counsellor and hadn't yet fully considered the implications for you. You were in complete denial. She asked you if she could take up your kind offer of lending her your car as she needed to go and arrange things with the wreckers about her vehicle.

You got all that done on the Wednesday. There was an unusual air of domesticity about the practical business of dealing with wreckers, cleaning out her car and hanging around waiting. Afterwards she invited you to her studio for the first time to see it and her work in progress. They were large, impressive canvasses in various stages of completion and she gave you some description of her technique and intent with them. You followed that up with dinner at a nearby restaurant, a good time as usual. You shared a duck dish. She even touched on matters from her past concerning sexual adventures that bordered on the flirtatious or suggestive, or could be given that interpretation. Had she made a decision to really finish with Will and was she now opening up to other possibilities?

You drove her home and helped her carry her salvaged items from her car into her apartment, the first time you had seen it. It was a pokey converted motel room and you were taken aback by its aspect of indigence, how this clashed with your perception of Delilah and what you thought she deserved to have in life.

You mentioned New Year's Eve and she talked about her invitation to a party at her friend's place near you, someone you knew vaguely, but she didn't make any suggestion about you joining her. Nor was there any hint of an invitation to linger, no coy glance at the bed, no manufactured excuse of sore shoulders needing a massage, or offer of nightcap, no warm hug of thanks that continued a little longer than it should have. You went home wondering whether perhaps she was simply shy, or out of practice, or liked the man to sweep her off her feet with a show of dominance. Given what you knew of her you found all that unlikely. Then perhaps not. What do you know?

On New Year's Eve she rings and asks if she can drop in on the way to her party. She does, and spends most of the time on her smartphone trying to arrange an Uber and there is scant mention of the past drama. You are not exactly sure why she broke her journey to drop in. In the end you give her a lift. Maybe that was why. No invite or apology that she can't ask you in. Nothing for three days after.

You're wondering now about your status as a doormat. You wish that some of the granite metaphor which is embedded in your name would manifest itself as grit. It hits you at last that she has chosen a rude mechanical over you, you an intellectual giant who has regaled her with your superior wit and wisdom and matched her profound insights and opinions over all these weeks providing stimulating company whenever she needed it. That he might be a hunk and possess extraordinary venereal talents is of no consolation. All that busy-ness of hers: she had been staying with him, going out with him, giving him presents, inviting him to stay over at her place where she had never invited you to even take a peep, having him as escort to her daughter's wedding, you imagine. She had probably shared duck with him. She is the consummate trickster. Enigmatic indeed. You get on with your writing which strangely seems to be going well despite the distraction. Perhaps it was all stimulating in a perverse way, just what a writer needs.

A few days later she sends one of her astonishingly well formulated emails thanking you for your help and suggesting a dinner the following week at her favourite duck restaurant, a secret one she would reveal to you on the night. Back into the old routine. It's so tempting that you weaken and agree, though you are now seriously considering the timing of the jettison, the end of throwing good money after bad, the giving it up as a lost cause. Faint hope is growing very pale indeed. But she is, after all, you have no need to remind yourself yet again, very attractive, profoundly fascinating, impressively talented, and with an imposing intellect. Nor has she actually dumped you.

She emails again: she's bought a new car and suggests a day for dinner and a whirl in the car – she has petrolhead tendencies as an earthy counterbalance to her intellectualism. You had never got a grip of that side of her but perhaps it explains the rude mechanical. You agree, and then she replies again, stating, unsolicited, how important this time is for her, this opportunity she has for her career path and how she has to determine her own fate, choose her own times and therefore cannot enter into a relationship, as if your mere acceptance of her repeated invitation to dinner has placed some pressure on her once again. That, or she's read your mind, which adds to the menacing respect you have for her.

It's the deathblow. Norma had been right. Delilah had had you for breakfast. You summon up the courage to write and finally tell her straightforwardly that she has behaved quite badly, and that it is best to end it:

Your last email was somewhat confusing, in part. I'm not sure what prompted you to write that as I had not seen you for two weeks and my emails were quite bland. I don't think I have recently put any pressure on you, waiting patiently for you to lead, and I have always been very supportive of your work. I've always said yes to anything and everything, as far as I can remember.

I would love to see you again, but I think this time I have to be strong and decline. To bite the bullet and call it quits, although it does hurt a bit. I know you're having a bad time with things right now but I think I have helped all I can, and you are getting over it. I also think that although we had a lot in common, a lot of similar attitudes and interests, there was a lot I liked about you, we might

not have been good for each other - we're both bossy, as you observed,
and you seem to have had trouble with men, and their egos perhaps,
as I have had with women, during our lives. In any case it seems that
"you are just not that into me".

It has been enjoyable knowing you, but for me it has been a
bit of a roller-coaster ride, not a particularly gut-wrenching one,
happily, but still with its ups and downs, its vertical loopiness. The
long gaps of silence and then the re-appearances, I wasn't really able
to connect with you, you seem to have some sort of wall around you.
I realise now that it is causing me too much stress. Mere friendship is
not compatible with this.

If you had told me you were struggling to exit a relationship at
least I would not have been so confounded by your coolness. Perhaps
you wanted me to sweep you off your feet and get you out of it, and
I would have been happy to do that, but there was always that wall.

This is not a rejection, it's more of a self-protective strategy. I'll
just get on with doing whatever it is I am going to get on with doing.
Pity about the duck.

But even now, at this terminal juncture, she maintains
the upper hand. She replies, agrees and apologises, understands
your situation, justifies her actions – says she didn't want to
"complicate" things and that she was "confused" - explains
her position succinctly and logically, patronises you, wishes
you well and hopes to meet again. It seems that her liminality
is not confined to her sense of self, her essence, but extends to
her relationship balance. Her explanation is flimsy and lacks
plausibility, as if she is still unable to face her reality:

The situation with Will was odd because he had been out of my
life when I met you but then later tried to reconnect. I did not want
to pursue a relationship with him and he did not really want that
with me either. It was too difficult between us. Having said that we
have both found it difficult to break the tie completely.

Nevertheless, her apology is gracious, is completely *mea*
culpa and attaches no blame to you. It is the usual perfectly

formed piece, except this time, to your sublime satisfaction, it does commit one clear grammatical error in delivering the coup de grace:

I felt that a relationship between you and I was never really going to happen anyway.

You don't reply, but she emails twice more asking for details to assist with her exhibition planning. She certainly has chutzpah. You send them to her without comment. She thanks you, and suggests any time you'd be in for a duck, she'd love to. Her dating profile remains active.

You think to yourself: "I'm sorry, Delilah, but I really just couldn't take any more".

The Virgin and "The Dud"

Robert, striding casually with thoughts only of his planned quiet evening ahead, turned the corner of the long corridor, doors closed to the rooms off it on each side, and immediately pulled himself up stark still, and stiff. She was suddenly there, almost upon him, sweeping silently in all her glory towards him from the other direction along another narrow corridor stretching out behind her and devoid of any manner of interruption: the woman he had been in awe of since he had first laid eyes upon her, the woman whose name he could not even utter in her presence, though he often whispered it to himself when alone in his bedroom. There was no time for him to react, if indeed there were anything he could do; they were alone, she was standing right there before him, face to face, eyes to eyes, body to body.

She said nothing, but swung her head around and hastily looked over her shoulder, pushed him backwards a little and peeked furtively over his shoulder, stepped back, put out one hand and grasped his, spun around and led him back down the empty corridor, still without speaking. There was nothing for him to do but comply. He was both mortified and exhilarated. She reached the door of her room, opened it swiftly with her free hand and entered, pulled him in, stopped, turned and pushed the door shut without hesitating, as if he were hardly there, led him in a few further steps, stopped again and whirled back around with a swish of her gown's skirt.

As their eyes met, and in that abrupt new certainty, there were no longer any questions to be asked, nor permission to be requested, no doubts to be raised, no hesitation to be suffered. The frustrated longing of years instantly overwhelmed them both and all their previous caution and discretion was abandoned. She released his arm and they threw themselves at each other, clenching in mutual embrace, their open mouths clashing together with a magnetic grip as they chewed and sucked and their tongues groped for pleasure and satisfaction, writhing like a pair of copulating skinks. Without parting, hands and arms flailing about, searching for the most acceptable position to settle into in what was formerly unexplored territory, they stumbled backwards and sideways to the huge bed in the middle of the room before falling over together onto it and shuffling somehow to lie crosswise over its cushiony welcome.

It was clearly going to be impossible in their feverish state to get clothes off, so sumptuously covered were they in the formal attire of the day's business.

She let him go reluctantly but necessarily and reached down, grabbing the hems of her dress and petticoats, and pulled them up manically, exposing enough of her body for the purpose. His hands now free, he tugged and pulled downwards from his waist whatever he had on, in total disregard to whatever was holding it in place but thankfully without belt or complicated buckle, releasing his swollen member from its confines. His mouth ravaged her neck and upper bosom which was bare and pressed upwards in the off-the-shoulder dress she was wearing, and so luminously white set off against the red-orange flaming pyre of her hair. They whimpered like blind puppies struggling to find a teat and sighed like the first soft soughing breeze stirring a forest after the midday heat. He manoeuvred himself on top and prodded her pubic opening with the tip of his penis. She reached out wildly with one hand, dipped her fingers into a bowl of some cosmetic lotion at her bedside and smeared it roughly over his thwarted appendage, and then around her vulva and into her vagina. The odour of their inflamed bodies mingled with the herbal fragrances of the make-do lubricant as they relished the sweet juice of each other's saliva. He thrusted and entered her with her guidance and she cried out with pain and rapture, her head thrown back over the edge of the bed, he biting her neck and pummelling with thunderous energy, she revelling in the penetration and colonisation of her body and the expectation of whatever was to come. They convulsed in rhythmic concord and their pent-up sexual frustration exploded in a short-lived frenzy, as he climaxed and ejaculated and she died simultaneously, crying out uncontrollably and without inhibition.

Then they were spent. He slumped down on her, her head hung limply back towards the floor. Concerned about his weight, he rolled off, withdrawing too soon. She winced, then pulled herself up to lie beside him. He turned to look at her and, propping himself up on one elbow, reached out and put his cupped hand on her forehead and ran it upwards across her hair. She found his hand and placed it down between her legs and he squeezed her gently. She smiled at him with the pleasure of it and mouthed his name. He kissed her tenderly on her lips and mouthed her name.

Before they could do anything more or even properly speak, and as their hearts gradually stilled, there was a pounding on her door. She raised her head to check and said quietly, indicating with her eyes:

"Through that door and close it behind you, quickly."

Panicking somewhat, and still in a state of half-awareness, he jumped off the bed, holding his nether garments up with one hand as best he could, and did as she had ordered, shuffling awkwardly but swiftly across the room and out of sight.

The pounding resumed.

She pulled herself up into a sitting position, smoothed out her clothing and composed herself.

"Come!" she called out, and the door was flung open. A man in uniform marched in and stood at attention. Two more men in the same uniform waited in the doorway behind him clutching weapons.

"Yes?" she barked, her mind spinning with hitherto unimagined emotions, her body still tingling with nervous energy, her spirits soaring, and all constrained for the moment now at hand. The man looked carefully around the room without speaking while she held him in her steadfast gaze, then looked back at her.

"The Spanish ships have been sighted to the south-east, Your Majesty," he said, bowing his head. "The fires have been lit."

Elizabeth smiled inwardly at the reference as she swung herself off her bed, slipped into shoes and stood proud and forthright, then strode from the room back into the corridor, the men parting to make way for her before following.

Lord Robert Dudley listened from behind the door of his closet refuge, and feared doubly for his future.

The Watched

Warren wandered into his study from the bathroom and stood at the large sliding-glass doors gazing out as he towelled his wet hair. The doors opened onto a small balcony and looked straight across the narrow street to the other apartments, the windows of which were always screened in some manner. This night, the one directly opposite had its usual gauze cotton curtain across but, because of the stifling humidity and heat, the window was open wide. A pedestal fan was running somewhere in the room, swinging back and forth so that the curtain was regularly blown up and away, revealing one corner clearly, before dropping and concealing everything again.

It was in that corner she was standing, facing just enough away to not spot the curtain's fractiousness, nor could Warren quite fully see her face. His attention had been caught when he noticed her taking off her earrings, though it was only one of them that he saw her remove as the curtain fluttered up, and back again. He watched as she lifted her hands to the back of her neck to release the clasp on her necklace. By the next frame her neck and throat were bare. He guessed then that she pulled off the band holding her hair back and that she shook her head, for he only saw the end result, as her long auburn mane settled around her shoulders.

She made a sudden movement of her legs, kicking out first one, then the other. Reaching down with her arms at her sides and bending slightly, she raised them again and straightened, pulling her dress inside out up over her head. She threw it aside and, with a momentary break in the continuity, revealed herself standing in her underwear.

She continued to look straight ahead, motionless, for a while. Warren could not quite make out the expression on her face. Without looking away, he leaned back and turned off the lamp on the desk in his room. He pulled over a chair from next to the desk and stood up on it so he could see her whole figure from the higher vantage point. His fascination was now complete and heightened by the forbidden nature of it. He felt the thrill of the chase. The near-nakedness of her body, as it came and went with the fluttering of the flimsy screen between them, excited and seduced him and he was enthralled.

Standing in place, she pulled her bra straps off her shoulders, bringing the bra down from her breasts and around to the front, undid the clasps and then took it off. Her bare breasts, with their appearances and disappearances through the flapping gauze, tantalised him. She bent and pulled down her panties, lifting one leg through, then the other, Warren assumed, only catching the resulting full nakedness of her as the curtain jumped around like a sheet on a clothes-line in the wind. He let his imagination fill in the gaps and feed his pleasure, and he found himself completely aroused.

Finished with her undressing the woman stood still, coming in and out of Warren's sight like an old movie flickering, he, transfixed on her exposed body each time it was in view. After a moment of apparent quiet reflection, she raised and held out both her arms in front of her, the palms of her hands open upwards. A second woman, also naked, suddenly entered the picture from another part of the room, and slowly stepped straight towards the first woman into an embrace, both clenching each other eagerly once they had touched.

With her head turned slightly to one side as she kissed, the second woman saw, through half-opened eyes and a billowing curtain, her neighbour, Warren, caught in the light of a street lamp, standing naked on a chair at his balcony window, holding his penis.

Orcastration

"Tell me about it, my son."

"Well, father, you know that I have always felt a great lust towards orchestral instruments as I have confessed to you often before."

"Yes, my child, perfectly harmless and I have given you absolution for it."

"Father, I have humped the cello, had sex with a saxophone, fiddled with violins of all ages from Stradivarius to Great Wall, violated various violas, banged the entire percussion, gone down on the xylophone, rooted the reeds, outdone the horns with my horniness, played around with the keyboards, soothed six trumpets, and have been quite base with several of that kind … "

"Very understandable my boy given your predilections but of no great consequence. These are not living things, though some may claim so at times … "

"But, Father, when it came to the harp … "

"The harp? Go on … "

"Each time when it comes to the harp, Father, I just adopt a foetal position around it and I … I … "

"Yes, my son?"

"… I … I … just can't let go … "

"And why can't you just let it go then my poor lost lamb?"

"Because my ... private parts ... get entangled in those little treble strings near its knee and I ... find it ... pleasant, Father."

"Bless you for your generous spirit. May the angel of God be with you through your torment and guide you on your way."

"Thank you, Father."

"Amen ... And, erm, stay away from the conductor."

Lorraine's Cross Purpose

Lorraine was in bed by the time Lawrence returned from the bathroom. She was lying naked, facing away. The bedside lamp threw its light across the wall so her silhouette was stark against the background. Her skin looked dark in shadow, with a golden rim along the outline where the finest of downy hairs glowed. She did not turn to greet him as he eased himself onto the bed and edged his way towards her.

He stretched out facing her back, snuggling in full length, his knees tucked into the fold of her legs, his erection fitting into the crack of her bottom.

He kissed her neck and put his hand on the angular roundness of her shoulder, spreading his fingers out so that they cupped fully around it. He explored its shape with his palm, feeling the bones under her skin. He kissed her again on the nape of her neck and used his nose to find the knuckling of her spine, nuzzling and playing with each bump. He could smell her warm sweetness, the odour of a woman's warmth, and took little sniffs like a dog. She had a smell that was hers alone. The smell of Lorraine, not the Cross. He was still distracted by intellect and not yet fully immersed in the sensuousness of the moment.

As he ran his lips down her spine as far as he could strain his neck, he let just the very tip of his tongue feel for the tiny fluffs of hair that grew in the small of her back and caressed them with barely a brush, savouring the tingling sensation and wondering how it felt to her.

The bones of her shoulder moved under his hand as she stretched out that arm and switched off the light. He ran his palm down her arm and back as she did so, and let it rest on her shoulder again.

Now he was aware of little else than the sensual pleasure of touch. In the pitch darkness he ran his curved palm down the length of her body, along the soft flesh beneath her armpit, past her breast which he touched with the tips of his fingers, lingering a little at the edge in passing, down the incline to her waist and then the sudden reverse upwards to her hip and the firmness of its bone; through the long flowing curve of her thigh, dipping so he could take in some of the great swell of her buttock along the way, though not yet venturing forward down the other side to explore the region of her sexual jewel; then as far as he could reach along her leg past the delicate indent at the back of her knee to the muscly firmness of her calf. All so soft and smooth.

He started back again. The image in his mind of the contour he was traversing was as if a laser was imprinting it on his retina, more intense than as if he were seeing it.

She had not made a sound and he wondered how in her way she must be enjoying it as he was. Up, along her leg, with the slightest rasp of shaven hairs, this time deviating more around the fullness of one buttock, toying with the crack that separated it from the other; then, as if now following his personal map, along the familiar form up into her armpit, the soft folds of which he squeezed gently, and down the underside of her arm with its skin as tender as a mother's kiss, and back. He let the palm of his hand return to her side and began to move it slowly downwards again, this time moving his fingers forward and cupping her breast, holding it firmly, and he broke the silence.

"It's wonderful how I can see in my mind's eye the shape of your body through the touch of my fingers."

As he reached her thigh once again she answered.

"For heaven's sake, Lawrence, stop *talking* about it and just get *on* with it," and he felt her hand grab his penis, pulling it with a jerk through her legs to her vagina.

The Infernal Triangle

Darj and Junie, Dahjeeling and Juniper to their respective hippy parents, at least for the first few months of their lives, had been an item for well over two years at the time. They shared one of the upstairs bedrooms. Though their relationship was sound, it had reached a stage of review, and then consolidation, or otherwise. So, both Darj and Junie were feeling a little restless. They had moved, some while before, into an upstairs room in a group house of friends from university days, all of them now professionals of some kind. Each of them was, however, struggling to find a job, let alone build a career.

Diamantina and Andrew, Di or Dime and Andie to everyone, lived in separate rooms downstairs, but were more often together in one or other of those rooms overnight. Andie and Darj went back a long way, to primary school days in fact.

Greek George was the true singleton of the place, though he managed to bring home the bacon often enough. He spent quite a lot of time in his room gaming and even made a bit of money from it, so he boasted. He kept the others in line too, so that the coupling thing didn't take over and ruin the group nature of their lifestyles which was what they fundamentally wanted, or claimed they did.

It was a mattresses-on-the-floor, milk-crate shelving, please-wash-up-your-own-dishes-before-they-grow-fungus type of household. Plenty of late-night parties, many of them spontaneous, and not always on weekends as none of them needed to be up early to go to jobs, except when they might have some casual work. Various friends would drop in regularly to add variety. Stay-in pizza nights with booze and maybe some dope and a free movie on DVD from the library, nights out to live music (free) at the local pubs, the odd bar-hopping, though that could be very expensive. Deep philosophical or political discussions around the kitchen table were practically a daily affair (and cheap) but keeping the grounds tidy was certainly not. There was always a bit of friction over housekeeping chores, Di and Junie needing to prod and cajole the boys constantly so they (Di and Junie) didn't end up doing everything except put the garbage out.

They lived a carefree existence of youthful exuberance and experimentation. They all got along really well; Junie and Di went op-shop crawling, the two lads watched footy matches, played pool at the pub or tinkered constantly on Andie's van, George picking and choosing as occasions arose. They would all head for the Saturday markets armed with recyclable bags and scribbled lists for fresh, cheap vegies and other food goodies to provide for the week's meals.

Sometimes, there was just a touch of flirting between a member of one couple with a member of the other couple, but this was held in appropriate check and never spilled over into an onset of jealousy and sulking on anyone's part. To outsiders, friends included, they presented a formidable fortress of compact bonding.

Occasionally there were breaks in the routine. There'd be a run up the coast in Andie's van for a few days of surfing; George headed off to Bali for a week. Dime got a job with a caterer and had to bivouac at some country estate for a couple of nights. Sometimes they would even manage to visit their parents homes for a dinner, and definitely for Christmas. Three of them played instruments: Andie was pretty handy on electric guitar, George could bash away on his drum set with sufficient energy to rock the rafters, and Junie had learnt piano since she was very young and had an electric keyboard. They would jam together every now and then when the mood struck, bluesy stuff mainly as that was always pretty easy and could go on and on, the other two joining in with bongos or loose and spirited mouth organ, or just singing along and jumping around.

One early evening on a long weekend with an atmosphere of holiday jollity in the air and after the two women had returned from a shopping outing together, they settled down for a meal quickly thrown together by Junie and Di. George had gone off somewhere for the weekend. Having finished the edible part they continued with the wine drinking and generally had some fun talking and laughing and listening to music. Darj had noticed earlier that the two in the kitchen had been more than their usual effervescent selves, exchanging looks, sharing secret jokes, laughing conspiratorially, glancing at him as they spoke, dancing around each other between stove and fridge and sink very energetically. He was suspicious and knew they were up to something. Di and Junie were quite capable of that.

After the meal, as they were lounging around in the second-hand armchairs and sofa they had salvaged from the street, the banter continued and eventually Di came and sat on the arm of Darj's chair and leaned over on him, feigning some tipsiness. He could see Junie watching and smiling and when Di fell into his lap and didn't make any attempt to get off, with Junie still watching and smiling, he realised that they might be moving into dangerous territory, and that even so he could well let himself be carried along for the trip.

Di was warm and smelled feminine and had that 'take-me' look on her face. Darj had always found her attractive and, occasionally, he had fantasised just briefly about their possibilities together. She, in fact, had been even more explicit about it, he recalled now, though at the time he had put it to one side. At least that is what he thought. He was never all too certain when it came to women.

He had never contemplated going further with it because of Andie and its obvious general risks, but just because of Andie mostly. Now he noticed Andie looking over as well and smiling. A bit unusual, weird even. Had it all been pre-approved, he wondered.

Di started to fondle him here and there, playing with his hair and beard, and finally put her mouth to his ear and said,

"Let's go upstairs."

He was nonplussed by the brazenness of it, but then noticed Junie again looking over and smiling, so he was in no doubt of their conspiracy and felt any sensible resistance he may have had fast dissipating.

"OK," he tossed off casually, "let's," and she jumped off him.

He got up and virtually ran to the stairs taking a couple of steps up, then stopped to look back. He caught her as she said something hastily to Andie on her way to darting after him up the stairs. Andie smiled. That was the final endorsement. Andie knew what was going on and seemed relaxed about it all. It didn't cross his mind to wonder what Junie and Andie might get up to while he and Dime were away, but that was a product of his general naivety and innocent detachment.

Darj reached his, his and Junie's, room, opened the door and stepped in a little, then turned around walking backwards towards the bed to watch Di come in after him. She left the door open and stood to one side. He moved forward to close it only to be confronted with Junie already there with a great beaming smirk on her face. She bounced in pushing the door shut behind her.

"Oh shit!" he said out loud, and then the full nature of it hit him. That was what it was all about. They had obviously been contemplating this caper for a while. Well, under the circumstances, he was for it. Why the hell not? It was obviously fully authorized.

They were all over him and each other in seconds, undoing buttons and buckles and yanking shirts and shoes off and pants down and hoisting tee-shirts up over heads with arms outstretched or doing the same to themselves, till there they were standing, fully naked in a three-way embrace and giggling like idiots. They did a six-footed sidle to the bedside and fell together over it, readjusting to lie lengthwise, talking nonsense and screeching all the while, Darj in the middle on his back and one of them on each side facing him. They frolicked with hands and legs and mouths, he from one to the other, they mostly with him, though there was some exploratory touching between them also he sort of noticed. It was all so novel, at least in certain ways, that none of them was too sure what to do other than follow their impulses. They were so comfortable with each other though that there was not even a passing thought given to taking precautions against risks, medical or otherwise, so there was no disruption to the matter's progress

Gradually the silliness subsided and the libidos took over as they became more aroused and focused. Di gripped his erection firmly in her hand and he realised at a deep level that it was her he wanted to make love to. The more superficial level went along with that. But amidst the feverish muddle of his current state he realised also that if he did it with Di first as he wanted to he would inevitably ejaculate, especially since he had not emptied his bladder, and then not be able to service Junie, which would trouble him and perhaps disappoint her, or worse, annoy her. After all, he didn't really know where all this was coming from.

So he leant towards Di and gave her a snappy kiss then pulled himself away and rolled on top of Junie and she took over, taking his penis and guiding it into her vagina. He could feel Di cuddle into them both and run her hands around his back and his buttocks. He wasn't able to feel where she went beyond that.

Fucking with Junie was pleasurable as always, but it was a well-worn track and there was a fork in the road very nearby leading to greener pastures. Thinking in that way in fact helped him hold back from coming, and indeed increased his whole enjoyment of it. What could be better than being agreeably with one woman while dreaming of another who happened to be right there waiting and expectant.

He had to stop. It wasn't easy since he knew what followed would entail a shivery frisson of disengagement and sense of loss as he withdrew, and an almost unbearable hiatus before starting again; but then there would be Diamantina.

He whispered, "I have to stop," into Junie's ear, "are you OK?"

"Yes, yes," she replied easily, "go to Dime."

He slowly pulled out and shuddered a little, shuffled across onto the waiting Di, and with her ready willingness he entered her quickly and they began the dance. It felt immediately different, not just the feelings of desire for her in his head, but also what his penis felt inside her. She was looser, less resistant, less squeezy. He wasn't sure if these feelings were genuine for their own part, or one affected the other, or if so which one caused the effect. It didn't matter anyway, he just went with the flow, and the devil could take the hindmost.

Junie had rolled towards them and was now caressing his body. He felt her fingers start to play with his testicles, bouncing them around and broadening his pleasure, but also reminding him she was there. And so he also felt a little guilty for his secret deception.

That didn't last long. Need replaced want and became irresistible necessity and he could not control it or himself which became the same thing. He needed to, and then needed to more, and came quickly, collapsing exhausted onto Di and over onto one shoulder to take some of his weight off her. He felt his flaccid member slip out after a short while and he kissed Di on the cheek as he rolled onto his back.

Junie seemed to be somewhere there, but he could do nothing more and left them to finish it off in any way they desired; he didn't care one iota by that stage.

He dozed off, totally satiated. It was probably not too long before he woke again, though he wasn't at all sure of the time, but it was still dark outside, the amber glow of the street light shining in through the window. He lay still for a time then put his arms out to each side and felt around, then looked to his left and right and quickly glanced around the room. Neither Di nor Junie was there. The door was ajar so he surmised they had left and were downstairs drinking again.

He could hear voices coming up the stairwell from below. He listened and could detect three separate ones, male and female. There was some laughter and some groaning and periods of quietness with a background of squeaking furniture. He noticed Di's and Junie's clothes on the floor where they had been dropped or thrown earlier.

The first sharp pang of jealousy and betrayal struck Darj in the chest suddenly, and then in stabbing waves travelled up to his throat and out along his arms finishing in an iron grip around his torso like crushing and terminal heart failure.

Pillow Slips

The taxi pulled up at the kerb and after a short delay while she settled the fare Elizabeth hopped out laden with laptop, shoulder bag and clutch, slammed the door shut with her hip, waited as the cabbie opened the boot and retrieved her wheelie bag, took it from him with a thank you, dragged it awkwardly behind her across the grass verge with her clutch hand, struggled over to the front door around the overspilling garden and up two steps, stood it upright, fumbled for keys in her purse and then found the keyhole with one of them.

Three days, three cities, three flights was too much. She wouldn't be doing that again, she decided. She would get inside, have a quick shower and pour herself a drink to relax before Bill got home. She turned the key, grabbed the handle of her bag and stepped through the open doorway, put the bag upright again, pulled out the key, closed the door behind her, and gave a big sigh.

She stood and looked at the room. She knew immediately something wasn't quite right. She ran her eyes around the space. There was nothing she could spot, nothing she could put her finger on, but it felt wrong nevertheless. Her heels clicked on the polished wood floor as she walked over to the bookcase filling one wall, stood in front of the middle section, squatted down and pulled out the third volume of the complete works of

Proust from the lowest shelf. She opened it and checked for the banknotes in the hollowed out centre.

She put it back, patted it in evenly and turned around. She caught herself in the large mirror with its ornate frame over the mantelpiece opposite and paused, taken aback by her frazzled appearance. The lounge in the middle of the room facing the large TV screen had been smoothed, the cushions puffed up and arranged diagonally overlapping against each other along the back and sides as usual. She sat down on it, slipped off her shoes and massaged her toes through her black pantyhose.

The coffee table had its magazines neatly stacked and the vase had fresh flowers in it. Maybe it was that. She had detected a hint of perfume giving the room a slight lift. Probably the flowers, she thought. Nice of Bill to think of that. She walked over to the entertainment console. The player was set to DVD: Bill had watched a movie, or maybe one of his current series favourites, but there was no sign of it or its case.

She looked all around again with the same vague feeling of unease. The corner lamp was on, as Bill usually left it. The Parker lounge chair next to it for reading was unchanged. The curtains were drawn on the full-length windows at the far end of the room. She walked around the eight seater dining table they had had made from the recycled wharf timbers and pulled on the drawstring at the left of the curtains to reveal the fading daylight on a manicured garden scene.

She looked out onto the dark greenness for a while, calming herself. Then she noticed a wine glass on the side shelf behind the furled curtain with some liquid remaining in it. She picked it up and sniffed it. Passionfruit: sauvignon blanc she guessed, not Bill's usual. She carried it out to the kitchen, emptied the glass into the sink and opened the dishwasher. It was empty. She put the glass in upside down and closed it again, not quite shut.

The kitchen was spick and span; just like Bill to do that. She opened the fridge: no leftover wine there. She looked in the door compartments and took out a full bottle of chardonnay and put it on the bench, screwed off the top with a slight crack, stretched for one of the Riedels from the overhead cupboard and poured some wine into it. She took a sip, turned and went back around the servery into the loungeroom, still surveying the scene in detail: the artworks - the Whitely and the Kngwarreye, the Boyd - all squarely centred, the African sculpture on the long Wegner side table, the large Venetian Murano glass fish at the other end, the two Pearlware candlesticks in the middle, the turned Bungendore karri bowl with keys and small change and various bits and pieces thrown carelessly into it. There was not a thing out of place.

She took another sip of the chardonnay then positioned the glass carefully on the coffee table with a cork coaster underneath it, went back to the front door, picked up her luggage and carried it into the bedroom not wishing to mark the floor. She put it down near the door of the walk-in robe and turned and looked around again. She had the same unnerving feeling as she had had in the loungeroom. Everything seemed in its place but there was just something.

She popped into the ensuite, stepped up to the vanity basin, checked her hair and rinsed her hands, dabbing some water onto her face with them before patting herself dry. She cast her eyes around the bathroom which reminded her of one of her recent hotel stays, nothing out of order, everything spotless. She stepped back into the bedroom and walked over to the neatly turned bed and felt the sheets. Freshly changed, and the pillow cases, all smoothed neatly with a slight hint of lemon from the laundry detergent. Bill again: he was good at all this. Sometimes it annoyed her that she couldn't nag him for not pulling his weight with the housework like others seemed always able to.

He was still reading the Jonathan Franzen. She walked right around the bed, stood by her bedside table and looked at it. She bent slightly and put her hand up under the lamp shade and clicked the switch. It didn't come on. She bent down further and turned it on at the wall socket. It came on. She straightened up and looked down again. Her box of tissues sat across the table at an angle. She pushed it back into place, then she picked it up. As she stood holding it in the palm of her hand from underneath, gently raising it up and down a little and looking at it, she heard a key in the front door, the door opening, and then closing again.

"Hi, are you home Beth? It's me."

Elizabeth walked out from the bedroom into the loungeroom and stared at Bill.

"Beth? What?" he blubbered as his heart pounded and the blood drained from his face. How was it possible that a man could stand right there in his own home, his castle, his refuge and appear so uneasy and out of place, naked almost?

She hurled the box of tissues across the room. "You bastard!" she screamed at him. The box landed with a clunk and slid along the shiny floorboards, finishing up against his feet as he looked down at it, head bowed before her.

Out of Toner

It was a shrill, piercing shriek that caught his attention as he slouched mindlessly at the sink washing the pots and dishes from the evening meal he had once again scraped together only to have it dismissed and discarded.

The distraction caused him to fumble and he had to reach into the now tepid and greasy water to reclaim the dishcloth. He noticed that it had a peculiar, metallic, snakeskin quality, as though it were made of finely-woven gold mesh. It exuded a sweet and pungent odour as he squeezed it, perhaps due to the dessert bowls and their sugary residue sitting at the top of the heap, perhaps simply due to his imagination. The bowls, along with the other plates and cups and saucers were mostly marked with cracks and chips these days as he had slowly slumped into the forlorn, impecunious lifestyle that his had become, the pots and pans with a scratched and weather-worn look, never likely to see their shiny, silver glory days again.

Helen's madness had gradually taken its toll on him, though he had resisted and fought back for a long time, for love. But the genius, the inventiveness of madness is akin to the resourcefulness of water seeping through, around, over and under a levee. It requires a united front of many hands to resist it and he was alone now, the team of supporters - his patient and confused friends, beaten medical troops, exhausted family, weary work colleagues - having peeled off one by one over time.

He heard another shriek. He was used to it. Another stab at revenge, revenge for something, anything, nothing. Another plea, another demand for help, for attention. Another malevolent chemical down the wrong neural pathway. He had grown inured to it all, but only by descending into his own debilitating malaise of acceptance and rout. It was close, but muffled, and probably the bathroom, the door shut and maybe barred, but not locked as he had seen to that extra obstacle long ago.

He draped the wrung-out dishcloth over the edge of the sink, reached for the dish towel and dried his hands. He shuffled in his scuffs up the hallway and opened the bathroom door without announcement to a scratching sound of a stool ineffectually placed against it.

She was sitting underneath the hand basin, legs spreadeagled on the tiles, her back propped up awkwardly against the fittings, like a drunken rag doll resting after some plumbing maintenance. Various containers were scattered around her, pulled out from cupboards and thrown pell-mell around the room, their contents spilled or squeezed out of them and adorning the display. Much had probably also gone down her throat, but again any potential risk there had been taken care of by removal in the early days of her suicidal tendencies.

He noticed a large toner refill container amongst it all which she must have deliberately brought in from his office.

"Ha, ha, ha, ha," she flopped around and cackled through smudged, ghastly, ink-stained lips. "Words, words, words; you always control me with your words."

"No more of your words floating around in my life, they won't last, they will just fade away, drift off into space, formless, powerless, meaningless ... unless I print them out for you. Ha."

He stood staring at her, speechless.

Blessed by Bliss

Peter had come to the party alone. He and Matt, the birthday boy, had been good friends since school, though they hadn't seen each other for quite a while. So when he had received the invitation he felt he should make an effort to turn up, despite not being really in party mood. He had been going through a serious personal crisis for quite a while but thought it might be about time to try for some resolution of it. He wasn't too hopeful of that, at least not in the short term. Adjustment would not happen overnight, that was clear. Still, a party, and people to meet and talk with, couldn't hurt.

Mary had come because of her considerably older brother, Jude, who had also known Matt for several years, since university days. She was an actress, or at least dreaming of it, but also working hard at it to become one, and had just come out of a difficult relationship. She felt in some need of comfort and was never one to be reluctant to take what she might need.

Matt's apartment was a two bedroom affair, neither expansive nor cramped. A small kitchen opening onto a lounge-room provided enough space for a decent number of party-goers to move around, bump shoulders, and get friendly in. With not much else on his plate Peter arrived early, gave Matt the usual hearty birthday wishes, handing over his gift, the perennial stand-by - a cellophane wrapped, blue-ribboned bottle of red, which

Matt promptly put aside without opening - and sidled over to where he spotted various opened bottles and glasses, nodding a few casual greetings to strangers on the way. He poured himself a substantial dose of medicine, not so much because he needed a big hit in a hurry, but so that he wouldn't have to brave the crowd going for refills too often. He looked around the room and spotted a safe perch on the margins of the action where he could watch the activity but not be called upon too readily to participate.

Mary turned up a little late, as was her way, and displayed far more effusiveness than Peter in her birthday greetings to Matt, as was her way also, thrusting a large bunch of purpley-blue and yellow bearded irises into his chest as she did so. She swung around and just as enthusiastically greeted her brother and several other people nearby, having known some of those there since she was a young girl. Matt returned from the kitchen where he had plonked the bouquet into the sink for safe keeping and held out a glass of wine to Mary, also substantial, though in Mary's case it was for rapid consumption rather than as a longer-term reservoir. With her usual roving eye she eventually spied Peter sitting on a sofa on the other side of the crowded, noisy room, looking a mite gloomy. Even so, she thought he seemed cute, perhaps a little too old for her, but then that in itself could prove interesting, maybe even challenging. She wondered, too, why she didn't recognise him, and who he was. In fact, Peter's life path had diverged significantly from Matt's after university while Mary was still quite young, and although the two men had rarely got together in person they had kept in touch and knew about the important things going on in each other's lives. As his much younger sister, Mary didn't feature in Jude's life once he started enjoying university life and they became closer only when she herself had broken free of childhood ways, which she did in her characteristic spectacular way by suddenly taking off to Africa at 18 to "save the children", briefly.

She excused herself from her brother and birthday boy whom she had continued to chat with after arriving and made a purposeful bee-line for the sofa through swaying bodies and waving glasses, her hands joined together holding the now half-empty glass out in front to create an advancing, crowd-parting phalanx. Peter didn't even see her coming and she had plopped herself down with determination next to him, squeezing gleefully in between him and another before he even realised it .

"Hi!" she said. "Cheer up, old chum, it's a party."

"Oh, I'm sorry," he replied, and grinned. "I'm suddenly a reformed man."

There was a brief moment of silent discomfort. His voice was deep, smooth and creamy and it was seeping through to Mary's subliminal zone.

"Would you like to dance?" He almost shouted into her ear with the music and hubbub now dominating the soundscape of the room. He didn't want to dance in fact, and had not done much dancing at all, but he believed that was a standard line to put, so chanced it.

She didn't answer. She looked at him and thought how terribly attractive he was in a restrained sort of way. The short spruced hair, the close shave, the fresh boyish complexion, all shiny and new. He even smelt fresh, like a newborn babe. There was something clean, pure, unadulterated about him that appealed to the perverted side of her nature, quite the opposite to her usual choices of dishevelled, dissolute young arty types.

She realised she was staring and that he was confused.

"No," she finally got out, "no, I wouldn't."

Peter looked nonplussed.

That feeling she knew so well in her gut and groin was taking over from the usual social restraint that most of the time she reluctantly, though necessarily, allowed to dictate her actions. She put her hand on his thigh and bent towards him stretching her face up to his ear, and whispered, just before she kissed his mouth:

"No, I don't want to dance with you. I want to fuck you."

The kiss was luscious as she leaned up and on him and he reeled both emotionally and physically from its power and suddenness. Wet and full and firm, he resisted opening his mouth even as her tongue tried and succeeded to force its way through his lips. Nevertheless, there it was inside him, feeling its way around his own tongue, and, amazed at its strength, he was transported into a land of new sensation. She had by now mounted him with one leg and had her hand wrapped around his genitals as best she could through his pants and at the angle, squeezing them gently as she bored her way into his mouth and his mind. For his part, the assault so stunned Peter that he could do no more than play the role his amorous assailant assigned him, while simultaneously finding it rather enjoyable and exciting, and definitely seductive.

Mary knew it couldn't continue the way it was going, there in that bustling room full of people, and in the midst of such a passionate situation she found the composure to work out what to do. The door to Matt's bedroom was open and people were spilling over into its space, so that was out. She had visited Matt here once before and knew there was another smaller room he used as a study just across from where they were. She could see its door was closed probably because Matt didn't want his work and private papers being messed with.

She leant back a little, looked into his eyes and could see his state of stupor, jumped off the sofa, grabbing his arm as she did so, pulled him up first onto his feet and then, with one hand, across the room behind her. In his dazed state, and with some deep underlying sense that something important was happening to him which he had to acquiesce in, he allowed himself to be taken without resistance. The way opened before them. Of course everyone was aware of what was going on but nobody was actually directly looking, except Jude who was vaguely concerned, but not inclined to interfere for the sake of harmony, and knowing full well that Mary would get her way no matter what. All par for a party like this one.

She reached the door and with her other hand out in front feverishly turned the knob and pushed it open, dragging him after her. In the room a desk lamp threw a dim light, enough to show there was an armchair as well as the desk, a bookcase and some filing cabinets. She led him in, slammed the door shut with her foot as she went, turned her back to the armchair and stood in front of him like a devoted supplicant. The din outside was muffled somewhat now with the door shut but was still enough to mask any noises their activity might produce so they both felt safe and relaxed.

Mary undid the buttons of his shirt and pulled it back off his shoulders while he stood in bewilderment as a mute witness to his own apparent downfall. He had a simple, old-fashioned athletic singlet on underneath the plain white shirt which added to her delight in this romantic apostasy of hers. She reached down without taking her eyes off his face and unzipped his fly, undid his belt buckle and yanked his trousers down to his knees as far as she could reach, letting them drop to the floor around his ankles. She quickly crossed her arms over the bottom of her tee-shirt and drew it up and off and threw it into the air with total disregard for where it might end up. As he lifted his singlet up and off over his head following her lead, though without the final flourish, she pressed her bare torso up against his, hanging her arms around his neck and pulling herself close. He gave a sigh of deep delight, he wrapped his arms around her and he bent and kissed her lips softly, though this time with his mouth open just a little. She returned his kiss, more gently than her first, and held herself there locked in conjoined pleasure. Her thumbs found the elastic top of his boxer shorts and, tugging them down with his help as far as they could reach around his knees, she stretched up in the kiss, and he bent forward and down. With Peter effectively hobbled at his ankles and knees they fell back into the armchair and completed the mutual disrobing as they writhed around, arms and legs flailing and mouths inseparable, gradually slipping down onto the floor.

She was very wet and beyond worrying about prophylaxis and safety. She took his very substantial tool and guided it into her body, and her self, and her future, eagerly and easily, and the pleasure of his entry and her own receiving it was beatific for both of them.

"Ah, sweet Jeeesus," she cried.

He was a wonderful lover. Perfect for her at this time. Tentative and attentive, he explored her as if it were the first time he had experienced a woman in this way, but without any sign of apprehension. He was slow, gentle and thorough. He breathed in her womanly odour, stroked the satiny contours of her buttocks and thighs, soaked in her sweet sighs. He seemed to be worshipping at her body as if at a shrine. The alabaster steeple of her neck, the altar of her mouth, the twin temples of her breasts, the inner sanctum of her vagina. They moved together in unison, deliberately and rhythmically like an incantation, pausing and savouring, then beginning afresh so that it lasted and extended and continued until they both could endure it no longer, and by some innate sacred sense they brought it to its rapturous orgasmic conclusion as one, as if by a divine grace.

They lay in embrace, exhausted and still, panting slightly and releasing occasional tender purrs of satisfaction, revelling in the swirling, tangy aromas of their bodies' excretions. After a while they managed to find some energy to move from where they had come to be spread out on the carpet and he pulled himself up into the armchair, gently bringing her halfway with him. She sat on the floor at his feet between his legs, which she noticed now were very hairy, like his chest, her head resting on his lap and her hand reaching up to hold his. The fingers of her other hand played absent-mindedly with his limp penis.

"So, tell me, what is your name then, wondrous hairy one?"

"Peter," he replied. "Peter O'Halloran … " and he hesitated.

She looked up at him, stretching her neck backwards, and waited.

" … Actually, until quite recently, Father Peter O'Halloran."

"Oh really?" she said, continuing to smile up at him and putting on her best, while nonetheless highly flawed, theatrical Irish lilt.

"Nice to meet you then, quite-recently-Father, and to be sure, until ever so recently, I was still the virgin, Mary.

Flamenco Football

Ernest Hemingway famously made Pamplona famous with his novel about its bull-running festival. But he never really strayed far from either the city's bullring where he had himself photographed hobnobbing with celebrities and near where a monument of his alpha-male top half was erected some time later, or the main plaza, where he hung around in bars, got drunk and terrorised locals, and where there is an oversized full length sculpture of him propping up a bar.

Doug Timbrell, on the other hand, knew Pamplona well. Almost every day he set out before three o'clock to have lunch somewhere in the old town. Occasionally he would venture further afield, to Hermitaganya for example, and Bar Los Arcos where they also offered a good 10 euro set lunch. He liked the waitress there, Lorna, who was very beautiful. She would poke fun at his mistakes in Spanish and make him laugh, and they would flirt a little. He would have liked it to go further, but it never did. Give it time, he told himself on a regular basis.

Most often, however, he would head for Jarauta Street, about the seediest street in Pamplona, where the Basque nationalists held sway, and Gypsies lived and congregated for dubious intent. Even these two groupings were mutually antagonistic, so the area was a seething cauldron of discontent. Or so it appeared. His conservative friend, Conchie, called it Comanche Territory, and wouldn't go there: off-limits, dangerous, scalp-threatening.

Doug liked it though. It had an air of an old Spain mostly swallowed up by progress and EU membership. The buildings looked much as they had done for a couple of hundred years and the people were rough and ready. Basque flags were draped from many of the little balconies, wall posters made unreasonably romantic demands for releasing political prisoners or proclaimed upcoming spectacles, canaries in cages cried for freedom or carolled in joyous sanctuary, cooped-up pooches yapped down at passers-by. This day, a typical drab winter one, Doug headed there around 2pm to check the menu boards outside each eatery along the way, but ended up as he so often did, right at the end of the street at his favourite, Askarza. It reliably had a four-courser, wine and bread included, for under ten euros.

By this time of day almost everything was shuttered up for lunch, leaving open for business only the bars that served the daily specials in their dining rooms out the back. They would not all be open, since each one had one particular day in the week when the staff took a breather. Doug walked across the Plaza del Castillo, buying a copy of the daily *El Pais* to read with lunch, and down Chapitela. He crossed the little plaza in front of the Town Hall where each year they kick off the fiesta - the one Hemingway made famous - with a rocket-firing, passed the Church of Saint Saturnino, whose bell was the highest point of the city, and ventured into Jarauta.

As he passed each open bar he would stop and check the choices for the day and remember them, even those he would normally not go to, just in case he did not find something suitable further on. He tried never to eat at the same place two days in a row. This didn't always work if the menus on two successive days were his favourites at one bar and those at the other bars not so appealing. Sometimes he would walk the whole length of Jarauta to check all the menus in order to decide on the best for the day, occasionally even walking all the way back to the first one if it proved to be the most acceptable, even though it might make his lunch quite a late one.

This did not matter so much since the lunch hour could be drawn out with considerable flexibility in Pamplona, like Spain in general. He always favoured the chickpeas followed by salmon, or the lentils with chorizo before the trout as mains, if they were available. The *jabali*, or wild pig, was another treat he would seek out, though less common and hence much prized. Price didn't come into the equation as they were all much the same. Bar Askarza was an incidental exception. Named after a Basque village, it was both the cheapest by half a euro, and the only one that offered an extra course, salad or soup usually, for starters, on top of the other three. This, as well as the decent wine, a small sparkling bottle of mineral water and reasonable bread, all thrown in, plus a relaxed and spacious atmosphere, made it a particularly good deal and the most attractive option for Doug.

He never had coffee at the end of his meal in whatever restaurant it was since he had other favourite places for coffee, and preferred in any case to have a change of venue. The trouble for Askarza was that it was the last bar-restaurant along Jarauta, and so there were odd days when he didn't make it that far due to an agreeable offering beforehand.

On this Wednesday however, with Bar Oreja closed for its day off, and nothing elsewhere catching his attention as especially enticing, it was Askarza that received his patronage. As he was coming to the last stretch, where Jarauta intersects with Eslava, he noticed a car with doors open both sides blocking most of the passage, as a car must, Jarauta being so narrow. Three men were leaning against it, Gypsies: long hair, rough features, darkly dressed, quite animated, with heavy-metal music thumping from the formidable sound system inside the vehicle.

This was probably a meeting place for a drug exchange, Doug decided. He wasn't particularly concerned for his safety.

Though he was sure that these types would very happily pick his pocket or break into his car given the opportunity, he was just as sure they wouldn't physically attack him in full daylight. Nevertheless, they felt menacing as he walked close by and they stopped talking and stared at him, checking out his conventional clothing and his foreign features. At least that is what Doug presumed. He maintained his stride, looked straight ahead, and remembered Deborah Kerr's whistling strategy from *The King And I*, while not enacting it outright.

Once outside Askarza, Doug checked the menu, committed it to memory so he would know what to order, went in through the small antechamber, down a couple of awkward steps and then straight through the narrow front bar.

Out the back, in the dining room, he was pleased to see plenty of available tables, especially his preferred one. The room was quite large, its tables neatly laid out in three rows and most covered with crisp white butcher-paper, two rows seating four around each table, and the third along one wall with seating for pairs. On the walls were framed photos of local football teams and historic scenes of bull-fighting, and a large jigsaw puzzle of a Paris street scene someone had proudly completed. And it was warm.

He peeled off layers of clothing, slung them and his shoulder bag over spare chairs and on wall hooks and sat down at a large table, recently used and still uncleared, where he could spread out. On a busy day he would have had to sit at one of the smaller twosomes. He had certainly seen the place totally packed on occasions, especially Saturdays when there was the local football clash. Sunday was Askarza's turn for the day off.

The patron was quickly scooping up the detritus, throwing a fresh sheet of paper over the table with a practised flourish, plonking down the bottles, two glasses and a basket of bread, and reciting the daily offerings. Although they weren't his favourites, a white bean *entrée* then lamb stew turned out to be just fine, with the soup first, and the rest as always. He liked the soup so much that, as he often did, he asked for seconds and the management obliged without fuss.

He was still sitting, reading the paper when the card-club members began to arrive at their usual four o'clock, coming through to the back after having a coffee or brandy at the front bar after a lunch at home. The old men, retirees and quite rowdy, wasted no time pulling two tables together and gathering enough chairs around.

"Who's coming?"

"Not Josexto today. He's in Bilbao."

"Where are the cards?"

"Up there, you get them."

More arrived and they sat at the table, all talking at once now with excitement. They were anxious to begin the game and it started suddenly with one of them dealing. The patron came over and, leaning on the back of one of the chairs, looked on. The game was away and it was furious. Cries of "*dos*", "*paso*", "*la hostia*", "*joder*", "*chiquita*", and the crucial "*mus*" flew around the room, loudly and demandingly, one on top of the other with increasing urgency, not all of them strictly required for the game. They were playing Mus, the game that originated in the Basque country, a game impossible to learn by simply watching others play, as Doug had discovered when he had tried.

He packed his paper away in his bag, took his overcoat from the hook on the wall and put it on, wrapped his scarf around his neck, put on his cap and walked past the group, nodding to them and getting just the merest recognition from one in response as they concentrated on the task, the patron deigning not much more of an acknowledgement than the first had given.

"*Que aproveche,*" Doug snuck in as he disappeared into the front to pay, the standard line for 'enjoy it'. He always loved to utilise this social mantra whenever he could, as it never failed to elicit some friendly reaction. On this occasion, however, he doubted whether they would even have had the nervous energy to snicker "*guiri*" disparagingly, the slang word for foreigner, once he had disappeared, the game having taken over their attention completely.

He handed over his ten euros to the co-patron, the one working the front who never smiled or spoke unless on the topic of football. His fifty cents change was slapped down without comment on the bar and he picked it off and popped it in his pocket. He had long solved his personal dilemma of whether to leave it or not as a tip by concluding that they could simply put the price up to ten euros at any time if they needed the extra. He would be happy to pay it, but in the meantime he would pocket the change.

He stood briefly in the vestibule again between the bar and the street putting on his gloves and then pushed open the door and stepped out into the crisp air and overcast glare of a winter's afternoon. He felt very satisfied and in the best of moods after the meal and the wine.

Heading off back along Jarauta towards the Plaza for a coffee he noticed again the Basque flags hanging from so many of the little balconies that could be stepped out onto through the french doors of the rooms overlooking the street. These flags reminded him of the British Union Jack, but in green instead of blue. It had a strange effect on Doug steeped as he was in the red, white and blue pattern, this colour shift, as if it were just a made-up plaything. It meant nothing for him, no recognition, no surge of nationalistic fervour, just some criss-crossing of unmatching colours on a piece of fabric.

As he turned a curve and looked up along Jarauta he saw that the car was still there, now with its doors closed and the music muted. He could see the two men were also still there slouching over the bonnet. How they managed to not have to have moved it for all that time was perplexing. Though it was very quiet being lunchtime and siesta, there would surely have been at least some traffic. Perhaps, he concluded, they had simply held their ground and forced any vehicle to turn off into Eslava. This would have been an understandable retreat for anyone confronted with such an intimidating obstacle.

As he drew closer with the saunter of his good-humoured postprandial mood he heard a young voice cry out, "*Senyor, Senyor.*" Looking around without stopping he could see nobody, but then heard it again: "*Senyor, por favor,*" and focusing on it this time, he looked up towards where it seemed to come from. Sure enough there, three storeys up, hanging over one of the little balconies was a young boy with his arm extended and finger pointing down with some agitation towards a spot near where Doug was passing.

"*Por favor, Senyor,* my ball." The boy knew to use English, and again Doug felt that pang of disappointment he often noticed passed through him at being recognised so easily as a foreigner.

He stopped and turned and went over to pick up the plastic football with his free hand, juggling it onto his open palm. He stepped back and looked up and contemplated how he was going to do this. It was certain that the Gypsies were watching him and so he felt under pressure to perform. He would be judged, as a *guiri*, as a man, as himself. It was a long way up. It would be an easy enough kick but the accuracy of a kick would be problematic, and that could cause further complications. He would have to throw it. He arced his straightened arm back behind him, leaning back as he did so and heaved it upwards as if he was bowling in cricket, except vertically rather than horizontally.

It was a reasonable effort, almost making the height but just to the left of the little extended balcony and so just brushing the wall of the building. It then plummeted down again to the street and bounced back close to where he was. The boy was now hanging over the balcony so far and stretching downwards so much that he looked like a rag doll, and Doug worried he might topple.

He retrieved the ball and this time put his carry bag down onto the cobblestones. One honourable failure was allowable, as something of a test run, but this time there could be no excuses. He was simply capable, or not, of achieving this manly feat. There were probably more people watching by now he guessed - he did not want to look around and check for fear of spoiling his act - from those balconies along the street, from doorways, others walking on the street, at the intersection, having stopped to view the action, all standing in judgement. The canaries had ceased singing. No dogs barked. The boy stared downwards in hopeful anticipation, as if his football hero was about to take a penalty kick to seal the match. The air itself seemed heavy in expectation, the drooping Basque flags somehow now displaying a defiantly challenging appearance. Doug was, however, mostly concerned about the Gypsies who had gone quite silent. Their fiery gaze was burning its way into his brain. How would he get past them unscathed if he failed, his pride dented, having categorised them as lesser life-forms?

Doug stood tall and looked up at the boy and the wall of windows and little balconies. "Don't worry," he told himself, "you have done this before and you can do it now. All you have to do is make one true shot. Make the truest shot that you can do." He drew his arm back again, leant a little further backwards than previously, and putting more effort into it, keeping his eye on the boy, heaved the ball up and away.

It was a good shot, the ball headed straight for the boy and balcony, rapidly at first but slowing quickly as it neared the top of its trajectory. The boy reached down with one arm and managed, it seemed, to just touch it as it momentarily hovered, but even as he did, it began its way straight back down, lobbing into the balcony directly below, and thus encaged, bounced around within it.

It was the worst possible result. The boy didn't have the ball, he couldn't come down to the street and get it, and he would have to wait for someone in the apartment below to let him in, perhaps not for some time if they were out, or to wake them up during siesta. Above all, Doug had failed the test. It did mean, however, that no-one else could now show him up by achieving what he had not been able to.

He cried up, "*lo siento*, sorry," shrugged his shoulders, picked up his bag and turned to take his medicine. He walked towards the gypsies shoulders back and smiling sheepishly. As he passed close by and their heads turned to follow him he shrugged again and said, without looking at them, "*imposible*," in the Spanish way, with the last syllable pronounced as "bleh".

And, after a slight interregnum as he took his steps very deliberately away from them, he heard his word repeated. Louder and louder, rhythmically in a sing-song style, lengthening that last syllable and moulding it into a typical mournful flamenco minor scale, so that it echoed for all to hear down Jarauta, then was joined by rapid hand-clapping on the offbeat and repeated over again with harmonies from the other man: "*imposible-eh-eh-eh-eh-eh-eh*".

Before Doug had walked too much further, relieved he had made it through and eager to cap it off with some fun of his own, he took a little jump and brought his heels down hard onto the cobblestones with a rat-tat-tat.

He threw his bag onto his shoulder and, lifting his hands over his head, clapped a few times to the beat, feeling confident that, as he looked forward to his coffee, to which he would now add a celebratory cigar, before very long a guitar would make an appearance, the tune would have evolved into a local standard, there would surely be a satisfying boy-ball reunion, and that Hemingway would never have experienced the thrill of flamenco football in Jarauta.

Bar Garazi, Pamplona

Against one of the pillars which line the cloisters around the main square of Pamplona, the Plaza de Castillo, where Ernest Hemingway once roamed engaging drunkenly with locals and foreigners alike, an elderly gypsy in traditional rags sits with a very modern white styrofoam cup in front of her, bemoaning life and her personal predicament in that life with considerable pretension to accuracy; a common hobo walks from café table to café table set outside on the terraces to snatch briefly an uncommon wintery sun, begging for alms with a paper coffee cup thrust towards patrons who sit and chat, smoke and laugh over their *aperitivos*. They avoid eye contact and continue their conversations, without pause, but the tension can be detected in their tendency to speak a little louder, to ignore the intrusion just a little too defiantly.

A tall, elegant Senegalese man smiles and politely places without speaking his cheap wares on other tables for consideration, one after another, with mannered and casual rejection from his potential customers; necklaces, bangles, always the pint-sized lucky elephant, carved in wood, as a last resort, just one euro, placing them delicately for a moment, then replacing them with hope persistently undiminished until finally he relents and moves on without acknowledgment from his lost quarry. As he leaves he gently puts down with a final smile a small multicoloured beaded bracelet and turns away. Whether to underscore his genuine graciousness, or to punctuate the embarrassment of their parsimony, is never clear.

Doug Timbrell, a young Canadian studying the Basque language at the local private university, and after a long, typically late Spanish lunch sitting under the cover of the retractable awning at Bar Txoko at one corner of the square, is accosted by a well-proportioned black woman, colourfully dressed and quite jolly who, spreading her fingers across her belly, asks him if he can help her financially with her approaching discomfiture. Doug suggests that perhaps the father would be better fitted to such a responsibility and she laughs heartily, gives him a quick kiss on his brow and saunters off.

Both the Senegalese man and Doug will be at Bar Garazi not too far away in the maze of narrow back streets later that night. There, Sagra, the bar owner, will be weaving her magic on the patrons and audience, as the evening moves along and into the more boisterous later hours. As always on Tuesdays it attracts the local musical talent to play jazz and soul and upbeat blues.

With her long silky black hair and full figure Sagra sways to the beat, in between pulling *canyas* of beer and mixing *gin tonicas*, offering *tapas* and little bowls of nuts as free accompaniments that create more thirst. She wears a clinging blue dress which reveals the bulging prominences of her body clearly, doing little to enhance her looks, and with an ironic smile permanently on her sagging face, indicates her enjoyment of the scene and her satisfaction with the large crowd, and perhaps a certain conspiratorial involvement with the musical mood.

Students from the local Conservatorium of Music get together with some of their teachers in jam sessions, producing sounds as good as you would hear anywhere. This is, after all, the city of Sarasate, who has a boulevard running off the Plaza named in his honour, as well as of the blow-in *toreros* who have a bullring to occasionally prance around in.

Martha Zapata has a voice belying her youth and diminutive figure, creating music of great splendour and purity as she sings a jazz classic. Patrizia (like Madonna and Pink, no surname) belts out R&B numbers with such power and energy that they infect the whole room, tossing her long locks from side to side and then back off her face, throwing her arms out and up in exaltation, to the whistles and applause of the excited crowd.

Hemingway brought the city fame with his promotion of the *encierro*, and the foreign hordes come each July for the annual fiesta of San Fermin, but the true essence of Pamplona is its music. Its music, its paradoxical conservatism, and the most gorgeous young women imaginable. Doug had come originally, along with many other thrill-seekers, for the fiesta, and had returned for the language, the music, and the young women.

Edurne, working behind the bar with Sagra, is the most beautiful woman Doug has ever come across, her eyes great, dark, pools of allure and intrigue, her mouth a marvel of sensuality which, when she smiles, lights up like an explosion of fireworks; all this, enveloped in a mane of thick, curly, auburn hair, giving the impression, under the lights of the bar, of a rose bush in full bloom. When she doesn't smile, her expression of concentrated serenity poses a promise of eternal contentment. For Doug, the thought of, in some way, coalescing with this divine creature, of entering into that perfect beauty, of experiencing some contact with that spirit made physical, is to love and adore her, to be transported somewhere not of his ken, of some future unknowable truth, as well as to wonder why she is here serving drinks in a little back-street bar.

She always wears striped tops, and every so often disappears, putting on a leather jacket against the cold and stooping under the bar to step outside and smoke a rushed cigarette. She manages to do even this with an air of detachment and sexuality. She has that fascinating quality of looking different in different moods, yet still ravishingly beautiful for each manifestation.

In the push and crush of the throng, Doug leans his back up against a wall to one side of the long, thin room and directly across from the bar, next to a tall black man, the same Senegalese man from the Plaza whom he recognises but does not acknowledge. There is piping running along the wall on which people can perch, though few do. There are hooks higher up for coats and scarves and hats, and, at a stretch further up, shelving, where some can manage to rest their glasses while they clap and cheer. The Senegalese man could reach it easily but does not need to since he is not drinking. From that vantage point on the side Doug can see the performers on their modular stage over the heads of the crowd as well as best avoid being constantly bumped. He can also watch Edurne as she works. He catches her eye more than once during the night, and each time he is buoyant with hope, and then drowned, his heart sinking into a reverie of fantasising.

People come and go edging past him, shouting at each other above the hubbub. His friend Roberto has stayed across from him leaning on the bar, and Doug also notices a small, seedy-looking man at the far end of the bar near the door, surveying the scene as if sizing it up. Doug has seen him before in Garazi, always sipping on a clear liqueur from a very small shot glass, shifty-eyed.

Two women work their way towards Roberto at the bar and say hello as best they can through the ruckus. Roberto leans over towards Doug and, shouting, introduces them. One of them, Isabel, squeezes through the congested passage to stand next to him, her back to the black man, putting her bag down on the floor between herself and the wall, under the piping. She speaks some English and bends over close to Doug's ear to be better understood. She's a teacher, of something, he can't hear what, but like so many young Spaniards after *La Crisis* of those years, out of work, just managing to get fill-in jobs to survive. She tells him she is going on a demonstration next morning and must leave earlier than she usually would. There are lots of demonstrations here in Spain these days about many issues. Her friend looks over from the bar where she is talking with Roberto and sings out:

"She's a communist. Tell him you're a communist, Isabel."

"I am a communist. I am a member of the Communist Party," Isabel says laughing. "It's quite unusual these days, and not very fashionable," laughing some more.

Doug's previously dismissive attitude towards her changes and he becomes interested in someone with such serious political conviction wedded to such a humorous attitude towards it. He now finds her proximity engages him and is somewhat seductive. She is not as stunning as Edurne, but her skin is porcelain white, she is tall and lissom, and very personable. And she is on the right side of the bar.

"Really, I am," and she reaches down to the floor pulling her purse out of her bag. She opens it and finds her membership card. He's never seen one before, a Communist Party of Spain membership card, and congratulates her, laughing along. In a previous time, possessing one of these would have got its owner executed here in Pamplona, in Spain generally.

He asks her to tell him more. She shrugs and talks about the demonstration in support of some factory workers who are being laid off. They communicate as best they can with broken English and Spanish over the noise of song and shouting.

Isabel goes to the bar and orders more drinks, asking everyone what they want, as is the way in Spain even for the impecunious, then comes back to get her purse from her bag on the floor to pay. She scrabbles around in it, squatting low, then stands up with the bag. She seems agitated and takes the bag to the bar to better peer into it. She turns around and says to the man from Senegal:

"Have you got my purse?"

She is accusing him outright. Doug is taken aback somewhat at her brazenness.

"No," he says and stands straight and tall, looking down on everyone from his height.

"I want to look through your bag."

The musicians are having a break and the crowd has thinned as some moved outside to smoke and cool down on the narrow cobbled street of the old town. Roberto and Isabel's friend and Doug are looking expectantly at the black man.

"I don't think he took it, Isabel, I would have seen," Doug says.

He is astonished at Isabel's forthrightness, and equally surprised when the black man calmly hands over his bag and she goes through it while he watches expressionless. She doesn't find her purse in his bag, unsurprisingly. The Senegalese man jerks his head back in disdain, grabs his bag and leaves. An illegal immigrant can't afford to have police nosing around, even if a paragon of innocence.

The four of them talk together, trying to work out how it could have been taken. Roberto says two thieves often work in combination, one picks a pocket and hands it quickly to a second, who walks past and away leaving the first culprit clean of any evidence. Suspicion, fed by impotence, turns on the seedy man at the bar, now gone, who, they speculate, might have been in cahoots with the black man.

Doug repeats he would have seen someone taking it, but even he doesn't believe that completely. He feels a little guilty. He had distracted Isabel and caused her to expose her purse and then leave it easily accessible.

Isabel and her friend decide to go to the police to report it. Doug follows them outside, trying to make up for her loss by offering his sympathy and concern. Isabel shakes her head with what seems to be some scorn, but could be despondency, and they walk off. Doug considers how her Communist Party card, along with everything else in the purse, would have to be replaced, and wonders about Isabel's apparent indifference. He begins to harbour doubts about whether it may all have been some bizarre performance. It occurred to him then that Roberto had paid for that round Isabel had ordered.

He does not ponder for long. The music has started up again. Patrizia, head thrown back, hair flying, hits high notes you could not imagine possible as she delivers her version of 'Natural Woman'. Edurne remains intact and glorious in her glowing shrine, while Doug returns to his yearning. Garazi thumps with the rhythm, and Pamplona swings on chords that soar all the way to the stars. Neither petty thievery nor shabby skulduggery will hamper a good night out for the crowd at Bar Garazi in the back streets of Pamplona, where Ernest Hemingway never roamed.

Culinary Capers

Mayonnaises may have at times brought mayhem and dismay to the streets and citizens on the island of Majorca but were never a problem for its mayor, Don Joan Ramon Llull, who revelled in the region's annual celebration of the world-famous dressing.

Except on just that one, and final, occasion.

The root cause for this near-perfect discrepancy was the annual 'Most Competent Condiment Competition', the florid flavour of the original Catalan title sadly losing much from its translation into the language of ketchup and HP Sauce.

For starters, there was the fierce rivalry with its smaller insular cousin, Menorca across the strait. Menorca claimed proprietorial as well as spelling rights to the saucy substance. To them it would always be *mahonaisse*, after its capital, Mahon, and the professed birthplace of the comestible concoction in question. The Menorcans also resented the Majorcans for establishing the competition before it had occurred to them to do so, as well as for being belittled as 'Minor', while their larger neighbour swaggered around as 'Major'. Why not a distinctive name, like 'Ibiza' for example, though they could never themselves agree on one?

Each year the Menorcans would comprehensively and publicly boycott the affair while secretly sending agents across the ditch on sabotage missions. These sneaky infiltrators carried out undermining activities by, for example, adding alien ingredients, such as chilli, saccharin, wormwood, and even Vegemite, to contestants' entries. Once, one particular judge - a Sardinian from Alghero, the Catalan enclave in the north-west of that island, such imports being favoured adjudicators as biased towards their Catalan brethren while still technically registering as Italian - upon tasting one of these adulterants, was seen running berserk through the narrow alleyways of its capital, Palma, where most of the competition was centred, foaming at the mouth and screaming blue murder, or *sacrebleu,* to be precise. But equally, these Minor alimental insurgents were just as often caught out in such devious meddlement, receiving their just desserts, usually in the form of an English breakfast followed by a baguette whipping, before fleeing back to the safety of their cosy kitchens across the straits.

Other flies in the soup were the French entrants, well-known for not giving a stuffed aubergine for any alleged achievements of non-Gallic gastronomy. These culinary artists, *culinaires* or *gastronomiques* as they liked to term themselves, would arrive in their Parisian finery accompanied by large retinues, commandeer complete suites of hotels, dine at the best restaurants, decry the quality of the product and service, and parade around town in grand *hauteur* under banners proclaiming devotion to their countryman Marshal Richelieu, supposed historical entrepreneurial genius behind the sauce's success.

Then there were the animal justice devotees who doggedly protested the abuse of chooks, filling the public places with their placards condemning the brazen theft and slaughter of the animals' unborn offspring for base human gratification. Violence often erupted between the cuisiniers and the eco-warriors as a result, the animal rights activists pelting their adversaries with rotten eggs and receiving barrages of rotten tomatoes in return. Plans by the ultra-radical vegan types amongst them to take more direct action and cripple the whole affair inevitably descended into fractious internal disarray as factions within the movement argued about the various merits of their specific principles on the matter: the casual and relaxed flexitarians ridiculing the extreme stance of the sanctimonious vegans, the self-indulgent lacto-ovo-pescatarians lashing out at the politicising of it all by the zealous climatarians.

Participants from the Spanish mainland treated all sides with imperial disdain. Rumours abounded of their teams, aided by a fifth column of anti-separatist Castilian nationalists, performing ritual beatings of hens hung by their legs from lengths of woven garlic rope strung between palm trees, held at secret locations in the island's interior to thwart any attempts by animal welfare champions to disrupt it. This activity was claimed by the Spanish *culinarios* to encourage premature shellless* egg production, a prized and rare ingredient, and was defended as being of great historical and social significance, part of that nation's cultural heritage as enshrined in its Constitution.

There were other international teams, of course, but none were taken seriously. The English were effectively ignored by everyone, except the madding English tourists, as they forlornly offered chips with mayonnaise, shepherd's pie with mayonnaise, and bangers with mayonnaise, in the network of English pubs that infested the island. The Irish teams in turn offered from their pubs a mayonnaisey concoction that was heavily dosed with Guinness, though in reality they wanted simply to drink as much as possible of the pure stuff, and watch the football.

The newest contenders, the Chinese, were not so much interested in the competition as gaining a foothold in Majorca which they saw as a potential stepping stone on the Belt-and-Road project route of global commercial conquest. The local government was keen to have them there too for the investments they might bring. and offered them inducements such as issuing them hotel rooms, car number plates and competition registration all with combinations of the number eight. In fact, the Chinese offerings were very popular, with variations on the theme involving Asian influences such as sesame or peanut oil, ginger, lime, soy, galangal and jalapeno, and novel combinations with noodles, tofu, dim sums and bamboo shoots, for example. The quantities they offered with such polite and efficient service, as opposed to the arrogance and parsimony of the Parisians, or the offhandedness of the local entrants, were much appreciated by the patrons. The other contestants, however, viewed them with intense suspicion, and there were whispered claims of certain other secret and illegal additives, such as MSG, and even opiates, being brought to bear for maximum effect in this calculated application of soft-power diplomacy.

The American contestants, naively sponsored by the Mayo Clinic on the basis of their wellness policies, of course applied all their genius for razzamatazz and marketing to the challenge, but their lo-chol, non-additive, GM-free, organically certified contributions in bio-degradable containers were universally scorned as tasteless gunk by other participants while still managing a small, dedicated, if rather eccentric following who could usually be spotted in joggers and spandex spooning themselves out calorie-correct quantities on the run.

Australian pretenders were regularly disqualified for refusing to call their product by its eu-sanctioned name, demanding that 'yolko' (pronounced as in "Oh no!") be accepted as the legitimate antipodean appellation. 'Peach Melba with Yolko' simply did not cut the mustard with the Europeans. Notwithstanding, the Australians normally turned up anyway, got roaring drunk, refused to believe there would be no bulls to run with, and routinely thrashed the local Rugby and netball teams.

A small New Zealand contingent always pitched camp adjacent to any Australian presence and made a point of offering Pavlova and lamingtons, with or without mayonnaise, decorated with sliced kiwi fruit on beds of silver fern. They would have liked to have stuck little national flags on the top but realised, accurately, that to foreign eyes it was virtually indistinguishable from the Australian national flag and would thus ruin the whole point of the exercise. At the same time it allowed them to spread the story that the latter was actually the new post-Brexit version of the British flag, the old Union Jack stuck away in one corner while the euro-stars flew off in the opposite direction. The Australians, shamefaced, could do little to counteract this telling slur on their nationhood.

All-in-all then, this was a recipe for a week of cultural chaos. Large marquees were erected in key spots around the island, best crockery unpacked, cutlery polished, special wines brought up from cellars, taste buds called to order, security measures quietly put in place, and clement weather invoked both by prayers to God and mammon, and by confident faith in the benign Mediterranean summer climate. The locals endured the inconveniences perpetrated on their casual holiday lifestyles with cool nonchalance, smug in the certainty their traditional version of mayonnaise with nougat and a finely balanced constituent mix was the supreme embodiment of the style, and that the festival ensured tourists would dump a shitload of moolah on them into the bargain.

And over it all hovered Don Joan, a symbol of calm, grace and excellence in all things Majorcan, as he toured around the island's scenic spots, checking the venues, encouraging participants, and especially, glad-handing potential voters with a sly nod to an inevitable local triumph.

Except that one time. As the multitudes assembled under clear starry skies for the awards ceremony in the Plaça Major at the finale of the year's festivities, the judges seated in full pomposity and hubris in the front row, the challengers congregating in their team colours waving flags and banners amongst the crowd, our portly luminary stood proudly in his civic regalia atop a podium decorated as an almond cake. A nervous young Majorcan apprentice chef, dressed in her pristine, gleaming white uniform, complete with apron and drooping oversized toque, scurried out from one side, handed Don Joan the sealed envelope and scurried away again. Don Joan, arms and hands in full flourish worthy of Liberace playing *Flight of the Bumble Bee*, opened it and read out the winner's name. The winner was, *quelle horreur*, a commercial German food conglomerate. Menorcan saboteurs had struck again by stealthily and cleverly insinuating strict EU standardisation requirements into the rules, ensuring an inoffensive though unquestionably bland and insipid victor!

General commotion ensued. Simultaneously, and spontaneously it seemed, Brexit agitators, Basque terrorists, Greenland nationalists and Catalan separatists leapt onto the platform, squirting a cheap, popular, generic brand of mayonnaise from beige plastic containers all over the mayor, the infamous product running down his official robes and around his big-buckled boots to form a sickly-white vomitus puddle, an anaemic give-away of the shortcomings of its ingredients. He beat an ignominious retreat, licking his existential wounds, but vowing to return for the sake of personal, tribal and epicurean honour.

And while the expression 'to have egg on your face' had long before been hatched elsewhere, poor Joan at that moment tasted the bitter sweetness of its local application, and the EU be damned.

* *q.v. Gary Rosenberg, malacologist, and his seminal work on shellless molluscs.*

Tricky Business

Conden was taking his usual break in the wide tree-lined pedestrian thoroughfare of Pamplona, Paseo de Sarasate. It was autumn and the once heavily leaved elms are beginning to look bedraggled. Unlike the plane trees in the nearby Plaza de Castillo they are not pruned back every year to create stumpy, amputated limbs which become thick and bushy each season but do not supply spreading shade. In Sarasate the trees are let to grow their way and are tall and wide and meet each other in their canopy, providing shade in summer so that sitting under them on the benches next to the flowers beds on the edges is a welcome respite from sun and heat.

This Conden liked to do, especially in that hiatus period between lunch and the evening stroll and re-opening of shops. At this time the streets were almost deserted and it was a time of quiet reflection, and for a *farios*, cigar. But now people had begun to reappear and Conden was enjoying watching them pass by. Many would simply be on their way somewhere, others including Sarasate in their route for the evening *paseo*, stroll, others still just hanging around Sarasate.

Conden, having finished his daily cigar, decided himself. to take a stroll up and down. He headed first towards the large statue which stood at the apex of the avenue, an imposing monument celebrating what may be equated to a Magna Carta of Navarra, beckoning, or daring, entry, something of a dead zone for strolling however. Just beyond and overbearing it in height was the giant Redwood, a gift to Pamplona from the Americans it seemed, though nobody could tell Conden how old it was or what would be done about it as it grew to its full and massive maturity.

Then he turned back to walk the full length towards the Parliament of Navarra buildings at the other end. As he did he passed a distinguished-looking black man dressed spectacularly in colourful traditional garb. Their eyes met and both nodded greetings.

Conden wandered a little further and sat down on a bench. A short while later the black man passed again on his way back, hesitated and stopped, then spoke with a deep, attractively accented voice.

"May I join you?'

"Certainly."

"I am Abdou Lubaki. From Congo. You?"

"Conden. Ireland."

"I find there are many Irish here in Pamplona."

"Yes, the lifestyle appeals, and there is always work teaching English."

"And were you a teacher in Ireland.?"

"No, I was a tourist operator, but I needed a change. And you?"

"I had a very successful career as an artist there but fell foul of the government. Either I had to restrain my artistic expression or leave. Or die."

"What art did you practise?"

"Sculpture. My works demanded very high prices. But I had to escape quickly and only managed to smuggle out a few pieces, the best."

"Have you sold any?"

"No, I can't do that openly as the government has a spy

network here who would trace me."

"So, blackmarket."

"Sadly, yes. The prices are much lower. I have one here if you would like to see it?"

"Sure."

The man reached into a shoulder bag he'd placed next to him and drew out an object the size and colour of an aubergine loosely enclosed in a couple of layers of bubble-wrap. He opened it up and handed a figurine to Conden.

"I'm taking this one right now to a potential buyer who works at the Museum and collects African art."

Conden took it carefully and looked at it by the evening's fading glow, the street lights partially blocked by the overhanging branches of the elms. It was apparently the figure of a fat, and also probably pregnant, woman. Conden's very limited knowledge of such things suggesting it was some sort of fertility piece.

"How much would it bring normally."

"At least 10,000 euros," Abdou sighed, taking the sculpture back. "Otherwise, just one thousand. She has offered me 500 but I will hold out for the thousand."

Conden saw an opportunity.

"Would you take 700 for it now?"

"Very, very reluctantly, but I am desperate. I could leave it with my friends at the *Vinoteca* in Eslava on my way home and you could pay them tomorrow."

"I could give you a little on deposit now to seal the deal if you like?"

"Oh, no, but thank you anyway. It is a great deal so I am sure you will want to finalise it. You will surely be pleased with your investment."

They shook hands, Conden asking him for his name again so he could check it out, and the man headed off back the way he came. That night Conden googled the name as best he remembered it, with inconclusive though promising results. There were references to the name, and prices for his work were certainly upmarket. So, starry-eyed, the following day he called at the *Vinoteca* having withdrawn the funds.

He asked the attendant about the man and what was the association.

"He asked us if we could help him out, for a commission, and we don't like to see these illegals doing it hard so we try," the young man said, speaking Spanish. "There are so many of them who struggle just to survive here."

Conden counted out the euros and the young man handed over a box of wine. Apparently the commission was in the sale of the wine, and Conden was getting a bonus. He opened the box and could see there were 11 bottles in the separated compartments, and a bubble-wrapped article in the twelfth. He pulled it out halfway and could see it was the figurine he was shown in Sarasate. He thanked the young assistant and carried the box home.

Back in his apartment he eagerly pulled his prize out and ripped apart the wrapping, revealing the statuette he had seen briefly the previous evening. In the bright light of his kitchen it looked very different: the blackness of its outer skin mottled, the features of the face rough, the body ill-proportioned. Perhaps it was the same one he had been shown, or perhaps it was a rough copy, he wasn't sure.

He ran his hand over its surface and pushed his thumb into a bulbous buttock. It seemed to give very slightly, aptly but worryingly. He scored it with a fingernail and removed a small piece. It was cream coloured and squeezy. He put it to his nose. It was soap, and he was more than certain that by the time he got back to the *Vinoteca* the man would have been and collected his money, less commission, and moved on to his next *paseo*, and that he had been well and truly conned.

Seeds of Gold

Julian Garcia Gutierrez, eighty-four years and forty days old by his own reckoning, being as he was very conscious of the significance of every day, just as those are at the other end of life's course, native of nearby Aldenueva de la Vera, sits in the watery afternoon sun at the gate to the German Military Cemetery of Cuacos de Yuste, close by to the Monasterio de San Jeronimo de Yuste, final resting place of King-Emperor Charles the First and Fifth. This is commemorated by an imposing statue of Charles at the outskirts of the town, down the mountainside from the monastery, where he majestically poses clothed symbolically in the vestiges of his mighty Empire, like some frozen giant swarmed over and overcome by midgets.

Indeed, it was literally Charles' last resting place, rather than the usual connotation as place of burial, since it was here he chose to rest during his final years after a life of dedication to others, those final years being all too brief. His bones were much later then exhumed and taken to Madrid for entombment by his son Philip, three hundred and forty-seven years before Senyor Gutierrez's first birthday. Here, now, Senyor Gutierrez sits selling his dried fruits and herbs, locally grown and collected. He has done this for many years, observing very much and very little, though he talks now more than he listens, and so observes even less, nor wishing any longer to observe much more.

Senyor Gutierrez speaks only the most meagre amount of German and English, which he has picked up inevitably and reluctantly from visitors to the cemetery through osmosis, rather than any effort on his part. He generally ignores any language barrier by rabbitting away indifferently in his native Spanish, or Castilian as some insist it be called in order that it not be considered the only language that represents, or has always represented, the voice of Spain. He uses the Castuo patois of the region, heavily accented, as a result of which almost nobody understands much of what he is saying, even the Spanish tourists. Yet he holds their attention, and thereby communicates his message, by the twinkle in his eye, the lean of his body towards them in secret brotherhood, his lilting inflection heavy in sibilants, the passion and enthusiasm of his continuous prattling, his liveliness despite his age, his local colour, their misplaced guilt at being so rich and free while he appears so needy and confined, the appeal of his products combined with his persistent refusal to answer any questions about their cost, or the added fascination, once having noticed it, of deformed legs giving him a dwarfish stature. This notwithstanding the competing pull of the wonderfully peaceful, intriguing and historically diverse, foresty mountain environment, currently denuded for winter.

He sits on the opened tray at the rear of his little hatchback vehicle, short, crooked legs swinging free. He has turned his bright blue baseball cap sideways to the right to keep the sun out of his eyes from the west in its low trajectory at this solstitial time of year, like some young rap artist gone to seed, his goods arrayed around him, some packaged in plastic, others displayed in small open hessian bags begging to be tasted or smelt, and in buckets on the ground in front of him, near where he has thrown his aluminium elbow crutches, easily overlooked.

Shrivelled apricots, figs and sultanas, dusted white with their sugary remains; almonds, walnuts and chestnuts with their russet shades redolent of autumn when they were gathered; desiccated rosemary and oregano, chamomile and a herbal mixture for tisanes, some seasonal apples for freshness, none with tags or prices, all beckoning for attention, while he draws it away from them to himself by his mesmeric jabbering, the waving about of his arms, the waggling of his legs, like a baby propped up on its father's lap, nodding his head now towards the monastery up the hill, now to the gates of the cemetery to his left, now skywards.

His face carries some of the characteristics of his products: tanned, leathery skin, dried, shrivelled and wrinkled by age and sun, eyes squinting and hardened by what they have seen yet still lively, mouth thin and tense with a slight ironic, larrikin twist, his neck wizened and reptilian.

In fact, for the few who might understand his babbling, he is telling stories: stories about the cemetery, stories of the men buried in the cemetery, stories of the visitors to the men buried in the cemetery; stories of the monastery, of the monastery's garden, of the giant exotic trees in its garden, of its construction, decline and renovation, of its destruction, rescue and restoration, of its inhabitants, original, past and present. It is never quite clear, especially to any listeners with the linguistic skills to understand the stories, whether they are true, totally fabricated, or a bewitching concoction brewed from any number of those observations he has made over the years, something akin to one of his mixed herbal blends.

And so, on this crisp, sunny, winter's day, he tells the story of the eucalypt trees in the monastery garden, the only trees there now with any foliage, having easily recognised that near-universal word eucalyptus in the otherwise incomprehensible question, to a young Australian from Warrnambool on that continent's southern coast. He has asked about them, in English, as any Australian would naturally ask about them having seen them in that alien environment, before they might ask why there would be a German War Cemetery just here in the middle of a Spanish nowhere, if they asked anything at all.

He has chosen the word eucalyptus carefully and avoided using the homespun term, gumtree, for reasonable fear of it being incomprehensible to anyone but Australians.

The young man from Warrnambool had just been to the monastery. He is interested in the history of those times of Hispanic glory, and, having noticed the gate and wall to the cemetery on his way up there from his hotel down the mountainside in the town of Cuacos, made a mental note to pull in and investigate it on his way back.

While at the monastery he had been struck by the massive trees native to and emblematic of his country, here in this isolated place on the other side of the world. He had questioned staff about the trees' history and significance, as best he could for nobody spoke a word of English at this major tourist attraction, but all he received were shrugs and shaking of heads.

So now he listened, transfixed, as Senyor Gutierrez began to tell him the tale, unable to disengage himself from the narrative's spell as it unfolded, beholden to him in the knowledge that the old man was telling this story especially for him, or at least so it appeared, and was clearly responding to his question, the import of which he had recognised only by that key word the young man had used, eucalyptus, the same in Spanish and English from its Greek origin meaning 'well-covered', referring to its flowers' little cap, weaving it back again and again into his otherwise almost unfathomable text.

The young man comprehended as much as his imagination could construct, with the bare essentials of that compelling word, eucalyptus, along with others like Terra Incognita, Terra Australis, some terms common to most European languages, and some basic Spanish he had studied before coming on his personal study tour of Iberian churches and monasteries.

Well then, Emperor Charles the Fifth of the Holy Roman Empire, and King Charles the First of Spain (indeed, he was also Charles the Second, the Third, and the Fourth, plus Duke,

Archduke, Count and Margrave of various other territorial concepts), maintained his rule for forty years in the first half of the sixteenth century, Senyor Gutierrez began, settling quickly into a rhythmic tempo which discouraged any interruption. He was a keen gardener and avid botanist, in addition to being lord of an empire where two temperate seasons, along with a tropical climate, as well as any hour of the day or night, prevailed somewhere on earth at any one time, as indeed on which, equally, the sun was always shining. Charles was Belgian, son of Philip the Handsome, also a Belgian and so-called for no apparent reason judging from extant portraits, and grew up in Ghent, whose inhabitants are known as 'noose-bearers' because of Charles' harsh treatment of them, a city with a very chequered history to this day. He lived his early life surrounded by perfectly ordered and maintained gardens of exquisite design which were not only beautiful but utilitarian, providing luscious taste sensations for the picking, something Charles liked to do as he walked around enjoying the ambience, learning, and making suggestions for improvements.

When it came time for Charles, or Carlos of course, here in Spain, to retire, it seemed reasonable that not only should he spend his time in prayer making peace with his God who had given him constant guidance through his momentous life, but that he should also allow himself some indulgence in his lifetime interests, interests which his duties had precluded him from fully enjoying as much as he would have liked to, at least at a level which permitted patient and practical participation.

The monastery at Yuste had been built by local artisans for the Jeronimite order over one hundred years previously. The area was well known to be particularly enchanting, as well as fertile and bountiful. Its climate also allowed for a greater range of horticultural produce to thrive than was the case further north. It was a perfect choice, and Don Carlos gave orders for the monastery to be refurbished, extended and generally upgraded for his occupancy, to include a chapel, his personal apartment, rooms for staff and extensive gardens.

He had always delighted in having botanists bring him exotic specimens from the many corners of his far-flung dominion and seeing them flourish on one of his estates. The orchard at the monastery, which lay just below his new apartment, had been generously - if it is possible to be said to be generous with regard to the request of an Emperor - given over to him by the monks so that he could easily wander down there whenever he desired.

The work proceeded piecemeal as he gradually extricated himself from his responsibilities of state, though it was delayed, as such work so often is at any level of engagement, forcing Charles to lodge with other equally generous subjects along the route to Yuste once he finally set out on that journey into retirement.

The period of Charles' reign had also been one of continuing world exploration and discovery on an explosive scale. Whenever he could, Don Carlos had immersed himself in the details of these endeavours, sending ships and navigators around the world on voyages into the unknown, among other things, and making sure he was kept informed of all developments in matters of general science, cartography, astronomy, commerce, language, public administration and botany.

The fierce rivalry between the Spanish and Portuguese monarchs was restrained by marital ties and their shared Catholicism, overlorded by their common Pope to whom they deferred, though this did not mean they would refrain from attempting to sway his decisions.

From this there had emerged a division of the entire world into two parts, one half, or close to one half, as there was some contention about it, for each side. While restrained at the higher levels, the rivalry was still cut-throat and at times erupted into outright, if somewhat controlled conflict at levels of daily engagement.

The stakes were extremely high, no less than world

domination. Both sides strived for gains and were willing to take significant risks to achieve their ends. Charles knew the Portuguese were planning excursions in search of a southern Terra Incognita and considered it his duty to match their efforts, even though these adventures could bring him into conflict with Portugal and threatened dire consequences for him if his representatives strayed across the demarcation line.

This imaginary, very imaginary, line was something in our age akin to us drawing a line around the moon before we had been there or even seen its dark side. Its positioning followed detailed research and argument, ran right around the globe as a meridian, extending from the north pole south to the spice islands and into the unknown, very near to where you come from, Senyor Gutierrez, nodding his way, acknowledged to the young man, and was sanctioned by the Pope himself.

Charles therefore secretly commissioned an experienced navigator, one, Manuel Rodriguez Garcia, in whom he had implicit confidence, originally of Plasencia, coincidentally not far from the monastery at Yuste, and from a farming family, which also therefore gave him a broad understanding of the natural world, to prepare two galleons and sail in search of Terra Incognita. The Capitan was instructed to make maps, look for commercial opportunities, collect botanical specimens, interact with native peoples in order to understand their ways and learn their languages, and naturally, to spread the gospel wherever possible, then to bring such information and specimens back to him personally. All of this would go undocumented in its preparation and would only be communicated personally to Charles himself on their return. This was crucial. Success was less central than secrecy.

At this point, with the afternoon shadows lengthening, the Australian needed to ask for a break as he had been hanging on every word that Senyor Gutierrez spoke, straining as best he could to pick up the merest understanding, and becoming totally immersed in the atmosphere being created.

He was helped in following the story more as it unfolded by the theatrical gesticulations of the old man as he rambled; that, as well as by the key words he would occasionally recognise, coupled with his knowledge of the history of the time, especially as it applied to the explorations of the unknown southern seas around his own country.

He interrupted the flow, indicated by gesture his dry mouth, and asked in English, though it might be of little additional usefulness, for a drink. The old man reached into the back of his vehicle and pulled out a leather bota, handing it to the Australian who managed to aim a stream of the wine into his mouth long enough to slake his thirst.

His legs had become very tired having stood for so long, so he then eased himself down onto the ground and sat cross-legged to listen some more, not unlike some schoolboy before his teacher. The old man bent down and picked out some figs to give him to go with the wine, indicating in a not uncomplimentary way his recognition of the Australian's capable manipulation of the traditional drinking vessel, and then continued, eager as he was himself to get on with the story.

Capitan Garcia, a name I share not by any coincidence with him by the way, a man of solid build, great internal strength, steadfast character and considerable talents, duly set off with his ships and crew from Cadiz to find the Great South Land one day towards the end of Charles' reign.

Nothing whatsoever was heard of them, partly because of the covert nature of the mission, but mainly because they had sailed literally into the unknown and therefore they were incommunicado, until, almost two years later, they suddenly appeared again, less one galleon and much of the crew, in Cadiz harbour, like some migrating bird which miraculously finds its way back to its nesting place.

Senyor Gutierrez broke off here and looked directly at the

Australian, adding as an aside in a softer voice, and hinting of a great significance:

"Of course, the story of the voyage of Capitan Garcia is one of great adventure and excitement, but must wait for another opportunity before it can be told."

Don Carlos, Senyor Gutierrez resumed in his former manner, by this time, though held in high esteem everywhere, was no longer King and only technically still Emperor, and had withdrawn and ensconced himself at Yuste, tending to his garden, his toys, his appetite and his soul. Yet, still, the Capitan, loyal to his liege and the oath he had made to him, refused to divulge any information about the voyage to others, insisting on making his way to the monastery at Yuste and presenting himself to Charles.

This he did, after a short period of recuperation in Jerez de la Frontera, travelling mainly by boat to Sevilla, as he was still wedded to his recent life on water and needed to ease his way back into terrestrial ways, and then by horseback through Extramadura to Merida and Caceres, Plasencia and finally Cuacos de Yuste. Charles had by now been well informed of the Capitan's return and approach, and had readied his court to receive him.

The Capitan left his small retinue to remain in the town of Cuacos, not yet adorned with its monument to the King, and rode the final stage up the mountainside alone so that he would be undisturbed in his audience with Don Carlos, one that had to be kept totally and forever secret.

They met in the private apartment that Charles had had prepared for himself in the monastery. It was not large, but comfortable, with a grand fireplace making the room quite hot when lit, and accommodated the special chair with an extension at the front to support one of his gouty legs in a raised position, for Charles was certainly not an abstemious monarch.

The Capitan noticed and admired the many fine clocks on the walls, several made especially for the King by his resident

Italian mechanic, Giovanni Turriano, (Juanelo we called him here in Spain), and all set at different times to remind Charles, it is said, of the reach of his former empire, although it may just as easily have been to remind him of the inexorable passing of his life, something which would have fed his tendency to melancholy. There were many rich tapestries, artworks by Titian, hand-made puppets and other toys, weapons, and a glorious sculptured falcon in solid gold given to him by the Knights of Malta, a special treasure amongst so many treasures.

Capitan Garcia could see that the once-Emperor was now seriously ailing. He moved slowly and painfully, had grown thin and bent, his lower torso distended, but, even so, his mind was keen and he showed a genuine enthusiasm to see his loyal servant again. Speaking, naturally, to his Spanish subject in Castilian, which he regarded in any case as the language of God despite his native French, he encouraged the Capitan to rest and eat and, only at his leisure, reveal the wonders he had encountered.

All this Capitan Garcia acceded to and they spoke casually of his family and the last part of his journey and some matters of local interest to them both. Present up to this point was Charles' chief steward, Luis de Quijada, in whom Carlos had the utmost confidence and to whom he confided some of his most intimate secrets, even to such length as his latter-day celebration of paternity of his illegitimate youngest child - Jeronimo by name, whether by coincidence or not - entrusting the boy to his care. Nevertheless, once the Capitan indicated he was ready to proceed, eager as he was to please his king, Charles motioned to Quirada to leave them; such was the profound secrecy of the mission.

Once Quijada had removed himself, after some fussing about to show his irritation, and they were alone, Capitan Garci began, adopting a less informal pose for his new purpose:

"Your Majesty, I can bring you wondrous tales of new lands and peoples, and information which undoubtedly will be of great value to you and all the realm, but, alas, I have been able to bring back few items of such value as I would have wished to."

Here, Senyor Gutierrez displayed a further dimension to his discursive abilities, making great moment of throwing his arms about, and creating a powerful image of the men speaking, to the extent of adapting his voice and even his accent to the scene.

"Tell me, and show me, all, whatever it may be, for I am coming to the end of my days and am greedy for as much in the way of knowledge as I can devour before it is all over for me here in this world and I go to meet judgment before my maker," Charles urged him.

"Your Majesty," the Capitan resumed, "there is indeed a Great South Land, a Terra Australis, no longer Incognita, so extensive that it rivals the Americas. But it is an inhospitable place, dry, hot, sparse and empty in parts, beaten by constant tempests in others, devoid of any riches such as gold and silver or spices or edible fruits or grains, peopled by savages as black as any Kaffir, but without signs of ordered society either present or past, with no dwellings of any substance, nor with a tongue that would allow any civilized man to ever understand them, and therefore sadly beyond the reach of attempts we might make to bring them into the Lord's flock; inhabited by strange animals, some with deer-heads and withered front legs, which bound in great leaps upright on their tails and whose offspring can return to their mother's womb and be born again any time they choose, but nevertheless which have no potential for any kind of human use, not even by the natives, being so wild and so poorly formed, save to be eaten, and then even with a harsh flavour and dry texture."

Capitan Garcia at this point leant forward a little.

"And there also," the Capitan whispered, "I was confronted by ships of the King of Portugal."

The Emperor frowned, leaned back and remained silent for some time.

"Tell me what then occurred," finally he uttered.

"We engaged with two caravelhos, sire, but the weather conditions did not allow us to approach them closely enough and they fled westwards. We did not want to pursue them in that direction for fear of violating the antimeridian and risking the consequences."

Charles nodded and listened intently while the Capitan gave more details of his expedition, the latter expressing apologetically his disappointment and shame with the little he could offer. Eventually, once he had described all he could, he paused and spoke in a different, lower, conspiratorial tone:

"Your Majesty, there are just two things of value I can humbly present you with, as a consequence of all my endeavours. The first are these maps, roughly drawn no doubt, but I believe forming the basis for any further exploration that may be carried out in the future, however unlikely and unprofitable that may be, for the benefit of the realm and to the glory of God."

The Capitan unfolded several parchment-like sheets and the two men spent some time then poring over and discussing with great interest and concentration these separate pieces of cartography which had been created on board ship purely by eye and judgement while sailing in all conditions, and were consequently of a rough style.

After some time Charles collected them together and passed them to one of his courtiers, summoned by him in German for this purpose, as Charles believed it to be the language of command, telling Capitan Garcia that they would be copied and reconstructed by the King's personal French cartographers and then be the subject of much more study later, and thanking him profusely. The Capitan then returned to his presentation.

"And second ..."

Here, he paused and reached into his apparel to pull out a large leather purse, untying its thonging and bringing out a few small, rough-shaped and knobbly objects, each about the size of a pebble. Some, which were waxy, in a turquoise colour with a bulbous cap on their tops, not unlike the skullcap or zucchetto of a priest or cardinal, could almost have been opals fashioned into brooches or some kind of bauble or button; others were a flakey, dark, woody brown without the cap, some of these with the shape of a cross on their flat tops, apparently created by some cracking of the indented surface.

"... in contrast to all the other plants and flora which we observed which were clearly of little value, but which I have brought back samples of and will provide you with nevertheless, in one particular place where we landed and explored a little, we came across some magnificent trees, giants in a forest of giants, taller than anything we had ever before seen in all our life or travels, straight as a galleon's main mast, hard and strong, and with enough timber in each of them to build one hundred ships. All around the base of those leviathans we found and gathered these nuts," (and at this point, holding them out for Don Carlos to look at, the Capitan used the Spanish word bellota for acorn, and not the word nuez for nut, or sencilla for seed – and indeed, these strange objects, though they were themselves whole, looked as if they could be the rough top half of some bizarre acorn) "which we have brought back so that, we believe, we can germinate and reproduce those great structures here, to the glory of God and the benefit of the realm, Your Majesty."

Don Carlos took the objects - which were in fact gumnuts, as I have heard others from Australia like yourself call them, Senyor Gutierrez said more quietly to the young man, he in turn astonished at catching that word, mangled but still recognisable, coming so unexpectedly from the mouth of the old man - turning them around in his fingers, squeezing and shaking them next to his ear, and finally sniffing them.

"Yes, Your Majesty, they have a very distinctive perfume, one which is not too unpleasant, and which is also highly present in the leaves (which sadly I have not been able to present to you as they dried and became brittle and were lost somewhere during the voyage) and indeed saturates the forest where the giants grow with its combined intensity, giving visitors to such place a heavy, heady feeling, but one which we could see no use being made of by the natives, nor can we see how it could be useful in any way for our needs now."

"It is indeed an intriguing new perfume and may have significant medicinal qualities, and it quite pleases us", Charles commented as he called again to one of the servants in German, his curiosity piqued by the possibility of some new life-enhancing balm, an area in which he had shown considerable interest and had extended regal encouragement to those exploring it during his reign.

"Summon Senyor Doncella to come here immediately," Charles ordered the servant.

—

Senyor José Enrique Doncella was the personal botanist to Don Carlos whom he had brought to Yuste to assist him with the gardens. He hailed from a village in La Mancha, the name of which I don't wish to remember now, Senyor Gutierrez tossed off to one side, not too far to the south-east of Yuste, also coincidentally. He was a thin, wiry individual with a serious and thoughtful expression permanently on his long face with its high-domed forehead, and wore a thick ducktail beard and a moustache which completely obscured his upper lip, and even his entire mouth when he didn't open it to speak or eat, giving him an impression of mumbling whenever he did either. He had worked for many years in the field, especially studying specimens brought back from the Spanish possessions in the Americas, learning much from the famed medical botanist Nicolas Bautista Monardes in Sevilla, with whom at one time while there he had shared accommodation.

When the botanist arrived in the room Charles handed him the bag with its contents and told him to take them away and study them and report back, without explaining anything more about them. Doncella was necessarily intrigued and excited but knew better than to engage in discussion with Charles if not invited to do so, and withdrew with a simple "Your Majesty".

Some days later Capitan Garcia said farewell to Charles, whom he would never see again, and returned to his home in Plasencia. Some time after that he moved to a property in the countryside near Navalmoral de la Mata, not far to the south-east of Cuacos de Yuste, where he would become a farmer again, retiring from any further public service and remaining in obscurity and forever maintaining the silence which he had vowed to uphold.

He had not, however, given over all the gumnuts to Don Carlos, taking with him a selected few which he kept, until one day he planted them crudely somewhere on his rural property, which is now, Senyor Gutierrez indicated with a nodding of his head down the road in the direction of the approaches to the area, an agricultural research and teaching centre, and home to two very old eucalyptus trees underneath and around which can now be seen flocks of merino sheep, crunching on the hard earth, their droppings mixed with the dry bark and leaves, just as in your own country; the very same breed your forefathers took from us here to such great advantage for you there.

Meanwhile the botanist Doncella investigated these intriguing new discoveries and reported his findings to Don Carlos within a few days. He told Charles that, after careful scrutiny and based on his extensive knowledge of botany and the anatomy of nuts and seeds, he believed that these objects were not acorns, as such, or even nuts themselves, but more like seedpods – now he used another Spanish word, vaina, for this – which held the seeds inside their globular bodies, releasing them when ripe by first throwing off a cap that covered and protected the contents, then folding back their inner compartments in which the seeds lay, allowing them to fall out into the earth where they could be succoured into growth.

He demonstrated to Charles his belief, which was an accurate assessment of the items in question, by turning one of the capsules upside down and banging it into the palm of his hand.

"You see, Your Majesty," the botanist declared, holding out his hand to Charles and at the same time blowing very gently to remove the chaff, "from inside the capsule come these tiny dark specks, similar to the specks we get when we grind the pepper spice seed, whereas in this case these specks, I believe, are themselves individual seeds, difficult as that may be to accept. We can only know for sure if this be true once we have induced one or more of them to germinate and grow, and this, Your Majesty, is what I would like to attempt to make happen."

Don Carlos took one of the darker capsules and did the same, resulting again in a peppering of small flecks across the palm of his hand. He picked some off his palm and placed them between his teeth and bit on them, moving his tongue around afterwards to glean any taste there might be in them, though this produced essentially nothing of interest.

"It is indeed a wonder, if it be so, and I believe that they have been put there, and sent here, by God who has guided us to reclaim them by his grace, and who has marked them with the sign of the cross, in memory of his only Son, as a symbol of salvation and rebirth. You must go ahead and do all you can, use all your knowledge of nature and all your skills and experience in the garden, to bring these tiny miracles to life, so that they may grow with the help of God in our northern earth into huge and magnificent trees, unmatched anywhere in the world, by what Capitan Garcia has told us, to the glory of God and the benefit of our children's children."

The botanist carefully gathered all the seeds and capsules together and withdrew, now even more excited by having some clue as to their origin and nature from the few words Don Carlos had spoken, assuring Charles that he would apply all his knowledge, energy and effort to the task, and keep him completely informed of developments.

He embarked on this arboricultural journey straight away, and although he met with Charles a few more times and discussed progress, of which there was little, indeed none, unless error and failure be counted as some kind of advance, Charles was never to find out if the tiny flecks were seeds from the south which would grow into monuments to the glory of God in the north, for he faded away and died during the course of his botanist's early ventures.

The botanist Doncella, charged with such responsibility, however, and though grieving, or in fact as part of his grief, redoubled his application to the job, testing various methods of which he knew, plus others which he experimented with, in his effort to unlock the life they hoped was encased in those grains. He also sent some specimens to his colleague, Monardes in Sevilla, to seek his involvement, and received back from him some helpful suggestions which he put into effect in his experiments, although to no benefit.

Here, once again, Senyor Gutierrez paused and leant forward and downward to speak to the Australian from Warrnambool in a different, calmer style.

Of course, being Australian, you would know that many of your country's native plants have special requirements to spur their regeneration, such as the seeds needing the application of some heat for example, whether for God's special purpose or not, but the ancient Spaniards obviously had no knowledge or understanding of this whatsoever. Now, this particular plant, fortunately for our botanists then, did not ask for such drastic treatment, yet they are still a little reluctant at first to release themselves upon the world, being partial to a period of cold, good solid, cold cold, before they burst into life when some warmth then arrives. To this end also, God, or nature, or both, have seen fit to give these tiniest, most precious of their creations, a hardiness and endurance to enable them to survive a very long time in the most challenging conditions until they are quite ready to fulfil their destinies.

The Australian was once again awestruck by the depth of Senyor Gutierrez's erudition, and felt particularly chastened since, if the truth be known, he was not aware of such important and fascinating facts about the flora of his native land. Still, he did not want to make any admission of his ignorance and by so doing interrupt the rhythm of Senyor Gutierrez's narrative, humiliating as that would also have been, not that it would have been acknowledged, of that he was certain, nor indeed understood by Senyor Gutierrez, though the Australian was beginning to wonder even about that notion, and allowed, if allowed might be the right word, the old man to continue.

Thus it would take some time for this to come about, Senyor Gutierrez continued, taking on once again his previous manner, given that Capitan Garcia had arrived back in Spain in early spring, having enjoyed a southern summer before that, and that there was now the advent of a northern summer, followed by an autumn, before any cold weather would provide the seeds with their germinating trigger. Only after that, meaning in the warmth of the following spring almost a year away, could any sign of life be expected from those recalcitrant storehouses of existence.

The deluded Spanish botanist, in his wisdom, which in this case turned out to be his ignorance, was striving in late spring, understandably, to bring about what could not occur till the following spring. It was only his native perseverance and dedication to his work, and the promise he had made to his now deceased leader, that meant he would not give up.

In many ways, in any case, he did do the right things for his diminutive charges. Most importantly, he kept them moist, and he kept his watchful eye on them constantly. With the abundance of seeds at his disposal - each of the capsules that Capitan Garcia brought back being capable of containing hundreds of individuals, and he had brought back many since it was a small cargo to carry, and he had harboured great faith in his belief that these capsules would provide at least some return for the King's investment in the mission - he was able to try all the combinations and permutations that he knew of in his experience as a practical gardener, and more that he devised to fit the purpose.

He sifted soils to make them fine enough to suit the miniscule seeds. He used soils from different locations. He mixed soils with river sand or crumbled animal manure and compost, or with husks from wheat and oats. He put glass over parts of the raised garden beds he had prepared for that function and where he had earlier sown without results. He placed some between pages of a book, a copy of a recent heretical version of the Bible by a German priest, Martin Luther, which he felt would be well-served by such treatment, and kept it constantly moistened with water, opening the pages every few days in ever-dwindling, but persistent hope.

From the same book he tore several leaves, rolled them into cones and filled them with some of his carefully prepared soil. With one seed in each he placed them tightly side by side in a small wooden box he had specially made by one of the village artisans. He layered it and stuffed it with straw so that each of the cones was snug in a straw bed which could be kept moist and warm as he moved the box from inside to outside, from shade to full sun, covered when he thought helpful by its lid. He knew that when the time came he would be able to transplant each cone separately without disturbing the roots. These would have grown long and deep as they felt their ever more constricted way towards the narrow end. He knew also that the paper itself would then rot away and become simply part of the plant's new home.

He soaked some seeds in warm water before planting them, an action that to some small extent unknowingly anticipated the special reproductive requirements of your country's flora which I mentioned, Senyor Gutierrez said, shooting another glance at the nonplussed Australian.

He planted in earthenware pots, keeping some inside through winter, leaving others outside but bringing them in at night, placing some in warm corners of courtyards, or on roofs where there was uninterrupted sunshine. He planted in woven baskets of reeds and hay, allowing him to hang some under eaves and inside, high, near the ceiling for warmth from the fires. He kept some in cupboards, thinking perhaps they needed the darkness as in their natural forest homes. He made deep holes for some, just in case, but kept most shallow as would be the usual way for such fine, delicate specimens.

He planted whole capsules, despite it being extravagant in its heavy usage of seeds, though only temporarily as he was able to salvage some of them later. Nevertheless, he felt he needed to try every possible route to existence the plants may have taken in their strange southern environment.

He reluctantly posted eagles' feathers and certain herbs in the corners of the gardens to bring good fortune to the process, a practice which he had heard about but which he had previously frowned upon as unscientific and therefore against his educated convictions. He planted some seeds by moonlight, a practice he believed may have some soundness in science, though he was sceptical.

He planted several in small glass bottles, both clear and light green, creating little hothouses along lines handed down from Roman times, keeping them just moist enough and moving them around to catch the sun, especially in winter.

By fabricating a type of enclosed ball utilising translucent animal gut he even hung some upside-down, believing that the embryos might perhaps require some reverse force of gravity or other energy, in the direction they would normally experience in their southern climes, to activate the life-force.

He could be seen on a daily basis working in the gardens, wheeling pots and baskets around in barrows, carrying his watering pots and buckets and jugs, a wet cloth and a sponge to squeeze gentle drops of water onto his vulnerable protégés, poking and prodding the soil with tools or bare hands, sitting quietly in apparent contemplation of the challenge before him, or occasionally bowing his head in what appeared silent prayer but could just as easily have been mild despondency.

By the late summer, without the least sign of any stirring in all his attempts to draw the sleeping trees from their shells, the botanist-gardener was near despair. He had little doubt that with the coming of winter nothing could now be expected to emerge, but he convinced himself that after that, with the arrival of another spring, he would succeed.

He continued his trials forlornly during the cold months, checking his garden beds and plots, his pots and bottles and book and everything to do with the seeds almost daily, moving some around to find warmth and sunshine, working on other parts of the garden to keep his mind off his central focus. He prayed regularly to his God to give him direction in his undertaking and strength to his purpose.

When the snows came and spread a white blanket over all his outside interests he stayed indoors in the old emperor's study and read whatever he could find about horticultural pursuits and botany and wrote letters to fellow gardeners and scientists seeking advice, but without being able to reveal the fully story behind his quest, a story in any case that he himself was not fully aware of.

There were inevitably no helpful responses to his appeals, unsurprisingly as there was nobody anywhere in the world at that time who had any expertise in the germination of eucalyptus seeds, although there were many responses with less than helpful advice.

Little did he realise that all the work that was necessary was being done just then right outside his door, without him having to lift a finger any further, as the cold damp snow worked its magic on the germ of those same seeds.

So that, one day in April, his patience and determination came to be rewarded. During one of his regular inspections, daily, at least, now that some warmth was in the air, he noticed in one of the raised garden beds the tell-tale sign: one of those thrilling landmark events, along with spring budding and flowering, first fruit set, and first picking, for which all gardeners wait and look anxiously. The surface of the earth, very slightly caked by the drying-out process after watering, had a small crack in it caused by something pushing it up from underneath. A little bulge from below, opening up the tiniest fissure which would widen and pop back its folds as new life pushes for freedom.

He recognised it immediately and knew what it meant. His heart raced and his hands shook with the excitement of expectation as he gently touched the little mound. He was sorely tempted to put his finger under the small crack on one side of the raised lump and pull it back, but he resisted, knowing the danger of damaging, or even in any way disturbing, anything underneath.

He calmed himself. Patience, in any case, is the true mark of a gardener. It could of course be a weed, though he had carefully and methodically cleared all the beds and pots of any growth during the summer, so his hopes were high and not too presumptuous about their absence. He checked all the other locations and this was the only one. So far. There was always a team leader which the others, he prayed, might follow.

He forced himself to go away. He walked down the long hill to the village, spoke with some folk about local matters of no importance, and walked back up again, tiring himself considerably. He went to the chapel and partook of the sacrament, remaining and praying for much longer than usual.

He spoke with the monks about complex theological matters, straining to keep his thoughts in the realm of metaphysics and to resist the pull of the down-to-earth at hand. He broke bread and drank wine. He had a siesta, though restlessly. He prayed in the chapel. He took a stroll in the peaceful serenity of the adjoining forest, now itself awakening for spring. He went to supper with the other monks. When he looked up at the end of his meal, dark was finally setting in. At least now temptation would be held in check until the morning. He went to bed and slept fitfully.

When the light first came in through the window and brightened the room, he woke up. It was very early but there was now no need to delay since the embryonic plant would be responding energetically to the call of the sun. He rushed out and found, not only had the seedling, for it was now no longer a mere seed, pushed off its confining cap of soil and was beginning to unbend its delicate pale stalk, but nearby there were three more little cracks in the soil's surface just where he remembered he had placed some tiny seeds almost one year before, as gardeners do remember. And he found comfort also in knowing, from his experience, that whatever might be visible above the surface of the soil would be multiplied many times below it as the new life sent its rooting tentacles down and down, searching for nutrients and moisture. He was overwhelmed with joy, satisfaction, awe and gratitude, and as tears welled in his eyes he dropped to his knees, gave thanks to his God and remembered his beloved King, praying that somehow he would be made aware of this stunning event.

The satisfaction, possibly the gratitude, if not the joy and awe he felt in his achievement was in fact misplaced, since all the work had been done for him by nature and the seeds themselves, apart from his mere sowing of them, though this did not occur to him in his elation. The next stage however was going to be very much more dependent on his horticultural abilities, for eucalypts, indeed most of the plants from your native land, Senyor Gutierrez directed his gaze and words straight at the young man with a modified tone of voice, significant in its insinuation since the old man seemed to be able to see right through him, are notoriously difficult to transplant, requiring some expert know-how, just as in their germination, as you would know.

The Australian nodded meekly in agreement, though he had been made acutely aware once again of his general ignorance of such matters of which he felt he should be more cognisant, wondering just how the old man could know all these things.

He used the opportunity, perhaps in reality as a diversion from more attention to his inadequacies, to take a long squirt of the wine and to nibble on an exquisite, dried fig, there appearing to be here a juncture in the story where, though success had been delivered to the botanist in his initial quest, a greater hurdle had suddenly arisen, unrealised by him in his focussing on the primary challenge, and so threatening the entire project. Senyor Gutierrez seemed to hint at this by a change in his manner and tone, pausing, taking a deep breath and then continuing more slowly and seriously.

All around for the botanist Doncella now, little seedlings of eucalyptus were popping up, their two light bluish-green cotyledon leaves - which the botanist also would probably have known as cotyledons coming as it does from the Greek, though naturally he did not call the plants eucalyptus in his interaction with the monks and servants, as this name was not applied to them until centuries later, but rather 'the trees that God has sent to His Majesty', or for short, 'the King's trees' or in Spanish, 'los arboles del Rey', which in turn gradually reduced to 'lodelrey' - searching eagerly for the light to make energy for those true leaves that followed, before their own essential stores were depleted.

Each day they grew a little more and he was delighted to watch as more leaves unfurled, these ones quite a different shape to the first two, giving him a better idea of what the final appearance of the trees was going to be like, he assumed, though mistakenly again, as these aberrants from the south carried with them in their nature yet a third kind of leaf, reserved for their maturity.

There was little for him to do except make sure none of them dried out, especially those ones in pots, which were also now popping up, and he had time to observe and contemplate, noting that most of the seeds that had been left out in the cold, either fully or partially, had successfully germinated, while those that had been kept warm had not. He decided therefore to store some of these latter ones, though not all, in cool dark places over summer and then place them outside the following winter in the hope of gaining a second crop in the future, and by so doing also testing the hypothesis by comparing the two new groups.

The days and weeks went by with Doncella giving daily attention to his previously dormant, now thriving wards. The seedlings had grown well and could now be called plants, or even little trees. The leaves had become distinctive, a light greyish blue-green with a waxy bloom on them like ripe grapes, and oval in shape, winding their way up their long thin stalk like a spiral staircase. The botanist was faced with more decisions.

Soon enough it was autumn and some chill returned to the air. The entire garden was showing the ominous signs of flagging energy and faltering resolve to continue. There were yellows and browns appearing in the heretofore ubiquitous verdure of the foliage; there was fraying at edges where for months heat and wind, or insects and birds had taken their toll; there was sad, resigned drooping where there had been excited waving and craning for advantage. Some leaves had already given up completely and were dropping and drifting to the earth to join those already lying there to begin their gradual disintegration and reintegration into the cycle of nutrients.

Dry, woody, dull remains, with their hollow bodies of what had once been bright and exuberant explosions of colour, and then swelling containers of goodness and new life, hung straggly and exhausted off twigs and branches. Previous sources of nourishment for first bees, then insects and birds and animals, were now only fit for the compost and to be the diet of worms. There was a cool dampness to be felt in the air or on the botanist's fingers after they touched the rough bark or lichen of a tree, where before there had been a crackle of parched crispness. With the moist blanket of cool nights and cloudy days a peaceful silence was descending to replace the noisy clamour of summer sounds. Meanwhile, Doncella's little new creations steadfastly ignored all these triggers and buttons of shut-down and beckoned him to intervene. He had already long considered the where and when and how of transplanting them; now he had to commit.

There were several spots in the monastery's grounds which he believed would be suitable, given that so little was known about how the trees would finally look, or how long it would take them to get to that stage, though he remembered the words of the King about their potential size. If they were to be very big he did not want to place them where they would obscure the view of, and from, the front of the monastery, with its entrance and gardens and walkways, nor did he want a result which would impose on or threaten the physical safety of the structure. There was one area, which was the approach to the chapel, and another area near that on a raised terrace section, or patio, further away from the buildings and near the external walls; the first which would be suited to an avenue of trees leading to the chapel's entrance, the second which would allow the trees to be seen clearly and therefore feature in their magnificence, a magnificence he believed without question they would develop, based on his memory of Don Carlos's words.

He therefore set in motion various works in those areas to prepare ground and space to receive the trees, and he put his mind to the question of when such planting should take place. Normally this would be in winter, late winter if possible, before the sap of the plants began to flow again in early spring and the roots could be safely bared, at least for the known deciduous trees. This would mean however that they, at least those not in pots, would have to winter over and may need some protection from frost. How they would take the frost he had no idea. He did not yet know even if they were deciduous or evergreen.

As for how he would do the transplanting, he assumed he would follow the usual procedures: cooler weather, towards spring, a misty day or one with some light rain preferably, maintain the integrity of the root ball, prepare the ground. The question was: this year, next year, or perhaps even the year after?

Before too much of his planning could be implemented, however, fate intervened and he suffered a serious setback, though he was able to learn from it as well. In mid-November, when the plants had still shown no sign of dropping their leaves and he had therefore deduced they were probably evergreens, although he did not dismiss the possibility of some other alternative, whatever that might be, in this hemispheric migrant, a sudden and unexpected early frost hit.

There was no warning of it in the afternoon or early evening, so once the morning came the damage of the night had already been done and it was too late. When he stepped out into the chilly early light with the hoarfrost coating every exposed surface with its delicate brushing of silvery-white, a full two-thirds of the little plants were nothing but shrivelled black piles, or small sticks with withered black or drooping green attachments hanging from them, none of which would survive. They were mostly the smallest ones, or the most exposed, or the weakest growers, so those that remained at least were the hardier and therefore best placed to survive more onslaughts.

He chided himself for not being better prepared and for not giving them all the protection they might need against such dangers. From that night he began bringing in all those in pots and baskets at dusk for the security of the warmer indoors, taking all of them out again at first light to gain the advantage of maximum sunlight when it was becoming a premium at this time of year. He began also to transplant some from the bed into pots, losing several within days but improving his skills and knowledge of techniques, noticing, for example, that those for which he maintained a greater amount of soil around the roots did better. Thus is the way of the gardener and the scientist, to accumulate learning from observation, by failing and modifying, by testing and reacting.

Just at this point the drone of a motor became evident as a car came up the hill towards them and the monastery. It pulled into the little gravel parking area, four tourists jumped out, speaking German, and headed straight for the gate, keen no doubt to see the place where their countrymen, perhaps relatives, had been laid to rest. Two of them noticed the little sideshow and peeled off to come over.

Senyor Gutierrez had already stopped in his narrative and had murmured '*guiris*' or foreigners, a derogatory term, almost, the Australian thought and hoped, as an expression of irritation for the intrusion, and a compliment to himself as some sort of honourable local and confidant, if albeit temporarily. They began questioning the old man in German and signing about the produce and the prices and he reacted in his normal perfunctory manner, using the patois without restraint, until the Germans finally chose some herbal tea mixes, handed over the amount of euros, which he finally allowed himself to request, without haggling, being easy to please in this regard, and joined their friends through the gate.

The Australian, who had sat quietly without wishing to be an impediment to the old man's business, and therefore his livelihood, in any way, though he would have dearly liked to have delved into the mystery of the cemetery with these Germans, was greatly relieved that it had been brief, as he was in a state of high suspense for the rest of the story. The old man, hardly missing a beat, simply took up the story where he had left off.

So the winter passed, the botanist taking measures to protect his little ones, laying straw around them, collecting wood from the forest and burning fires on the coldest nights, screening them from harsh northerly winds, checking them constantly for any signs of problems, while carrying out his other chores around the gardens and in between his devotional and temporal duties.

One thing he had now noticed which was very much to their advantage was the absence of any predators, insect or microbial or fungal threats to their wellbeing, something he mused on with great interest, wondering what might be causing this, what their defences might be, how this might be useful for application elsewhere. It could not have occurred to him, nor to anyone else in those days, that this was a portent of terrible problems to come, when new life takes root in alien lands. You, Senyor Gutierrez said with some sympathy, will no doubt be painfully aware of this through the destruction wrought on your land by our rabbits. The young Australian this time was able to give an honest nod of agreement.

He had determined a strategy for the transplantation stage, by now also it having been confirmed by their leaf retention right through a winter, that the King's trees, the lodelreys, were definitely evergreens. He would go ahead and transplant as many of the young trees as was needed for the sites he'd had prepared, about a dozen, and leave the rest where they were, in case he needed to replace any.

Hence, towards the end of winter, he did just that, taking most of the specimens, the largest, from the open beds, keeping as much of the soil around their roots as he could, as well as three from baskets which had had some protection over winter, burying the complete basket with its guest undisturbed, knowing that the basket's material would simply rot away and even provide some nourishment and texture.

Within days some had begun to wilt and show signs of distress, and within weeks they were all dead. Don José, for the botanist had gained a level of respect by maintaining a position of established authority, and had reached an age where he was being referred to in this way, was again on the edge of despair. If he could not transplant his babies then all would be lost. Some may be left to remain in the beds but they would be poorly positioned there, and risked being removed if they grew too large in the future. The onset of summer precluded another attempt at transplantation that year, believing, based on his experience, and correctly this time, that transplantation would be more perilous for the plants in summer than in winter or spring, which had itself just failed. The botanist had no option but to prepare to spend another winter, caring and waiting, and he went about this task with his usual patience and determination.

This patience and caution was to be rewarded again, because, again, what he could not know was that these little eucalyptus trees, his lodelreys, relished the opportunity to strengthen themselves further through another dose of cold while they were in their established positions, without the shock that a transplantation would bring, though paradoxically not for too many more seasons, since the larger they became, the less likely was the success of transplantation.

Thus, the next time Don José transplanted his dozen, this year's batch somewhat bigger than last, they were far more ready to thrive, which several of them did, though again he noticed the ones that had been protected by over-wintering indoors, did not. His expertise was building year by year. He took a further chance and replaced the few early failures of that year quickly, being particular about keeping them well watered, and by the end of the summer of 1561 all but one of the sites he had chosen were happily hosting a thriving little eucalyptus tree, or lodelrey, so-called at that time as I have said.

The Australian, whose body had been straining and stretching itself to attend to the story as much as his ears and mind had, felt a great sense of relief at last, to know that some milestone had been successfully reached and passed, and gave a sigh and relaxed himself. Senyor Gutierrez paused, feeling much the same way, shifted his position slightly and looked up towards the monastery as if to check to see that the scene he was describing was actually still there. No longer thirsty, the Australian now realised the time of day it was, and became concerned about his return to his hotel while there was still light. The old man recognised this and proceeded more rapidly towards an ending, to round off the story and bring it up to the present.

Don José, the botanist and gardener, tended those trees for several more years, replacing as best he could some that died or appeared weakened or diseased in any way from the stock that remained, and also thrived, in the garden beds. Before he died he had passed on the knowledge and expertise he had developed to many of the local peasants and artisans who had come to the monastery for the various jobs that needed to be done.

By this time the true leaves, long, darker green, thin and curved like a sickle, had replaced the younger ones, and the form and appearance of the adult tree became clear to him. He was able to notice also a novel feature of this woody specimen from the southern forests in that it began to shed its bark in long ribbons, revealing each year a fresh and healthy new surface of its trunk, much in the way a snake sloughs off its skin each year. He was also to enjoy the fruits of his labour and determination in seeing a completely new species prosper in its exotic environment, by walking amongst them and sitting in their shade and especially by breathing in the special aroma that they had brought with them from the Great South Land.

He sometimes picked one of those long angled leaves

and bent it over putting it to his nose to breath in the reviving freshness of its perfume, and always when he did he remembered his king who had done much the same all those years before with the original gumnuts.

———

Over the decades and centuries the memories of these great adventures were slowly lost or distorted, particularly as no documentation was ever made of their origins or connections. However, legend lived on in the minds of local people, like those of my forefathers from the villages here around who have worked at or assisted the monastery in various capacities for centuries, and the wisdom, such as I have passed on to you today, has not been entirely lost, though obviously, in your country, this knowledge and expertise has now become commonplace.

Once the eucalypts were well established there seemed no need for further extension of their domain as they had little utilitarian value, no fruit or edible nuts, even for animal fodder, no timber better than what was already known and appreciated, caused shading in winter when as much sunlight as possible was desired, and grew far too big and too quickly to be manageable. They appeared, also, to suck dry the soil around their bases, causing the area to become bare and prohibiting the growth of grasses and other plants, making their presence incompatible with other crops, or pasture for animals, and therefore unpopular with farmers. The bark that they regularly shed, more and more as they grew larger and larger, along with branches and sometimes large boughs, gathered around the base of the trees and caused unsightliness, danger and spaces unfit for use. Despite the hopes of Charles, the heroic efforts of the Capitan, and the unwavering faith and dedication of Doncella, it seemed that the seeds of gold from the south were destined to fail in their assumed promise of bringing untold benefits to the north.

Reports started to filter in of similar trees growing in other parts of Spain and Portugal, and sometime, around two centuries ago, the name eucalyptus surfaced as the accepted description of the tree and the oil that was being extracted from it for medicinal use, just as the King had foreseen, so that the local term, lodelrey, and the botanist's reference to the 'King's trees', became superseded and lost, although occasionally you may catch it in some obscure vernacular reference locally, even today.

Around that time the French were here as occupying invaders and in a mongrel feat of vandalism burnt the monastery almost to the ground, utilising, it is rumoured, the highly combustible fallen bark scattered conveniently on hand to start and spread the fire. Here, Senyor Gutierrez hesitated, and for the first and only time the Australian thought he detected a note of sincere emotion in the old man's voice.

We are all, he said regaining his composure, both here and in your country, also aware now of the propensity of your eucalypts to blaze uncontrollably and of the destruction that sometimes results. Some injury was suffered from the heat and flames by the trees nearest to the buildings, just as they possibly contributed to the conflagration, and a couple had to be removed and were replaced nearby, in this case by seedlings which were now becoming available, brought from elsewhere.

It is true that they do not always grow here exactly as they do in their, your, native land, as you will recognise I am sure, seeming somewhat bedraggled at times, as if they are uncomfortable being where they may not be entirely welcome, or pining for the familiarity of their own natural surroundings. Still you have up there, Senyor Gutierrez nodded his head towards the monastery, what you can see today, the magnificent giants that Capitan Garcia promised his King they would become, by the grace of God, by the persistence of Don José, by the foresight of the Emperor Charles or by the absolute certainty that life, through nature, will doggedly prevail.

The Australian was exhausted and dumbfounded. He

pulled himself together and got up onto his feet. He pointed to the figs and almonds and apricots and indicated with his cupped palms that he would like to have such a quantity of each, unable to speak in any manner or form. The old man scooped out such a quantity of each into three plastic bags, tied their tops in a knot, and handed them to him, mumbling "ten euros", without adding a "please".

As the Australian took them and pulled out his wallet Senyor Gutierrez suggested,

"You can give me more if you like."

And so he did, handing over a large note, which the old man grabbed and stuffed into his trouser pocket without speaking as he jumped off his perch at the back of the vehicle, surprising the Australian by just how short he was with his crippled legs, and bent down to pick up his crutches, turning his back on the young man while he began to pack up his goods, saying nothing more.

The Australian mumbled a "thank you" in a language, which one he was not certain, but whichever it may have been, it seemed of no consequence any more, turned, and walked over to his car. He decided he wanted to take another look at the monastery and the trees before the fast-diminishing light ended any chance of that.

He had read in his guidebook about the history of the place, how it had been revived on the insistence of the dictator Franco, how it was now a state heritage monument and tourist destination, of how its only residents were four Polish monks of the Pauline order, not Jeronimites, about Verdi's opera which was set there. But nothing about the massive gumtrees in the gardens.

He started up the engine and pulled out of the carpark, braking sharply before entering the road as a vehicle rushed past on its way down the hill, the last of the workers at the monastery scurrying home.

He drove the short distance up the hill, parked and walked over to the wall where there was a grilled gate leading into the monastery grounds and the garden. The monastery was closed now to visitors and locked. He walked around a little, bewitched by the heavy sweet smell of figs and the earthy dampness of fungus and humus which filled the air as dusk pressed down upon the forest and the constant twitter of birds broke the otherwise oppressive silence and stillness. He found some acorns and chestnuts fallen on the ground and noticed a large walnut tree in the rear walled-off garden

He walked back to the gate and looked through the bars at the trees inside. He marvelled at their massive trunks and buttressed boles as they secured their grip in the earth, looking all the world as if a group of monstrous camels or elephants had gathered and were stamping their feet upon the ground. He gazed up at the canopy blotting out the sky above. He smelt the heady perfume of the eucalyptus and could imagine, just as Verdi imagined the return of Charles' ghost to rescue his son Philip in the very same place, the botanist Doncella and the King conferring in the garden over their plans to bring to life something of the southern hemisphere here in the north.

The giant trees' branches far above spread out over the wall so that there was a thick layer of debris on the ground at his feet. He scrabbled around in it and picked out several nuts and some green leaves, crushed and pressed them to his nose and breathed in deeply, experiencing the rush of familiarity and remembrance, and then stuffed them in his pocket. He would, he thought, try to rekindle something of the transplanted north back in the south when he returned to Warrnambool, using the knowledge that he had learnt from the old man, and combine that with modern methods. In the meantime, he would carry with him around these northern latitudes something to remind him of home.

He went back to his car and drove down the hill towards the village of Cuacos, past the statue of the Emperor Charles keeping vigil over it, and on to the restored 16th century abbey which was his accommodation for the night. As he passed the spot where he had spent such an entertaining and inspiring afternoon he slowed and noticed that it was now deserted and that the gate to the mysterious German Military Cemetery was closed. He felt a strange sensation in response to its emptiness and lifelessness, as if it were a different place altogether, as if in fact the whole episode had not occurred at all.

Next time that cemetery, he promised himself, and continued on without stopping.

Redfern, _My_ Redfern

Travis took a deep breath, straightened up, pulled his shoulders back and ventured one tentative step from his front entrance directly out onto the footpath. He looked up and down the street. It was deserted as he had expected, and had hoped. At this time of night, especially Sunday nights, it was always like this, a complete contrast to the noisy congestion of the day. A lone car appeared at the crest of the hill to his left, headlights beaming, and cruised quietly past and away down the hill, towards the airport. It only served to reinforce that contrast as the peace reclaimed its temporary dominion. He decided to head left up the hill towards the station for his wee-hours jaunt, revelling in the silence, the calm, the dark, and the intensity of it all. This was when Redfern was all his and he could be, and feel, and act, his true self.

The exhaust fumes of the car lingered awhile before being absorbed into the night's fold, and no more would follow for some time to prolong that unpleasantness so constant during the busy hours. The closed shopfronts he passed one by one were resting from their daytime labours of display, some with shutters down like eyelids shut for a sleep, others, insomniacs, still proclaiming their worthiness under artificial lighting. But there were no madcap teenagers careering noisily down the strip on skateboards, no bikes swishing by him from behind causing him to suddenly start in fright, and anger. No beggars asked for enough for a bus ticket home please mister. No cars pounced out in front of him from the service station, blocking his way across the footpath; none careered in from the roadway with complete disregard to pedestrians. No sirens wailing and hee-hawing as police cars and ambulances screamed past to some unknown place of emergency, no gawking media helicopters hovering overhead, no gurgling motorbikes revving for explosive effect. No crowds rushing to or from the train station twice a day in the peak hours. No scorching, blinding sun above or cold, buffetting, southerly wind at his back. No nosiness, no intrusiveness, no officiousness, no judgmentalism. It was like being in a forest with only the trees and animals to deal with, and they would give no trouble. He strolled along happily and confidently, with a jauntiness in his step, embracing the quiet, claiming his proprietorship, expressing his autonomy. "Ah, the serenity," he chuckled to himself in a Darryl Kerrigan moment, with a recollection of jets roaring low overhead to land at nearby Mascot outside these cossetted curfew hours.

Travis continued up through the tunnel of hoardings erected for the new apartment development, towards the intersection with the pedestrian thoroughfare to the station. There, more hoardings proclaimed more apartment development. The intimacy of the old individual street-front shops was being replaced by impersonal global blandness. Redfern was changing. Yet, thankfully, this had not brought with it a bustling night life. Not so far.

He came out of the tunnel with its clomping wooden boardwalk back to the quieter rhythm of the pavement and open to what stars managed to twinkle through. He debated whether he might take a left up ahead for a quick turn around the mall, or cross to the right at the lights and check out the route to the Town Hall. There was always the option of straight ahead and into the city, but that should probably be left for a while longer, he decided.

The two men appeared abruptly, just a few steps ahead, turning the blind corner from the mall towards him, as if they had been beamed in from another time zone. His whole body tensed as he saw the two hulks, swaying a little and bouncing off each other for balance, muttering nonsense at the top of their voices in the way of drunken comradeship. Despite the brief shock Travis didn't falter in his stride. He knew he had no choice but to keep walking straight at them. To stop would reveal his apprehension and have them front up to him anyway. To turn and walk away would only have them following him with its own drawn-out tension as well as putting him at a disadvantage as the hunted. To turn and run would simply indicate panic and cause them, invite them even, to chase him and if caught inevitably have a barrage of passionate retribution unleashed upon him, apart from it being challenging in itself. And they were between him and the police station in the mall around the corner, so there was no comfort there.

So he braced himself and stormed straight ahead, keeping as neutral an expression as he could manage, peering between them into the distant city skyline as if he were oblivious to their presence. It was only a few steps, and he heard their spluttered taunts well before he reached them. The hatred and menace showed on their faces and in their manner. They had drifted apart so he headed doggedly for the space between them, head high, chin out, long bold steps. Like a ship trying to steer safely between the turbulence of dangerous reefs. He felt the heavy bump to one shoulder as he passed through, and then a painful grip on his opposite upper arm. The abuse that spewed forth from them washed around him like a nerve gas attack.

His mind raced. Trying to sweet-talk them would be futile given their toxic physical and psychological state. Screaming for help would only provoke them and was not likely to elicit any assistance in time anyway, even with the police station so close. A weapon, perhaps something the builders had left lying around, but there was no time for that. There was only one weapon he could use, one that he already had on him and was cocked to go: his shoes.

He let himself revolve to his left on the arm holding his, pirouetting a little on the ball of his left foot while bending his right leg at the knee and then kicking powerfully forward and upwards with the point of his shoe into the groin of the arm-man. Travis caught the effect of this in his side vision as the arm-man crumpled and fell to the ground with a loud yell just as he felt two hands take a grip on the back of his shoulders. This in turn enabled him to re-balance and aim as he followed his frontal assault with a reverse action directly backwards. He kicked hard like a mule, bringing the tapered end of his stiletto heel into contact somewhere which he judged to be a similar region to his first blow. He felt the grip release as shoulder-man yelled out in like fashion to arm-man, doubled up and collapsed onto the pavement. Travis regained his balance on both legs and then reached out with his right and stomped on the face of arm-man with his full sole, toe and heel, trusting that his victim would have had a clear view of that bright red sole as it descended. Then he turned and gave a solid blow with the point of his pump to the kidney of shoulder-man.

Enough. Prudence was called for. There was no point in pushing his luck any further that night. He certainly had no desire to dally and gloat over his victory nor did he want any witnesses appearing. There seemed little chance of the two men regaining the ability or desire to retaliate any time soon, so he stepped over arm-man casually and headed back down the street towards home with no more urgency in his gait than someone with business at the post-office not far from there. He could hear their moaning recede as he went, mixed with some defeatist expletives.

"Redfern is mine!" he half-whispered, half-shouted jubilantly, as the clip-clop of his heels coming down hard on the pavement echoed around him and reflected the determination of his step. Back down through the hoarding tunnel, past the shops lit and unlit, across the service station entry and exit and onto the footpath protected from rain by the overhead awnings where people would linger during storms. Now almost swaggering in triumph as he went, he congratulated himself on choosing the Christian Laboutin Biancas with their solid platforms, points and steely stiletto for his promenade that night, and not the peeptoe cork wedges, while making a mental note that they were pinching just a fraction at the toes. Then he gave a final, cheeky Yellow-Brick-Road Dorothy-skip as he stepped back through the entrance into his Redfern refuge, and disappeared.

So Much Pleasure

M urray Coady had been a boxer. A champion one, if he was to be believed. He had even written about it all, or rather a ghost writer had for him. A younger woman, an intellectual type, whom he had also then had a relationship with, if you could believe him. Now he worked the tables for all it was worth at the local corner pub in his breathless, frenetic, detached way, with his deep, woolly voice and backblocks accent, selling his book to the unwary, talking sport and betting on the horses and the dogs, shaking hands here and there with a less than impressive grip and a hail-fellow-well-met approach, and doing whatever other deals he could come up with.

He no longer drank, he said, which you could certainly believe because it was clearly observable. Or did drugs which was probably also true. This was thanks mainly to that ghost writer who steered him onto the path of righteousness, he said. The pub was purely a convenient social and business venue in his reformed abstemious state. He always kept a car or panelvan parked nearby so that he had a ready supply of promotional material on hand. This consisted of photos of himself standing with various other, infinitely more famous, champion boxers. He had an inexhaustible supply of his book ready for sale as well, and an offsider on tap to help. Murray looked the part of an ex-boxer, the muscles turned to portliness, the face wearing the grim acceptance of many rounds of punishment survived, a short concentration span, and a victorious attitude.

He was, above all, proud of his accomplishments, and was currently showing great magnanimity in the distribution of invitations to his birthday party to be held at a local sporting club. He was coming into a significant anniversary very shortly, one that would mark a technical knock-out of sorts, and a large crowd turning up would confirm his self-assumed status in the local hierarchy.

Donna Starr, sitting at a table alone, and unacknowledged by Murray Coady as he made his rounds, reminded everyone at that same pub of Whoopi Goldberg, with her big wide lumpy cheeks, a smile as big as an inverted Sydney Harbour Bridge, and teeth as white as the tiles of the Sydney Opera House. Her long, lustrous, coal-black hair was brushed straight back from her face to reveal a broad, smooth, domed forehead, draped itself over her shoulders, then splayed out like the wedged tail of an eagle across her back. She was holding her newly-found treasure that night with hands that looked like they had been dipped in the smoothest, liquid golden chocolate, unveined and unmarked, with long, slender fingers hardly creased, even at the knuckles. This new treasure of hers was wrapped loosely in a green plastic supermarket bag of the kind that finds its way into the oceans and disintegrates into miniscule pieces that fish mistake for plankton and ingest so it then becomes part of the food cycle. But tonight this green plastic was playing a role as glorious in its way as any precious gold leaf enfolding some ancient pharaoh's bust had ever managed.

Donna clutched that green bag to her shiny golden brown cheek with those velvety hands and laughed a satisfied laugh, and said "kumbaya" out loud, for no good reason other than it sounded a happy thing to say. And it was thus that she absently addressed the noisy and heartless and totally uninterested and distracted gathering of motley groups assembled to take part in the trivia night at Abbotts Hotel in Redfern that Thursday night. Inside the green plastic supermarket bag was her coffee-table book on Audrey Hepburn. She was as thrilled as any mother holding a newborn babe swaddled in sumptuous finery had ever been at having this book about someone who had brought so much pleasure to her life, perhaps simply as entertainment, or perhaps as some role model that strengthened her as a woman, despite being in so many other ways her complete opposite,

"I've got a book about Audrey Hepburn," she cried out to nobody in particular, and nobody took any notice, as the MC assured everyone that the composer, whose work he had just finished playing twelve bars of, was in fact Edvard Grieg. This revelation drew a dull moan from most of the crowd, along with one isolated excited cheer.

And so, as Donna repeated her short paean to her heroine, sounding very much akin to an incantation, Aaron, who was sitting with friends one table away from Donna, this time did take notice. It seeped into his consciousness through the general noisy babble that here was something that may indeed be of interest to him; that a book on Audrey Hepburn, who had also brought him so much pleasure through his life, could be worth looking at. It carried the added novelty of its provenance in this situation, with its improbable owner, in this improbable environment. On the other hand it occurred to him as he prepared to act on his curiosity, that there was something quite appropriate about it too, it being a trivia night.

He got up from his table and, taking Donna's kumbaya invitation literally, stepped, hardly more than leant over, and asked her if he could have a look at her book. She stared back at him blankly, appearing stunned as if she had never supposed her words would garner a response, let alone such positive interest.

She glanced over at the mess on the table he had come from.

"Move your plate first," she said very authoritatively, practically and unexpectedly.

Aaron turned back and did so, wiping his place at the table with a paper serviette into the bargain. He looked back again with a smile he hoped assured her of his understanding of the responsibility he was taking on.

Donna handed him the book without further comment. He put it down on the table with the newly clean surface in front of him and opened it. He could see clearly that it was a book about Audrey Hepburn, confirmed by a photo of her on the cover smiling puckishly, eyes heavily made up and closed shut, head tilted slightly to one side. It was a photo of her which was unfamiliar to him. Printed underneath in large letters was simply 'Audrey Hepburn', as if any reminder was necessary.

He leafed through the book with friends at his table watching on, discovering it had plastic pockets attached to some of the pages, with inserts. Checking these inserts, he found a postcard from Mexico signed by Audrey, a personal letter from her to her son, and her ID card from the time when she was young and lived in Belgium under German occupation. They all became quite excited about this astounding find, though in the dim light of the pub and its trivia night, and goaded by the nature of the event and the atmosphere, it was easy to jump to inflated conclusions, which they did.

Aaron had been caught out by Murray some time ago and, as an unwary wide-eyed innocent on his first visit to the pub, had bought his autobiographical book, so that Murray did not have much interest in him anymore. But Donna did. She was quick to see an opening for some pocket money. She came over to sit at his table now, and joined in the excitement at the wonder of this potentially lucrative find, mentioning that a woman had already offered her twenty dollars for it. Aaron was thinking of considerably more amounts than that and hinted that way to Donna. She talked lovingly about Audrey Hepburn and how she had other mementos of her at home. She wrote down an address on a beer coaster and, getting Aaron's phone number, said she would ring him about visiting her the next day.

Without warning she leant over and gave him a big kiss,

right on his lips. Then she just as suddenly got up and was gone again, clutching her Aubrey book to her bosom, and disappeared, completely absorbed into the throng of the pub on that busy night, with the extra hubbub as the jackpot question was about to be asked. Aaron did not win the jackpot and did not expect that he would ever hear from Donna.

She rang the next morning, asking him to drop by and check out the book in good light, and at the same time to take an opportunity to look at some of her other finds from the street.

Aaron set out up Regent Street after choosing a fresh lot of movie DVDs at the local rental, still referred to as the video store, although video tapes had long disappeared in the face of the onslaught of digital discs, themselves facing oblivion before the unstoppable advance of internet streaming. The store had in the meantime become a mecca for movie buffs, expanding relentlessly as it cannibalised the stock of other stores forced to close down, then re-selling them frenetically before it must itself succumb. He passed the newly-opened café where a waitress had been trapped for hours the day before during a quick visit to the back toilet, just as scaffolding on yet another ritzy high-rise development collapsed, crashing down on adjacent buildings, the clamour of the crash resounding around the blocks as if an airliner had ploughed straight into them on take-off from Kingsford-Smith airport not far away.

Just a little further on he caught someone calling to him from a dark corner.

"Got a spare dollar for a bus ticket, mister," said the voice.

Tired of being constantly asked for money in this way, he snapped back a loud "No!" without looking, and immediately regretted it. He saw then that it was a mere boy asking, and thought that perhaps he did just need the money to get home. But being in that state where a couple more steps had been taken, and the indecisive thought process of feeling like a heel versus easily continuing on your way was using up the time needed for action, he didn't stop. Nor did he then apologise, even though the boy shouted after him:

"Everything's good, brother, everything's good," and he walked on, regretting that now as well.

He continued on past Redfern Station, along Lawson Street and across Abercrombie, down Ivy Lane where he always felt inclined to whistle or hum The Beatles tune *Penny Lane*, to the address in Boundary Street which she had given him when she had rung him that morning.

She lived in a little bald-faced terrace house with an upstairs wrought iron balcony identical to all the rest in the same row and typical of the area. Unlike most of the others around hers, however, it had not been renovated as the area privatised and gentrified, thereby revealing its character as public housing. Aaron noticed the house next to it was up for sale at auction and knew it would bring plenty in these days of real estate fever, being as the area was, so near to the city and the university. Still, it was a far cry from the Tiffany's of Audrey Hepburn in 5th Avenue, New York.

Donna was out on the little upstairs balcony apparently waiting for him, and leaned over it to say hello, in much more restrained tones than the night before.

"I'll be straight down," she called out.

She was clearly excited about Aaron coming and, with a slightly hoarse voice, introduced him to two others in the house, both men. Aaron could not work out what their position was as they looked on intently. They all sat down in the small front loungeroom cluttered with ornaments and pictures, vases with paper flowers, books and toys and objects of an indiscriminate nature. Pinned to the wall was a large poster of Audrey as Holly Golightly in *Breakfast at Tiffany's*. Everything, it seemed, had been collected from household rubbish put out on the street. She handed him the Audrey Hepburn book, gingerly this time, as if now they were really getting down to some serious business.

Aaron took it from her carefully and opened its pages wherever they fell. It did not take him long, no time at all in fact, to see that the book, though interesting enough, was a special edition of reproductions. Feeling his culpability, he realised that his main task from this point was how to break the bad news gently to Donna so that her disappointment would not be too devastating.

He started by showing how, by feeling with the fingers, the surfaces of some of the documents were smooth, without any raised points, which would be the case if they had been originals; that creases which were there for the eyes were not there for the fingers, a little like a *trompe l'oeil* on a garden wall; and how if tilted into the light, the unbroken smoothness of the reflections showed that they were photos of some kind, and not true etchings or woodcuts. Donna took it on board quickly and, resigning herself to the overwhelming case, passed on this formerly hidden evidence to the two men, who nodded acceptance of her learned analysis.

Still, it was obvious that she was a little shaken by the disappointment, having had expectations unfairly raised. She began to displace that disappointment by talking rapidly and almost intimately about Audrey, how she felt about her and what she knew of her life. Aaron noticed her eyes had become a little teary and was moved by this emotional display of such devotion by someone so far removed over someone so very different.

There was a brief lapse of concentration in her thoughts and she stumbled over some minor fact about Audrey, using the present tense then correcting herself into the past tense.

"Oh, a blonde-hair moment," she murmured, almost to herself, and recovered her composure quickly.

Aaron, after pausing while the full comprehension of Donna's comment grabbed his attention, chuckled in appreciation, but then also wondered whether Donna had in fact realised the irony of what she had said, or not. He looked hard at her, into that strong face full of character, and was simply not sure.

Having lost the initiative with the book, Donna was still not going to be beaten. She suddenly jumped up and headed upstairs calling back as she went that she had something else to show Aaron. She returned, after some time, bearing a box of photographic equipment which she said had been left out on the street, plonked it down in front of Aaron and asked him if it was worth anything.

Aaron happily went through it, amazed that such museum pieces had been recklessly discarded. He noted details of the various pieces down on a pad which bore the insignia of the university that Donna hastily supplied, also obviously from a heap on the street. He assured her he would do his best to find a buyer, though not with the same tone of excitement in his voice as the night before over the book in the green plastic bag.

He felt now he should begin to edge his way out. He asked if he could take a photo of Donna and the book. When he looked at the photo later he noticed that it had captured in the background another small framed picture of Audrey's face peeping out from a bookcase, something he had not noticed when he was there. After some more idle chat among all of them he got up. He grabbed his coat and cap and was making for the door, mumbling words of meek gratitude and nonsense. Donna came up to him and put her arms out open wide and wrapped them around him in a long, warm embrace, but without the kiss as on the previous night.

Aaron left, promising to be in touch about the cameras, and retraced his steps back up Ivy Lane and further on towards the train station at Redfern, then changing his route to go along Caroline Street and past its painted chocolate-box house of black pride. A little further on he came to the protest enclave that had been set up amongst the rubble of demolished houses, with its green, orange and dun-coloured tents flapping in the ever-present wind. Aboriginal brothers and sisters pitted against each other over The Block, that remnant of a vast landscape that was once all theirs, a broken bastion of urban aboriginality.

Men and women, white and black, sat around a perpetual fire crackling away in its rusty colandered oil drum and stood in quiet groups talking and laughing. A large tent, opened at the front for general access, housed a makeshift office with a table where a white-haired local elder sat and supporters could add their names to a petition against the planned development. Their Aboriginal flag, itself an alien notion, was painted large and proud on the side of one of the remaining terraces facing them, with the city skyline as its background, like a colourful scream of defiance, and a barricade against the shiny latter-day fortress of the conquering occupiers.

But these were not Aaron's thoughts as he walked through, smiling and basking in the realisation that, though he had been born and had spent his whole life in the country, he had never until then been hugged or kissed by one of its original peoples. So, as he detoured into the tent and signed his name in the book of protest, he offered his silent gratitude to Audrey Hepburn for that benefaction.

A Momentary Passing

Even now, in the middle of the day, the street shadows are long. They will get steadily longer as the day progresses, and though the sun is bright and warm in colour, it is low and has little heat in it. The breeze is light but cool as it flows up the hill along Regent Street from the cold south. It flows ineffectually against the constant one-way traffic that heads down the hill towards the airport. The trees, migrants from the northern hemisphere and dumped irregularly along the footpath wherever enough space allowed, are denuded, divulging their origin. People are clad in clothing heavier than that which merely a week ago would have been oppressive. All of this combines to give this day its winter setting, a day which has another, unnatural, distinction as the first day of the financial year.

As he walked further up the street towards its major junction with Redfern Street, Aaron Buswell passed a billboard on a bus shelter crowing a newly-released movie with the inscription: 'The Moment That Makes The Difference'. He wondered as he glimpsed at it whether or not it was any or every moment that made the difference, each step taken this way or that or indeed not taken at all, that made a difference, a cascade of every-moments, or whether it really had to be something momentous that changed life's course

The gulls were taking an afternoon rest from their

incessant food-gathering on a tiny patch of grass next to a mottled shades-of-grey-barked London plane tree. Leafless now, it rose straight out of the cold, hard, asphalted earth like a spikey-haired flagpole with an elephant foot. Cope Street used to run into the main street here but had been ruthlessly truncated at its zenith. Now ibis stalked around looking ridiculous, with their long legs and outlandish curved beaks without obvious purpose here far from the swamps.

Aaron walked around the sculpture civic authorities had placed triumphantly on the spot where the streets had previously joined. It reminded him as it always did of an anti-aircraft missile cluster arrayed against potential air attacks by evil enemies of Redfern. He chuckled as he connected that to The Martian Embassy playroom for children he could see across the street, and fantasised about a war of the worlds centred on Redfern.

Further along, coming from a newly renovated and still-vacant office building, a weird whooping noise of some fire or burglar alarm yet to find its proper role in the scheme of things erupted. So now all thoughts on the subject of moments of import lapsed for Aaron as he wondered what use such alarms were these days when they were everywhere and nobody much took any notice of them except to be irritated by their intrusion.

He waited to cross Regent Street watching for a break in its torrential stream down the hill from the traffic lights. The cars and trucks would bank up regularly but briefly for a red light, like a logjam in a river, then rush on again with the flow released by the switch to green. In the moments between, more cars would sneak around the corner from Redfern Street and accelerate down Regent to catch up with the previous flurry. There was little time for a pedestrian to beat the successive waves.

He scurried across two lanes and a van in the third lane honked as it flashed past. He banged on its side and swore at the driver and thought how just gripping a steering wheel transforms people. With the safety of the footpath he relaxed, stopped and chatted to a woman with a kelpie dog and a baby in a stroller. He patted the dog though the woman cautioned him. He was good with dogs and knew how to approach them, putting the back of his hand out slowly so the dog could sniff and check for malintent. He had seen the dog and the stroller with a man pushing it the day before, and the woman confirmed that was indeed the father.

He walked on, passing the Chinese restaurant that specialised in duck, with glistening red carcasses hanging obscenely in the window. Aaron liked to call it the Viaduck, partly because he could never recall its true name, and partly for a chuckle. Aaron liked chuckling to himself over his private jokes. He thought of the campaign being waged against the inhumane treatment of farmed ducks and wondered whether he could ever eat duck again. That was the trouble. He liked them so much, and the ones from this restaurant were as good as you could find. He considered the possibility that they were so good precisely because they were treated very badly, and was immediately angry with himself for stumbling onto such an awkward awakening.

Aaron turned left along the small pedestrian thoroughfare created between towers of commercial space to head towards the train station. One pair had originally been ominously named the TNT towers after the national transport company that built them, though without any dire consequences ensuing. The RSL club was now not much more than a facade since it was gutted and converted into ritzy high-rise apartments. This had created such a wind tunnel that even today, with only the mildest breeze elsewhere, people were pulling coats around themselves and holding caps against the artificial gale.

Aaron passed the spot where a man had been shot dead in the cabin of his truck when he tried to outrun a police chase by turning into this short-cut. He had somehow lodged himself and his truck irretrievably under the awning of the club as he cut the corner in his panic, even as he threw the gears from forward to reverse, spinning the tyres backwards then forwards uselessly. His final moment came with a bullet from a police service revolver which shattered the windscreen on its way towards and through his brain.

Now a man, originally from India Aaron reckoned, with a rag spread in front of him, sat there half cross-legged with a bowl on the rag and a small cardboard sign pleading sympathy. It felt strange to have an Indian there where there were usually Aborigines, the strangeness underlined by the similarity. He appeared to be doing rather well financially-speaking, if in fact financial could be applied to such dealings. Passers-by were showing him due respect even though they had to walk out further to get around the corner. The dead man almost certainly did not rate a single recollection.

It was not so busy here now as it would be later when the commuters started to come home from work in the city, but it was still full of bustle and the crowd was still as diverse and wondrous as it always was. Aaron waited to cross at the lights where he usually waited to meet friends who might be coming by train to visit. The traffic coming up the hill in the three-lane road from the airport suddenly stopped quietly and patiently in its roaring rush as if by a miracle, or for a short respite from its stressful mission.

He passed through the turnstiles, putting his ticket in the slot to flip up the guard, although he noticed just as he did so that an adjacent gate was open and most people were simply going through that way in both directions. It surprised him because he was aware of the problem the city was experiencing with fare evasion and thought that this would simply encourage it. He noticed also that the police were there again with their sniffer dogs, all floppy ears and deceitful wagging tails, on the look-out – or should it be the smell-out, he chuckled to himself again – for drugs. Aaron recalled having read that, despite their frequent swoops here at disreputable Redfern, their success rate was higher in more affluent areas. They persevered nevertheless.

As he moved along the concourse looking at the faces coming towards him and avoiding bumping into the hurriers and the head-down screen-addicts, one man on crutches with crippled legs approached swinging himself along surprisingly quickly in the manner of a child between its parents, and just as gleefully. Aaron couldn't help but let his eyes linger briefly as they neared each other. Then, just as they passed, he was taken aback as the man, short by circumstance, stopped, though Aaron continued to walk on. He swivelled on his crutches by lifting one and swinging around on the other like a spinning toy ballerina, and with a big smile called out to him by a name which was not his but which he knew was directed at him. It was too soon for Aaron to have walked far enough not to have noticed, or to have others not notice. Because Aaron did not want to embarrass the crippled man in the midst of the crowd by ignoring him, he stopped and turned.

The man, balancing on his crutches now, held his right arm out gawkily with elbow bent while the crutch lodged in his armpit, and repeated that wrong name and shook Aaron's hand and asked him how he was and said how good it was to see him and how long it had been since he had seen him. He did not mention his own name which suggested to Aaron that the man really did believe he was well known to him causing Aaron to stare intently into his face for recall and to ransack his memory.

When he found an opportunity, as the crippled man was talking effusively without a break though without saying anything that might contain some clues to his identity, Aaron asked him whether he did indeed know him and what his name was. As he did so he looked into the man's face searching for some recognition in the way that sometimes we do after not seeing someone for a very long time, finding the resemblance and the visual memory gradually combining like computer programs that morph together people's faces over time, bringing us up-to-date on the person we used to recognise so effortlessly.

He thought that perhaps this person did know him and that he had just got his name wrong, so he mentioned his own name and found out that the crippled man's name was Michael. This was of no assistance, nor did Michael's discovery that he had got Aaron's name wrong make any difference to the warmth of his greeting nor to his excitement at the reunion. So he asked the crippled man, in an offhand way so as not to offend him, for his surname, to be given it, without a flicker of disappointment or surprise, as O'Reilly. There then followed some family history of the O'Reillys and confession of his own staunch support to that day of the Church, together with an expression of his confidence that they had both been strengthened throughout life by their commitment to its teachings and values.

Aaron realised he did not have to make any further attempts to remember the crippled man from his past, and that it was only now necessary to extricate himself politely from the conversation that had all the power such encounters do have to embroil us and make us captive to their invisible bonds. And so he did, assuring the crippled man finally that it had been good to meet him, leaving "again" hanging in the air unsaid or perhaps implied or even possibly just missed. He wished him well until next time when he was sure he would recognise him, he being so memorable in appearance. He suspected however the recognition would not be mutual, nor did he say such.

So Aaron made his way, now a little late, to catch his train, though he was not anxious since the trains from Redfern to the city ran regularly and often. He used the opportunity to consider the proposition that the moment he had just experienced and the delay it had caused him had made some difference, but that he would never know for sure what difference.

All That Matters

Though winter, that day in Sydney was spring-like, as it can be in June in Sydney: the air still, the sun just slightly warming, the sky a washed-out blue brushed with wispy cloud, like dissipating aircraft vapour trails, which perhaps they were; ibis, cockatoos and pigeons, noisily thick on the ground vying for their share in the little park named after some long gone local identity, where the local bakery regularly throws them its surplus loaves, and where sometimes you can feel the trains rumbling underneath as they approach Redfern station, it all bringing the denizens out to enjoy in good-humoured fashion on what could be described as a perfect day.

This they did as they usually do by walking their dogs, not always leashed as decreed, or doing their supermarket run, or strolling looking in shop windows, discussing their contents and occasionally entering to check that which, more often than not, they only briefly and fickly dream about adding to their homes or wardrobes.

Aaron decided to do his laundry at the local Redfern laundromat, run by a silver-haired, taciturn Cambodian in his fifties, or maybe older as it is often hard to tell. He sat patiently most of the time, sometimes with his female companion, possibly his wife, possibly his mother, watching what sounded like soapies in Asian languages on his laptop, perched in front of him on the counter, he himself hardly visible.

Having gathered together his clothes and bed linen, divided between whites and coloureds as always, Aaron headed down the hill with stuffed bags in hand. He noticed as he passed by the new Sonoma bakery with all its fancy, though what he regarded as extraordinarily expensive loaves, an altercation going on between two tradesmen and a well-dressed woman standing between what appeared to be their respective vehicles, one a ute the other an expensive limousine, one of the men shouting angrily that she hadn't given any indications of pulling out and pointing at his damaged tray, the woman on her part standing calmly and writing something in a note book.

Aaron went through the usual process of buying the tokens for the washing machine, checking the pockets, especially for tissues and bank notes, and arranging his clothes around the central column so that they wouldn't become tangled, adding the correct amount of liquid detergent, setting the water to 'hot', pushing in the slotted mechanism and listening to hear for the water flowing. He took a copy of the local paper from a pile and sat down to read in order to pass the time.

When the cycle was through he transferred his finished load into one of the driers. But the coin-operated mechanism having failed, the coins used being, he had previously noticed, ten-baht ones from Thailand with the distinctive Thai King's head, a portrait of whom hung in the nearby Thai restaurant, and which he assumed were used because local coins of little value could not be substituted for them, he called for assistance. The owner's wife, or mother, shuffled over in a begrudging manner, her entertainment having been disrupted, told Aaron to change over to another drier which Aaron, also begrudgingly, did, to find that she then, with some dexterous manipulation of the knob of Aaron's former machine, had it running.

He threw a withering look at her and asked why she had not just done that for him instead of making him go through moving his load from one drier to the other.

"Now go for ten minute, not seven minute," she replied.

Confronted with such logic he retreated to his new drying corner reprising his complaint meekly, for which he received a further explanation that it was necessary to let the coin drop properly before turning the knob and that this was only common sense. Rashly pointing out that it was not so much a matter of common sense than learned technique he was finally and soundly ticked-off that "it really not matter, nobody die".

It occurred to him that for her, given her background as he could imagine it, this was philosophically unquestionable, and that he should pull his head in.

So, finished, and walking back home along Regent Street now in a mood of happy resignation for small mercies and buoyed by the weather-fuelled atmosphere of amiability, Aaron passed the latest high-rise development, one which would soon overshadow that same little obscurely-named park, to the rhythmic throbbing of a pole-driver backed by spasmodic jackhammering and rumbling cement mixer, putting him in mind the inspiration for Rhapsody in Blue, though unlike Gershwin he could hear no music in it. He saw that the two men and the woman previously engaged in heated confrontation were now standing nearer each other next to the woman's car, the woman still calm and silent, the angry man now speaking quietly with a sheepish demeanour. As he left them he could hear the words "very sorry about that" drifting apologetically around the scene.

Then, further along, he noticed two people, forty-ish, on the footpath ahead, standing talking to each other closely, face-to-face. One, a small and curvaceous woman with her back to him, in clunky high-heeled boots of the cheap Chinese-made variety, was looking up at the other, a large gorilla-like man built square rather than oblong, probably a Pacific Islander, dressed in black including a neat jacket, like a bouncer at a city club would wear, who was looking down into her face, his head bent forward and slightly cocked with concentration.

As Aaron passed he realised it was the woman doing all the talking and saw as best possible out of the corner of his eye, since he didn't dare turn his head to look straight at them, if only so as not to disturb them as much as not to get caught eavesdropping, that she was Asian, attractive and glamorous in whory style, and her speaking was firm and constant.

Ears pricked he caught just a slightly accented "love and feelings are the most important things" before it dropped out, so he resolved to unload at home the two bags of laundry as fast as he could, which not being far was easy to do, and head back down the street for another skerrick of this conversation.

They were still there, still transfixed in the same position. This time approaching from the other side he could see the woman's face unflinching in its resolve, that without her shoes she would barely come up to the man's nipples, and that from the back the man looked even more like a brick wall than before.

Once again, as he floated past, feeling like the little dickie bird, Aaron found them continuing the theme, she emphasising "this is all that matters", and he talking over her at the same time but hesitantly and softly, with "I understand that".

Having grabbed what he could during that brief passage he walked on a little and effected a subtle half-circle manoeuvre to take him back again for a further dose, in the manner of a bullfighter's veronica, although in this case he was more the bull than the torero, but he was intercepted in this run by a neighbouring shop-owner, referred to by some locals with a mixture of awe and affection as the Recycled-Iron Lady, to whom he whispered, "a very interesting discussion going on there," nodding towards the couple.

She grinned and explained that they had been sitting for some time on the furniture which she displayed on the footpath outside her second-hand shop, already then deeply into the preliminaries. Though she could not tell what the subject had been, Aaron thought he could guess.

This conversation delayed him enough to miss a further encounter. The final glimpse he had was of them crossing Regent Street diagonally, then arcing to be parallel to the busy three-laned one-way street with the traffic stopped by red lights, or it could have been even in deference to their state of grace, he head down, she face up, both oblivious to the rest of humanity's business, something of the look of a garbage truck accompanying a mini-car heading abreast down the road in the direction of the currently interrupted flow, and Aaron imagined that words such as love, feelings, caring, understanding, were still being bandied around, by her, and that, whatever the underlying nature of it all may have been, it was going to end well.

Aaron had never seen them before and would never see them again. It was as if the scene was really being played out in some other dimension, time or place, and some warp had occurred to drop it there and then. He returned home to sort, fold and put his fresh laundry away, and think about things that matter.

Waiting for Crumbs

Night, when it comes to Redfern, comes as it does to any city anywhere in the world, stealthily and imperceptively. It descends from above and closes in from the sides, leaking through the spaces between buildings and seeping along the streets with its dark embrace. As it does it brings with it a feeling of confinement and with that a re-focusing on the things that are near around us, without the distraction of anything above, no overarching canopy of brightness nor even of stars, in a city. A different reality engulfs the scene. Its inhabitants are so much more aware of that closeness that is their true world, without views or panoramas. Sounds and smells become enhanced in the dimmer light, like the enhanced other senses of the blind and the deaf, becoming a oneness that envelops and comforts. We become different, and we act differently. Some hide from it because it is too confronting and long for release, which comes soon enough.

That day in Redfern the night came early in its wintery way, while the traffic still streamed out of the city at the usual time by the clock, and the workers made their way to the cosiness of their homes in an atmosphere created by the season. It was as if the humans with their puny ways had tried to awaken a sleeping giant only to arouse it slightly, it then rolling over and going back to sleep again. The night places were gearing up for their turn to star, though it was far too early for most people yet to adapt to the inevitability of this temporary change.

The interior of shops along Regent Street with their retro-living set-ups, ironically hidden behind the reflecting glare of the day on their glass feature windows until then, now became highly prominent as the lighting from the spots under awnings or from inside flush out the details for drivers in cars held up by red lights or bottlenecking to consider. It made the street look like it might be a series of intimate living rooms, with an expectation of seeing someone reading a book, or reaching out for their drink, or greeting a returning family member.

The local supermarket in Regent Street, well-lit and visible from outside through its glass doorways, is always very cold. A blessing in the summer heat but daunting for the winter cold. Going into the supermarket from outside in winter was like stepping out of an airconditioned room into a freezer. Aaron had complained about it a few times and was given the explanation that all the refrigeration around the walls on three sides was the culprit.

One day at the checkout he had joked about it to the woman on the cash register, a Maori with a flat oval face which looked like it had seen some hard times, though the smile and general air of jollity about her belied that, or at least indicated her resilience. She reminded him of Billie Holiday in her wasted later days, just a certain similarity in her expression of weary resignation. Aaron had noticed she was wearing short sleeves and asked if she weren't cold. She chuckled away and said "Nah", that she had her husband to keep her warm, loudly enough so that it was picked up by her colleagues on duty nearby resulting in general merriment.

So the next time she served him at the checkout he asked if her husband was still keeping her warm. She looked askance at him, not remembering the earlier incident, and then guffawed anyway, replying that he certainly was.

This time he had only come for a carton of milk, but Aaron had remembered he had previously been overcharged on an item, so he had brought the empty container with him along with the receipt for it. She took a little time to work out what it was all about, but then, having grasped it sufficiently, said she'd go and check the shelves for the correct price. She was back soon enough and applied herself to the task and to the cash register, first passing the container over the laser reader, which brought up the overpriced amount, then passing the milk over it. The result was an amount that didn't make much sense, so Aaron asked her what the price of the milk was, and then explained that the amount therefore was more than it should be after the refund.

She said "Take a look", and turned the screen towards Aaron so that he had a look and could see that the problem was that the milk subtracted from the full amount as credit of the original purchase left a minus amount which was what was showing. He pointed out the simple arithmetic that when the correct amount was subtracted from the original overcharged price the result was 50 cents.

So she then asked, and checked, to see how Aaron had paid for the original purchase, which had been by credit card, and said that she would credit it to the card, which seemed to Aaron to have nothing to do with calculating the correct amount and was probably done by her more in the way of a distraction from the difficulty of solving the problem. He suggested it was a bit of a bothersome solution and that all she had to do was subtract the refund from the milk and then he could pay that amount in cash, which he then dropped on to the counter for emphasis. This was not the way she wanted to go however, and becoming more confused than ever, took out the little calculator and did some calculations on it which she didn't reveal to Aaron, and then turned to the register confidently again, passing the original container once more over the laser reader, and then the milk, and announcing that everything was fine, she would give him $2.60.

"Great," Aaron said, "and then I'll pay you for the milk separately."

"No," she insisted, "I just have to give you $2.60."

Accepting that she was not to be convinced otherwise and now getting quite tired of it all, as were the people in the queue behind him so that two more registers had been opened to accommodate the backlog, Aaron decided to take it, enough was enough. He checked, as she contemplated the receipts once again with a worried look, and asked if everything was OK, and with that left, thanking her. He didn't ask about her husband.

Aaron passed through the automatic sliding doors and left the shop. With the coins in his hands it was easy to let them slip into the bowl of the legless man who was often there for hours on end in his wheelchair, patiently and silently, since he had no need to explain or beg, waiting for such crumbs.

Aaron went on to the video store which stayed open late and took his time picking out a few fresh thrillers. As the nerdy young man went through the catalogue drawers matching numbers to DVDs he asked if Aaron had seen *Zodiac*, which must have had some connection to one of his choices, so he asked him to hum a few bars as he couldn't recall it. This feeble attempt at humour fell flat but it occurred to Aaron how hard it was to remember whether he had seen a movie, after having seen so many, simply by its title or description. Even knowing the actors or the plot or specific scenes didn't always help. But just a few seconds of the opening scenes will trigger instant recognition. The visual memory, he concluded as he watched the young man match codes to discs, seemed a much more basic one, immediate recall, while verbal description was so much weaker, second-hand in a way.

He left swinging his white plastic bag full of hours of entertainment. Further along he passed a young woman who walked along Regent Street carrying clumsily two larger bags slung over her shoulders by the cords crossways, the blue plastic ones usually used for garden waste, and two smaller ones tied to her waist, like a mule. Both of them were confronted and assailed as they walked by the smells and odours emanating from so many of the businesses along the way, sometimes lingering well after they were closed.

From the bakery comes a glorious, overwhelming thick perfume of baked flour perhaps mixed with dried fruits and sugars, olives and nuts, but mainly hot baked flour. This can strike you a long way away from the store itself, especially if there is a good breeze and they are at their baking busiest, much more so than the other whiffs. Next comes the coffee, that wonderful smell that entices you in to taste it in the flesh. and a little like the smell of cigars, or cucumbers, the promise better than the reality. The butcher follows a little way along, not so enticing at all, in fact, quite the opposite and for many thoroughly revolting; slightly, mildly acrid but with a surprising sweetish cleanliness about it, and very distinctive once it has been experienced. Dogs on their walks invariable hesitate and try to hover when they are taken past. The Vietnamese restaurant, and if the current is flowing in that direction, the Thai restaurant directly opposite across the road, have their complex food odours wafting out their doors. And finally on the corner the rankish smell of stale beer from the pub whenever someone opens the door to go in or out. During daylight hours the natural perfumery of the florist further back contrasts with the chemical abrasiveness with its addictive quality of the panel beater's, surpassed in its foulness only by the hairdresser and matched in its headiness by the cabinet maker, all in a row.

But this night they did not entice or seduce the woman, as she was far more tired than anything else. It had been a long day for her after having spent the previous night at Prince Alfred Park near Central Railway. She had gone there after being forced out of her more comfortable spot underneath the viaduct arches of the old rail lines, now the new light-rail lines, next to Johnstons Creek further west. The local council had moved in after complaints from residents, and while others were more defiant, she had preferred to avoid confrontation.

In any case it was good to move, necessary to move, to keep moving. Why it was so she couldn't explain, but did know she did not want to deal with anyone in this world. The fragrance of the coffee from the late-opening pizza café sickened her slightly, as did the perfumy sweetness of the early bakery, the one that started baking for the following day even before some other shops had shut for the night.

As she walked down Regent Street the young bag lady suddenly started. She felt fingers playing at the nape of her neck which then continued up to ruffle her hair where it emerged from under her close-fitting cap. With a disconcerting mixture of pleasure from the sensuality of it and fear of its implications she remained calm. She had learnt the hard way in her life that the best reaction was often no reaction. She tried to think of who it would be, who she would know well enough here in Redfern to do that, realising that there would be nobody.

She slowly turned her head while continuing to walk at the same pace and saw two men in their thirties, the one nearest with long blonde hair, and swaggering somewhat.

"Do I know you?"

"Do you want to know me?"

"Under the circumstances, no," she replied, revealing an American accent. She slowed and they passed leaving her to watch them cautiously as they mercifully disappeared around a corner and down the alleyway linking Regent and Cope, brightly lit at night by an orange glare highlighting both its potential danger and the large murals that serially appear on its walls.

Across the road she could see clearly, now that it was dark, the display windows of the retro furniture shops in a row, lit up, the warm homeliness appealing to her need for both some rest and a sense of security, however false and misleading.

The young woman turned and crossed using one of the breaks in the traffic which were coming more often now, lumbering across as fast as she could manage with her bags of burden, before the traffic lights brought the next surge down the hill. She dumped all her belongings in front of and to one side of the bright window with its armchair and coffee table, standard lamp and bookcase and various porcelain adornments, running even to a heavy Venetian glass ashtray and, on the false wall behind it all, a large clock with its art deco features.

Pulling out from one of the blue bags a folded plastic sheet, she flapped it open and spread it on the concrete footpath in front of the window, pushing it neatly right up to its base, as if tucking it into a mattress. From the large bags she took smaller plastic bags containing clothing and put these, along with one small cushion, on the tarpaulin, then also placed an overnight bag at one end. She sat herself down on and amongst these makeshift bedding materials, propping her back up against the window and stretching her legs out in front across the tarpaulin. In her tight-fitting knitted woollen cap with flaps she could have been straight from the middle ages, save for the jeans and rubber thongs. Her eyes were unnaturally wide open with large black pupils and a circle of white sclera showing around them, set in a dark sunburnt face, giving her a staring, crazed appearance. She crossed one leg over the other and, reaching down, began to pick skin off the bottom of her foot, holding it up to feel and taste with her tongue before flicking it away onto the street.

Aaron had continued up Regent Street to try to get some takeaway. It was getting late and by the time he reached the Chinese restaurant, the one that specialised in duck and which he liked to call Viaduck, where vermilion carcasses of ducks hung glistening in the window under bright, hot lighting looking bloody as if they could have just been slaughtered and skinned, there were none left and he had to settle for a pork spare ribs as they closed down for the day. He gently pulled on the sliding door, which the owner fought a constant battle to get people to open slowly, posting on it large hand-written signs appealing for care. He walked on a little further just to kill some time then turned back, passing the Indian place which was always suspiciously devoid of patrons, though perhaps explained by the quality of its fare which he had suffered on several occasions, now also closed, but still with its heavy curry smells. He braved the open expanse of the entrance and exit of the petrol station, still operating mostly for the convenience of taxis, and with its security window and microphone now the only means of communicating between operator and customer, on past the corner church whose only congregation these days was a Samoan evangelical group who he often heard on Sundays singing their hymns with the most exquisite voices.

And then Aaron could see indistinctly, as he looked further along the footpath, a heaped bundle of bags, and he wondered what it could be. As he got closer he made out a young woman and a makeshift bedroom arrangement and guessed that it was the woman he had passed in the street earlier. He slowed and stopped next to her and stood for a while, waiting to see if she would say something first. She had half-covered herself with a second plastic sheet now in preparation for sleep and as some protection from both the elements and busybodies.

Finally, after some time without any recognition, he said to the woman, "You must be cold", but she looked blankly at him with her staring eyes, saying nothing.

"Would you like to come home with me and sleep on my couch?" he added, but she remained silent and unresponsive.

Aaron waited a little longer and then ventured, "I could keep you warm here if you prefer."

Now that he had broached the possibility he felt emboldened and so persisted with his approach with some more encouragement to her. Still she did not react, so he sat down on the blue tarpaulin putting his plastic bag with the pork spare ribs to one side. She rolled over towards the window. He talked a while, asked her where she was from, where she was headed, why she was there, but got no answers. The street had become quite deserted now and the traffic flow was very spasmodic, it being a Sunday night. The new bar almost directly across the road closed earlier than on other nights. He thought that since she had not clearly rejected him he might continue on a course that had now taken on a momentum he had not anticipated nor planned.

Pulling back the top sheet he twisted his legs around and shuffled himself into a position under it lying up against her back.

"Isn't that nice and cosy now?" he asked, again without a response. So he let himself lie there, readjusting his position every now and then very slightly, partly to try to reduce the discomfort of the hard surface he was on by edging himself more onto the cushions and bags, and partly because it did feel cosy, and partly, mostly, to further his cause. His penis was swelling and was becoming uncomfortable, being held in place by the pouch of his briefs. He twisted a little and reached down with one hand and pulled it upwards, still inside the underpants but at least free to choose an angle of comfort. Then she moved, in three or four stages, rolling first a little onto her back, then shuffling away to give him more room, and then to face him some more, then finally further towards him. His throat tightened with excitement and his heartbeat quickened.

She was familiar with this situation and would handle it in the way she had learnt to, from instinct and experience, in order to survive. Aaron felt her hands exploring for his belt and zipper and then manipulating her own, then seeking out his penis and wrapping her fingers right around it, which felt vey good, and guide it to her pubic parts, and as she did he thrust a little with his pelvis. He enjoyed the moment of entry as her vagina seemed to grip his penis and draw it inwards as a welcoming gesture, and he sensed her pleasure with that as well. He pushed in until as if locked in place and then shifted his body to be comfortable. Although his hip hurt as it was touching hard concrete through a gap in the padding, he ignored that, and she shifted to accommodate him, though they did not put face to face or mouth to mouth. He bowed his head and placed his chin on her shoulder and after a moment of settled pleasure he pulled out just slightly, then thrust back, and he felt her respond and enjoy and heard the slightest of sighs, and so he continued very slowly, allowing his mind to swim with the flow. He let his basic animal take over his mindfulness as he was both repulsed and compelled by her physicality, then stopped momentarily to savour the pleasure of stillness, and then back again with the motion. She did not require much from him, simply following in the beat of his tempo easily and sympathetically.

He could smell her unwashed putrefying odour like bad cooking oil from a cheap café and it made him think of the pork spare ribs nearby, and he let himself drown in its intensity and the rhythmic pleasure, and so on and on, until time and place and person were lost, then he also was lost to the demanding force of necessity as the need ratcheted up and up, and even his self was lost and all he wanted was to be absorbed into their mutual sexual being, and then the uncontrollable paroxysm of otherworldly bliss prevailed and there in that otherworld absolutely nothing else existed except the orgasmic pleasure which held him in its brief thrall then let him go in pulsating steps, and he was done.

He did not know where she was in her journey and now he did not care. All he wanted to do was wallow in his physical satisfaction. His arms and legs went slack, as if the blood had drained from them into his pleasure, and he let his head fall to the side as he rolled backwards, while at the same time she pulled away, breaking the spell with a brief unpleasant frisson of finality, and rolled herself back to face the wall and away from him. He felt no inclination to kiss or stroke her as he would normally have done and no words were called for, so he drifted off into sleep before a sense of disgust could fully overtake him.

Aaron did not know how long he dozed but it was probably not for long. When he woke and became aware of his situation he moved quickly, adjusting his pants first and then pulling himself away from underneath the plastic sheeting which now crackled in a way he had not noticed before, looking around and standing up. The street was deserted, he checked with relief. He picked up his white plastic bags of pork spare ribs and rented DVDs and walked casually away towards home down Regent Street, feeling a mixture of self-contempt and triumphant elation over his deed. He would phone the local police station and report a homeless woman sleeping rough and possibly in danger when he got home.

Passing the supermarket again, where the legless man had sat, but now deserted, he thought once more of those who are satisfied in one way or another with the crumbs from the tables of the better off, and his face did carry a smile of satisfaction, though there was nobody around to notice.

Good Vibrations

Sheila woke suddenly, reached for her phone and checked the time. Oh hell, she thought, I've set the wrong alarm time. She threw back the covers and sprang out of bed, squeezed into, pulled on, stepped in, clicked, and buttoned up her standard black uniform and dashed to the bathroom.

Only time for the basics here, I'll finish in the taxi, she relented.

She rummaged through her shoulder bag quickly for essentials: purse, keys, make-up pouch, torch, capsicum spray, hand wipes. What else? She garnished her neck with a pale blue silk neck scarf, darted into the study, found her violin, thankfully already in its case, and was out the door.

The journey would take forty minutes even without much traffic, not counting taxi-waiting time. Down the steps and onto the footpath she turned left and made for the corner of Selsdon Road where she'd have a better chance of a quick hail. One appeared within a short but nerve-wracking period. She waved it down, it pulled to the curb, she opened the door and bent to step up and in, violin first, placed on the floor as always, for safety.

"The Palladium, please," she managed, slightly breathless from the hurried walk, "and don't spare the horses."

"Sorry, luv, do me best, but there's a lo' o' traffic into the city, Sat'y night an' all."

"Well, they can't start without me, so that's a blessing. And a curse I suppose."

"By the look of tha' case I reckon you'll be ticklin' a fiddle tonigh'?"

"Something like that." She gave it a terminal severity and pulled out her make-up to finish off putting on her face as she had no desire to chat.

It took fifty minutes and she was in a state. The taxi managed the last crawling mile in a time she could probably have crawled it herself. She paid the fare, hunched, and stepped out, turned and retrieved the violin case and raced to the entrance.

There was a long queue for patrons which made her feel both relieved, and more anxious. The recent bomb scares and terrorist attacks had meant security was tight. Nobody was excluded. It felt like she was boarding a plane, not about to embark on a night of Vivaldi concertos. She moved over to the performers' section which had a clear run, placed her violin and bag on the conveyor belt, stepped through the metal detector and on to collect her things. The belt had stopped and she waited. An officer came around from the back.

"Would you mind stepping this way, please, madam."

Sheila was puzzled as he led her to one side where her bag and case sat on a table hovered over by two more officers.

"Can you explain the noise coming from this case, madam?"

Sheila froze as she heard the familiar sound. She remembered what else she used her violin case for when she travelled, with its convenient and hidden velvety compartments. In her rush she had forgotten to take it out. She blushed and burbled something incomprehensible about forgetting and being terribly sorry. She couldn't bring herself to answer directly.

"Could you open it for us, please, madam?"

She did as required and there it was, underneath the bow and cleaning cloth, to most appearing like an innocuous and mysterious part of the musical ensemble paraphernalia, except that now it was vibrating away in all its pink, frantic, frustrated endeavour.

The officer plucked it out, holding it up for all around to see. She made herself as inconspicuous as it was possible to do in the busy, very public and open lobby, failing miserably, or so she felt. He switched it off and put it back.

"Thank you madam, that will be all."

The large man waved her through, his heavy jowls hanging loosely, pulling his face into a permanent look of despondency, on this occasion tinged with either professional disappointment, or personal salaciousness.

Sheila closed the case with a sharp clap and fastened the clasp, grabbed it and her bag and scurried off head down towards the backstage. She could hear the tuning of instruments and prayed that 'Spring' would bring its promised release.

Unsprung

The flight had been uncomfortable. Not because of any greater physical discomfort than usual but because of his state of mind. Van had not been able to put aside his intense nervousness. He had heard they could tell just by suspicious demeanour if you were up to something.

As he walked down the long corridor, so like all the other airport corridors he had walked down, hand luggage feeling weighty on his shoulder, passport and customs declaration in hand at the ready, he felt as if he were covered in flashing lights and tried to switch them off, unsuccessfully.

For minimum human contact he used the electronic passport facility and then headed straight for the baggage retrieval area, a cavernous hall with rumbling carousels from one end to the other. Silent people stood around watching lonely luggage doing the circuit, like despondent sheep around a water trough in a drought.

Van knew the place well. His plan had had its genesis in his experience here over the years. Originally he had discovered the toilet in the far corner for pure practical necessity. But because it was tucked away and difficult to see, and because most people were simply anxious to grab their luggage and get away, it was little used.

The run with his bag there was the most dangerous part of the whole operation. He could see one border security officer preparing his sniffer dog on a side bench. There were several uniformed people walking around idly here and there. Of course if they were surveilling him he wouldn't notice. But there was no real reason for that to be happening, he was not a known person to authorities as far as he was aware, all the risk was with the baggage.

Van stood sheep-like watching the ceaseless dreary parade for a while then spotted his bag which he had secured with strips of brown duct tape. Daggy, but it stood out, easy to identify, but most importantly it was intact. This was the moment, do or die. He stepped forward, grabbed the handle and yanked the unassuming suitcase off the conveyer belt, shuffled it onto the lower rack of his trolley, spun around and headed for the distant corner. He wanted to sprint but knew he mustn't. The restrained pace made it feel interminable: the hand on his shoulder expected any second, the officer with the sniffer dog intercepting him suddenly from behind a pillar, his name called ominously over the loudspeaker.

He reached the door and rammed it with the front of his trolley. It swung open violently. Inside it was empty. He pushed to the furthest cubicle, parked the trolley, reached down for his bag, snatched it off, used its weight to push open the cubicle door and swung it acrobatically to sit across the top of the toilet bowl.

He closed and locked the door, used the tip of his pen to puncture the duct tape around his bag, ripped that off and crumpled it up, unzipped the bag, pulled out the parcels wrapped in heavy plastic and threw them on the floor. His hands were shaking now and his actions clumsy. He rearranged remaining items to fill the spaces, zipped the bag closed, placed it upright on the floor and placed each parcel in the toilet bowl.

He heard the main door squeak open and the rattle of cleaning equipment outside his cubicle. He summoned his courage and half-whispered, half-croaked: "spring."

"Has sprung," came back a reply.

Van opened the cubicle door, took his bag, placed it on the trolley and wheeled it outside without looking up, ineptly banging into walls and doors as he went, keeping his head down the entire time, only partly aware of a woman mopping the floor, but being particularly careful not to look at her or let her see his face clearly.

He made for customs in complete but supressed panic, but also now confident he was safe. He was waved through. When he stepped outside Van looked up at the bright sun of an opposing hemisphere and shouted, "spring has sprung!"

The Road to Riches

With each plodding step the four of them, Sven, Aliana, Lori and Chet struggled against the mud and strangling vegetation along the poor excuse for a trail. It was obvious that it had been several months, perhaps longer, since anyone had been through. Their clothes, soaked in sweat, clung to skin already overheated by exertion and the atmosphere, skin now being smothered just when it was gasping for air.

They could all feel the blood from leech attacks squelching between their toes, but dared not stop to clean them out nor walk without the protection of the heavy boots. Flies and mosquitoes buzzed around their eyes and exposed skin, forcing them to expend more energy and create more body heat by constantly waving them away, fearful that by giving them a moment's chance they might land and inject them with some debilitating parasite or virus.

The lushness of the growth combined with the hothouse environment produced a stench of permanent rot. Unfamiliar and menacing bird and animal noises occasionally punctuated the otherwise deathly silence of the oppressive, tangled surroundings, raising pictures in their minds of frightening prospects.

This had been going on now for uncountable hours, though in reality it had only been about four, with no end in sight. They grunted and grimaced and cursed each entangling vine and fallen branch. They had started out early but the light would not last forever. The density of the canopy not only gave the impression of constant twilight but also meant they could never be sure of how long the light would last. Once darkness set in they would not be able to go on and the thought of a night in the jungle terrified them all beyond description. The one animal they should have feared the most, their own species, seemed a strangely comforting proposition, in whatever guise it may have assumed to appear, and however false that proposition might be.

At least it hadn't rained. Yet.

They had come to this predicament through their own foolhardiness. Chet had warned the others that to take only one vehicle through such perilous country, four-wheel drive with plenty of gear or not, was a risk to begin with. A breakdown, accident or bogging would leave them stranded. There would be no mobile coverage and they didn't have time to arrange for a sat-phone or a location beacon. To some extent they were also avoiding the notion of any contact given the secrecy and riskiness of the operation and by doing so subconsciously denying its need and any possibility of failure. Sven had concentrated on the GPS receiver which he said was essential and would always tell them where they were, which would be enough.

Then, when the signage had stopped and the road forked several times - in both directions so that returning would also be a lottery - they made no efforts to stop and mark the route back. And when the crunch came it didn't even involve a crunch, or at least the crunch part had long gone.

An enormous tree had come down almost lengthwise across what was now a two-wheel track. Their puny chainsaw would be no match for its girth, plus there would have been the challenge of moving the massive cut section out of the way even if they had succeeded in separating it, or slicing it into manageable pieces, challengeable in itself. On top of that its enormous weight had created a deep furrow in the track which had filled with mud and water, and so even if the trunk were removed it would have probably been impassable anyway, or at least problematic and highly risky.

All this was discussed and debated at length. One measure of caution they had managed was to check the odometer at the first fork without signage, and the time. They had travelled 41.6 kilometres into the jungle and it had taken five hours. The decision was to go back. They would use the experience to re-plan and try again, although the delay might possibly mean the whole project could fail. The target was a mere five kilometres further on, according to the calculations at least, so the decision was a disheartening one. In any case that decision would be taken out of their hands.

It was a matter now of turning the vehicle around. It couldn't be done where it was, with steep embankment one side and drop, however slight, on the other. And looking back along the track it appeared to be much the same. Sven, the driver, maintained he could drive in reverse until a place could be found to turn. So, with his neck craned around and them ducking down to clear his view he started off, swinging the steering wheel back and forth with one hand. But within forty or fifty meters of this effort he stopped, turning his head forward and swivelling it around to relieve the strain.

"Not so easy," he said. "Perhaps someone could walk ahead to check for anywhere to turn."

Nobody stirred.

"OK, then, I'll give it another go."

This time he did not turn his head but looked up into the rear vision mirror, both hands on the steering wheel. It was a skilful effort but the vehicle was swerving more dramatically as Sven attempted to keep it on track.

"Not so fast!" Lori screamed out.

"Shut up!"

Sven shot a glance around at her distracting him from the mirror for just long enough to lose his reverse sense of direction and the vehicle careered to one side, rear wheels over the edge, stopped abruptly from plunging further by a tree, the passengers jolted but cushioned and saved from injury by seats and headrests.

"Shit, shit, shit!"

Sven opened his door and climbed out. The others followed, on the uphill side. They gathered in a bunch on the track staring at the sidelined Toyota.

"Right, new plan." Sven broke the silence.

"I don't think there's much damage, mainly the rear door so I think we can get it out of there, but it will take some time. Too late by then to try to go back, even if we could turn around. So we'll set up camp for the night at the roadblock, up at dawn and off on foot to the target. We'll stick to the track; follow our nose and the GPS. It's just five kilometres and we should do it in a long day. "

"But surely, the point was to have the vehicle to transport the load back, how is that going to work?" Lori broke in.

"We've got our backpacks. The wreckage site was never going to be on the track, or a track, we were always going to have to lug a load, or loads, from the site to the vehicle. Now it will just have to be one load, five kilometres."

"Bloody hell," Chet said.

"Well, fifteen kilograms is easily manageable, twenty-five kilograms possible. That's one-and-a-half to two million dollars a load. You might want to be greedy and try for thirty kilos. Worth the walk?"

They were all silent and thinking hard.

"The gold bullion wouldn't take up much room at all, spread around in the pockets; the heroin would pretty much fill your pack and the bills would depend on their face value, with a bit of luck they'll be fifties or hundreds. Lori and I have estimated there was at least 200 million aboard all up so you can pick and choose."

"Unless it was destroyed in the crash."

"Yes, the notes and heroin could be gone or scattered. But we know from our research, imaging and the like, as best possible, that the wreck didn't burn and is mostly intact so the chances are good. The gold, of course, is the best bet. You know all this already."

"Just working it over again," Chet said. "Yeah, I'll go for gold."

"And the walk back will be easier with the track cleared; we could even decide to do a second trip."

Lori chipped in.

"We have enough supplies for a while, we got that right at least, so it's possible. There's not much point in trying to reverse out empty-handed when we could do it with some sort of a haul."

"And when we do try again we will need to do it carefully, checking the way ahead … "

"With a full day to do it in," Aliana expressed her disquiet at last, but also it seemed, her acquiescence to this plan.

So with time and considerable effort, and some worrying backsliding, they had the vehicle back on the track and to the fallen tree camp before dark set in. They opened some cans and packets, ate and drank, decided to forego a fire, even if one were possible, and therefore coffee and tea, and hit the sack early. The two women and Chet took one of the Toyota's compartments each and made themselves as comfortable as they could there, inevitably sleeping poorly. Sven set up the camp bed next to the chassis, covered by netting, and braved the elements and the nightlife.

Daybreak was very gentle in the thick closeness of the forest, but Sven was up and about very soon after, waking them all and getting ready for the hike. They discussed what to take: the backpacks could be filled if they liked as long as most could be discarded or consumed. High energy food and drinks, light plastic ponchos, torches, a few basic tools in case they were required for access or removal. Sven had already checked and packed the all-important GPS receiver. Lori suggested salt for leeches, an inspired thought, and a first-aid kit kept in the vehicle, but none of them had remembered to bring mosquito repellent so Aliana added toothpaste to the armoury, for the bites. Each brought some spare clothing and special personal items. Chet threw in a pair of canvas sandshoes, knowing from experience they were very practical in wet situations. The rifle was left hidden near the vehicle, deemed too awkward to carry and unlikely to be needed, or at least worth that risk.

Sven, who had more experience with bushwalking than the others, and was the strongest and fittest, led the way, following whatever signs he could detect of the old trail, less and less the further they went, hewing away with the one machete they had brought, hacking at vines slung directly across the path, bending and swinging low at alternate sides to undercut bushes, then sweeping them away with his arms. Watery blood dribbled down to his hands from the cuts and scratches the thorns were patterning on the bare skin of his shoulders and arms, and then flew off into the air as he threshed about against the tangled barriers.

The rest of them had to keep to Sven's struggling pace, not that they could have gone faster given the opportunity. Chet was next directly behind him but keeping some distance to avoid his swinging frenzy and the whiplashing of cut stems and bent branches which was unpredictable. Despite Sven's efforts Chet still needed to push back and duck under prickly and jagged leftovers. He could feel and hear each squelching step he took, the splash of his leading foot sinking into the mud and the gurgle of the suction as his back foot pulled up out of its gluey grip. Squelch, gurgle, hack; squelch, gurgle, hack, they plunged onwards.

Behind Chet Lori strove to keep up. He could hear her feet making the same squishing as his were, though a little quicker. She would give little grunts of effort and whimpers of frustration at every step. At the rear was Aliana who, carrying her considerable frame and bodyweight, risked falling behind and so needed to be checked on regularly. Chet expected to hear her start sobbing at any point but she managed to persevere. He would cast glances back over his shoulder and occasionally paused to allow her to catch up a little.

Twice Sven stopped for a rest, standing sweaty and steaming, bent, with his arms hanging limply by his side, elongated by the machete and knife he held, producing a simian appearance, breathing heavily and staring out into the curtain of vegetation surrounding them. They would, one-by-one, reach him and stop, equally exhausted and silent, and grateful for the chance to recover, however briefly and unsatisfactorily. Eventually Sven would say something about getting going and resume his slogging task. Squelch, hack, grunt, would begin its rhythmic accompaniment to their progress once again.

After what seemed to them an eternity, but in reality lasted only as long as they would have spent on a leisurely lunch with friends, they emerged into an open space. It could not so much be described as a clearing as it had not been cleared, but at least it was devoid of growth. As such it appeared a great relief to them as they each broke free of the dense encirclement they had suffered so long and could see beyond just the few paces in front of them. It was a short-lived reprieve however. There was no corresponding brightening, and no sky became visible as might have been expected, the canopy formed by the taller trees opportunistically stretching itself across the divide with their race to gain an advantage in the search for sunlight, the outermost phalanxes of their leafy troops intertwining in battle, like slow-motion wrestling.

And as they took one step into the welcoming openness, their feet slipping then subsiding further down into the now-yellowy mud, they realised with sinking hearts that this island of hope was a mirage, as fabricated as any shimmering image in a desert, and worse, since any attempt to grasp it or embrace it would result in a struggle to survive even greater and more immediate than that which they had been facing.

A bog, a quagmire, or quite possibly quicksand, did not even allow the opportunity for rest let alone a refuge for the night or a point of rescue if that were to happen. The only consolation was the knowledge that the vehicle could have gone no further than this.

As Aliana took one step too many and began to be sucked into the ooze, with Sven and Chet rushing to grab her under the arms and drag her back to safety, she did finally break and start a sobbing which she could not stop and which took over her whole body in repeated tremors, nor could they offer her much comfort themselves being so exhausted. They just waited and let her recover.

There was nothing for it but to edge their way around the bog and return to the challenge of the vegetation. They followed one another closely, picking the spots to tread cautiously and clutching any outcropping twig or leaf for balance and support, but even so occasionally slipping downwards into the mire, grasping for any lifeline and being helped back up by one of the others. The going was no less stressful than fighting through the undergrowth.

They reached a point which they felt was diametrically opposite where they had emerged from the gloom onto the openness and, estimating the same direction as before, renewed their efforts with the trail. Sven was no longer even certain he was following any trail at all. Aliana was now recovered from her sobbing but was in a state of despair and lagging behind. Sven himself was tiring and Chet offered, with no great enthusiasm, to take over his job as leader. Just as he was reassuring Chet he was still capable they heard a cry from the rear and turned to look back. Lori had also turned to look behind her and they could see Aliana sprawled out, face down, and rolling back and forth in pain. In stepping over a branch across the path her foot had locked into a smaller branch growing from it at a sharp angle and she had toppled forward, her ankle then twisting in the fork as she came down, her right hand also suffering as she put it out to break her fall and it took her whole weight.

Lori reached her first and helped release her foot from its snag, then Sven and Chet managed to get her into a sitting position as she moaned in agony. Lori and Chet were speaking to her calmly and doing their best to settle her down, but Sven had stood to one side and was becoming silently but obviously agitated. Chet loosened her boot and eased it off gently, and then the sock and could see the swelling already starting. Within hours it would be black-blue and puffed up. There appeared to be no breakage but serious straining of the ligaments and it was already incapable of being walked on. Chet pushed the boot back on carefully and tied it loosely, leaving the leeches he could see there thinking they might in fact help keep down the swelling by reducing the blood build-up and inflammation. Her hand and wrist also appeared unbroken but with ligament damage, though this in their circumstances was less serious. The implications of the situation were immediately obvious to them all.

Sven broke his agitated silence with a loud "Shit!"

"This was the last thing we needed!" he let out, fists banging at his temples. It was clear all he wanted to do was get going again. He was red-flushed and soaking wet, skipping back and forth with little steps on the spot.

Lori looked up at him and said "Take it easy, Sven."

She and Chet helped Aliana up onto her good leg and Sven headed back to his station to start hacking again with the intention of hurrying them up it seemed. With one of them on each side of her and with arms around their shoulders she attempted to walk. Chet could feel her take the weight in her arm on his shoulder as the pain in her bad foot forced her to lift it quickly off the ground. She took another step to try again and this time cried out just in anticipation as her foot merely touched the muddy surface. It was impossible in any case for them to continue three abreast along the narrowly sliced track so Chet told Lori to go on ahead and leave Aliana for him to help.

"If she can't manage with the two of us how is she going to do it with just you?" Lori said as she undid herself from Aliana's arm and stepped in front turning back to watch.

"We'll give it a go," Chet said in genuine hope.

It was slightly easier with just the two of them side-by-side but Chet was still having difficulty with finding places to step safely without getting caught in tangles and he was having to constantly brush aside foliage with his free arm. They were making achingly slow progress in this manner and there was no way it could continue. Aliana simply stopped, head down, her strained foot off the ground with Chet taking her weight, she in grim despair.

"Let's just take a break and consider what we can do," Chet offered, helping her down to sit out of the mud to one side. Lori, who hadn't gone too far ahead, was already headed back. Chet could hear Sven swishing and chopping further on, then he too stopped.

"Perhaps we could fashion some sort of crutch or walking stick out of a branch," Lori suggested as she reached us.

"Not a bad idea, we'll need Sven's machete and knife for that."

"It's useless," Aliana murmured. "We're stuffed with me like this. I can't go on. You'd better leave me and keep going. Pick me up on the way back."

Her tone sounded as if she either lacked conviction in her urging or had resigned herself to her fate, so it offered no help for their deliberations as to what to do.

Lori injected some logic.

"Look. If you and your backpack don't make it there we're down a quarter or so of the loot. If you can just struggle to get there you will at least be able to bring something back. Even if you only get there by the time we're ready to head back we can quickly load you up. Or if you don't quite make it there we can share your lot around amongst us and then unload it onto you when we meet up on the way back. We must be over half-way there by now so it's not so far. The trail will be clear both ways by then. But whatever it is, you are going to have to struggle back to the vehicle."

She paused.

"Otherwise you're dead ... weight."

Aliana pulled herself up onto her good leg.

"Get me some sort of walking stick and let's go then," she said with a grimace and forced smile.

Sven arrived to check on what was happening and together they soon found a suitable branch with a crook as handle and cut it to length. She tried it out and told them to be off.

"I'll be fine, fine and slow, and I'll see you at the wreck site."

"Good luck, but if it gets dark you will have to camp. Whatever you do don't leave the trail," Sven warned her. "Especially if the light begins to fade, it may be deceptive."

The three of them set off again back into the routine, casting glances back to Aliana until she was obscured by foliage. Sven had tired and Chet took over the lead and the slashing, the other two finessing the job as best possible. This continued for another couple of hours at which point Sven began checking his GPS receiver regularly.

"We are getting close to the turn-off point," he shouted

eventually, and this encouraged them to greater effort in their excitement.

Soon enough he shouted out again.

"OK, this will do it. We are at the closest point the trail will be, we strike out directly left here. It should be no more than two-hundred or so meters."

It would be harder going from then on as it was no longer a trail, as overgrown as that may have been. Sven took over the machete role again, telling Chet and Lori to take a break as it would be slow progress.

They found a couple of spots to sit facing the new route and watched Sven slash and hack into the tangled maze. Even so it was not long before they had lost sight of him though they could still hear him cutting and grunting. Suddenly though there was a sharp scream of pain followed by loud whimpering.

Chet and Lori jumped up and ran through the freshly made track to find Sven writhing on the forest floor, blood soaking through his clothing running down his legs. It seems he had slashed himself with one wild swing opening up a deep gash down his leg. Lori put her hands on the gaping, bleeding wound and Chet dived into Lori's pack for the first-aid kit, pulling it out then changing his approach by ripping off his T-shirt, tearing it into some ribbons and wrapping it tightly around the length of the wound and above. Having stanched the heavy blood flow they set about to make Sven as comfortable as possible and checked what they could use in the kit. There was codeine and they gave him some.

The wound needed stitching and though Lori had done some elementary first-aid training she had no experience of stitching. Still, the equipment was there and it would have to be done. They used some coconut water, fortuitously included in the provisions, to wash down the wound which made it look a little less alarming and she set to work, managing through Sven's squirming cries of pain to achieve some reasonably secure attachments. They used adhesive strips and bandaging to finish the job and gave Sven some energy drink to suck on as a distraction for him as much as for any medical value. They had not brought any alcohol with them.

They sat down with Sven to work out what to do. They were so close. Sven handed Chet the GPS receiver. They decided Chet would take over the trail blazing but would reduce its thoroughness to basic so they could make more progress quickly. As Chet went off and started slashing Lori sat with Sven. She took off his boots and socks carefully, revealing the blood and leeches. She salted the whole lot, the leeches shrivelling up and dropping off to reveal their suck spots which would become sores, and she cleaned it all up with more coconut water.

"You need to go with him," Sven told her. "Fan out as much as you can but stay within earshot. Keep calling to each other. Once you've gone around a hundred meters head off at angles, then double back. But keep in contact."

Lori listened and nodded.

"Off you go. I'm fine, the codeine's working and I'll take nutrients here and rest."

Lori got up and left to follow Chet. She made her way diagonally off through the tangled foliage as best she could, calling out to Chet who eventually replied. This continued for at least an hour, the calls shifting from left to right for Sven who remained in place as an aural touchstone. Chet at one stage returned to this base, checked on Sven and headed off at another angle, always calling out to Lori who was doing it tough further out.

This went on for another hour when suddenly there was a shriller call, a "Here, over here!" Very soon Chet reappeared, paused briefly and headed towards the calls from Lori, and towards which Sven was pointing, swinging as he went. Lori had come across some pieces of wreckage and once Chet was there they surveyed a wider and wider area until Chet called out, "Here, here, found it", and Lori joined him.

They had found it. The fuselage had more or less remained intact as it had slid along the ground snakelike through the undergrowth though the nose had been destroyed as it finally crushed against a tree and stopped, skewing slightly. The wings had long been torn off and were probably some distance away and scattered, but they were of no interest to the searchers.

Driven on now frenetically by the nervous energy of excitement Lori and Chet found openings and worked their way inside. What was left of the cockpit area was a grisly scene of decayed and ravaged flesh and bones amongst smashed instrumentation and equipment. But in the main fuselage space were bundles and packages and crates of cargo, strewn around but mostly undamaged. Chet stepped over some, bent down and stood up holding out a bar of dark golden colour for Lori to see. They both cheered.

They made their way back to Sven, running where they could, Chet slashing wherever necessary, in a state of euphoria.

"It's there, Sven, all there, just as we hoped."

Sven did his best to look pleased and was, in fact, as elated as they were.

"Let's get you there and make camp. We should leave some items here and towards the plane for Aliana to find and follow."

Sven objected.

"I think it might be best if I stay here."

"But the night will be closing in soon, you'll be here alone if we stay in the plane," Chet said.

"Yes, but for me to make the move there now and then back again tomorrow would be inadvisable for the sake of this wound, it needs rest. We can set me up here for the night with food, medicine, energy drinks, bring me something to lie on from the plane, and you can be back again after dawn. I'll rest and sleep. It will be better if you can carry my share of the loot here too, save me that part, then we can go back to the vehicle from here together. And I'll be here for Aliana."

It all made good sense, as long as Sven was prepared to spend another night with the jungle, this time alone.

"OK, then," Chet said, "if that's what you think. Let's get going, maybe we can even make a couple of trips back and forth before dark."

"Or even after dark if the track is opened up enough, we have the torches. Just to check on you," Lori added, feeling concerned.

They set Sven up with whatever was necessary and set off towards the wreckage site again, slashing and clearing the pathway as they went. Back in the plane they ransacked for anything usable, piling up cushioned seats, bottled water, the planes medical supplies, blankets, and broke open some of the crates and packages, releasing gold bars, banknotes and heroin bricks.

They loaded up their backpacks with whatever they thought might be useful for Sven that night, plus some gold bars, as many as they could for the short trip. Lori suggested taking a cut of heroin as a last-minute thought, in case it might act as an analgesic for Sven, and they headed back. Once there Lori decided she would stay with Sven for the night. It was the obvious thing to do. There was no sign of Aliana.

So, having left with the others all he had brought, Chet hurried back once again to the plane, and with only an empty backpack to burden him was able to make good time and to clear even more of the track. He estimated it would take around ten minutes each way now without distractions. He decided he could spare a half hour before loss of light to make another trip with a load of bullion. Together with what they had already shifted this would then cover both Aliana's and Sven's share and save time in the morning. He quickly smashed open another crate and deposited the gold ingots around the pockets of his backpack until it was heavy and sagging, as much as he thought he could haul for two-hundred or so meters.

Chet arrived, temporarily exhausted by the weight he had carried, deceptive because of its lack of bulk but hefty nevertheless, to find Lori and Sven settling in and reasonably comfortable. He didn't linger, explained his thinking for the trip and headed off again.

Back at the wreckage site again and with light now failing Chet prepared a bed with the plane's seating, ate, salted the leeches and cleaned his bloody feet, and slept. Towards dawn he woke up in a sweat. He tossed and turned until encroaching light allowed him to get up and move around. He had something to eat and drink, but without fire it was limited to packet snacks and water. All the medicine had been left with Sven for his pain so there was nothing he could take for the fever. By the time Lori arrived he was feeling quite wretched. She checked him over and was quite concerned suggesting he take a little of the heroin which he did. They set about packing gold bars into their packs, much more than they could carry the full distance. On a whim Lori decided to place a few under a rock she spotted a little way down the track. "Just in case," as she put it.

Chet threw a brick of heroin into his already heavy pack, just in case as he put it, and they headed off again. There was nothing left to do at the wreckage site. If the plane was now discovered it would be obvious someone had been there but this did not concern them unduly. If not, there was always the possibility of them coming back for another raid. In the meantime the jungle would do its job once again and cover over their rude intrusion.

By the time they reached Sven they were both quite exhausted, Chet especially so though he was feeling generally much better with his temperature lower. Sven was also in better spirits despite his leg having swollen. It appeared from his state he would need antibiotics. There was still no sign of Aliana. While Chet and Lori rested and recovered they discussed what to do.

"I feel I need to get back along the trail to the vehicle as soon as possible to look for Aliana. But also we need to get medical assistance for Sven," Chet said.

"And we really need to get out of here generally," Lori added.

Sven agreed, though reluctantly.

"It is going to be hard for me. I feel I'd be better off continuing to rest and allow my leg to improve. But I can see your point. I'll need a walking stick like Aliana's. And I might not make it in one go and have to spend another night camping. I am not at all keen on that after hearing those pigs grunting around so close last night."

"Well, we do have a good twelve hours of light. We should be able to reach the car, top up supplies and make it back to you to either help you on or stay the night with you," Lori said. "How do you feel about the heroin as analgesic?"

"I can't be sure whether it's the codeine tablets or the heroin but I certainly feel on top of the world."

"I've only taken heroin and I'm feeling pretty good too. I'll keep taking small amounts I think."

Lori jumped up.

"OK, it's decided. Let's find Sven a staff, load up and get going then."

They had 117 gold ingots stacked around them now, 117 kilograms, each about half the size of a bar of Lindt chocolate, much more than they could take with them. Lori looked around the camp site and could see the odd rock here and there. There were probably more but rocks were not easy to spot in the undergrowth.

"We will have to leave some. It's important that we can find them again if we need to, and that others can't, at least not too easily. Putting them under small rocks, or next to big ones slightly buried is I think going to be our best bet."

Chet and Sven agreed with nods.

"If Aliana is where we left her we should try to get her lot to her so I suggest we take thirty-five kilograms each, leave twelve bars here," Chet said.

"That's a helluva lot to carry, thirty-five kilos each, and Sven with a bad leg," Lori objected.

"Yes it is, true, but with lots of rest stops ..."

"... and a pinch of heroin," Sven chimed in.

"... we can do it," Chet finished off, with a laugh.

They went about getting ready; Lori and Chet took some gold bars each and went looking for rocks nearby to hide them. Leaving two or three at some places they were able to reduce Sven's load an extra five kilos. Once ready they helped each other on with the backpacks, straining and heaving them up high on their shoulders.

They set off together but Sven immediately fell behind. Chet had taken another small dose of the heroin and was full of energy. Lori lagged behind to check on Sven but soon became impatient and put forward a different plan.

"I'll go ahead for a bit and then leave my pack and come back to help you out," she stopped and said to Sven, who simply nodded.

Sven struggled on for a short while but soon had to give up and find a spot to drop the pack and rest. He waited for Lori who turned up walking easily without her pack and sat down next to Sven.

"I can't do it," Sven. "We will just have to dump some of the load."

"Alright. Let's try it. You take a bar and keep an eye out for rocks. We'll leave one under any rock we see near the track. I'll carry the pack till we reach where I left my pack."

Moving slowly along the track it took around an hour for them to reach Lori's dumped pack. They managed to secret away under or next to rocks along the way eight of the gold bars, the idea being, of course, to retrieve them at some stage once they had recovered and returned, especially if the plane wreckage and its cargo was discovered by others before then.

There was no sign of Chet who had been able to keep ahead of Lori. He was, however, feeling the strain by this time, with his fever returning and a general debility taking hold. After one episode of dizziness and collapsing he decided to remain down and wait for Lori. He found the heroin pieces he had broken off the brick and put in his pocket and swallowed a small one.

The other two rested awhile. Sven's leg was beginning to throb so he took some more heroin. The pain passed and they hoisted their packs onto their shoulders once again and resumed their trek. Despite the lighter load Sven was still struggling. Even Lori was feeling the accumulating effects of carrying such a load. She stopped and waited for Sven to come alongside.

"We'll try the same again, I think. I'll go ahead; you dump a few more bricks, as you can. I may have to do the same. I'll be back."

Sven was happy to go with that. He limped along, looking for any possible hiding spots, deviating off the track if he caught sight of a rock to position another bar under, finding the lighter and lighter load helpful but not enough to take the serious discomfort out of the effort he had to make just to walk.

Lori appeared on the track ahead once again, much to Sven's relief. He was down to thirteen kilos by then but still suffering. They rested briefly, Lori hoisted Sven's pack up, grateful for the lesser burden of it, and they started off, edging along slowly at Sven's pace and pausing to leave a gold bar under any rock they spied. Again it took the best part of an hour to go half a kilometre at best. They rested again once there but were now also getting hungry. They had brought very little in the way of food and especially drink to save on weight but ate and sipped what they had in the hope of reaching the roadblock camp before needing more.

"I'm pretty buggered," Lori said after a spell. "I'm going to have to shed some of my weight too otherwise I won't make it."

"Yes, you'd better. You go on ahead again and take any rocks. I can manage with the five or so kilos I've got left. At least for a bit till you get back again."

Lori shouldered her backpack once again and started down the trail but found it extremely taxing on her remaining strength to be dropping the pack in order to hide one bar and then heaving it up again. After two stops at rocks she noticed right next to the track a very large and distinctive tree with buttressed roots forming well hidden canyons between them, so she unloaded her pack and pushed five bars down into the lowest part of the crevasses where they could not be seen, and then covered them with forest litter. It would not be too difficult to remember and recognise that tree, she thought, and she would tell the others as well.

With the next rock she stopped for and turned over she was taken aback to find a gold bar already in place. Puzzled briefly she surmised that Chet had resorted to the same method of reducing the weight of his pack as they had been doing. She carried on for some time more, her pack growing lighter surely but imperceptively, slowed somewhat by more rocks already having been claimed by Chet.

Chet meanwhile had continued on, placing gold bars under rocks whenever he could but was becoming increasingly confused and disoriented by the infection streaming through his body and compounded by the opposing forces of the heroin he had taken to cover it. Although he had shed nearly half his load he was now stumbling along the trail hardly able to keep himself upright. He had reached the open area they had come across on the way in and had gone around, earlier passing without noticing the place where they had left Aliana. Befuddled now by the fog in his brain he raced straight ahead into the clearing, almost immediately tripping up in the soft ground and then falling full length face forward into the sludge. He passed out as he hit the muck and suffocated, his body sinking slightly into it with the weight of his backpack, leaving only it showing on the surface.

Lori did recognise the place they had left Aliana when she reached it, confirmed for her by a half-empty water bottle and some snack wrappers and then a little distance away, her backpack. She shucked off her own pack and checked the area around, depositing three more gold bars as she did so, discerning from the disturbed ground some evidence of activity, but found no further traces of Aliana and feared the worst.

She began making her way back to Sven, realising it was now around noon and beginning to become concerned whether they could make it to the vehicle before nightfall. She found Sven propped up against a tree, his pack as a cushion for his back, one leg bent up and his bad leg stretched out, his hands holding it as if trying to keep it from exploding. Lori knelt down and gently shook him awake.

"How are you?"

"Could be better," he replied, attempting a smile.

"We are going to have to try to get to the vehicle now as quickly as we can. I'll stay with you from here and help you along. Have you taken anything?"

"Nothing for a while, no energy."

"Alright, then, let's beef you up and make a run for it. No more pack for you, we'll stop briefly now and then but try to keep moving. We should come across Chet at some stage and he can help, unless he's reached the vehicle in which case he'll probably come back to find us and help."

Lori found the heroin in Sven's pockets and picked out what she thought was an appropriate sized piece and gave it to Sven. She pulled him to his feet, he groaning from the pain, slung the pack over her shoulders, handed him his stick and guided him on the way. It was slow and painful going at first, manoeuvring awkwardly over fallen logs, sidling carefully up or down the slightest inclines, but as the heroin kicked in as morphine relieving Sven's pain he moved more freely, while at the same time depending more and more on Lori for keeping on top of the task as he became less and less lucid.

It was well over an hour before they arrived at Aliana's camp. Lori had noted the rocks along the way where she had left bars on her previous trip and picked out a couple more for golden hideouts leaving Sven's pack near empty. She was favouring larger rocks now as being easier to spot and so find again, pushing the bars down into the soil next to them and brushing over with any forest litter around. They did not stay long, Lori wanting to make good progress while she felt Sven was capable. By the time they reached the clearing she had ridded herself of five more gold bars plus two of Sven's. She had not found any more rocks already with bars attached and wondered about it, thinking that perhaps Chet had dumped his whole load.

She sighted Chet's pack easily from a distance as they approached and hurried towards it leaving Sven to catch up. As she picked her way carefully through the slush it did not become clear that Chat was underneath until she was right there and attempted to lift it from the bog. She froze as Chet's body became visible and dropped the pack, shuddering with a long agonised moan.

She bent down again, pulled on the pack and released it from Chet's limp arms, carrying it back to where Sven was watching.

"Chet," she said simply, turned and went back and pulled Chet's body by his ankles to the edge of the mire, noticing he had changed into his canvas shoes, and leaving him as he was rather than having to look at his face. Sven joined her and sat down.

"Oh, God, what'll we do?" he said.

"There's not much we can do just now. I think we just need to get to the car, save ourselves and get to help. Let's go."

Lori transferred the remaining bars from Chet's pack to hers, hoisted it up, and they edged their way around the bog the way they had come and set off along the forest trail on the other side. It felt like they were finally on the last leg and would make it, albeit with some effort.

Lori kept placing bars from her pack under rocks where she saw them close to the track. Sven was now shuffling so slowly that she could still stay ahead of him despite the detours and interruptions. She had removed and abandoned his pack now and disposed of the last bars in it so that there was only the one pack left and she estimated there was about twenty-two kilos left. She was herself exhausted, muscles everywhere aching, scratches and bites sore and itchy, and hungry. What she did not know was that sepsis had set in with Sven, masked and delayed by the opiate medication, and that he would not survive without urgent attention.

Sven did not go much further. Delirium had set in, his mind had become addled and his body soon collapsed. Lori rushed to him and did what she could to make him comfortable. She realised the heroin would be of no further benefit and she could not revive him, nor was it feasible for her to somehow carry him to the vehicle. She crouched down and hugged him, kissing him and sobbing, then pulled herself up, grabbed the pack and threw it over one shoulder, and strode off. She moved quickly and deliberately, taking confident steps, watching out for suitable dumping spots and acting quickly to unload.

In less than an hour she had done over a kilometre, finished with the gold and freed herself of the backpack. She was now rushing along, almost running, operating on nervous energy, her mind full of getting help for Sven, getting to the car as fast as she could. What she would do then she wasn't considering at all, assuming without thinking that things would just fall into place, that disaster would simply not befall her, that she would be with her children again, that she would be talking, smiling, laughing with them again, sharing food and games, that it would all go back to what it was before. Before the gold.

She was running now, in short bursts where the ground was clear and allowed it, slowing down again to brush foliage aside and skip over litter when it returned. It was when she had hurdled over one fallen log and landed on the other side without looking first, something she would never normally do as a seasoned bushwalker, that she felt the sting on her thigh. She had landed on the tail of a snake and with lightening speed it had reared and twisted and struck against its attacker, sinking its fangs deep into her flesh and pumping the poison. Lori screamed with terror and jumped around lashing and grabbing at the twirling horror which was still attached to her leg. She finally took hold and threw it off into the air so that it flew momentarily, gyrating around, then came down and disappeared into the undergrowth.

Lori's heart was pounding. She did not know what type of snake it had been nor whether the venom might be lethal, but the fact it had bitten was a bad enough sign. She sat down shaking and found the puncture marks, wiping the area. It was beginning to swell and discolour and was becoming more painful. She scrabbled around and found some thin vine, broke and chewed it off with difficulty then tied it around her leg at the groin, pulling it as tight as she could bear. She had little by the way of clothing left but managed to rip off a lower section of her shirt and then tied it around her thigh closer to the bite. She knew she should not use the leg as this would pump venom up to her heart and to other organs. But she could not just lie there and wait to die, if that was going to be the case. If the venom was lethal she would have to get medical assistance, and that meant the vehicle. If it wasn't lethal she needed to get to the car anyway.

She heaved herself up, hobbled along a little and found a walking staff. Then, keeping her bitten leg as stiff as she could, she stumbled along the trail, falling occasionally, struggling up again and continuing. She estimated she was possibly just half a kilometre from the Toyota and could get there within an hour if she just kept at it. But the poison was seeping through, pumped along by her muscle action and she began to feel nauseous. Before long she had to stop and vomit and this in turn brought on a throbbing in her head. She forced herself to go on, the headache worsened and she began to shiver. She found her breathing started to become difficult. She was tottering, leaning on the staff to stay upright, sweating profusely, and gasping for breath. Finally her legs gave way and she collapsed in a heap, head spinning, mouth gushing with saliva, muscles twitching uselessly, unbearable pain around the wound mercifully relieved first by loss of consciousness, then death,

---

I learnt the outline of this whole enterprise because Lori and Sven were my parents. I was in my teens at the time and so gleaned a lot about their enterprise only through a sort of subconscious osmosis from their conversations and activities because they certainly did not take me into their confidence about it, I guess for security leakage reasons. And I had adventures of my own to distract me. After they had gone, and I had grown into adulthood, amongst their possessions I came across notes and documents relating to the research and preparations for the project to recover the hoard.

Aliana and Chet had received private information of the illicit flight and its cargo from personal contacts. My parents had become aware of this through their friendship and had followed it up. With the advances in satellite technology it became possible then to almost pinpoint the old crash zone. From this, my memories of my parents and what they were like, along with the public reporting of the aftermath and my own involvement with that, I have put together a dramatised, perhaps somewhat fantasised version of how it may have unfolded, partly to preserve the memory of my mother and father, and partly for my own closure, painful as it has been.

But this I do know for sure: it took two weeks before the four were reported missing, after a group of hunters came across the Toyota. My sisters and I were not unduly concerned having become used to their adventurous absences. In any case we were enjoying our freedom with friends. And of course they had not told anybody of their true plans, merely saying if asked they were off on a camping tour. The resulting search starting from the stranded vehicle at the roadblock found a rifle hidden nearby, two near-empty backpacks, some miscellaneous items, and scattered human remains at different points along and near the track. Later forensic investigation identified three separate individuals. Chet's body was not discovered as it had sunk further into the bog, assisted by some heavy rainfalls.

A by-product of the search was the surprise discovery of a plane wreckage and its remaining cargo of gold bullion, cash and drugs, all of which was impounded by government agents. Various pieces of equipment from the plane were also found in one location not far from the wreckage and there was speculation over whether the four had salvaged and hidden any of the treasure. But nothing was ever found, the jungle proving to be a worthy guardian of their careful placements.

Many years later, however, when the large international tourist development on the pristine coast adjacent to the forest was underway, and the main access road was being built along the route of an old track, a fairly well-preserved body of a man was recovered when a large bog was being drained. Before that a road worker had come across a solid gold ingot under an overturned rock. He confided only to a couple of close colleagues in fear of any consequences but knowledge of the find, and the regularity of the treasure being hidden under rocks, quietly spread through the workforce. As the path of the road was gradually cleared more and more were uncovered by many of the labourers checking around rocks before bulldozers churned it all over, amounting eventually to ninety-three ingots. By the time the secret reached management and then authorities, well over one hundred employees had curiously left the project and drifted back to their homes in villages spread around the country.

And so it was that the lives of many were forever changed for the better by a highway lined with gold, yet for me and for my family it was a hellish road of dubious good intentions.

Anemotion

Ana hoisted her bag up onto the deck of the carriage, turned her head back around, made a silly face, waved with her free hand, then grabbed the rail with it and pulled herself on board.

On the landing she checked it was the right carriage then bumped her way down the aisle to find her seat. Several passengers had taken their seats along the way. Hers was empty, she was relieved to find, as was the one next to her which was pleasing. How long would that last, she wondered. An elderly woman behind her made her impatience felt through her expression and body language while Ana blocked the passage, unzipped her bag, took out the few things she would want during the journey and threw them onto the seat. She was well practised at this and knew what she would want and that it was worth doing it all properly and without rush. She heaved the bag up onto the rack opposite her, slightly forward. She always did it that way and not directly over her head as most people did so she could keep an eye on it easily.

She edged herself into her seat next to the window and the elderly woman passed by indicating her displeasure at the delay through a beady glare. Ana could see out the window now and there stood Nan, Joe and Roberta in a line looking for her face to appear. They spotted her, came alongside and waved enthusiastically, as if they hadn't seen her for ages and she was about to return.

She looked around at her surroundings a little, the backs of a few hairy heads peeping over seats in front, some including the nape of a neck, others truncated at half-skull: thick curly hair, close-cut hair, lustrous long hair pressed flat against a head-rest, one cap covering a shaven pate. Across the aisle was a young couple, restless and full of energy, lost in their digital world together. They could be written off. She couldn't look behind her now and had already forgotten those who had taken seats before her as she shuffled through. They might now be checking from behind her straight brunette bob propped on top of her own head-rest.

She turned and looked out again. The three smiled and waved again. She waved back again, then looked straight ahead. She felt a little like someone strapped into the electric chair waiting for execution, with a morbidly fascinated audience watching. Ana wondered if some languages had a word for this, these frozen moments of, not so much suspended animation, but suspended emotion. That awkward feeling of not knowing what to do, what position to assume, what expression; that unease of not knowing how long it will last, like holding a pose for a photograph while the photographer fiddles with the camera. She couldn't think of one in English. She knew words like *schadenfreude* from German, the Danish *hyyge*, or the Chinese *fengshui* and Portuguese *saudade*. Maybe 'anemotion' would do it. Ana allowed herself an inner smile of satisfaction. Actors would know how to handle it, she guessed, this 'anemotion'. Writers might try to describe it, ascribe it to a character at some key point in a novel.

She detected movement next to her and looked to see a man taking his seat. She nodded and smiled and he returned both as she made pointless manoeuvres to establish the virtual dividing space between them, like a dog settling in its bed, twirling itself around and around and ending up exactly where it began. There was something about his eyes, his look, his presence, perhaps even an undetected smell, pheromones that appealed to her, exciting her subliminally, and she felt herself blush slightly.

Then she stared ahead. More frozen moment, and 'anemotion'. Except this time it felt different. It felt intoxicating. It had potential. She wanted more.

Ana turned her head and looked out the window again, smiled and waved, again. But that earlier anemotive state had passed, along with the changing scene. She was all about what was going to happen next, as the train made its first little jerky movements away from the platform and into her future.

Out of Order

It was not without good reason Colm had chosen this place for the penultimate stage of the project, this place of such marvellous natural beauty, though the reasoning did not include its charm.

It was remote, allowed for perfect access by boat, even, because of the massive pier, a large one, and had no mobile phone coverage. Yet it did have, by some freakish twist of fate, or oversight on the part of BT in this digital age, a public phone of the classic Dr Who variety. He needed that to make his one crucial triggering call.

They did have the option of driving the two hours or so from Glasgow towing a trailer and its perilous load, though even that would still necessitate a launching somewhere. But using a boat and travelling up the loch from the Mull afforded more protection from both interception and detection, accidental or otherwise.

Colm knew the loch well. As a boy he had occasionally been taken fishing there by his father. He remembered one particular Saturday morning when the farmers' market was on, his father buying marshmallow made in the traditional way from sap of the mallow bush freely gathered along the verges of many local roads. They had taken it back to the loch where they had toasted it on sticks over a little fire his father built to cook the first salmon he had ever caught.

He remembered too the thrill of finding shiny, smooth, round marble stones amongst the shingles of the foreshore and skimming them out over the dark waters of the loch under low leaden skies. Each of the stone's bounces created a small, expanding explosion of refracted light on the loch's surface, themselves like ephemeral stepping stones for fairies to skip along, only then to disappear under the returning and enveloping blanket of darkness. He liked to try again and again, counting the bounces each time in the hope of breaking his record before the stone suddenly gave up and disappeared forever into the molten depths with a final exhausted plop.

But they certainly did not want today to be a market day. They did not want crowds of people coming into the normally tranquil town from surrounding areas. The less roving eyes about, the better for their purpose.

Colm moored the boat to the pier while Brendan scrambled aft and severed the towline holding the tender. The small, mostly submerged, old and waterlogged vessel drifted away very slowly. He knew from his research into the currents it would float towards the headwaters of the loch, towards its target, circling the edge, its wooden fabrication and chemical explosives in plastic containers, along with its near-invisibility, circumventing defensive measures. But he knew also digital activity was monitored and he did not want any local inquisitiveness to interfere. He would phone Mary for the final stage from that phone box. It would not be monitored, and would give anonymity in any case, untrackable, unlike smart phones which they would not carry for that reason.

Colm, the collar of his coat pulled up around his neck and face against the biting wind, and not just for concealment, hurried up from the pier to the phone box. Brendan stayed at the boat ready for getaway back down the loch, around the Mull and across to the Republic not too far away.

He yanked open the door and stepped in closing it firmly

behind him. He pushed coins into the slot and dialled the number.

There was a click.

"Hello?"

"I'm sorry, this service can only accept emergency calls."

"Hello! Moira?"

"Please dial 999 for emergencies."

"I don't want emergency."

"I'm sorry, this service can only accept emergency calls. Please dial 999 for emergencies."

"Hello?! What's the … "

"I'm sorry, this service … "

He slammed the handset against the main box, screamed some obscenities at it and jerked the door open against its will, jumping out and racing back down the hill and along to the end of the pier.

Brendan was waiting ready to cast off. Colm threw his arms up into the air as he approached to indicate his frustration and failure. They both stood staring out at the loch trying to spot the drifting hulk but its freedom had also aided its eclipse beneath the surface and it was lost to them. It would meander now with the currents for the unforeseeable future until it sank completely or was somehow discovered.

The submarines on the other hand would survive to float and dive and cruise another day. Colm would need to skip a lot more shiny stones across the loch and watch them disappear before he would get a second chance.

The Wrong Way

The car was heading towards white-capped mountains now. Their massive form filled the windscreen from pillar to pillar after the freeway had curved gracefully around to the right, then straightened into a lengthy stretch. The countryside was flitting past each side in their peripheral vision, back from the edges of the windscreen, and attracting their gaze away from the view to the front now and then. The view had transformed quickly, from open grasslands to forested hills, from wide panorama to embracing closeness.

In the cabin of the car they felt protected, yet disconnected. They would not have known whether outside it was stifling hot or shivering cold if it were not for the digital thermometer on the dashboard telling them. They had not spoken for some time. He had been keeping one eye on the car's instrument cluster and was responding by minor corrections of his driving to various suggestions they were issuing to him about speed and fuel consumption. He enjoyed trying to get the optimal fuel consumption despite the meagre savings involved. A man thing he had concluded. She seemed to be focused on listening to the music and checking the read-outs from the stereo system which accompanied it from time to time. She had switched the CDs from country-and-western to classical, perhaps to reflect her responses to the landscape.

She had not consulted him. He preferred the country-and-western but did not comment.

He noticed the odometer had clicked up some hundred kilometres by the time she spoke.

"This doesn't seem to be anything like what we expected. Where are the signs?"

"We must have missed them. I'm sure this is right though. Just a little further."

"I'm worried we're going the wrong way."

"Well, let's just see what comes up next."

"We'll run out of daylight if we just keep going and it's the wrong direction."

"Maybe we should have leased that GPS."

"Yes, I told you, I wanted to."

She opened a compartment, reached in and pulled out her smartphone, pressed some buttons, contemplated its screen for a short while, pressed some more buttons then put it back into the compartment.

"No signal."

"There was one. What did it say?"

"I missed it. I think it said Gloucester, which means we're completely lost."

"Maybe it didn't."

"It did."

"You said maybe. Do you want me to turn off at the next opportunity then?"

"Yes, I think we'd better. You said 'maybe', not me. I said 'I think it said'."

"Here then, here's one coming up; I'm turning off."

They drove up the exit ramp and stopped at the intersection at the end of it faced with a simple left-right choice between two places they had never heard of.

"Which way then?"

"Let's just go across the freeway and back the way we came."

"Where's that going to get us?"

"Back to where we came from at least and where we know where we are, unlike here."

'But we're trying to get to Gerard's and going back is not going to achieve that. We need to keep trying, so left or right?"

"Hell, how do I know, I've told you go back."

"That's easy for you to say but I'm driving and I have to do the deed."

"Do whatever you want then."

"That just doesn't help me at all, Margaret."

"I've told you what I think, Gordon."

The landscape brooded all around them, snow-capped mountains far ahead, forested hills, empty and quiet and still. The car sat motionless, its digital read-outs glowing red zeros. Vivaldi's seasonal cycle had reached winter. The transparency of the glass windows seemed to have become opaque as their world imploded.

Whichever way they turned they were going the wrong way.

Furnace

Bangkok. Who the blazes would want to live there? Polluted, crowded, frenzied, dangerous and unconscionably hot and humid. And make sure never to insult the king.

As Mal was driven from the airport to his hotel he focused on the task and ignored his surroundings and his discomfort. Tomorrow he would get away early and make the four-hour trip north with the organiser. There he would meet his guide and prepare for the hunt. Success was not guaranteed. Indeed, quite the opposite, it was very much a matter, more a matter, of good fortune as much as of careful planning.

The next day brought a clattering, bone-rattling drive on rough tracks followed by a long trudge to an isolated campsite and a sticky and restless night in a tent fighting off the insects and the adrenalin surges, ineffectually in both cases. Up at dawn tired but energized by expectation and nervous energy, and fitted out, he was off into the wild.

A Thai jungle begrudges movement through it and does not give up its secrets freely. The sweat dripped off his forehead into his eyes, stinging and making him blink, constantly blurring his vision already struggling with the dimness of the light filtering through thick canopy. His shirt was soaked through, sticking to his back and shoulders and around his waist. He could feel his feet squelching inside his heavy boots and he suspected there were leeches in them slithering around in his sucked-out blood.

He tried wiping his face with the inside of his arm while grasping a rifle and sweeping its muzzle back and forth across his limited range in what was beginning to feel more and more like a green-lined, overheated coffin. He stepped slowly, cautiously, as silently as his human frame and its awkward accoutrements allowed. Insects buzzed and bit, branches and vines and thorns kept challenging his progress. Were the screams of the monkeys to warn of tiger, or man? Did their vocabulary distinguish the two, he wondered, and wished he could understand them.

He heard the swish of brushed foliage and spun around. His guide crouched, finger to lips. Mal could feel his heart racing; his head throbbed, his palms slippery on the stock, his finger greedy on the trigger, his muscles tight, sinews twisted, his mouth dry despite the sweat. He stepped back and surveyed, trying to spot spaces between leaves and trunks and tangling vines to peer through, trying to detect any tell-tale orange burning bright amongst the flashes and patches of vegetative browns and green-browns and the blackness of gaps in that forest of the night.

Another swish and he spotted for a fleeting second the shadowy movement of colour he had dreamt of. Jackpot! His heart jumped into his throat. He wanted that skin like nothing else.

What more could life offer him or money buy him now? He had paid handsomely for the opportunity, the privilege, the glory. He had endured the hardships, dared this deadly peril. It would grace the floor in front of his fireplace back home. People would be dazzled, demanding the full story which he would dramatically deliver again and again. The guide would claim the penis and bones and even the whiskers for the merchants of traditional medicine and death to sell to humans for the dubious pursuit of longevity and fecundity. The meat would probably be left to the treepies and the rats and the maggots. Perhaps only three hundred of these magnificent creatures remained and one of them would be his forever. He hoped it would bring him a whisk of immortality as well as fame. Infamy was of no account.

He swivelled around, swinging the rifle with him, now barely capable of any thinking, all instinct, all animal, all hunter. Where was it? The guide was nowhere to be seen and the jungle was a prison wall surrounding him that would allow passage in only one direction, his. Just him and a monster, his prey; or was he the lamb to the slaughter?

Cock, point, sweep. Wait, watch; wait, peer. Hold breath just when breath is most needed, heart thumping on ear drums. Stay steady, stay calm. Ears pricked, eyes straining; oh for keener senses. Now silence has descended like a shroud. What do those monkeys see, hear, say? Another swish of foliage.

Stare, spot, squeeze, nothing. Jammed! Sheer terror gripped him. He click-clacked the bolt, hands shaking, legs buckling. A long, deep, gurgling, guttural growl like the beast from hell itself flooded the place; a huge, fearful, symmetrical flaming orb centred with two great, wild, fiery, pitch-black pearls framing a cavernous pink tunnel pillared by a pair of gleaming white sabres exploded out of the forest deepness at him front on. He felt the dread of doom as time choked and then stopped. Hold steady. Dare to hope? Courage and success, or bewitchment and eternity?

Point.

Cock.

BANG!

My Island Realm

Early each school day I raced along the full length of the wharf near our home in the firm belief that if I dawdled I might be swallowed up by its planks collapsing beneath me. I ran with all the enthusiasm of morning, the distinctive plinkety-plonk hollow sound that jetties make following each step. I ran all the way to the walk-through shed at the end, with its wooden benches along both sides and the ferry timetable pinned onto a notice board behind locked glass sliding doors. Without stopping I skipped right to the outermost corner of the wharf where I could grab hold of the faux-antique lamp, its ethereal nature so seemingly at odds with the solid dark mass that surrounded it, and be safe again. I always wondered how the lamp got its light from such a watery nowhere down below.

In the depths of winter I would arrive early enough that the light in the lamp would still be glowing. Its reflections would dance around on the surface ripples, mingling with those coming from the street lights nearby and the big neon signs of the skyscrapers further away in the city. I was almost always alone so I would stand then with my thoughts, listening to the little wavelets lapping at the piers below me, the popping and cracking of the tiny molluscs which encrusted them, the mild creaking of the jetty timbers, and the distracting plop of a fish jumping, together creating a minor musical water suite, befitting its barge-like setting.

In the misty morning dimness I would stare across the bay at the island with its single giant ancient fig tree and square brick structure at one end. A flagpole occasionally sported the national flag with its twirl of stars and funny crossed box in one corner, or sometimes a black and red one with a big yellow circle in the middle. My mother had told me it was for the people who first lived there, and I preferred it to the other, messy one. Often a bra, or knickers, or sneakers dangled from it as well, though I could never understand why, or what they stood for. My mother would only say: "Just people being silly, dear."

On early winter mornings, devoid of any lighting of its own, the island was a dark blob, discernible only because of its invisibility in the midst of the sparkle from all the reflections off the water and the street-lamps, and from the awakening households behind it further across the bay. It was like a black hole in a twinkling urban universe. But in summer it glistened in the early sunlight and I could make out its paths and flower beds, rocky outcrops, fencing and litter bins, and the sign that proclaimed dogs were prohibited. That always made me wonder what it was that made dogs so unwanted there, and why not pigs or cats or cows. I could just distinguish the word 'LADIES' marked on the wall of that small, square building at one end.

I was fascinated by the island in a way I was not by any of the other shorelines I could see when I cast my glance around in a wide arc, simply because it was an island. It was as if it were a separate country, distinct and unaffected by the surrounding land which was somehow made weaker through its commonness. This connected part was full of the ordinariness of school and homework and chores, of people always getting in the way, and of nothing exciting happening, like battles and exploration, or carnivals and circuses and crusades, or vampires and wild animals, or magical adventures like Alice had. The island was special. It was a dogless society, very ordered and tidy, with an advanced network of roads, strong fortifications and a castle with mysterious underground bunkers and secret passages, a unique and well-preserved ecology, a proud history which was regularly commemorated by patriotic ceremonies involving displays of national symbols, and I, well, I was its ruler, and could make it into anything I wanted. A ruler in exile who longed to return, and would, in triumph, one day soon, and whose subjects, the island's enchanted citizens, waited anxiously for that momentous day.

The ferry always arrived to break my trances. Sometimes it emerged suddenly out of a mist, at other times gradually becoming discernible in the distance, silent amidst the early morning glitter, then with its low throbbing, and finally its bow waves splashing in its rush towards the jetty, as if it might slam straight into it. It would inevitably pull up just in time with a wild churning of water at its stern, causing me to think about all the poor little fish that had to get out of its way or be mashed up. I would clamber on board as it bumped and turned, and immediately be carried off into the cares and commonplaces of the day, with school friends vying for my attention, and me for theirs.

One clear autumn morning, after I reached the end of the pier in my usual way and jumped to a sudden stop grabbing the lamp post, I looked over to my island realm from my place of exile to notice a strange figure moving slowly around from spot to spot, apparently checking this and checking that. It was tall, I could tell, as it stood next to the no-dogs sign, and was draped in a large, dark cape which came right to the ground, dragging behind like a monarch's robe, and with some type of headwear that could have been a military helmet, or in fact a crown. I knew immediately that this was my usurper, the leader of an invading force now arrogantly surveying his dominion, and that this was the time for action.

I would commandeer the ferry as soon as it arrived, rally my troops around me and, taking my place of leadership on the foredeck, head to my island for the assault and reconquest. I would call on all my subjects to return from wherever they had fled; from my regal platform high up in the old fig I would convoke a meeting of the new parliament to be held beneath, in the shade of its spreading branches; I would overturn the anti-dog rule and welcome all strays, of whatever colour, size or breed, to make my island their home, pulling down the despised sign and replacing it with one displaying the symbol for a smile; and I would take up official residence in my red-brick castle. There would be peace and prosperity, art and music festivals, dancing and games, and I would be revered by my adoring people. It would be the first United Ladies Republic ever in the world, and I its Queen Eloisa.

The ferry was on its way, as always, and I could feel the excitement of approaching action. It pulled up in its usual manner. I leapt on board brandishing my painting homework in its postal-tube sheath out in front like a marauding pirate ready for the fight, but was immediately enveloped by quotidian cares and commonplaces, friends vying for my attention, and me for theirs, as it was every day.

By the time the ferry pulled back again into the jetty that afternoon, with darkness approaching, I was weary, the burdens of the past day weighing me down. I plodded homewards along the wharf, leaving behind me that dark world of drudgery, confident as usual in my personal certainty won through experience, that no planks would collapse while I was heading in that direction, and not the other way. I had forgotten the strange figure on my island, but if I had remembered, and looked for it then, I would not have seen it. The man, cold and hungry, had been picked up by an outreach service for the homeless, having spent two nights curled up in a corner of the toilet block, wrapped in a blanket, with his beanie pulled down over his ears and cheeks, and having exhausted the discarded leftovers he had scrabbled for in the bins. It remained unclear to the carers how the man had found his way onto the island, perhaps amongst a group of tourists or party-goers, the type of fun-seekers who would hoist a pair of pantyhose up the flagpole.

Still, calm had been restored to my island realm after such a turbulent and disruptive era. Its isolation was re-established, with all dogs expelled and excluded once again. As I reached the top end of the jetty I hopped onto the grass verge where my mother had waved me off that morning and was now waiting, as she did every school day.

"Hello, Eloisa, how was your day, dear?" she asked, lifting my backpack off as I stretched out my arms.

"Alright," I hesitated in reply, with nothing much at all in my head as I ran off towards home.

Flighty Connections

Joel stared up at the departures board. He saw his connecting flight was delayed and shook his head in mild despair.

What would he do for the next four hours? Not long enough for a decent snooze, even assuming somewhere could be found for one in this humungous hangar for humans, cunningly designed to prevent such dangerous distractions. Only so much duty-free shopping was possible. A tour of the concourses and their string of gates would be good for exercise and soak up some time but was limited in its attraction. People-watching was probably the best way he could while away the hours, he thought, as he sat on one seat and plonked his hand luggage on its neighbour.

He pulled out his smartphone. Three hours, fifty-six minutes to go. Why does time crawl in these situations and zoom when you're running late for an appointment? That subterfuge not available here, as far as he could determine. Pity he didn't smoke or he could shorten his wait and his life just a little more by doing a spell in the smoking room with all those idiot addicts, he thought. He might have chanced it anyway except for all that smoke. He could have taken a shower if he'd been a frequent flyer, heaven forbid, and a member of one of these mile-high elite clubs tucked away around the place. No, there was nothing for it but to patiently tick off the seconds.

He made another circuit of the concourse and lobby. It hadn't changed much. A visit to the comfort station would get some superfluous minutes out of the way. He spent much more time than necessary staring at the uninspiring back of a toilet door, then washed up. He wet his hands and ruffled them through his hair, combing it back with his fingers to spruce up. He felt braced to face another spin of the concourse. Three hours, ten minutes to go. Take away standard boarding procedure, maybe two hours, fifty-five.

He shouldered his bag and set off again. He began recognising people he had seen on his previous rounds. After stretching it out for as long as he could he found some spare seats and sat down. There was always the internet: wombats behaving badly, Mariah Carey, Netflix. That seemed to be what most everybody else was doing. If he could just figure out how to connect. He was never too good at these things.

There was a big sigh from the next seat. A woman had dumped herself into it and slumped back. She turned towards him.

"You killing time too?"

"Yes, delayed flight," he smiled. She was attractive, similar age.

"Where to?"

"Colombia, UNESCO conference."

"Oh? Me too … serendipity."

"Serendip indeed!"

She laughed.

"The waiting just makes it worse for me."

"Why so?"

"It's a bit of a confession …"

"I'm a complete stranger … trust me."

"I have a fear of flying."

"Well, you've come to the right place."

She laughed again. "Thanks a lot."

"Joel," he proffered, along with his open right hand twisted awkwardly in her direction.

She took it limply but easily with her right. "Aranya."

"Wow. Nice. Unusual. Sounds like a security-web to cling to when you fly might just be the trick."

She laughed again. "Something like that, I'd feel more at home. My parents didn't speak Spanish, my father just liked the name. I'll be Anya in Bogota, avoid any spider-woman digs."

"Oh, I dunno, could give you real street cred!"

She tossed her head back and scoffed good humouredly. He looked and lingered.

"Anya it is then. What's your seat number?"

"56G."

"Oh, double serendipity. I'm across the aisle. Maybe we can do a deal with 56H and I could hold your hand for take-off. That's the worst stage for nervous Nellies."

"You're so kind, and unkind." Again, a smile.

They talked. Time flew. Other passengers passed back and forth. Last call came and went. They missed their flight.

The End of Colour

The drably dressed middle-aged woman meandered aimlessly around the large open space. Eventually she wandered up to the glass-walled room and glanced in. She pulled herself up abruptly and stared. Children were swarming around inside, spilling over bright-coloured chairs and big balls, climbing up little ladders onto platforms and jumping off onto piles of happy foam, bouncing and giggling and squealing with glee.

The woman's face gradually distorted and it became unrecognisable from how it had looked only minutes before. The colours of the playthings incensed her. The outrageous brightness of the yellows, the aggressiveness of the reds, the arrogance of the blues, the insolence of the greens. There was no subtlety, no compromising, no tolerance in these colours. They were absolute. And dangerous.

She swung herself around, searching for whatever might lay at hand to defend herself. She dashed over to where she spotted a fire extinguisher hanging on a wall with an axe inside a glass box next to it. She ripped the fire extinguisher from its bracket and smashed it against the glass, shattering it, and grabbed the axe.

An alarm bell blared out its urgent appeal. Shoppers everywhere looked up from their coffees and muffins or stopped in their tracks to see what it was all about. The air not only filled with the clamour of the clanging but was also suddenly charged with the electrifying sense of panic.

Holding the axe tightly with two hands and brandishing it above one shoulder she raced back and into the glass room. People jumped out of her way but did nothing to stop her, stunned by the speed and outlandishness of it. She lifted the axe higher above her head and brought it crashing down onto the first piece of furniture in her way. A little plastic red chair buckled under the blow, splitting and shattering into several pieces which flew off at all angles with an almighty crack. Children screamed and ran off in every direction like cockroaches disturbed after opening an old box of biscuits.

She raised the axe again above her head and, yelling out some unintelligible gibberish about colours and "Benetton", careered around the room, bringing the axe down on each chair and table she came across. The noise was terrifying: children screaming and crying, the woman yelling, the axe wreaking its clattering havoc, the alarm wailing. Adults, mainly women, had come running from all directions into the room, calling out their children's names and grabbing them up off the floor into their arms, whisking them away in flighty panic.

Summoned by such hue and cry a man and a woman in uniform appeared from around a corner, headed straight for the woman, tackling her to the ground in mid-swing then sitting on top of her while she struggled and shouted "Fuck Benetton!", over and over.

As she lay pinned face down on purple lino, colours began to swarm around each other in her mind, colliding and overlapping and melding to form other colours, like great swirling blobs of paint thrown into a swimming pool, into which she then dived and floated around flailing, enveloped and buffeted on all sides by colour, colour, colour.

She felt a silver sting on her arm and she saw pink and white and brown featureless ovals with golden-brown halos staring down at her. The colours slowed their madcap dancing; she could see green and knew it meant revenge, then red and sensed anger, then blue and felt melancholy, yellow for confusion. They all began to line up and organise themselves and stretch out and she could see a rainbow forming.

She realised that was what she was seeking, that was what she had been after. The rainbow of fulfilment. If only now all those colours would squeeze into each other and make a white bridge of attainment so she could cross over it into paradise. Then there would be no more colour, ever again. Just the sweet, eternal blackness of peace.

School's In

Three knocks, three hard knocks. Elaine wasn't suspicious, she knew the drill.

More hard knocking. She went to the door and opened it confidently. There stood yet another one. She was getting used to it.

"Come in," she shrugged. "May as well join the others."

He had an uncouth look about him. It was her father. He had abandoned her mother and her when she was three. She recognised him from the photos. She led him down the hall into the crowded room.

"This is my father," she called out over the hubbub. Eyes turned upon him with little interest, and then away again.

She led him around.

"Dad, this is Mr. Murphy. He was my teacher for two years in primary school. He was sadistic and quite a bully, picking on me to such an extent that I turned against school altogether, leaving as soon as I was able, at fifteen."

Mr. Murphy scowled slightly, but with just a touch of trepidation in his demeanour. This was, after all, the girl's father.

"Maybe if you'd hung around you might have sorted him out."

Her father gave Mr Murphy a dirty look then shrugged his shoulders.

"I had better things to do."

Elaine turned towards two more men, younger, huddled together in conversation.

"This is Andy and Tim. Andy took up with my best friend, Teresa - she's over there - while we were still together, and Tim turned around and did much the same a couple of years later. With my younger sister. Remember her? Maybe you heard?"

Andy and Tim looked at her sheepishly then carried on joshing around with each other. She took a few steps into the crowd, pulling her father along behind her.

"And here is Derek, my ex-husband, he with the magnetic personality and gambling habit. He ran off with a younger woman just as the children were starting school, then dragged me through the courts for years to get custody and the house, but mainly the house. He didn't, but the process was the worst part. That's my lawyer over there. She did better out of it than either of us. Did I mention the violence?"

Derek turned and walked away. Her lawyer smirked.

"Come and meet Kate. She was my drinking mate when I went on a downhill spiral and helped me go all the way down before disappearing with my boyfriend of the time, and my credit card. They did leave me a little something by way of memories, a stint inside, and tiny guests that required medical attention."

Kate gave her an air kiss and pulled a silly face.

They moved along and Elaine stopped again.

"And here's Damien, my boss at a time when I was just getting myself together and making something of my life. He tried it on with me, then made things difficult until I finally brought up his sexual harassment with management, at which point they sacked me."

Damien stared straight at her expressionless, then winked.

"Meet Joyce, Dad. Joyce was my financial adviser when I was in need after the court business and managed it all very well, for herself. By the time she finished I had to sell the family home to pay off the debts that had somehow come my way through her strategic investing."

Joyce nodded with a wry smile, fiddling with the collar of her flowery dress, and they passed by, stopping again in front of an older woman with a hangdog look and no eye contact.

"Let me introduce you to Bernadette, certainly not the least of our students-in-waiting. She was driving under the influence when she mounted the footpath and struck my youngest boy walking home from school. He never came home again. I go to see him as often as I can."

They moved along.

"And Dad, Dr. Thomas, the specialist who looked after my body through its cancerous journey but made me feel I might have been better off dying in the process."

Dr. Thomas looked at them both and adjusted his spectacles.

"And of course you know Mum," she said turning towards a woman crouched alone in a corner.

"She brought us up all by herself, as you surely know, and was never less than wonderful while she was able. It was so sad later then, her deepening depression, the bi-polar episodes, the medication that robbed her of herself, and us of her eventually, though not before draining us of much of our time, energy and finances."

Elaine turned back around and clapped her hands loudly.

"Pay attention everybody now, and take your seats. We are here to learn, and there is indeed a lot to learn."

She was grateful, and proud, that her children had been able to attend quite a different school.

A Certain Sanctuary

You climb the stairs wearily homeward as you leave the world behind you. Your right hand reaches around into your back left pocket as you plod upwards, the three long fingers probing for the key you routinely keep there whenever you go out. You retrieve it with two of those fingers, then secure it with your thumb and lift it out of your pocket and up to the keyhole just as you take the final step to your door. You always like to get that timing, the rhythm, the flow, just right so there is no interruption in that treasured transition from the public to your private world. You are wondering what was going on down near the entrance when you arrived, two people apparently at each other's throats, some curious onlookers, but you were just too exhausted to become involved with it. Not that you would want to anyway. You had slipped past with only a sideways glance at them.

The key turns with the help of a vigorous wiggle and the door opens, allowing you to step into a room that sings out welcome to you, come on in, escape, hide, relax, recover. The bookcase with its familiar titles where you had lost yourself in fantasy worlds; the sideboard and all the bits and pieces you had brought back from around the world to remind you of those wonderful times; the Joshegan rug under the coffee table you had bid far too high for at auction; the old sofa, the photos and artworks on the walls, even the functional pieces like the heater, the television, the lamps, the old stereo with its turntable, all of them so friendly and comforting. Homely joys. The side table provides its usual service for you to dump your bag and empty your pockets onto it. Hardly missing a beat, you take a few more steps to slump into the armchair, releasing a long sigh as you do so.

You consider getting a drink from the fridge in the kitchen but you need to rest a minute first.

There is a knock on the door.

"Shit," you say out loud, though not loud enough for anyone else to hear, and you refuse to respond.

There is a harder, insistent knocking.

You repeat the same word but resign yourself to the inevitable. This time you force yourself up out of the slump, turn and drag your sorry legs back towards the door. You remind yourself to have one of those peep-hole things installed soon. And a security chain.

"Who is it?" you ask by way of a temporary substitute for chain and peep-hole.

"Your neighbours. From downstairs," comes a voice, flat tone, male, maybe forties.

You put your hand out and onto the doorknob thinking what was the point of asking who it was and then opening up to someone you don't recognise and who could be anybody, even though he says he's a neighbour. For whatever that's worth, as well. Just makes you look and feel weak, or stupid. You open the door anyway.

A man is standing there, back from the door, safely, smiling in what seems to be a forced way, in his forties, with a woman, younger, standing behind him. She looks serious. They seem vaguely familiar.

"Hi."

"Hi there."

"We've come up about what happened."

"What happened?"

"What happened downstairs."

"What?"

"Just now, when you came past."

"Oh, yeah, I saw something going on but don't know anything about it," you shrug.

"It's about what you said."

"What I said?"

Your face reddens but it is not the blush of ingenuous shame; it is from the realisation of serious menace.

"Yeah."

"I didn't say anything, just came straight up."

"What you said to my girlfriend," the man adds, and takes a small step forward.

You lean back a little. You should not have.

"What did you mean by it?"

"I didn't mean anything; I mean, I didn't say anything so couldn't mean anything."

"Don't you think it was a bit rude?" The man had stopped smiling.

Oh hell, now you notice he's got a ring in one ear and a tattoo on his neck around the area of his carotid artery which is bulging slightly as he becomes more aggravated. You wonder how could anyone bear having something like that done to them there when you squirmed just having an ultrasound done on yours? You recognise him now as the man who lives downstairs. Why the hell did I open the door? No choice really.

"Well, seeing I didn't say anything I can't think it was a bit rude, can I?" Oh shit, you tell yourself, now I've started arguing with him about something that didn't happen. You go to back-pedal but he interrupts before you get the first word out.

"Well, whether you think you said it or not, we want an apology 'cause she's very upset about it."

"OK, I'm sorry she's upset, but it can't be about anything I said since I didn't say anything, but I am sorry about the whole thing, whatever it is." You wish now that you hadn't looked at them as you passed.

"That's a cop-out. You said it, and she wants you to take it back and apologise properly." The man's voice had gone up a notch, in both volume and pitch. He is roused now and has moved forward somehow, maybe a step, maybe a lean, you couldn't tell anymore, you're just panicking. The woman hasn't taken her glaring eyes off you the whole time. You feel your heart thumping and your throat tightening.

You've got to talk your way out of this, quickly.

"Can you tell me what I said, then?" you squeak.

Mistake.

"No, smartarse. You know what you said. Anyway I wouldn't repeat it in front of my girlfriend."

"Perhaps she just misheard me. Look, I ..." you say, and raise your open hands in front of you, palms out, as some mild symbolic pacifying protest, waving them from side to side to try to ward off, what: misunderstanding, distrust, confusion, anger, accusation?

What they don't ward off is the clenched fist that flies out towards you, spearheaded by its bony knuckles, straight through the space between them, landing directly on your nose and jerking your skull back with its force, and, oh, the pain that explodes through your whole head and streaks down your wrenched neck like lightning across your shoulders and out through your arms to your fingertips and jumps to your stomach as nausea and at the same time shocks you in its unexpectedness, so that you are floored, in every way.

And now he's standing in your room, your refuge of only minutes before, looking down at you and bristling with anger and you are terrified as your hand holds your face and your nose feels it is swelling like a balloon that will burst open and you see the blood and feel its slippery ooziness with your fingers and you picture a big, bright-red, wet, balloon about to burst.

His face contorts and you first wince to take the strike and then cry out as he kicks you in the side, right where you think your kidney might be. He screams "ARSEHOLE!", and turns and walks out and you fear amidst all the pain that you might lose a kidney as well as your nose and what that would mean for your future welfare. You hear his girlfriend throw "arsehole" at you as she follows him down the stairs from the position outside she hadn't moved from the whole time, and you think, "bloody bitch". But you hadn't said that, nothing like it, nothing at all; Jesus, what the hell was all that about?

You lie still for a while, gaining whatever composure you can muster, more grateful they have gone rather than resentful at the injustice of it. Realising they have left the door open you stretch with one leg to push it closed with a kick. It clicks shut but that still leaves the deadlock to be completely safe. As completely as you can be unless you make the mistake of opening it. You gather your energy and reach out to the sideboard to pull yourself up. You feel wobbly and stagger to the bathroom after securing the door. You resist looking in the mirror for fear of what you might see, and with your head down splash water on your face. The sense of injustice begins to rise and take over now against the tide of pain, and you begin to consider how to respond.

Call the police? There would be a good case against him: unprovoked assault, home invasion. But the police would ask questions and start delving and probing. They might discover things, almost certainly. They would speak to others, and others might talk, might begin to suspect something and repeat, or start, rumours. What if they were to check your computer? This had always been a worry for you. They seem to be able to find things even when you delete them these days. You probably should go to a hospital but wonder how you are ever going to get out of the building now, running the gauntlet every time you try. Those two from downstairs will start talking to others and an alliance of neighbours would form against you. Maybe it already had. You would never be able to explain it all away once they start gossip mongering. You will have to move and find somewhere else to live, but that has already happened so many times. And still how will you get past them until then?

You could do nothing, accept it, lay low, sneak in and out at ungodly hours, but they would waylay you again eventually and it would be so stressful. Or, you could fight back. The only way would be with superior power. You remember, and go to check in the bottom of your wardrobe to see if it is still there, and loaded. It is. You take it out and feel its cold steeliness and patterned form, that snug fit into the palm of your hand, its simple, inviting mechanism, its functional fascination, its existential significance. It reminds you of your father who you got it from after he died and you cleaned out his house. What would he think of you? Why should you care what he might think after all he had done? You remember your mother, cowed, always cowering, imploring, placating, accepting. retreating. How realistic is it anyway to consider such retaliation? If you simply were to go downstairs and shoot him where would it get you? Even with the mitigating provocation gaol probably, and all that implied,. Any sweetness of revenge would be severely soured.

As you close the wardrobe door and look up you catch yourself in the full-length mirror. The mirror tells its story and it is not a pleasing one. Your nose is swollen, your eyes puffy and the bruising is spreading. The blow has added ten years onto the already galloping ageing of your appearance. You are putting on weight and losing any hint of a youthful shape. Your attempts at preserving some claim to youth with that hairstyle and those clothes you persevere with just make you look ridiculous. You despair. Everything seems to be closing in on you. The refuge is becoming a prison and a hell-hole. You can't go out, you can't stay there, and the time you have to do anything at all is running out.

You go to the window and peer out. You see the man who lives downstairs standing on the other side of the street, first looking up towards you then quickly turning his head down the street one way and back up the other way. You move to one side behind the curtain so you won't be seen, but the man downstairs had spotted you already as he looked up again and stepped off the gutter. You can sense the determination in his stride as he heads, slightly jay-wise, directly towards the front entrance, dodging a cyclist nimbly, like a rugby player side-stepping a tackle, before taking one final long jump up onto the footpath and disappearing, now almost running, under the entrance's awning.

While you stand paralysed by indecision and by the lack of any hope of having anything to decide upon, there is a beating on the door again, this time a thumping created by the use of the soft padded end of a clenched hand, ominously, like a curfew's knell. There are voices, more than one of them male, and one also you recognise from earlier, shouting, though you can't understand what they are saying, as if it matters. Terrified, you look at the pistol in your hand. You consider the window as an escape route but there is no comfort there. If they force their way in they will bash you and find things. You would be within your rights to shoot, surely, then.

You rush to your study, yank out electrical cords from sockets in a frenzy, grab your desktop computer and run with it to the bathroom, throwing it into the bathtub with a crash, grabbing the plug and jamming it into the drainage hole and turning the taps full on. You dart out to the laundry and come back with a hammer and start pounding the black box frantically. You realise that if they get in now it will be a dead giveaway like that. But it's too late: you can't hide it anywhere, there is nowhere.

You race back to your study and start pulling out drawers with photos and papers and files and toss them on the floor. You scrabble in another drawer for matches and strike them furiously one after the other, flicking them onto the heap until one catches. You spot your camera on a shelf, grab it and hurl it against the wall. Then you notice the pistol you left on the desk when you went in there for the computer, pick it up and stagger blindly out to where the thumping has intensified into a continuous growl. The men are shouting, and you hear the word you fear the most amongst it all, the word they claim describes you, and it does, but they never seem to understand its proper meaning. You love children and would never hurt them.

You turn your back and lean up against the door sobbing, deliberate in your intentions despite the hysteria storming through your brain. The doors of mercy seem to have all closed on you. You bend your arm and place the barrel of the pistol in your mouth. The door is thumping against your back. It is as if its throbbing accusation is displacing the beat of your heart. You feel the resistance of the trigger as the soft, sensitive pad on the underside of your index finger presses on it, and then you feel it give, just slightly, to your pressing, and then you feel no more.

The banging stops abruptly, the men outside jump back when they hear the explosion, and there is a brief stillness. They look at each other and back away further. They cautiously move forward and start the thumping again, tentatively, then more demandingly.

"What's going on in there?" one of them shouts. "Open up!"

Silence. From downstairs someone sings out. "Fire! There's smoke coming out of that window." The men put their shoulders to the door without effect. They step back then pummel it with the soles of their boots, but the door merely gives a little at the corners. More people gather at the foot of the stairs. The two men finally stop kicking the door as they hear sirens approaching and pull back feeling both helpless and slightly foolish.

You hear nothing and are no longer troubled by their demands nor fear their threats nor care about their entreaties. You are beyond even the concept of hearing nothing or of fear or of caring. You feel no injustice, no struggling pangs of conscience, nor relief. You have left explanations and conclusions for the world to sort out, but the merest sigh will not be passed in tribute to you. And so you have found a certain sanctuary.

The Sun Also Sets

Sunrise. What a letdown. Each one much the same. First the vaguest hint of light, like some remembrance of a childhood aroma. Promises of shapes where before there had been total denial. But soon there would be no denying it. With imperceptible stealth the sky would be back, again. Then the main event, the dancing nuclear furnace, the starburst, the full reveal. Again. Did the universe lack imagination? Could it not come up with some creativity for a change?

Carla managed a droll chuckle: "for a change," yes, please!

What was so special about this day? The whole world, it seemed, considered it some fresh beginning, some automatic clicking over of a major leaf in life's journal. In reality it was just another day, like the one before and with firm expectations of another to come. Today, and today, and today, replays itself creepily until … well, until it doesn't. Carla was surely down in the dumps, and she could see no hope of a groundhog redemption.

She pushed herself up from the sand where she had flopped and lain in the dark when her bicycle had run off the track to a sudden halt. She stood brushing herself down and stared for a while at the regenerated world sheared in half, just-blue sky and ink-black ocean, shielding her eyes from the shards of brand-new sunbeams, and walked towards it.

She flipped off her sandals and felt the wet softness of the edge of that half-world on her feet, then the wash of the waves up her legs. The cold braced her, not just her body but her spirit. She waded further into the surf, her horizon now more complex with a crest of swirling white against an upper layer of deepening blue. The force of the water on her body stopped her easy progress and she stood still, taking each gentle surge with a steadying resistance.

Carla had certainly seen hard times in the months past. She had been isolated, feeling not only alone but also angry, then bored. She had been surprised and disappointed at the patient acceptance by most everybody of the restrictions forced upon them, for reasons she could see no sound logic in or rational justification for. She chafed at the off-handed dismissal of opposing argument. Her views had served to isolate her even more through estrangement, including from long-time friends. Her plans for travel and a business had been thwarted, perhaps destroyed. A sudden uncertainty in life's course, her own and generally, had possessed her. She had found herself rudderless, lost, and leaking. That signature smile and infectious laugh which could transform a dour gathering in a moment had abandoned her. As had the gatherings.

A larger wave unbalanced her. She flailed backwards and went under, regaining her footing quickly and standing up soaking wet but revitalised. She stared down the next breaker with its glistening reflections and refractions of the impending onslaught of light. Then she turned her back to the rising sun with its promise of another day of struggle and frustration. She ran awkwardly with her skirt hitched up around her thighs, splashing her way towards dry sand, shaking and squeezing salty water off clothes and from her hair, the taste of the salt in her mouth as she tottered and fell and picked herself up again.

She would not succumb to the dispiriting times, to the regular and incessant battering of quotidian life. She would shun tiresome sunrises, face the west and revel in its fulfilment. Though there seemed no longer anywhere to hide in a world overcome by a pall of uniformity, of bland sunrises, she was sure she could still find a forest to thrive in, or a gorge, or go near one of the Poles, join the project to Mars, move to a west coast. Where exactly no longer mattered much. But Carla knew she never wanted to see the sun rise over an ocean again.

His Secret Sanctuary

The silence imposed on the cavernous room by shelf after shelf of books lining each wall from floor to ceiling was broken only by the siren call of their contents.

A man in a bedraggled suit and sneakers clutching a rolled-up magazine came in through the wide entrance, with its great carved doors folded back, walked along the carpeted aisle and took his usual place at the long oak table with its built-in lamps and grubby chairs. He heard, he felt, then he succumbed to that call of silence as he sat down. He placed his hands palms down with fingers spread out on the pale wooden surface, shiny with the rubbing of paper on wood over the decades, as the noisy, intrusive silence interrupted his train of thought.

The murmuring in the background, which had until then been impossible to recognise as anything but inconsequential distraction, grew louder. It was coming at him from every direction. He put his hands up to his ears and pressed against them but it wouldn't stop. He could not discern any specific words or message but it all seemed to be human voices, speaking in English. The volume kept increasing and the hubbub became a cacophony of unseen, unknown people shouting. He stood up rapidly and looked around. He could see nothing but books. The noise, the shouting, was coming from all the books.

He shuffled over to one of the walls and stared at the row of books. As he did the shouting became clearer and then crystallised into a man's slightly scratchy, high-pitched tones, drawn-out and well enunciated though a little slurred. He looked at the shelf closely. It was a section of Hemingway's stories. He pulled out *The Old Man and the Sea* and opened it. The voice hesitated briefly, then roared out, dwelling on certain words:

"For God's sake get me out of here! This ain't Pamplona. Sure, I got the Nobel for it. Sure I did. But that's no reason to trap a man inside a story forever. Trap a man and he is likely to go to any lengths to escape. Any lengths. I am not that Old Man. Give me back my self-respect!"

The dishevelled man slammed the book shut and stood back, confused. He took some steps sideways and found Joseph Conrad. He eased *Heart Of Darkness* from the rest and opened it.

"Mr. Kurtz, he dead!"

The foreign accent of the English wasn't fake.

"Can't anybody appreciate the horror of it all. Not being allowed to die. That's what it's like for me. The horror! It's not a game. Leave me be to escape, to disappear, to die, for the love of Jim!"

The man again closed the pages sharply, replaced the book and recoiled. He looked further up the row and took some long, hurried steps and stopped again. He heard a woman's voice now and saw he stood before several Anita Brookners. They all looked the same, none of the titles grabbed him. He pulled one out at random and opened it.

"You're not my mother," the voice droned. "I've been so trying to get my mother to do something about this mess I've got myself in. Yes, I know just because I've written the same story over and over, it really shouldn't condemn me to an eternity in that very same story. Do you think you could find her for me. I should think in France most likely. Or perhaps Camberwell, or Ealing. She'd get me out of here."

He reeled back and spun around. Another voice, a woman's again attracted his attention. He moved a long a little and came to the source, a row of Patricia Highsmith. He reached and selected a Ripley. He opened it cautiously. Her speech was measured, the accent refined. It was deepish, a little husky and there were brief intervals of silence sometimes accompanied by a slight sucking sound.

"Why must I endure these constant attacks? Psychopaths everywhere. I've been bashed and stabbed, poisoned and shot. I've been drowned. I'm stalked everywhere I go, I'm hunted. Some stranger wants to murder me, I know that surely. And what have I ever done to deserve this? Made them up, nothing more than that. I need to get out of this place, be alone again. Venice would be nice."

He recoiled again, this time dropping the book in shock. He rushed across to the other wall. He spotted several rows of Georges Simenon. A voice, this time with a strong French accent, sidled out from one as he opened it.

"*Sacre bleu!*

"I am not French.

"I am certainly not Inspector Jules Maigret!

"Yet here I find myself condemned to perpetually tracking down imaginary criminals.

"Of course I have created a character that lives in the hearts and minds of millions.

"But he is not me, nor I him.

"When will someone solve my predicament as surely Maigret would have?

"Or must I forever spiral around the arrondissements of Paris and roam the blasted provinces of France trying to solve it myself?

"I need a drink.

"A pastis please, if you can find me one. Try a brasserie."

The general babble resumed. They were all crying out for help, screaming at him to release them from their self-created, self-imposed purgatories. How could he? There was only one solution for him.

He ran his finger along the rows and rows of books looking for the one that would save him. He found it, wrongly catalogued and misfiled, opened it quickly and jumped in. It was the only book he'd ever written. It was called, *Literarily Limbo.*

Love Mars

*L*et the record show that the interview with Mr Leroy Robert *O'Brions commenced at 17.01 hours, Friday, the 23rd of April, 1988. Detectives Boudleaux and Bryant in attendance.*

Mr. O'Brions, why did you go to your wife's home Monday of last week?

I wanted to see her. I wanted to tell her I still loved her, and that I was hurting.

And what happened when you got there?

The door was locked. I tried to use my keys but she'd changed the locks. That made me angry. She didn't have to do that. She had no need to do that. But I wasn't going to hurt her. I can take a lot of pain.

What did you do?

I knew another way in. I do know a thing or two. I've really learned a lot. I always kept it secret, just in case I forgot my key sometime, you know. There was a window I made sure couldn't be closed properly.

And when you were inside?

I found Cass in bed asleep in our bedroom. I went and checked on the kids and they were already asleep. I shut the door so not to wake them and then went back to Cass and shut that door on my way in too. I woke her up and started to talk to her but she kept telling me to leave. I didn't want to leave. I wanted to stay with her and the kids. I loved them and it was my home too, my place, my place to be. She wouldn't understand that. I told her again and again that I simply loved her and wanted to stay and be the father of our kids and love her forever. I always dreamt of us being happy together forever but I guess I was just fooling myself. I can see that now.

So what happened?

I had no choice. I had to do something. I leant over and put my hands around her throat and squeezed tight.

And why did you do that?

She laughed. She just laughed at me when I told her I loved her and would always love her. She just laughed. She has a wonderful laugh. We used to laugh a lot. She would always laugh at my fooling around. I could always make her laugh. But when I told her I would always love her, that's not something you should laugh at. What else would you expect me to do? I kept telling her I loved her and that we would always be together and she kept laughing. I bent down and put my cheek against hers and she did stop laughing at me then.

What happened after that?

I went and got myself a beer from the fridge. I didn't make her a hot chocolate like she usually had because I knew she wouldn't want it anymore. I checked on the kids again and they were still asleep so I gave them a little kiss and made sure they would sleep very deeply, and then I went back to the bedroom and got into bed. She was mine now. I had her forever. She would always know I loved her. It was the last thing she heard. I cuddled up to her to keep her warm.

Why did you do that?

We always used to cuddle like that. I would put my arms right around her and hold her tight and snuggle in and she would snuggle back. She was getting cold, and I could feel her big belly and something move inside. I liked doing that, cuddling together. It felt familiar. And now we'd always be together, happy, as a family. But love, that's just a lie.

Man Oh Man!

Five-four-three-two-one.

Mick got the feeling his time was up. The looks he was getting from them, the snide comments on his laid-back style, unfavourable comparisons to Moonie, or Dave Clark. As if someone whose greatest claim to percussive perfection was a tambourine would know. Meanwhile they were fussing over Davie like he was a new-born babe. A bass player, for fuck's sake, as if that was essential to a rock band. Despite Paul.

But if they wanted him out, he would not go without a last hurrah.

Like the charge of that light brigade, into a valley of death he would ride. Metaphorically speaking anyway; he was no hero.

Rather he would insinuate himself, more like the Greeks did in their wooden horse. He'd play them for Trojans. Sneaky rather than brash.

A germ of an idea wormed its way into his ear. 5-4-3-2-1. It was partly his, he could use it anyway he wanted. He would go out with a bang. Literally. After all, that was pretty much what and all he did: bang. Countdown to blast off. Ready, steady, out we go, uh-uh. A rock legend, never to be forgotten. Unlike Davie.

He kept to himself beforehand, stayed in the hotel room, ordered in, didn't answer the phone, drank lots. Toked some. Toked more.

He got himself ready. The usual: black skivvy, tartan strides, high-collared buttoned-up heavy grey jacket, black boots. He pulled the pistol out of his suitcase, wrapped in his pink sock. He held it and looked at it, checked the cylinder for bullets and placed it gently on the side table. He went into the bathroom, ruffled his hair, pulled up the skivvy around his neck and nodded in satisfaction. He went back to the pistol, picked it up and put it into his outside jacket pocket. It felt weighty and awkward there so he moved it to the inside pocket. The knock on the door told him they were ready for him.

The hall was a choppy sea of faces and a volcano of voices. The others were there already, all smiles and buddy-buddy. The words of someone at the microphone were echoing around the cavernous emptiness; he heard his name and those of the rest of the group amongst the clamour. The cheering became thunderous. He ran out onto the stage arms in the air with the others and stepped up to his personal little platform, spinning on his stool as he threw himself onto it, crashing the cymbals and giving the bass a few thuds.

They worked through their standard hits list, the fans screamed their worst, he got hotter and hotter in his heavy outfit and banged and banged harder and harder. He knew the order the songs would come in, and waited. The familiar organ chords fired up, sucked in and out, and off they went, those crass words of his. He banged and banged more and more manically until the final climactic flourish, then stood up, kicked over the cymbals, picked up the bass above his head and crashed it down onto the kettle and tom-toms. Pulling the pistol from his jacket he screamed out "5-4-3-2-1", and fired into the air. Then put the barrel to his temple.

The crowd loved it, the band jumped and yelled and cheered him on. He jumped off his platform and ran to the front of the stage, counted down and fired into the air again. This was fun, he thought. He put the barrel to his temple, shouted "Ready?". The crowd went wild, but he was beginning to wonder whether this really was the time to end it all, centre stage, top of the world.

Suddenly Davie was in his face.

"Hey, steady man, take it easy!" he shouted. "It's my last night, don't spoil it for me."

"Whadya mean?"

"They're dumpin' me, man, superfluous to needs."

Mick let the pistol drop to his side and stared at Davie. The screaming continued, Davie grabbed the pistol, fired it into the air till it emptied then threw it into the heaving mass below, took his bass guitar off his shoulder and smashed it over and over on the stage, threw his arms into the air and ran off.

And so Mick discovered it was not him they wanted to replace but Davie, the humdrum bassist. Poor Davie, all that pampering from guilt. Bloody paranoia.

And years later, a spicey reversal added a silver lining, as he was channelled into fame on 1-2-3-4 ... 5, Go! Lyrics were still crap, though.

Flicks

Bernard slumped into the armchair, staring around the room, thoughts of what had just happened to him swirling through his head. People. How they treated you, how they reacted to you. He tried hard not to run foul of others but it seemed there was something about him people took offence to. Maybe it was the types he mixed with. He was sure drug-taking was involved with some of them, but what could he do? You were who you were, did what you did. He would never understand fully, he concluded.

He looked at the painting of a cattle dog on the wall directly in front of him. His grandmother had painted it before he was born and given it to him just before she died. He liked it a lot, even though he had not known the dog. It reminded him of his grandmother whom he had loved, and it made him want to have a dog for his own one day.

He swept his gaze around and glanced briefly at a couple of other nondescript landscapes he had picked up in junk shops, hanging not quite squarely on the other walls; at the bookcase with its motley collection of mostly unread volumes propped up in a certain ordered disarray and interspersed with porcelain figures, an empty bottle of whiskey he kept in a vain and cheap attempt to recall the taste because it had been so good to drink, a vase of dried flowers, some photos of what family he had, a wax-caked candle holder, river stones and sea shells he had brought back from places where he had spent holidays, a large clock ticking almost indiscernibly; at the shabby sofa-bed he had dragged in from the street one garbage night and which he took naps on occasionally but never extended because nobody ever visited him; at the standard lamp in the corner, the coffee table with its oversize ashtray in front of the sofa. The television was on the blink and sat like a dark, brooding, malevolent alien in a corner, just waiting to pounce.

His eyes finally fixed on a clear bowl of water on the sideboard under the windows screened by jumbled Venetian blinds overlooking the street. Apart from the almost imperceptible seconds hand on the clock it offered the only action in an otherwise bleak, boring scene. He watched the goldfish flick its flashy feathery tail fin and wave its pectorals, then glide around the bowl, then flick and turn and glide the other way, its pouting lips now and then up against the glass, as if trying to get a taste of the outside world. Slurp, slurp; lick, lick. Did they have tongues, Bernard wondered. He recalled discovering how soft a cockatoo's tongue was, though it had more the appearance of a granite rock, when he stuck his finger in one's cage and the rock had touched it ever-so-unexpectedly gently. Those bulging pop-eyes of the goldfish seemed to be staring right back at him. It almost seemed as if it was expecting or even pleading to be fed, and probably was, like a dog or cat would, but in its fishy way. Or to be released, perhaps. Did it know it was a fish and recognise him as the human Bernard, his keeper and protector? How did it feel in that transparent prison? Trapped, or secure? Was he, Bernard, any better off than that goldfish, any more secure, any less trapped, any more or less happy?

The clock propped up between the books ticked time away. A knock came at the door. Bernard would have to get up and answer it, while the goldfish could carry on its contented, undemanding existence. He pushed his hands down on the arms of the chair and raised his reluctant body to its feet, hesitated, took a few steps over to the bowl and sprinkled some specks of fish food flakes from its container sitting next to the bowl onto the surface of the water. The goldfish spurted to the top and sucked them in eagerly. No tongue to be seen, Bernard noted.

More knocking. He turned and ambled over to the door, disengaged the chain lock, pushed down on the silver lever with one hand and turned the knob with the other, then pulled open the door to face his visitor, hardly knowing what he was doing.

The muzzle of the pistol was already pointing straight at his forehead and there was no registration by Bernard of the blast that came instantaneously, nor did the word "CUNT!" which was screamed at him find its way to his brain's language centre for conversion into meaning and understanding, nor was there any awareness on his part of the projectile that passed effortlessly through his skull and brain tissue, smashing the goldfish bowl on its way towards lodging itself in the gyprock-and-mortar wall beneath the window and its tangled louvres.

Bernard had ceased to exist well before his body lay crumpled on the floor, but the goldfish had just a little longer to contemplate, in its way, over the lingering pleasure of its last meal, the new freedom it had been afforded beyond the security of its transparent world, as it also lay, though not crumpled, on the same floor.

Flick, flicker, flicked.

A Brooch of Trust

She was front and centre of the group, all of them grinning enthusiastically into the camera, probably jiggling and fidgeting as well in anticipation of the indulgences to come, though that was not captured. A photograph could not lie. At least in those days. You can't be sure nowadays of course. Lies, fakes, fraud and spin abound. What can you trust?

The ruby was clearly visible pinned to the dress of Dior design over her heart and just below the large lapel of the low-cut shawl collar. It was hard to miss with its moody, 538-carat, deep vermilion depths surrounded and offset by a clustered ring of small sparkling white diamonds. There was nothing fake about this broadcast of success, though it was not so clearly explained whether it was truly owned or merely borrowed on account.

The police had been called to the luxury hotel in the early morning of the Sunday after the fancy-dress ball of the night before. The flamboyant billionaire had booked the entire establishment for himself and his young wife of four years, extended family and close friends, plus a few not-so-friendsy but necessary hangers-on for a week of socialising and fun and, no doubt, on the side, some arm-twisting business arrangements and forward planning into the bargain.

But not all went to plan. The ball was the centrepiece of the occasion and as the night drew on the abundance of food and drink, the intoxicating rhythm of the music, along with the conviviality, carried everyone away in a maelstrom of frivolity and excitement. They laughed and twittered amongst themselves and danced away as if the wonder of it all would never end. Sometime well into the wee hours of the following morning, however, somehow, someone noticed that the red ruby brooch had disappeared from the leading lady's chest.

There was no indication of how or when it had been removed or by whom, or if it had simply fallen off, though the over-confidence of the owners undoubtedly contributed to an opportunity afforded.

A high-pitched scream of horror cut through the general clamour. The anxious billionaire was quickly on the spot and, assessing the situation as heinous, demanded:

"Stop the music! Check everywhere and everybody, and then re-check. These crooks, these illegals, can't be allowed to get away with their crooked, pathetic deed."

A normally ruddy complexion which had become even more florid from his initial apoplectic reaction was now beginning to grow pale with the gloomy prospect of his failing to hold on to what was his, and of all the fun being cut short where it should have gone on indefinitely.

"I fought and worked hard and long for that amazing bauble so that my fabulous wife would have the pleasure of its beauty to complement her own. I will not see it pass from my grasp. This fantastic gem was a phenomenal turn-on for me. And now, my erection has been stolen!"

The breathtaking brooch was not found that night, nor for a few days more, but turned up again soon enough, the ruby miraculously transformed into a deep blue sapphire, worn proudly on another's breast, albeit suspiciously, contentiously and enviously, and as always, temporarily.

And despite how much the bloated billionaire trumpeted his displeasure, despite all his wealth and power and connections, despite all the half-crazed searching his friends and family did for him and despite all the trust he placed in the immutability of precious stones, the blue sapphire would not change back to ruby red.

The Lost Hour

Ray dumped himself on a stool, slumped against the bar and lifted his head to look at the clock, a huge antique creature which had probably adorned the wall since time immemorial. It was late. But not too late, nor late enough.

There were other shadowy presences in the place but Ray didn't care. He was only interested in the passing of time, and filling it in. The barman was a hunk, young and sullen, man-bunned, making sure his gaze was off into some superior distance and definitely not in Ray's direction.

"Can you do me a decent Old Fashioned?" Ray slung at him very loudly across the vast existential gap between them so the obnoxious prick couldn't ignore him by feigning otherworldly distraction.

The barman gave Ray the very slightest of disdainful acknowledgment by cocking his head and casting a brief glance towards him. He swung around and reached up to a shelf at the back of the bar, selected a tumbler with casual weariness, brought it down and slammed it on the bar, produced a sugar cube from somewhere under the bar and tossed it in, covered that with dashes of bitters also from somewhere under the bar, swivelled around and reached up again, snatched a bottle of whiskey from another shelf without seeming regard for its quality one way or the other and added some to the mix, stirred it all with a long-handled spoon until the sugar had dissolved, scooped in some ice, stirred again, stuck a slice of orange by its slit on the lip, dropped a spiked cherry in with a final flourish, and pushed it along in front of Ray, immediately walking away to the other end of the bar with a swagger and without a word, nonchalance intact.

Not bad, Ray thought, holding it up to eye level and tipping it slightly, contemplating the colour spectrum before him, from the deep red of the cherry through the golden brown of the rye to the orange and cream of the citrus rind and flesh, all fractured by the glistening glassiness of the ice-cubes, and was pleased. He drained the tumbler of liquid, sucked the spirit out of the ice as much as was useful and, leaving the adornments, banged it down on the bar.

"Same again. Hold the cherry. What time d'ya close?"

"Don't," the barman countered. Haughty, as if having to work all through the night attending to the fleeting demands of a bunch of inconsequential blow-ins was the supreme achievement of life.

The barman repeated the routine, minus cherry and flourish. Ray contemplated the reduced colour effect and part-emptied the tumbler, letting it drop onto the bar with the orange slice intact and the ice clinking.

He looked at the clock. It was later, but not enough later. Time was of the essence, and alcohol its flavour. Some of it needed killing. Bill Joel's *Piano Man* provided appropriate ambience and Ray hummed along.

"Same again. No orange."

The barman reprised.

"Cherry?"

"Just a passing fancy, didn't move me," Ray retorted with a self-satisfied grin. "Gi'us a double whiskey on the side."

Ray transferred the whiskey into the tumbler. He found it

easier to sip without fruit in the way. He looked around. People were huddled, murmuring amongst themselves. Occasionally excessive explosions of raucous laughter would erupt from one corner or another. *Piano Man* had given way to *The Pina Colada Song*. A couple sidled in and waved to the barman.

"Hey, Jackson."

"Hey, Jane, Billy."

"Same again, Jackson. Ditch the bitters," Ray giggled. He took a gulp and looked at the clock. It was getting later now, but so slowly. What was that about a watched clock, or was it a kettle? He put his head down onto his arms crossed on the bar.

When he looked up again Jackson was on a stool moving the little arm of the clock forward one wee, small hour. Time had killed itself. That hour was lost forever; Ray was saved temporarily. He looked at his glass. It was lighter. The ice had melted. He swigged it down and grimaced. He could venture home now, she'd be packed and gone. She would not be coming back, summer or winter.

Frank Sinatra was crooning *One For My Baby*. Ray took the cue.

"Jackson! Same again, double," Ray slurred. "And Jackson: skip the sugar, and spare the ice."

The Ninth Time

Tom had just begun loading his laundry into the third machine along from the entrance, the one he always tried to grab for no other reason than his being a creature of habit and it had been the first one he'd used there, when the old woman came in. She was po-faced, bedraggled and carrying a large, Union-Jack bag hugged up close against her chest.

Tom half-watched her with the cursory interest he would take in anybody at a laundromat. She didn't look at him or anything else with her head slightly lowered and eyes fixed on the floor, but went straight to the end machine with its lid up, awkwardly closed it with two free fingers and released the bag gently down onto it.

He thought he saw the bag move after it settled onto the lid while he was absentmindedly unravelling each item of his clothing and bed linen and dropping them into the tub of his machine.

Tom dribbled the detergent around on his jumbled bundle in the loaded tub,. He always brought his own with him to save money on the overpriced in-house offering. He pushed in the slot with its loaded token, pressed buttons, cocked his ear to listen for the sound of flowing water and then thought about how to kill the next thirty-six minutes.

Taking a seat on a bench with its daggy cushions, his back to the light from the window, he pulled out his paperback, found the turned-down corner where he had left off, and settled back to read on.

The woman had gone over to the counter where the Laotian owner sat watching raucous Asian soapies, banged some coins down, held up one finger followed by several fingers, picked up the tokens the owner had replaced the coins with, counting them out as he deliberately placed them in a row before her to avoid any confusion, and returned to the washer, not a word spoken. She put one token into the machine, pushed the slot in and the machine started. She picked the bag up off the lid of the machine and went with it over to the drier nearest the window and furthest from the owner, again fully involved with his televised silliness, put the bag on the floor and opened the porthole door.

Tom's cursory interest had continued between the lines of his novel and he was watching her more closely now. He felt certain that she had put nothing into the washing machine. The woman bent as if supplicating to the drier and unzipped the bag, pulled it open, reached in and pulled out a large ball of what looked to Tom like very dry rolled-up blankets, lifted it up in two arms to the porthole and then shoved it through and into the drum of the drier, pushing hard on the ball to get it all in. She closed the door and clicked several tokens into the drier's slot. They each dropped with a clink, she pushed a button and the drier started its rhythmic tumbling.

Tom was perplexed. She had an empty washing machine and a drier with dry bedding in it going simultaneously. She had taken the seat nearest her drier and was now watching it steadfastly. He stared at her quizzically and finally induced a glance back and eye contact, so cast a quick look at the washing machine and back, shrugged his shoulders and raised his eyebrows. The woman simply pointed to a sign Tom had seen before but had not taken much notice of.

'NO WASH NO DRY' it warned pointedly and clearly, with no need of superfluous punctuation.

Tom went back to his book but could not help checking on the woman and the drier occasionally. Round and round it tumbled, thick with reds, greens and black, yellow, blues and white, tossed around in a jumbled, uninterpretable mess, sometimes hovering in mid-air tantalisingly, then whipped suddenly out of sight.

Before Tom's wash had finished the woman's drier rumbled to a silent stop and she hopped up off the bench, popped open the porthole door, disgorged the contents, still a large ball of blankets much as before, stuffing them back into her bag on the floor in one go, squatting to finish. She lifted the bag with both arms hugging it to her chest as before, turned, and headed towards the door.

As she passed Tom she said: "They can die, y'know, if they stay wet too long after a wash and get cold."

Sadly though, neither Tom's curiosity nor a warm thirty minute tumble-dry was going to save this cat, this time.

Afterglow

Sylvia had lived in her small cottage sequestered away in a forested valley of the mountains for many years. She had built the cottage herself, beginning with just one room, slowly, section by section, until it was comfortable and suited her and so that any further extension would have been wasteful. A fireplace provided warmth for her and heat for cooking as well as some light at night, and she cut and split the wood she gathered from the forest floor for the purpose.

She had dug and hoed and fenced a vegetable garden and planted fruit trees, watered reliably from the perennially running stream nearby. She spent many happy hours pottering around in her garden. Along with the pulses and grains she stored in large air-tight vessels on shelves lining her kitchen walls, this produced more than enough for her nutritional needs, and her appetite.

In summer she washed in a shaded rocky pool in the same stream; in winter she sponged herself down while standing in a big tub in front of the fire. She read the books she had gradually accumulated, in the case of favourites usually more than once. Sometimes, especially on long winter nights, this was by the dull light of a single candle or a kerosene lamp. In later years she discovered the miracle of miniature light bulbs powered by small batteries and adapted them for her reading requirements.

She did not need, or want, the company of people. Apart from a few hens which scratched around the orchard and supplied her with eggs daily, roosting each night in a secure corner of the cottage's verandah for safety from predators, her own thoughts and the company of the forest and its creatures were more than enough companionship to keep her contented.

As often as was only necessary she would make the trek into the nearest town to replenish supplies she could not furnish by her own efforts. Occasionally old friends looked in, though less often as the years passed, or strangers blundered through. It never concerned her that she did not make such interlopers feel comfortable being there. She was always glad to see them go, and to be free to return to her routines and undisturbed contentment once more.

Among all the other delights the forest offered, fireflies had been welcome, regular visitors on hot summer evenings. They would float ethereally around amid the trees, like stars twinkling away in a dark foresty firmament, or teensy fairy lights flashing as Yuletide decoration, arrayed by forest nymphs for their own amusement. Sometimes they would be counterpoised by the faint high-pitched peeps and shadowy flitting of the tiny bats that lived in the crannies of the rock face above her garden. On such nights each month, when the moon was at full beam and any clouds had rolled away, it would cast faint, long, chiaroscuro patterns across the hillsides of the forest and down through her garden, resembling an ink-wash landscape by Sydney Long, and a fit setting for a bush idyll.

Many times she had interrupted her cooking or sewing or reading and dashed out to chase those elusive scintillations, often even simply gambolling amongst them in lost delight. She would let out little squeals of pleasure, wave her arms about and clutch at them, her hands fluttering like the pale moonlit wings of moths as she made her fruitless efforts to catch some. She dreamt of whisking them into and through her hair with her fingers and dancing around in the night like a character from Shakespeare: an enlightened Titania in her enchanted forest madness, or an incandescent Ophelia in the willow tree with her flowers, driven to her madness by men, though Sylvia did not make that connection in her musing, however accurate it may have been.

One time, spotting their arrival around her cottage, she thought that if she could collect some of these bright sparks she might use them for reading by in her little candlelit home. She had darted back inside and grabbed an empty jar from the shelf, then back out again to try to capture some, running amok, one hand waving the jar wildly in the air to scoop up specimens, the lid vainly at the ready in the other to thwart their escape. Each time she swooped, however, they had disappeared before her very eyes, just as miraculously as they would then suddenly reappear, out of reach somewhere else on their frolicking in the woods.

To this day she was unsure whether they had been real or not. Observing them as she did, free and fleeting as they rollicked around in their natural surrounds, was not enough to convince her or others - since she wanted so much to spread their story - that they actually existed, that such fantastical creatures could really be. Perhaps they were, in fact, sylphs, or from a faraway galaxy.

When such thoughts entered her head her mind would shoot off in imaginative flight through the forest searching out secret lairs and magical rings where these pixies might dwell and play. There were such places she knew of: glades and circular clearings and ancient trees with hollowed boles where she was certain gatherings of mystical creatures took place. Or she would soar radiantly through the ether to distant stars to find what might be hiding there. At other times she wondered whether the spirits of the forest were not communicating with her, sending messages to her by means of some arcane code which she had to decipher but never could. She tried flashing her torch at them to see if that would evoke a response; she trilled and yodelled and ululated but all to no avail. They merely kept up their silent, puzzling, dazzling behaviour for Sylvia to dwell upon.

On one of those balmy evenings a member of these ephemera became entrapped in the folds of her flowing dress, flaring frantically in its distress. She rushed inside and released it onto the table beneath her makeshift candelabra hanging overhead only to discover nothing but a dull, unremarkable bug in its place, and so remained just as uncertain as before about the secrets of their luminosity. Her fascination at the brilliance of their feat in drawing mysterious light from puny little exoskeleton frames which contained nothing but their cargo of squashable gunk never dulled. What worlds and realms there are beyond our ken and kin it made her think.

But those times were now gone. A combination of war and other human actions along with the forces of nature, some unleashed by the ravages of that war, devastated the entire landscape in every direction around her and no doubt beyond, though she did not know that for certain. Nor, ultimately, could she escape from what occurred beyond, but she could endure. She was resourceful, flexible, patient, independent. In some respects the new order suited her disposition. There were no longer any people to interrupt her solitude, nor it seemed were any were likely to appear again. After a short period of higher than normal activity the planes with their vapour trails and eerily delayed rumbling high above and the occasional low-flying military jets and helicopters with their disturbing and intrusive roaring and clack-a-clacking had completely stopped.

She kept her kitchen garden going as long as possible, harvesting everything, storing and preserving what could be. It was hard to say goodbye to all but two of her hens, they being like friends, but she honoured them by thanking them and saying a little prayer each time she consumed something of their bodies, even including the bones for flavouring the various pulse meals.

The two remaining hens she kept scratched around in the dying earth for less and less sustenance and she had to sacrifice some of her own victuals to keep them healthy. That was worth doing for the one or two eggs a day providing her with essential protein and vitamins, and delicious enjoyment.

As her forest slowly succumbed, taking its creatures with it, the paltry supply of berries and greens that it had once supplied also faded away, though mushrooms provided some welcome addition to her diet. She spent many hours searching them out and collecting them, having learnt from one of her books early on to distinguish the edible from the poisonous. At least firewood was plentiful for dealing with the cold that took hold of her world, so she kept her little house warm day and night.

After several seasons of darkness and little rain the skies gradually became forever clear, except for the clouds that sometimes billowed red at sunset on the eastern horizon, like the spectral sails of a giant heavenly vessel come to salvage remains. Sylvia steadily re-established her garden, managing to water it from the trickle in the stream that once rushed in excess as a torrent past her verandah. She was soon able to recharge batteries for her torch too, reclaiming her nights for reading.

But the fireflies didn't come any more. They stopped once the bush had all died off and the animals had all vanished. There were no other insects, nor flowers or leaves left for them to eat, no trees to play and hide in, nor even birds to sacrifice themselves to. The soil that cradled their newborns was still there but dry and rocky and lifeless, providing no succour. The gum trees that had shed their fawn bark every spring to stand gloriously in their fresh new pale-blue and green regalia had shed their bark one last time and were now a field of dun telegraph poles with limbs outstretched to a lifeless backdrop. The forest spirits had fled too, if indeed they had ever been in residence, since there were no longer any signs of them, no whispering noises or shrill calls, no vanishing silvery shadows at night, no musky, musty smells.

Sylvia in her starry-eyed and self-absorbed state had made no provision to preserve the forest or to renew it, by collecting seeds or growing potted seedlings, before it was too late.

And so, in her continuing melancholy of missing her otherworldly visitors and the futile longing for their return, she eventually draped strings of fairy lights, like those same miraculous ones she had first used as her reading lamp but now switched to fast-flashing mode, through a scaffolding of the branches of dead gum and wattle trees, now readily rechargeable with her solar collectors and the relentless sunlight. On some dark nights, when she ventured from her beleaguered hideaway, she switched them on so she could watch and dream and remind herself of what it had once been like in her mountain forest, those warm summer nights, long ago, although she no longer had the inclination to dance or sing.

Caved In

Sef cowered in his bunkered basement as usual. He had been cooped up there now for many months, overwhelmed by the burden of mandates, and was certainly feeling the strain of it. Cower was possibly an overstatement of his posture, but accurate metaphorically. He had ended up like this because his usual resilience had been undermined by constant warnings from authorities of impending catastrophe. He had learnt the word 'catastrophise' when he had received some counselling for depression and was warned not to do so, but it never occurred to him that governments and their agencies could fall into the same trap, with similar but more universal consequences. Now his devil-may-care attitude to life had deserted him as his confidence had been chipped away, so he had chosen to isolate himself from the imagined dangers. He was fortunate, in these circumstances, not to have family to miss or lose, job to keep, friends to stay in contact with, classes to attend, health issues to set aside for a while, no significant personal milestones to be celebrated, the public ones having been cancelled. His independent nature, his loneness, was now an advantage, though he was not too sure to what eventual end.

He was almost running out of wood for the small fire he managed to keep going at a low glow for cooking, a little warmth and its companionship. His food intake was down to what he poured and scraped from cans and packets and jars. He was able to keep his water supply topped up from dripping rainfall overflow. It was naturally filtered and went nicely with the whiskey he enjoyed in the evenings to unwind, though he missed the ice. There was not much to unwind from, but that was itself the problem: boredom, frustration, lack of human contact. It certainly helped him to get to sleep, though not to stay asleep.

He had long ago given up showering, the drainage in any case being totally inadequate to the task, making do with the occasional rub-down with Smart Wipes of which he had stocked up on early in the crisis, along with the whiskey. Flushing his waste was out of the question likewise, and he had failed to act quickly enough to ensure his supply of toilet paper which supermarket shelves had quickly been denuded of. Wrapped in newspaper and left to dry before the fire, the hard matter was a minor supplement to the fuel supply, encouraged along by the paper. He stored his urine and used it as a cleaning agent, or to spray on the bugs that appeared regularly, until there was too much and then he poured it under the verdant bushes growing around his entrance hoping for a reliable fuel supply.

The refuge was deeply embedded in its earthy environment. He had lived nearby for years, so he knew its secret. Most of what had been around on top had been demolished and razed and it now acted as an occasional carpark, but the basement cellars had been left like wombat burrows under ploughed fields. There was never any hope of getting radio or television reception, and it predated any provision for fancy cables or pipes.

His main entertainment and contact with the outside world had come from the newspaper, in addition to its peripheral usefulness. It was delivered each day, sometimes a loud thump from above in the early morning heralding its arrival. He had achieved this anomaly in his disconnection by signing up to a special subscription deal before he had succumbed to the bureaucrats' demands, the payment automatically deducted from his credit card, in perpetuity it would seem.

But as Sef cowered this particular day he felt uneasy. There was something amiss. The idea of venturing from the basement to go further afield and check things out began to stir in his thoughts. He had not heard a thump for several days and had found no newspapers when he had scrabbled around outside and fertilised the bushes. Perhaps a visit to the newsagent would be necessary. Then he could go to a supermarket as well. Re-stock, though he did not have high hopes for toilet paper. He decided he needed a list and over the next three days jotted down stuff as it came to mind. There had been no further newspaper thumps and his list was getting extensive.

The following day Sef put on his best outfit with his new sneakers which along with his other personal effects had remained aimlessly stored in closets and cupboards since his embunkerment, loaded his pockets with all the necessary accoutrements for a business trip, pulled on his gloves, donned his mask, climbed the stairs, checked once again for the newspaper in vain, fed the bushes, and set off.

There was an eeriness in the air from the start. A silence, a stillness. As Sef walked he saw nobody, heard no signs of human life whereas previously there had at least been some brave souls willing to defy the various decrees. By the time he reached the town it was clear to him there was something terribly wrong. Or rather, more wrong than it had been up to date. He recalled reading in the last newspaper delivered something about military activity in the Taiwan Strait and troop build-ups in Europe. Perhaps this time 'catastrophic' may be the accurate description.

He wondered a minute, then turned around, discarded the mask which suddenly seemed a useless relic of another age, no more than a badge of compliance even then, and headed back to his bunker. He felt he might be going to need that for some time yet, mandated or not.

Toeing the Line

He stood momentarily shivering, the towel he had been given wrapped around his waist. He stared at the nape of the neck of the man ahead of him. When he ventured to peek over the taller man's shoulders a little, to the left and right of that solid column of flesh and bone, the line of people stretched for as far as he could see. They had all also been provided with a length of plastic piping which they were to hold out against the lower back of the person in front. With the dividers being held between each of them it looked like a continuous human shish kebab.

He was not game enough to swing his head and check behind to see how far the line extended back, but he had the feeling it was much the same. They were all shuffling slowly forward as one. Without turning around he could not make out any expressions on faces, but a heavy silence hovered over the scene. He imagined the towel was for reasons of modesty and was grateful for that at least, though he did not understand why more protection could not have been supplied for the cold against which the towel achieved little. He wasn't sure how he had come to be in this endless line of people, it had just seemed to happen, had crept up and overtaken him. He was not a stupid man, he was well educated and experienced in life, but it was as if he had been mesmerised in some way, taken over by the primal power of a herd mentality.

He reached out and leant forward a little to tap the man's shoulder. The head turned slightly in acknowledgement.

"Where are we going?"

"No idea really, but I know we need to go there in order to survive, and that we are very lucky to do so."

He remembered something of the mess life had become in that past, not just for him, but was confused about why it had happened. It had simply crept up slowly and taken over for no good reason other than it was deemed necessary by authorities. Most had complied without protest, let alone defiance. He had not wanted to cause any trouble either and the pressure to conform was overwhelming. It had surprised him how easily he had forsaken parts of his lifestyle that meant so much to him: his family, his friends, dining out, theatre, cinema, live music, the beach and tennis, travelling overseas.

The line continued to shuffle forward as one, like a conveyor belt. As he came up a slight rise he could now see there was more than one line, many in fact, and that they were converging towards an area ahead where a great mass of people was congregating amidst much activity. But he could not see beyond that. Looking back now he could just pick out in the far distance people lining the horizon, still, and apparently just watching.

"What's that up ahead?"

"That's where everything will become safe," the man replied, turning just enough to direct his words back.

He felt excited now, with hope all would be well, that the sacrifices they had had to make were for the common good and the common good would be good for him.

As they approached the large pavilions with the thronging crowd his heart raced. He could see attendants in plastic robes wearing full facial masks with painted-on smiles guiding the towel-girt crowd through turnstile-like passages, all in silence except for a general murmuring of encouragement, reassurance and congratulations.

He was handed a map showing the way forward and crossed over, feeling nothing more than a slight tingle physically, but experiencing a definite relief, a lift in his emotions, a feeling of well-being and camaraderie with the crowd. Once through, everyone spread out and began to speed up. The man was next to him, walking swiftly.

"What now?"

"We are going to see how we can fly."

They were all running as fast as they could, dropping their towels and their plastic rods as they went. And as he hurtled over the cliff off into the precipice he did fly, just for a moment.

But a Whimper

The end of the world is coming. Sort of. Not the whole world. Just humankind. But slowly. Perhaps. Not with a bang, but a whimper.

Xinhua News Agency, 16th January, 2032

The Chinese Government has announced the implementation of a childbirth-free period to commemorate the year of the rat, a sign renowned for its intelligence and sociability. In order to stabilise and balance the development of the population in the interest of the nation's future prosperity and well-being, the Government will provide financial and other incentives to all couples who chose to delay starting their family for one year. It added that any children born under the sign of the rat this year would suffer throughout their lifetime the stigma of their birthdate.

The UN Fund For Population Activities welcomed the announcement adding all and any measures by governments which promote the fulfilment of every person's potential was to be applauded. China watchers in the West have however questioned the Chinese Government's motivation for the decision and have expressed bewilderment as to its actual demographic function given that country's previous relaxation of natality restrictions and impending problems with regard to the ageing of its population.

—

The Standard (circulation 74,000), Kenya. 20th January, 2032, page 7.

The Agha Khan University Hospital Nairobi Early Pregnancy Clinic has reported an unusually low number of women presented for pregnancy in the month of November and that no new pregnancies were registered in December. The clinic Director, Dr Marlene Mwaniki, has issued a statement saying that such an aberration was unprecedented but that various undocumented and as yet unknown factors could be at play.

—

The Zambia Daily Mail (circulation 13,000), 18th February, 2032, page 5.

The Maternity Teaching Hospital reports that no new pregnancies had presented for the year so far. The unusual statistic had been referred to government authorities and investigations were taking place to ascertain explanations for the phenomenon.

—

The Standard (circulation 74,000), Kenya. 11th March, 2032, page 3.

The Agha Khan University Hospital, the Karen Hospital and Gertrude's Children's Hospital have issued a joint statement expressing their surprise and concern at the absence of any new presentations of pregnancies since December of last year. They have set up a consultative committee with the Department of Health to look into the matter.

—

The Guardian Newspaper (readership 2,134,0000). London, 5th April, 2032, page 9.

Jessica Newby writes:

Maternity Hospitals and neo-natal clinics in East African nations have been reporting surprising turndowns in pregnancy presentations since the beginning of this year. Some reports coming through and responses to enquiries seem to suggest that in many areas no new pregnancies have been registered at all. Government agencies in Zambia, Kenya, Zimbabwe and Tanzania are investigating the situation but no official statements have yet been forthcoming. Unconfirmed reports have been quoted as claiming similar marked reductions or absence of new pregnancies have also been noted in parts of South Africa and Namibia. Investigations and enquiries are continuing, but international agencies claim reportage inadequacies are probably the cause of the inconsistencies.

—

The Australian Newspaper (circulation 198,500), 21st May, 2032, page 8.

The Australian Antarctic Division has lodged a complaint against the Chinese Antarctic Administration (CAA) following their refusal to allow inspections of their four Antarctic bases against the rules of the Antarctic Treaty. The Australian team had been carrying out a routine tour of various bases and was planning on making a return visit to the Chinese bases after the Chinese had sent teams earlier in the year around bases of several other nations along with other reciprocal inspections. The CAA has not responded.

—

The Guardian Newspaper (readership 2,134,000). London, 2nd June, 2032, page 4.

Jessica Newby writes:

Reports circulating widely concerning the absence of new pregnancy presentations by East African women have now been confirmed by government and non-government agencies. The causes of this apparent divergence from the norm is currently unknown although any diminution of the usual associated behaviour as a prerequisite for pregnancy has been discounted on the basis of general observation and hearsay. In any case the situation now has many officials both government and private very concerned. It is believed that the matter has been referred to the United Nations Economic and Social Affairs Secretariat for investigation.

———

The New York Times (circulation 2,101,000), 14th October, 2032, page 1.

Benjamin Cohen writes:

The United Nations Economic and Social Affairs Secretariat has issued a statement based on its latest collation of figures gathered internationally stating that it can confirm that there have been nil new human pregnancies registered anywhere in the world since September this year though it is possible there have been unnotified ones. It added that in the pregnancies that were known to be in progress there had also been a marked increase in miscarriages.

———

Frettabladid (circulation 70,000), Reykjavik, Iceland, 29th June, 2033, page 1.

The Government has issued a statement reporting the latest birth of a baby boy in Reykjavik last night taking the population to 346,238. As there have been no further pregnancies presented for the past nine months in Iceland it is believed that this birth will be the last until human fertility returns and that the population will now steadily decline. Following UN studies it is also believed to be the last birth that will occur worldwide for at least the next nine months, the total human population of the world therefore reaching around 8 and a half billion, and now falling.

———

The Guardian (readership 2,126,000), London, 23rd November, 2033, page 3.

From Jessica Newby, Chief Investigative Reporter:

As the world reels from the unwinding catastrophic news of total human infertility that has swept through one country after another, scientists, technocrats, politicians and academics have begun applying themselves to the task of sorting it all out and most importantly, finding a solution. Now known as the Human Infertility Precipitating Virus (HIPV) it is part of the same family as HIV which caused the disease AIDS that swept the world in the 1980s. Reaction to the critical hidden sterilising effect of the viral infection was retarded since infection with the virus caused no obvious immediate or even long-term symptoms in those infected. Nevertheless, infection with the virus seems to have been universal. Many months were lost while the virus spread globally, authorities failing to instigate crucial quarantine measures, oblivious to its world-shattering consequences. Unlike the Covid-19 pandemic from 2020 which the global community dealt with rapidly and efficiently and which, ironically, distracted medical, scientific and political leaders from the much greater threat, by the time the world became aware of what it was dealing with the virus had reached virtually all points of the globe and meaningful intervention was futile. Lockdowns, shutdowns, quarantine, social distancing, self-isolation, border closures, were all pointless with this pandemic. The latest report from Reykjavik of the last known human birth has triggered announcements of feverish planning into research and technological application, as well as the arrival of a new world order: peak humanity. From now on, for nine months at least, and more likely several years unless something drastically changes naturally, the world human population will be in continuous decline. Other crises such as climate change, natural disasters, the war on drugs, financial or economic challenges, resource sufficiency, famine, endemic diseases and certainly overpopulation - although, unfortunately, probably not war - have suddenly paled into insignificance before the terrifyingly real possibility of the end of humanity and civilisation.

What we know or at least best understand so far is that there was a minor mutation in an adeno-associated virus, the type often used as a vector in gene therapies utilising the fairly common and relatively easy CRISPR method, and that this mutated virus was used in some medical procedures in China. The virus causes sterility in human males by interfering in some way with sperm germ cells. What appears to have happened then is that the virus slowly spread through contact, and possibly also through airborne transmission, and spread rapidly through international travel and exponential growth until it had gained a foothold in every corner of the globe where humans are found. The large number of Chinese now working and living in east Africa, as well as Africans travelling to and from China are thought to have been the first to spread the virus. It is possible that officials in China knew earlier of the fall-off in pregnancies but kept the figures under wraps. So, scientists are currently focusing on how this virus can be stopped from infecting men (and even women as it also seems it can cause miscarriages), or even better, reversing the action of it in men already infected. The problem is that apparently all men and boys including the newly born, though this won't be verifiable for a while yet, may have already been infected. Hence the development of any vaccine may be of no use whatsoever since there is, and will be, nobody to inoculate. Three cosmonauts currently resident in the International

Space Station hold out some hope for humanity that they have not been infected. Again, there will be no way of ascertaining whether they managed to escape infection before leaving earth until they have been tested. Tests will be carried out on them once reliability has been proved and kits can be safely delivered. Decisions have been made to hold them in orbit indefinitely until such time as the situation clarifies. The possibility of any temporary inhabitants of the many national bases in Antarctica being virus-free have been discounted due to the regular interaction amongst them. With the exception of the Chinese bases, testing has been carried out and no male has been found to be fertile so far. As it seems that the virus had its origin in China it is believed the Chinese were already infected before being stationed in Antarctica and spread the virus to other bases there. Apart from these slim prospects the only option is for a 'cure' for those infected. If its effects can't be reversed the future looks bleak, very bleak indeed. In fact, as bleak as bleak could be.

———

The Times of India (circulation 3,153,000), May, 2034, page 6.

The Government of India has announced that it has reinforced its blockade of North Sentinel Island in the Andaman group as a *cordon sanitaire* to ensure the biological security of the Sentinelese people. Indian warships are on permanent patrol around the island and have been ordered to allow nobody through the blockade, without exception. The Government has stated further announcements concerning the situation there will be forthcoming. It is understood however that a relaxation in the prohibition on visiting the island that occurred in late 2018 has allowed some scientific contact to take place in secret since then opening up the possibility of contagion. There have been suggestions also that there were fatalities among islanders from Covid-19 in 2020 indicating contact had probably taken place reducing the prospects of exclusivity.

—

The Bay Of Plenty Times, Tauranga, (Circulation: 11,254), October, 2035, page 5.

Roger Fraser's Local Affairs Column, 'Plenty To Talk About':

The maternity and neonatal facilities at Whakatane, Tauranga, Murupara and Opotiki, which have been running on empty now for over 3 years but have remained on standby just in case a little miracle popped up, have finally given up hope and been closed. They will be re-fitted by the Health Service for general medical use. Obstetric and neonatal specialist staff will receive re-training in general medicine. New Zealand's youngest citizen, Ian Fraser, yep, relation, my son in fact, who happened to be born right here at Murupara, is doing just fine and will turn 3 next April. You can expect another big party for him, all welcome.

—

El Pais, (circulation 1,157,347), February, 2038, page 1.

The World Health Organisation, with the new powers to determine certain international matters conferred upon it recently, and in conjunction with the governments of all the world's nations, announced today that every male human on earth, man and boy, would be tested for his fertility. "This is not something in the light of developments that we can leave to natural circumstances. If there is a man with viable sperm anywhere out there we must find him. The fact that no pregnancies are occurring does not mean that there is not viable male human sperm somewhere - not every male human tests his fertility naturally", a representative of the British Government added. The WHO statement added that the testing would be mandatory for all males and there would be penalties for non-compliance. Individuals who refused would be given one month to agree to testing after which they would be forced to submit a sample. Few were expected to dissent. Each nation would conduct the tests in its own style. Civil liberty groups in the United States and Europe have protested but they have been virtually ignored by governments and supra-national organisations.

———

The Los Angeles Times (circulation 900,000), 21st May, 2041, page 3.

Scientists have admitted failure in their attempts to clone humans from female human eggs, stating that "the infertility virus that had affected male spermatozoa seemed to have also caused irreparable damage to human eggs." They have stated however that considerable advances have been made in the combination of stem cell research and cloning. Already there have been successful examples of the cloning of mice and rabbits using the procedure. Experimentation with human tissue had begun some time ago and progress has been made. Governments have lifted all previous restrictions on such work and it is expected there will be intensified research into this promising line of enquiry.

———

The UN Convocation On The Survival Of Humanity.

Media Release, 1st January, 2042.

It is estimated that the current population of the world is around 8 billion people. Given no extraordinary events such as pandemics, war or multiple natural disasters which would cause the human mortality rate to increase dramatically, it is expected without further births that the decline in population will continue at a steady rate and result in a human population of around 6.5 billion in 2067, about the same it was in 2004.

———

The Bay Of Plenty Times, Tauranga, (circulation: 10,129), August, 2045, page 3.

Roger Fraser's Local Affairs Column, 'Plenty To Talk About':

The Education Minister has reminded us that the last primary school will cease operating at the end of this year and flagged the end of secondary schools by 2041. The former primary school buildings will be used with minimal conversion for adult further education initially, as will the former high schools and colleges once they are decommissioned. There are plans for them later to be converted for other uses, particularly housing for seniors. Ian is off to college in the new year and is looking forward to that, for sure. Big celebrations are planned for the last-ever class at his local primary school before the Christmas break.

———

Leipziger Volkszeitung (circulation, 97,000), Leipzig, 22nd November, 2046, page 7.

An announcement from the Max Planck Institute for Evolutionary Anthropology has thrown new light on the causes, challenges and possible solutions of the human infertility catastrophe. They have confirmed that it is the AAV virus that started the devastating disease and that there has been little progress in devising some way of reversing its sterilising effects in male humans. It appeared that the virus affected humans exclusively and no other animals seem to be susceptible. Though the virus could now be stopped that was no longer of any benefit given that all males had been infected and sterilised. They have put forward various options for areas of future action: cloning, DNA and stem cell technology, cross-species fecundation, artificial intelligence and hybridisation, medical advances in longevity, cross-species transplantation, prehistoric archaeological expeditions in search of frozen individuals, synthesis of the entire human genome, and experimental research in hitherto unknown territory. Analysts have subsequently pointed out that this announcement in reality does not augur well for any rapid progress in finding a solution.

—

The Washington Post (circulation, 386,000), 5th February, 2049, page 1.

President Angelina Jolie, in her address to the nation yesterday, with Vice-President Elon Musk in the Speaker's Chair behind her, said, in part: "We now live in a childless world. In this doomsday scenario in which we humans find ourselves, this unprecedented challenge that faces humanity, there are no invisible enemies, no evil empires, no demons, no battlefields, no line in the sand, no final victory to be strived for, no struggle for supremacy. No longer can we dream of a future in which we have colonised other parts of our solar system. There is only hope for a deliverance which we must hold securely in our hearts as assuredly as the sun will rise tomorrow, though it may have set today. There is no quick fix for this, the greatest threat to our species ever, greater even than the threat of total nuclear war that has hung over us for a century. I have directed, as my predecessors have done, that every possible resource at our disposal, at the expense of all other projects and programs, be focused on finding a solution, no matter how long that may take. The best minds in science, all over the world, are directing their ceaseless attention to the problem. They are working together since there is no cause for competition between nations in this universal challenge for humankind. The task is daunting, but we have many years yet, in fact the rest of our lives, in which to succeed, and we must keep our resolve. In the meantime we will live life to its utmost and maintain our humanity towards all our kind, wherever they may be, and to our fellow creatures of the earth we share, and we will keep the faith."

—

www.aljazeera . com > news > 2052/10/18

President-Protector of Turkmenistan, Serdar Berdymukhamedov, 70, has announced their current policy of not permitting any citizen under 40 to leave the country will be amended to include those under 50. This policy, which has been in place for decades to prevent population decline, has for the last 20 years also served to maintain the lowest possible median age for the country now standing at 55. Other countries have followed suit over time including even some of the liberal democracies which have used laws such as Public Health provisions to enforce them. It is expected more countries will implement such bans.

―

Pet Life Magazine, June, 2054, main article.

A marked increase in pet ownership has accompanied the progressive decline in the world's human population. The lack of children worldwide and the prospect of never having children, especially for those of what will possibly be the last human generations now embracing the age of parenthood, has led to a desire for a substitute brood. And what could be more suitable than a couple of dogs or cats or indeed a whole menagerie? As an example, from an estimated 200 million pet dogs in the world in 2020 there are now calculated to be more than 1 billion pooches in over 500 million households. The numbers for felines are similar, and for other animals, particularly birds and fish, even greater. In non-urban areas with a tradition of keeping animals, the increase has been less. Nevertheless, horses, cattle, sheep, goats and various poultry have become part of families in larger numbers. With a relaxation in the laws, or application of them, the times have seen a growth in the number of unusual pets, particularly primates, perhaps as an attempt to replace as closely as possible that which is now missing from human family life.

―

The UN Convocation On The Survival Of Humanity.

The population of the world today, December 31st, 2057, is estimated to be around 7,000,000,000 and falling.

—

The Baltimore Sun (circulation 95,000), 16th August, 2059, page 5.

Scientists from the MIT today admitted they had succeeded in fertilising chimpanzee ova by inserting human genomes but that the results had been "disappointing" and experiments concluded. Further work would now be carried out applying new technology to a variety of prospects involving other simian ova and human chromosomes. Scientist expressed their optimism over the latest developments. Opposition from ethicists, while being expressed, has been muted.

—

National Geographic (circulation 3,250,000), March, 2068, page 7.

'Triumph Of The Unwanted'

Environments all over the world have long been under threat, and often overcome, by animal and plant species alien to them. With no natural predators to keep them under control, superior competitive capabilities or simply having human patrons, they flourished and survival of the fittest became explosion of the blessed. Rabbits, crown-of-thorns starfish, cane toads and prickly pear cactus in Australia, Australian black wattle and paperbark trees in return, Asian carp in Europe and America, water hyacinth, foxes and mongoose, camels, goats, cats and horses, starlings and mynas, crazy ants and mosquitoes. And the most successful global coloniser of all: humans. It was ironic that human action was generally the only defence, or at best rear-guard action, against these exotic invasions. And so now that human intervention has become gradually less and less viable with the reduction in our numbers (ironically again) the reality and finality of the incursion of these interlopers has become part of the accepted new natural-world order.

—

Beijing Daily (circulation 230,000), 2nd June, 2071, page 10.

Government officialsdmitted that scientific experiments on human ova using spliced human and simian sperm impregnation have resulted in some viable embryos, all of which were male and were discontinued. Further work is planned and officials expressed their "hope for positive developments".

—

La Repubblica (circulation 98,000), 8th February, 2073, page 1.

The Italian Minister for Immigration today announced that Italy would open its borders unconditionally for all people under the age of 50 who wished to come and live in Italy. Some financial and other incentives such as free travel to an Italian city of choice would also be offered for people in certain professions such as doctors, nurses, trained aged carers and cooks, but there would be no restrictions on all others except for convicted criminals.

—

Suddeutscher Zeitung (circulation 134,000), February 9th, 2073, page 1.

The German Chancellor today matched yesterday's announcement by the Italian government stating that anyone in reasonable health under 60 with the capacity to join the workforce would be welcome to migrate to Germany from that moment. All new citizens would be given a home of their own on perpetual lease, a motor vehicle of German manufacture, a preliminary lump sum payment and would be provided with a suitable job within one week. Reports from reliable sources suggest that other European countries will shortly follow the lead of Italy and Germany.

—

Jane's Defence Weekly, August, 2075.

The United States Armed Forces are now considered by most experts to be entirely automated, computerised, and run by artificial intelligence. All frontline fighting weapons are pilotless, driverless, human-free. Satellites and lunar-based control systems determine all military responses, overseen by human decision-making at the Pentagon, White House and other management centres. It is believed that the Chinese had already achieved this status some time ago and that European military machines will join them within two years. This is partly due to the rapid advances following enormous investment in technology, and partly due to the growing dearth of potential warriors in these jurisdictions. Meanwhile, in the recently formed United Islamic Crescent comprising the Moslem nations Indonesia, Pakistan, Bangladesh, Iraq and Egypt and others, and in India, both with more in the youngest cohorts, and between whom serious conflict has already occurred, frontline troops remain predominantly human, at least for a few more years.

—

The UN Convocation On The Survival Of Humanity.

The population of the world today, December 31st, 2080, is estimated to be around 5 billion people and falling. The lower figure than previously estimated is mainly due to the large loss of life through famine and communal conflicts, plus declining health services. The revised population estimate for 2090 is 3 billion people, about the same as in 1960.

—

The New York Times (circulation 467,000), 22nd June, 2085, page 1.

President Donald Trump Jr today announced that the Mexican Wall, built by his grandfather of the same name and title over 65 years ago, would be pulled down and that entry into the United States for all able-bodied people under the age of 60 would be encouraged. Housing, employment, motor vehicles and initial financial support would be provided to all those eligible for entry. The realty was that the Wall had become of no practical purpose for many years and had bcome considerably dilapidated as migration from Mexico to the United States had gradually slowed to a trickle and then essentially stopped. Living conditions in Mexico had improved while opportunities for employment in the US had diminished. The median age of the US now standing at 72, that is half the population was between 52 and 72 and the other half over 72, meant that there was an increasing, indeed snowballing need for aged care and carers. The case of Mexico was similar, though less pronounced, but with the family and family ties being more solid and important, fewer people were interested in or prepared to leave family members who were growing more infirm and needed ongoing daily assistance. Analysts believe that the latest measure to encourage younger Mexicans now to migrate would have little effect on migration numbers. Indeed many commentators are predicting that migration could start to go the other way as older Americans decided to up and move to warmer locales in Mexico where they could set themselves up very comfortably and tap into a younger reservoir of potential aged carers for their twilight years.

—

Media Release from International Olympic Committee, 24th January, 2089.

The Executive Board (EB) of the International Olympic Committee (IOC) today announced that the 2096 Olympic Games, the Games of the LI Olympiad, would be the last ever.

"It has now been very many years since the IOC has been

able to call upon the youth of the world to gather to celebrate. Nevertheless, humankind, of an ever increasing age, has managed to continue to come together to celebrate human achievement in sport and physical exertion, as has been done every four years for almost 200 years. In 1896, 280 participants gathered in Athens to compete in 43 events in the first modern Olympic Games. At that time there were around 1.5 billion people in the world. We have decided that it will be only appropriate for the last ever Olympic Games to be held in Athens in 2096. By that time it is expected there will be around 2.5 billion people living, all over 64 years old. We expect at those final Games there will be a strong focus on the dignity of elderness," said IOC President Momiji Nishiya. "By 2100 the youngest person in the world will be 68. We do not consider such age to be an insurmountable hurdle for physical competition and outstanding performance. However, the infrastructure, organisation, communication and transportation support mechanisms for such an enterprise would by then be impossible to implement. We expect, and will encourage, individual national Olympic Committees to continue to hold their own celebrations of the expression of human vigor well into the 22nd century."

The New York Times (circulation 325,000), Fall, 2093, page 9.

The World Convocation on Human Species Survival has reported that the youngest living human being was 60 years old. In its statement it also advised that the present population of the world was less than 3 billion and was expected to fall more rapidly than previously due mainly to the ageing population. The revised estimate for 2103, by which time the youngest person will be 70 years old, and with no new births, is now less than 2 billion, similar in number to that in 1950, though with the decline in support systems of all types it is possible it could be considerably less.

—❧—

The Bay Of Plenty Times, Tauranga, (Circulation: 500), 22nd April, 2097.

Ian Fraser's Local Affairs Column, 'Plenty To Talk About':

Hi everyone. Another birthday rolling around and everyone is invited as usual. We're all getting a bit long in the tooth now and with things as they are you need to keep your pencils sharpened. All those skills we thought would be taken up by the young-uns for our benefit are going to have to come from our own tool boxes. Another milestone next week: 65. All welcome.

—❧—

The New York Times (readership 394,000), Summer, 2098, page 5.

The UN Convocation on Human Infertility (UNCHI) today released its latest report on the human population crisis stating that there were no longer believed to be any female humans of child-bearing age. However, they added, there were many thousands of human eggs being held in cryogenic conditions in the hope of future scientific breakthroughs. It added that the human population could now only be roughly estimated due to conflicts and deteriorating record-keeping and communications, but is now less than 2 billion.

—❧—

The New Yorker (readership 158,000), June, 2099, pages 1-9.

Special feature: 'The Great Revival' by Lucien Lee.

(In part)

The extinction viral pandemic which has terminally afflicted humankind for the last 67 years has taken its inevitable toll on humanity but has had some very different, some might say ironic effects otherwise. With populations, economies and societies everywhere contracting and ageing organised warfare has virtually ceased, for example. Localised unrest still occurs but is generally of a much more benign nature. The reality that most people are now in their 70s and 80s being one key factor. And just as conflict has been localised so have most other aspects of life. Overseas trade and travel have shrunk to almost nothing while the use of bicycles and horses has increased as has neighbourhood walks, with or without pet dogs and chimps whose numbers have soared ... There are more and more shortages or some products, particularly highly processed or manufactured items of all varieties, but local produce has been successfully substituted, along with the large stockpile of unused and unneeded non-perishables ... Homelessness is a thing of the past, legal ownership of developed property having long fallen into disarray. High rise apartments were the first to be abandoned as uninhabitable, then apartments generally, and most fell into disrepair and ruination creating urban deserts in previous mega-cities. Everyone now lives in fully self-contained housing, predominantly alone but within easy walks of each other ... The great strides that were already being made in sustainable energy, small-scale solar in particular, and storage, have fortuitously ensured the continuation of power supplies, another key factor in the maintenance of a civil, functioning society ... Medical and health services have shown surprising resilience, partly due to the advances in medical science made in the early decades of the pandemic plus the easy availability of pharmaceuticals which were produced in enormous quantities, accumulated in storage and privately hoarded by a market rapidly decreasing in numbers ... And then there is the environment. Pollution is virtually unknown. Climate change back to its natural cycle. Nature is reclaiming its dominion everywhere. Fish stocks have exploded, whale protection is no longer necessary. Indeed, there is no longer any need for protecting any species, the inexorable constriction of human activity has done that automatically. Cattle, sheep, pigs and poultry are the exception, their numbers already severely depleted and many gone feral, but they will just have to adapt. Widespread regeneration of deforested areas of Amazonia, Nigeria, Congo and Borneo and elsewhere has been reported as occurring more rapidly than expected ... Whether we like it or not, and obviously we don't, the human extinction pandemic has proved a saviour for the world at large.

—

The Australian Newspaper (readership 47,000), Special Edition, 2101, page 3.

Simon Patel reports:

Information has been filtering through in the last few days that agents of the National Geographic Human Vestige Team in New Guinea, part of the worldwide network of questors in search of any sign of human resurgence in remote parts, have located a 30-year-old man in a near-inaccessible valley of the highlands of Papua. It is believed images and DNA samples of the man were taken and will be available in the next few days. Intense interest has provoked a wave of speculation and expedition planning in the hope that there may be other humans, particularly females, of similar age in the area.

—

The UN Convocation On The Survival Of Humanity in its final statement today, December 31st, 2109, before it ceased operations forever, stated that there were estimated to be less than 500,000,000 people alive in the world, about the same as is estimated in 1600, that this was about as much of a guess as it would have been then, and that the youngest known person was 76 years old. Most of these survivors lived in the developed world since, while Africa and parts of Asia had the youngest populations, their health and social systems were not up to the task of maintaining an environment capable of sustaining an aged population. It further estimated that the last person on earth, probably a woman, would certainly die by 2140 at the latest but more probably by 2123 or even earlier - though this would never be known for sure - as all support systems collapsed or disappeared making life sustainability at great age untenable. It added that most repositories of human ova had also now ceased operating due to power failures or war and other causes and that it was assumed any deposited examples had now become unviable. Further, it said, reports of younger people existing in remote areas such as Papua and Amazonia had not been possible to confirm and were therefore dismissed as unreliable and false.

The Bay Of Plenty Times, Tauranga, (Circulation: 15), 25th April, 2115.
Ian Fraser's Local Affairs Column, 'Plenty To Talk About':

Sadly, we have to announce the death yesterday of Charlie Wrack, aged 92, and also that of good ol' Wiley, although I'm sure you all probably knew already. Charlie had lived in the same house he was born in all those years and Wiley, you'll remember, wandered into town looking worse for wear but with a permanent wag displaying a happy disposition and took up with Jean about 12 years ago. That leaves me and George, but we're still kicking so you girls watch out (except for you-know-who course because you've got each other, lucky yous). That will also reduce our weekly circulation to just 14 (Jean used to read it to ol' Wiley because he never learnt to read of course) but we don't plan to shut down the photocopier yet and we promise to keep getting all the latest news to you as it happens, or not too long after anyway, and always provided we can keep finding supplies of that bloody photocopying powder ink and the copier doesn't break down. Oh, and don't forget my birthday in a couple of days, the usual big shindig.

—

Word of e-mouth, 2116.

Reports filtering in from Africa through to the outside world are suggesting that a totally isolated human-like population has been detected living in a huge underground cave complex somewhere in the east of the Democratic Republic of Congo. The area is so remote that its exact location is unknown but stories, some circulating widely and with reasonable prospects of validity, indicate that there has been certain cautious observation recently. There are no plans to verify the reports and in fact there is little ability to do so in any case. The stories that have been circulating for some time suggest there is an enclosed eco-system sustained by underground watercourses and sunlight streaming through complex chimney systems, but that access is near-impossible.

—

The Bay Of Plenty Times, Tauranga, (Circulation: 9), 25th April, 2107.

Ian Fraser's Local Affairs Column, 'Plenty To Talk About':

Hi there all. Thought I might as well put down on paper what we all talked about over the last week - those of us who can still talk that is - especially since I came across a brand spanking new ream of paper up the back of the storage shed yesterday, should see us out I reckon. No news as such to write of and everyone knows about everyone else's aches and pains and comings and goings, but heck, got a tradition to keep up here. Except to mention the rumours scurrying around the withernet of a humanoid race supposedly holed up in a giant, ah, hole, in the Congo. Well, I'd have to say these stories are, a bit like those old internet scams, straight out of Africa.

Continental Capers

Joshua, as always, had taken the seat one away from the window so that Jessica would get the view without having to crane her small body over his, not that Josh ever minded having Jess' body pressing against him. So it was that they both peered out the oval window as the SupRa Skycoach they had boarded just three hours previously approached the rugged coastline. Its sola-wings glistened like mirrors as it banked and descended to land at the recently completed airport, close to that coast. Josh leant right across Jess to see fully, and they were stunned by the breathtaking sight. They could have donned the drop-down augment-viewers for a panoramic tableau, but sometimes there was simply no beating old-fashioned reality.

What they saw was an overarching greyness, unrelieved by any organic green, as the defining tone of a wild, craggy landscape. It stretched far into a distance where mountain ranges, impressive even from this height, formed a jagged horizon, topped with the brilliant whiteness of snow spreading down the slopes into the valleys, all bathed in intense sunlight. As the stratocraft flew closer and lower they could see that that greyness came from the granite rockiness of it all.

They passed over the littoral and watched huge white-water sprays crashing against shoreline boulders and reaching high into the air, but nowhere near as far as the top of the enormous precipitous cliff faces. These were dark from the constant wetness, and possibly moss or lichen clinging to their rugged facades, and provided a kind of formal entrance feature to the lighter grey beyond, like an enormous, endless protective fence in both directions.

The Skycoach glided in, wavering slightly as it adjusted itself, then touched with a tiny bump and correction, and they were whizzing along a tarmac. Buildings now dominated the scene, flashing past on both sides, all of them shiny and modern, products of the huge investment that had been made here in anticipation of even greater returns. They slowed into taxiing mode and finally swung around to pull into a disembarkation module, came to a halt, and the various unloading procedures began.

Jessica and Joshua, chattering and peering around in every direction like children to take it all in, tripped along and out through check-points, all efficient and welcoming. With their luggage trundling along closely behind them in e-tow they found the autodock and claimed their pre-arranged rental vehicle, a late-model autonomous all-electric number: the Solrayzer Aura self-balancing two-wheeler - as smooth as riding a sunbeam, the ads proclaimed.

As Josh checked over the styling and mechanics he chuckled.

"It's so cool how these things are being called 'autos' again."

"I thought they were always called 'autos'."

"Yes, early on, but it came from 'automobile' and fell out of fashion for a while."

"So it's a sort-of updated upgrade, an example of a same difference, then. Let's just call it a car and hoon off into the sunset," she urged with a giggle.

"Well that'd sure be a helluva long drive here," Josh shot back as they touch-opened the sliding doors and peeked inside for a quick inspection before hopping in.

There were, they had been assured, plug-in sockets right along their route so there would be no risk of outages.

Inexhaustible amounts of power were available here apparently, all sourced from the solar arrays and wind turbine farms, both forms of energy abundant, along with the oil, gas and volcanic thermal. They had done plenty of research and had decided on the road-driving option and not the magrail-tube which ran alongside the paved Payway. They wanted to take their time, stopping where they felt like it in the purpose-built, self-contained units, and utilising some of the walking tracks that had been constructed by the Tourism Co-ordinating Authority at interesting sites along this, the only route across the vastness available to the public. As they stepped out into the sunshine for the first time, they could feel the dry, cold, crispness of the air, taking deep breaths, delighting in its obvious pristineness.

The sleek vehicle was primed, pre-programmed as requested and waiting, and they drove off singing 'On The Road Again', the old Willie Nelson version from 1980, at the top of their voices. It had become a tradition for them to burst into the song as they set out on any of their road-holiday adventures. Josh could remember his father and mother doing the same thing when he was a boy heading off on holidays in the family's old internal combustion Toyota. Traffic was heavy at first but they had known this would be the case now that the previously off-limits territory had been opened up for tourism and had become so popular. The congestion eased off once they were out of the System Commercial Zone – Ess-See-Zee they had heard some Americanos at the airport pronouncing it confusingly, they would have rhymed 'Z' with 'red' - and the Payway was wide enough to accommodate the flow, so they settled down into cruise mode to enjoy the scenery as it passed by.

And what scenery it was, desolate but magnificent, unlike anything they had experienced before. The coastal heathland with its low level drab-coloured shrubbery gradually became more dispersed and finally disappeared giving way to those rocks and boulders and the stony desert they had seen as a Lilliputian countryside from above. Now it stretched out on both sides into the distance, broken occasionally by streams and rivers bringing water down from melting snow and ice visible on the higher slopes. They also knew from their virtual preparation exercises there would be lakes to come and icier mountains to skirt but that it would be practically devoid of animals and vegetation. They would have liked to have detoured to check out the volcanic zone of recent eruption but it was too far out of their way and it could also at any time become a no-go zone. They had already spotted one of the Special Exploitation Zones in the distance with its pump towers and pipelines and knew there would be more of these, as well as the DormaZones where they would stay. ZzzZones, or Zeeszones they would discover it to be in the vernacular of those who worked in them. They had estimated the journey would take them five days at the high speed these new autos could do, so they would sleep over on four occasions. It was expensive, but they reckoned it would be a once-in-a-lifetime thing to realise, and with time on their hands now they had elderized, why not.

And so the starkness rolled past. They were able to lie back, relax, chat, eat and drink, even social network if they wanted to on the Aura's interconnective system, but they had decided not to while moving. They could take it all in from any position they chose as the vehicle looked after itself. The vistas were immense and comparable only with the great expanses of the North American deserts and prairies, Outback Australia, the Sahara, the Andes and the Siberian wilderness, all of which they had visited.

Yet this landscape had a special uniqueness. There was an other-worldly, newly-formed feel about it. They could be zooming across Mars, albeit a dry, more bluish and dustless one, or a moon of Jupiter. It was bleak, imposing, silent and barren. It confronted them with their sense of insignificance in a universe of such dimensions. They were also conscious of being living things in this otherwise lifeless world.

After two hours of travelling along the Payway, orientating themselves to their new and wondrous situation, they commanded the Aura to stop at the next way station so they could immerse themselves in the atmosphere they were just beginning to mentally absorb. The auto soon pulled off the main road and hummed its way along a side track to a parking area where it locked itself into a re-charge station. They jumped out quickly, stretched and twirled around in glee.

"Golly galactic!" shouted Josh out loud. "Just take a gander at those mountains, Jess. And that's a glacier there between those two monsters."

"It's just stunning, Josh. And clear as crystal. No cloud, no mist, no haze. What's your Spand-e-shux readout giving you?"

Josh telepathed the thought and checked his sleeve.

"99.7 for atmospheric purity. Crisp at -2 centigrade, and very dry. But peril level for UV."

"Same here. We might have to put some zinc cream on our noses if we stay out too long," she quipped and they both laughed.

They took a brief walk around the area, Josh scrabbling around in the rocks for a couple of samples, Jess simply embracing the scene, and they hopped back into the Aura and headed off again.

Another couple of hundred kilometres of gawking and gaping and the vehicle began to slow as its programmed first daily layover kicked in. Jessica and Joshua sat forward and prepared for the break from travelling as they pulled off onto a service road, then entered the DormaZone, the vehicle finding its way to the pre-booked pod, locking in and starting its recharge. They jumped out eagerly, stretching and checking out their layover space. Here now was some vegetative relief, albeit carefully landscaped and manifestly exotic. There were various cold-climate tree and bush varieties in a grassy park-like environment. Jess, the gardener, found some soil to poke around in.

"Hey Josh! Look at this soil. It's like a desert soil. Very pliable but not much in the way of organic matter. And they've got all sorts of watering methods in place. I bet they're putting fertilisers into the watering too."

"There are bugs here, look, so life follows life."

Other vehicles were pulling in to their own pods and there was a bustle of people unpacking and orientating themselves. Jessica could make out several languages being spoken. She'd had a linguochip embedded some years before and could aurally download the translations if she wanted to. She wasn't so interested just there and then though. She did pick up that there were Eurusskies, Islamians and Chongolians amongst them, by look and by sound, and this made her feel a little uneasy. She could discern the Americanos generally, but with almost everyone wearing Spand-e-shux it was not always clear-cut. The Africans with both their black skins and their colourful overclothes were standout easy. Josh had decided not to go with the implant and had stuck with old-fashioned virtual language learning programmes so it was always a bit of a competition between them when it came to meeting foreign speakers. Signage pointed to the Caterzone along a walking path one way and to the personal Dormapod areas the other. They followed the directions and tracked down their pod for the night's stayover. They nodded and gave the universal greeting "Hey!" to anyone they passed.

The pod was pleasant and comfortable. It had self-catering facilities and all the technological installations they would need for connecting to their medical and e-information updating and social networking sites. A pers-E-spex floor-to-ceiling touch panel in the recroom afforded a marvellous panoramic view. Josh looked in realtime over the stark, rocky landscape towards the rugged crags in the distance, now with some reds and paler shades merging with the earlier uniform, dull grey. They took turns to touch various spots on the screen to zoom in on particular features they wanted to check, expressing their wonderment with outbursts of delight, like children with a new toy. They could discern what looked like a few Special Exploitation Zones too, but they were well screened by earthworks.

Jessica tore herself away and went over to the techno-centre. She faced up to the ID-ifier for a retinal and shibboleth check to complete her medical survey and receive her regular neuro-bolst while taking a dry-douse, and then looked over the vegetallic pantry provisions on a screen.

"It seems deliscrumptious," she called across to Joshua who was still playing with the view, though it was now gradually dimming in harmony with the fading light from above.

"We could have a banquet by candle-light here, or try what's on offer in the Caterzone. What d'you prefer, Josh?"

"Let's eat together here. I'm just a little reluctant to mix with all those foreign cultures tonight. I'm feeling so invigorated and inspired by this environment, it would be romantilious to stay in together. Holy hothouse, Jess! Have you noticed this?"

Joshua was looking up at the ceiling where there was a pers-E-spex dome giving a fish-eye view of a night sky. It seemed like all the sparkle of the heavens, including a crescent moon, had been brought down to form a magical roof over their heads.

"Oh, Good Gates!" Jessica chimed in and they both stared at the vision with amazement, finding it difficult to accept that it could not possibly be real with the sun still high in the sky outside, as it would be through their whole trip.

Joshua portalled the e-Medicentre, did his techno-audit and update and received a slight cardio-rhythm correction while taking his vitameds, by which time the food was prepared. He gave his long, curly, thick hair a quick tousle. He was very proud of it after years of having shaved his dome as his hairline receded followed by the truly bald era. And so they did have a romantic dinner alone together in their pod that stopover, the Ovenwiz reconstituting a great smoked fishish entrée, a vegemeal roast with sides, a chocolatey dessert, and a rehydrated top-shelf Danish cabernet-malbec to wash it down and continue with afterwards. They settled in to enjoy a digintensed classic film-noir movie. The cuddling on the sofa followed its usual course to sexual playfulness and they finished the day in the sleep-pod, making gentle love, and then dozing off in each other's arms.

The programme in the Aura's computer woke them via their vidi-phones at the stipulated time and they readied themselves for another day's adventure. For the next three days, to their own pre-set timetable, they continued their cruise through that remarkable landscape. Around dark lakes and across turbid turquoise rivers, winding through bare mountain ranges with canyons and gullies and cliffs of a primordial ruggedness such as they had never witnessed before; far-flung plateaus and wide valleys under sunny, cloudless skies; stopping once each day to take a hike along prepared trails into hidden canyons, up along rushing rivers or around lakesides; resting at stop-over pods, dining, relaxing, making love at the end of each day's travel. Everything about the landscape seemed so new, so fresh, as if it had just been unwrapped from its clingfoil after arriving direct from the factory.

They had hardly spoken with anyone the whole time, the landscape had been so overwhelming, and it was that they had come for after all. The tourists had remained much the same mixture of cultures as at first. They had not come across any Britons or Australs, surprising given the populations involved. Occasionally they had glimpsed Special Exploitation Zones, which they had learnt, and now loved, to call Ess-Ee-Zees, and heard rumbling and thundery noises which they guessed were associated with them. They had seen quite a few wind turbines bunched together at intervals on ridges, and, sparkling in the distance, were what appeared to be solar collectors spread over large areas, though, being so flat, it was hard to tell how extensive they were. The big mines, it seemed, were well away to the east and west with completely independent infrastructures.

But mostly it was quiet and simply untouched and, in many ways, yes, sterile. Joshua had noticed on their last day, birds, which could have been gulls, flocking in the hills, perhaps nesting in safety there. He'd also spotted in some places a tussocky grass growing, which he assumed must have been brought as seeds on the wind, and he wondered whether it might be supporting some life amongst it, if life could have managed to migrate here yet somehow. Rats had always seemed to be the first to do that, he thought. Or was it humans? There would be more he surmised as nature took its course.

They had chosen to go back on one of the latest Dirigicraft Aerostats with wrap-around viewing, so getting window seats was no problem. It was quite a sight hovering just above ground level with its huge carbosil-surfaced sola-dome top glistening like an enormous lampshade. Boarding the craft tethered in the middle of a large field of crushed rock was more like boarding a cruise ship and they had no problems with their luggage weight limits. Not that this was much of a problem given the paucity of souvenirs to accumulate, but Josh had collected a variety of rocks along the way as usual. They each took a lounge chair facing straight out and settled in for the ride as the airship silently lifted off and rose before turning slightly and heading slowly away from land. As they flew-floated once again across the demarcation line between land and sea and out over that very dark inky-blue ocean, they could look back at the cliffs and waves and then into the distance, more and more as they climbed, at that rugged countryside they had traversed, and now believed they understood so much better. There was the sadness they always felt when something was over, cushioned by the happiness of the memories that would remain, and the prospect of reliving them for the benefit of others, and of course for the boasting kudos.

Two days later they were back on home ground, the airship delivering them very close to where they had started out from.

"Hi Grandma, hi-ya Gramps," said Zelna as she gave them

both hugs. "Glad to have you back. How was it?"

"Sweet! Out-of-this-world terrificulous, magnificentitious," said Josh laughing.

"Splendiferous, awesomeful," Jessica added.

"Oh, my Apple, what a place! Just perfect, natural, exhilarating natural beauty. We went from one side to the other, right across the middle. North coast to north coast. No choice with that. In the final analysis though, a little overwhelming, even intimidating. One week is enough. But wonderful, cool, clear summer weather the whole trip."

"And wicked nightlife!" Jessica quipped with a sly glance at Josh. "How lucky we are that it's been opened up for everyone now since The Big Thaw. You've got plenty of time to see it, Zelna, before the next Glacial brings The Big Chill. And you must!"

"Or maybe not if another volcano or two erupt and it's gone overnight," Josh added a cautionary note.

"Yeah, I do want to get there sometime, and you never know how suddenly things might change," Zelna said. "Just for now, though, 'fraid I've got grandmotherly duties to attend to. Freeda and Josh Jr. are completely tied up with work so I'm collecting the twins from the Educentre and taking them for the night. I'll drop you off at the Elder Zone on the way. Elderization for me can't come soon enough."

"The good ol' Ee-Zee," Josh drawled conspiratorially into Jessica's ear, and she smiled.

"How much has the index increased while we were away?"

"Oh, the standard predicted rise, about point-one of a millimetre daily, another 4 or 5 square kilometres of coastal lowland underwater at high tide. Another refugee turn-back crisis. As expected, nothing out of the ordinary."

Zelna grabbed a bag in each hand and headed towards the exit, calling back, "So, did you get to stand on the actual South

Pole then?"

"Yep, but only one of them," Josh replied. "We did a jig on the True Pole but we would have had to tread water to stand over the Magnetic one. Even with the warmer climate down there now, and the Spand-e-shux on high, it would still have been too darn cold for our liking. As for the third one, the Geomagnetic, well it seems to lead everyone a merry chase, and that would have been cuttin' capers too far!"

Joshua, as ever, could never resist a wisecrack.

Fitting in the Fittest

All the preparations were completed. The hard work had been done. It was simply now a matter of concluding the key final phase: the gathering. The old man emerged from his cabin, stood and watched, then walked around to the other side and stood again, shifting his gaze along the full circle of the horizon. He could detect rain clouds cumulating and knew it was time.

The figures started appearing in the distance soon after dawn. They approached from every direction, their indistinct forms gradually growing larger and larger until, at various points, different for each depending on their size, it became clear what each of them was. The, just when some came into perspective, new ones would appear as dark dots behind them.

Eventually the surrounding scene was one of sheer swarming movement, on all points of the compass. From near, and getting nearer, to afar, the swelling flurry converged on the centre where he waited patiently. There was no rushing, no unruliness, though all those feet pounding the earth had raised the distant dust that first announced the disturbance. Along with the voices chattering and calling and murmuring and bellowing, the wings flapping and buzzing and swishing, the pounding of paws and hooves and feet made a roar that grew and grew until it was intimidating in itself, simply as noise, and not by any design. It reminded him of a Roman legion coming over the crest of a hill, then advancing inexorably and menacingly downwards toward its target. Except in this case it was barely upwards to a slight hillock which stood out from the flat plain all around it and there was no malign intention.

He knew the gathering would go on throughout the day and then into the night, which would itself bring a whole new set of participants into the exercise. It was all unfolding as planned. He gave orders that commenced the final operations and threw himself into supervising the frantic activity, regularly taking gulps of strong red wine from a jug he carried with him as he paraded about. It proceeded in the gradual and ordered pattern that had taken years to organise and he congratulated himself on his foresight and diligence as it progressed steadily amidst the commotion.

Then it was done, almost suddenly it seemed, as dawn broke the following day. Quiet descended and stillness prevailed with little notice being given. But then as he was looking down from his commanding position onto the now vacant scene around him his gaze was drawn to the distance once again where various marsupial macropods from some remote region were thumping towards him, along with others he could not recognise or name waddling and scampering, fluttering and striding, apparently the long distance meaning their journey had taken them just that much longer.

Shouting questions and demands the old man ran from side to side and from end to end. It became clear that it would be impossible to fit the strange surplus animals in what room was left, and that therefore the whole enterprise was compromised. If all were to be included there was no other solution than to enlarge the ark somehow, but by those foreboding clouds there would be no time for that.

He castigated himself for his miscalculation. Yet there was one other way. Something would have to give, though not, he avowed, his wine barrels. He dropped to his knees and raised his hands in supplication and waited for some indication, an answer, a sign, a direction, anything that would absolve him from making such a judgment over the survival of others.

One of the new alien birds, of a stocky build with dark brown wings and a white head and breast and strong solid beaks, just at that moment began to let out a raucous rising cackle akin to laughter that filled the whole wide basin with its jollity, before descending into a satisfied gurgle.

That was enough. Reluctantly, and to his everlasting damnation perhaps, he wondered, he decided to favour the unusual latecomers; the scaly and feathery dinosaurs would have to go, they were simply too big, leaving only the smaller birds to represent them after the apocalypse. He gave orders for them to be disembarked and they complied without protest, wandering off once again into the distance, not comprehending the eternal ramifications of their acquiescence.

Thus, as the deluge began, Noah wept fittingly for the loss, and for his last-minute failure in what should have been this, his finest hour, causing him to doubt his faith and to question his purpose.

And so he stared out at the relentless downpour, and drank more wine.

The Winning Party

Quyen "Kuey" Nguyen sat forlornly watching the television broadcast of the election results as he had done on election nights so many times before. In his forties, he had been born in Vietnam and came as a refugee with his family when only a baby, starred academically and was now a top-shot lawyer.

As always a handful of supporters milled around, though nobody was particularly interested in the results; why would they be? The motley collection of candidates standing in a scattering of electorates around the country for the House of Representatives and the 40 quixotic hopefuls for the Senate were garnering the usual paltry number of votes.

Kuey wondered why these loyal followers continued year after year to throw themselves into the firing line and take inevitable defeat for the cause. And what was the cause? A fair go for everyone, justice and decent opportunities in life. But how? They were continually shifting ground on how they would achieve this. Still, their aim was always true.

Whatever the case, Kuey knew he had the numbers to take the party leadership after the election and he would persevere with the battle, however disheartening it sometimes became. He had a vision and he was committed. He was also very, very ambitious.

Krish Kumar, native-born with conservative Indian parents who had migrated separately then married by practical arrangement, came and sat down next to him.

"Same old, same old," he said, looking at the figures.

"Yep. But those people out there keep believing in us; we gotta do 'em right. And there's all the others that need us but don't realise it yet."

"But what can we do, we need more … we need new ideas, or a better marketing director."

"Well, we'll have me up front soon."

"And you need to bring something fresh with you to the mix."

"Perhaps so. As soon as this is over let's sit down and do some brainstorming. Meanwhile we can drown our sorrows."

Joining the others in the kitchen for some lighthearted banter and booze, they both knew however that something radical would need to be done if they were to make any headway in politics.

———

A month later the large group around the oval table came to order with Quyen Nguyen presiding. They covered various procedural motions then proceeded to dissect the election results and their campaign performance. They all agreed that the party's platform needed sprucing up, needed something novel to distinguish them from the rest. They had already taken up drug reform, the legalization of marijuana, though this was not something unique to them, and were moving towards supporting government control of other illicit substances.

Krish chipped in. "There's no joy in pushing climate change, everyone's on that bandwagon already."

"And they've all got copycat policies on health and aged care and defence and the rest," added Nikki, a defector from one of the major parties. "We need a big issue that's neglected … or not being properly handled."

"Free dental care …" Amy suggested. A single mother in her thirties, she had recently been to the dentist and was given a prognosis that would cost her a small fortune.

"Yeah, not bad, but small change and hardly going to start a publicity fire," Kuey said, throwing a wet blanket over it.

"Free beer," Krish said with a flourish.

They all laughed.

The matter of homelessness and its solution was brought up by Sondra, divorced, in her fifties, a welfare worker and struggling renter.

"This is an issue that requires some imaginative new policies, including on home ownership challenges for young people. There's already subsidies for deposits and loan assistance and so on but with prices as they are these days it's a drop in the ocean," she put to the meeting with some passion.

Finn, a more introverted type, also in his forties, raised his hand a little and people turned towards him.

"There have been several experimental trials around the world with the notion of guaranteed regular payments for everybody. Known as 'universal basic income'. We could take it on?"

"Yes, I've heard of them," Kuey said, "but they weren't particularly successful."

"True, and there're reasons for that, not least of which was they were only trials. It has to be implemented thoroughly, and with confidence and courage if it is to work. Or at least that's the theory."

"Even so, it seems a bit socialist, and dull, and we don't want to be burdened with either of those descriptions. But having said that, maybe we should look into it." Kuey showed interest.

"An academic bloke built on the idea and has taken it further, into the area of lump sums or some such. He's also added a twist about how to make it work. I'll find out more and report back."

The meeting broke up with lots of lively discussion as they hit the bar, a trestle table at the end of the room topped with plenty of bottles of cheap wine and a tub full of ice and beer, courtesy of retired teacher Rob, the dogsbody.

Finn went to work on his research later that night. He was a night owl and the internet never sleeps. What he discovered was an idea which seemed so outrageous at first, so bizarre, he was almost inclined to drop it completely and move on. But as he read further he started to believe an approach such as was being proposed to what is fundamentally an age-old and persistent blight on society, that of poverty and economic inequality, had some merit. And in particular it was the sort of creative, left-field thinking that the party was looking for to draw attention and gain the spotlight.

At the next meeting of the party committee Finn outlined the concept as he had researched it. Finally, in summary, he said, speaking quietly and deliberately:

"It is a proposition to ensure financial security for everybody by providing enough funds through lottery prizes for all who need it to purchase a comfortable home."

There was a period of silence once Finn had finished as the idea sank in and the shock subsided.

Lin Huang broke the silence. She was fifth-generation Chinese-Australian with parents who had a work ethic based on self-sufficiency and determination.

"That's crazy, utter nonsense," she scoffed.

"Exactly what I thought at first," Finn said.

"You can't build serious policy proposals on the basis of luck or lotteries."

"A reasonable reaction," Quyen intervened. He had been given a briefing by Finn before the meeting and had immediately seen potential in the idea. "But it is not quite so revolutionary or unprecedented as you suggest. Remember, not so long ago, the New Zealand government used a lottery to choose who might be allowed to return home from overseas during the covid pandemic."

"And right here in Australia there was a lottery draw, dubbed the 'Death Lottery' by some, based on your birthday, to determine who would be called up for military service during the war in Vietnam. I lost that one, or won it you might say! My lucky day, 23rd April. Still haven't been there, must do so soon, eh Kuey? I hear it's nice, changed a lot since then."

Alan Thorley was the oldest on the committee and liked to bring some historical perspective as well as flippancy to the discussions whenever he could. Like Nikki he'd defected from another party, disillusioned with their constant in-fighting, and lousy sense of humour.

"But how's it going to be funded? Sounds very cargo-cultish." Nikki was sceptical, and practical.

"Theoretically it will fund itself," said Finn, having prepared for the question. "There'll be savings - social security payments, for example - and a special tax impost could even be welcomed knowing that it was going to be returned as prize-money. There'll be our new drug excise income. It should also act as an economic stimulus: pay somebody to dig holes, then pay somebody else to fill them in, increase demand, multiplier effect. The building industry would explode with new projects."

"Keynes," Alan nodded knowingly.

"And keep in mind enormous sums were paid out to prop up financial institutions during the GFC, and then even more for people to stay at home during the pandemic."

"Why not just hand out the money to the needy and be done with it?" Nikki's practicality reared again.

Kuey was ready for that one. "No fun in that. Sliced flat white bread in a brown bag as opposed to fluffy chocolate cake with candles. Same calories. We have to make it appealing and exciting. And we don't want to be accused of being commies."

Finn went on: "Lotteries have traditionally also been run and controlled by governments until the economic rationalists took over and privatised everything within reach. But there is still a lot of experience and tradition in this country in the running of government lotteries."

"It's the case worldwide in fact. Governments, generally speaking, run lotteries," said Sondra, warming to the idea.

"What about the gambling angle? There's a strengthening community push against gambling because of the damage caused by addiction." Amy had known a gambler, someone close, and was intimately aware of its dangers.

Finn had prepared for this one too through that omniscient night-owl internet route.

"Most people don't regard lotteries as gambling, Amy. It's looked upon more as an integral part of normal daily life. Go to the shops, get some bread, milk, eggs, newspaper and a lottery ticket. You know, eight million Australians buy a lottery ticket in any year, and half of those over 50 regularly indulge. And they're all voters."

"I buy lottery tickets, and I vote," Krish joined in. This was right up his alley. He weighed in:

"So, we could expect a favourable response from almost half the electorate and at least a synpathetic response from a large section of the other half who might benefit. Especially if we keep the details a bit vague at first while we build our public profile. Home ownership for example in the 25 to 44 year-old cohort has dropped a lot in the last few years, so there's another pool of a few million voters. This will appeal to young people seeking their first home and older people, either to underpin a comfortable later life if they're needy, or save them from having to bankroll their kids if they're comfortable. I'm liking the numbers."

General commotion broke out as everyone became increasingly excited.

Quyen tapped the table for order.

"Okay. This has legs. Let's get a sub-committee onto it for details and give it a run in the park. We'll need ready responses to the crap that will be hurled at it from the other pollies and the academics. The usual claptrap they throw at every new idea - how it's nonsense, unworkable, and the rest."

"You know, there was a pollie once who said we could fuel all our cars with water and got a drubbing for his vision, you may remember? And now? A major hydrogen-from-water clean fuel industry in the offing." Alan injected an historical pivot again.

"It certainly will differentiate us," Kuey continued. "It's all about individual autonomy, if not effort. We'll just throw in the motherhood policies to go with it: universal health insurance, the US-British alliance, strong defence, improved aged care, superannuation guarantee, tax the rich, first nations rights and reconciliation, climate action, integrity in government, women's issues, free dental if you like, whatever. What's more, it sounds like fun … put some fun, and luck, into politics, could be a winner. Anyway, what've we got to lose?"

"The Winning Party," Alan piped in.

They all looked at him, smiling.

Various media outlets and internet sites one week later:

The new leader of the old Fair Go Party, Mr. Quyen Nguyen, last night announced its re-formation and re-naming as the Winning Party. In doing so he offered as the main plank of the new party's platform the policy of ABC - Aggregated Basic Capital.

This innovative programme, he said, would be implemented by a series of national lotteries which would result in all those in financial need achieving the status of home-ownership within the shortest possible time. That is, Mr. Nguyen promised, the period of two electoral cycles, or six years from the time they formed government.

Details would be released as the policy was unrolled over the next few months but it was believed each lottery would have substantial prizes and that there would be a large number of winners on a regular basis.

He said the party would be in a position to offer a full outline of the plan by the time of the next election as part of its overall election pitch.

The party has previously secured between 1.5% to 3.0% of first preference votes in various local, state and federal elections over the last few years but has never secured representation in any parliament or council. Mr. Nguyen claims this will all now change with its new strategy of wealth redistribution without wealth diminution.

"Our new policy to eliminate poverty and bring about greater financial equality in our country," Mr. Nguyen said, "is as easy as ABC, but will bring about the greatest benefit to society since the equal-pay-for-women victory 60 years ago, perhaps even since the basic wage Harvester Judgment of 1907."

"Our vision is the next logical step for economic justice," he said. "A perfect example of aligning the common good with individual advancement through financial autonomy."

There was no immediate reaction to Quyen Nguyen's statement from any of the other political parties or commentators, though social media was abuzz with chatter.

Within days a viral firestorm had erupted across multiple social media platforms with cries of fake news and accusations ranging from creeping socialism to fiscal dictatorship. Those in favour simply demanded to know where they could buy a ticket, and those voices were increasing exponentially.

The mainstream media soon picked up the story and began

reporting on the breathtaking new proposal. The reaction was as expected and forewarned. All the political parties condemned it as irresponsible and dangerous. Political pundits poured scorn on its naiveté. Almost all academic economists and commentators shot it down in flames in language that had no negative impact whatsoever on its popular reception. None of it had any effect on dampening interest in the possibilities of instant wealth. It was all music to the ears of members of the new Winning Party. The kerfuffle was everything they had hoped for.

There was, however, one exception to the outcry. In a restrained, old-fashioned paper press release sent through the post to a select number of newspapers, Professor Simon de Nursas, the Italian-born econometrician who had spent most of his professional life quietly and painstakingly working out of Harvard University, author of the seminal work in the field, *Winning Equality*, wrote as follows:

There is, or should be, little or no dissent amongst economic scientists that the elimination of severe poverty is the primary goal of our work, and the reduction of all poverty generally the major focus.

Only when this is achieved can humanity live without the suffering, hardship and uncertainty which poverty brings with it, lives of quiet desperation, either directly, or indirectly in the form of war, social unrest, ill-health and environmental degradation.

Once conquered we can then turn our attention to the next challenge, which is the pursuit of further economic equality and the fair redistribution of wealth.

I believe that both goals can be achieved in general unison by the notion of a Universal Basic Income, and its extension, what I am calling an Aggregate Basic Capital, that is, a minimum amount of assets that each individual in a society owns.

It is a very straightforward concept, indeed as simple as ABC, and I believe it can best be achieved not by simple handouts from government but by individuals winning financial security through lotteries, gradually, over a relatively short period of time. The amount

of prize money involved would be approximately the median price
of a modest house in the community, or whatever economic unit it
entails.

It was a stunning affirmation of the party's position though
it had not come without some gentle nudging via various useful
contacts certain party members kept in their inveiglement quivers.
Once again controversy raged but it was too late. The dream of
freedom from financial hardship had lodged firmly in the public's
imagination, and was not going to be easily dislodged.

In the first opinion poll taken after the policy's release and
general circulation the Winning Party had leapfrogged to third
most supported political organisation, and 'financial security'
had surged to second place after 'climate action'.

Now it was going to get hard. The party would have to
hammer out the details while at the same time remaining not too
precise about the process.

The sub-committee met and in a mood of runaway
enthusiasm fuelled by rampaging success came up with an
initial plan. They were now also being aided by a number of
amateur, though no less expert, economists who had gleefully
come forward to lend a hand. Ex-Treasury bureaucrats with
careers curtailed or ambitions frustrated by previous conservative
government policies, retired academics with axes to grind over
rejected or purloined theories, computer geeks who just liked to
grind the numbers for any hairbrained enterprise.

They decided their opening gambit would be simple and
easy to digest and just as easy to remember. Each lottery would
have 3 prizes of $100,000, $200,000 and $700,000 dollars, a
total payout of one million dollars. There would be one thousand
lotteries drawn each and every day of the year for a total outlay
of 365 billion dollars per year. In the first term of a Winning
Party government there would be one million new homeowners
drawn from those who otherwise would not find it possible.
There would be a further two million receiving a significant and

life-changing financial boost. Tickets would be free and assigned by computer-generated algorithms from a new section created within the social security departments to those selected from taxation, unemployment and other records of income and assets. Registration for tickets by those eligible outside the system would also be available. First prize could only be won once, but the minor prizes would not disqualify winners from further entry. Selection would begin with those deemed most needy and work upwards.

The sub-committee chose to go no further than this rough outline at that stage. They thought it best to throw some morsels to the hungry hordes and gauge the response. They would not mention issues like funding the scheme, dealing with fraud and errors, or selection criteria apart from the vague reference to need. There would be a time for all that.

The response was immediate and mixed. The same critics as before blasted and lampooned the proposals bringing down all manner of condemnation on it and its purveyors. But the next opinion poll had the Winning Party in second place with a 32% approval rating from all sectors of the electorate. It seemed even the rich could find some benefit to them from the concept either as a painless way of spreading the wealth, salving their consciences over those living amongst them in lesser circumstances, or just keeping society on an even keel so they could go on being rich securely.

It was time for Quyen to step forward and take the initiative. The new government, only recently elected, had fallen to third place in the polls and was showing signs of panic. Nevertheless, it had almost three years to attack the proposals, make counter-proposals and recover. Unless, of course, the government could be brought down early. If the momentum of the policy's initial burst of success could be maintained and built upon perhaps there would be opportunities. There were, for example, four state elections coming up. Incoming newly-elected Winning Party state governments calling for immediate implementation of the scheme nationwide would be very destabilising.

Quyen began a tour of the country, speaking at meetings and giving media interviews. He was in great demand and he was happy to oblige. He was very mindful of the dangers of revealing too much of the plan, though in reality there was not much more to reveal. Journalists and commentators constantly pressured him for more details about how the scheme would function but he was adept at palming them off, reiterating its simplicity and returning over and over to other policies of the party, while leaving the lottery policy dangling tantalisingly in full view.

Party membership had boomed, some joining no doubt in the hope of having an inside run for the lottery, and a complete restructuring of the party's organisation to reflect its expansion had been put into effect. State divisions were primed for electoral campaigning, and candidates endorsed for every corner of the country.

Krish had taken leadership of the party in the country's largest state in preparation for an upcoming election. It was also the section of the country where the housing pressure was most critical due to the high prices and overheated market. Polling showed the party had every chance of taking government, so Krish and his team were ramming home the lottery proposal. Though it was only a national government which could truly fulfil the scheme's full potential, they were offering a mini-version to kick it off: just one lottery per day until the national scheme took over.

That was enough. It was a landslide win. Krish was the premier of the state and he had a mandate for all the party's policies and only a minor responsibility towards the lottery proposal. They would have to tread with care so as not to risk failure with it, but because of its limited nature that would not be too difficult, plus it would provide a good deal of opportunity for trialing.

It was in any case only the early swelling of a popular

tsunami. Reading the political signs anxiously, six members of the government party and four independents in the national parliament joined the Winning Party, giving it instant parliamentary representation. The opposition, with the new Winning Party in support, was in a position to bring down the government.

And so it did. They were just ahead in the polls and surmised they could still achieve government, and that it was best to do so before the lottery scheme took even more hold of the public's imagination once it was up and running in the state where the Winning Party was now the government.

But they couldn't. The momentum was with Quyen, Krish and their party of winners. They barnstormed the country, campaigning on the lottery concept of financial security and a new equality, keeping the battle cry simplistic with a repetition of the slogan - 'One thousand winners a day, every day' - and avoiding any engagement over the fine print.

They won, of course. Quyen Nguyen was the country's first Vietnamese Prime Minister, and he assumed the role with relish. The ABC lottery was not top on his list of priorities from then on. He was happy to have had it as the vehicle for overall success. They now had an army of experts - bureaucrats, academics, advisers - and foot soldiers to carry it forward.

Even so, it took six months for the first day of lotteries to take place. The publicity leading up to it was intense, but nothing by comparison to what followed after the draws. Media crews tracked down winners all over the country, personal stories of hardship and then salvation were featured, lights lit up on maps showing all the locations where the prizes had gone. Day after day it accumulated until the entire country looked like a satellite photo taken at night, glowing with pride and contentment.

This continued for the remainder of the first Winning Party government. The economy boomed. New housing projects were everywhere, having sprung up as soon as the party had won government, in anticipation of the good times ahead. The housing rental market had nosedived as more and more renters became home owners, countered by rental housing investors selling up fueled by the same economic pressures. Problems with the scheme began to manifest themselves - many seethed with envy for not making the cut because of their own successful efforts to accumulate wealth over the years; anger fermented in those left out because of bureaucratic bungling and ineptitude, or from integral weaknesses of the plan; fudging and outright fraud increased; unemployment soared through people giving up work to become eligible, bank accounts were drained for the same reason.

None of this particularly concerned the new government. They quietly buried damaging information that was emerging, shrugged off criticism, patched up holes in the legislation and simply relied on the widespread support the scheme enjoyed for smoothing its progress.

The re-election of such a popular government was a foregone conclusion. The Winning Party controlled both houses of the parliament to an extent rarely before witnessed. They could do anything they wanted, within the constitution naturally. Quyen Nguyen bestrode the political landscape in the style of a modern antipodean, cornucopian colossus. Interest in the scheme had extended beyond the country's shores and similar policies had been adopted by several political bodies internationally with the firm likelihood of replication. Professor Simon de Nursas was nominated for the Nobel prize in Economic Sciences for his studies into poverty and contribution to overcoming social inequality,

The party took the opportunity provided by the distracting publicity over the lottery to pass legislation to legalise and control various recreational drugs for personal use (with a welcome injection of funds for the budget), for the establishment of a nuclear industry and a monopoly over new hydrogen fuel production in the cause of climate change (with the prospect of more funds flowing in from licensing and royalties), for a super tax on the rich, and the multinationals and, ironically, on all other forms of gambling (more for the treasury), the re-imposition of death duties and an increase in the general consumer tax (still more in the coffers), not to mention the special lucky-lottery surcharge tax as had been quietly hinted at during campaigning (even more for the budget's healthy bottom line).

They increased ministerial salaries and emoluments and found it was essential to travel overseas often, on fact-finding missions and in order to cement security and trade ties with select nations. Radical electoral reform was in the pipeline.

Amidst this euphoric political atmosphere the leaders, the team, the government, the whole party neglected to consider the final upshot, that is, the lottery scheme would eventually create a society where most, indeed all who wanted it, were no longer financially needy. After almost five years of the scheme operating, nearly two million people had received the top prize enabling them to be unencumbered home owners, and a further three to four million had received substantial sums, enough for most to have enough for a deposit and mortgage on a home.

Eligibility had been progressively extended to where it was now at the point of exhaustion as far as being 'needy' could be defined. Polling was reflecting this as the Winning Party's approval rating showed steady decline. Voters are always happy to support policies which promise them benefits, but their gratitude afterwards is short-lived as they re-align their loyalties.

Faced with the real possibility of losing the next election, Quyen called a special meeting of the inner-circle committee, re-named the steering committee. Most of the original members were still on it though they were now well-paid ministers, premiers or top bureaucrats, but their number had been swelled by newcomers as the party grew and matters became more complex.

With Prime Minister Nguyen presiding, they all agreed that

their platform needed sprucing up, needed something novel to distinguish them from the rest again.

"Nothing left to wring out of public housing measures or entrenched unemployment," Finn, the Finance Minister, offered cheerfully.

"And they've stolen our policies on health and aged care, drugs, taxes and energy and the rest," added Nikki, now the Minister for Foreign Affairs. "We need a big issue that's new and exciting, something out of the box."

Alan, special adviser emeritus to the Minister for Veterans Affairs, piped up.

"Annex New Zealand … and Papua New Guinea? They *were* both ours once. And Eastern Antarctica, it's ours already. We'd have the world's largest Exclusive Economic Zone, second largest land mass, and the continental shelves would give us sovereignty over the largest area on earth. Call it Austranzica."

There was a brief silence.

"We will need a marked increase in military spending, a space program and a nuclear capacity," Lin Huang, the Minister of Defence, mused.

"A win-win situation," Quyen Nguyen declared.

They all looked at each other, and smiled.

Home and Hosed

It was a dark and stormy night outside as Mickey sat at his computer, head in hands, tormented by words: words that had been used millions of times before, and often in the same sequence. But he couldn't shake it off, he was in pain. Still, you can't look a gift horse in the mouth, he reminded himself. An advance was an advance was an advance in any language.

Yes, his tail may have been lodged firmly between his legs but he was determined not to get his knickers in a knot about it. Chin up, he told himself, every cloud had a silver lining. But just at this moment, for Mickey, the writing was rather on the wall than on his screen. Up popped "time flies" in his head as he watched the clock tick away, but he certainly wasn't having much fun. He knew all too well that time healed most wounds, and hopefully writer's blocks too. Even so, he felt he was all thumbs in that normally razor-sharp brain of his. Damn, there was another one, they just kept coming, as thick as treacle, or was that thieves.

He told his literary subconscious: Be silent and still, just get a grip on yourself and all will be well when it ends, erm, well. Somewhere at the end of his personal rainbow there would be a heart-shaped gesture of thumbs and forefingers to give him the thumbs-up. He would again feel that golden glow of success, that warm fuzzy feeling, like a delicate perfume, as he had done before, once upon a time. He would not buckle under the pressure but would instead buckle down and put his shoulder to the wheel and, um, nose to the grindstone. Damn it again!

Mickey knew as much as anyone that fact was stranger than fiction. Perhaps there lay his creative salvation. Better safe than sorry. If he was going to be saddled with this cliché-ridden commission he would saddle up and ride it with verve, as roughshod as that may prove. Then, in the blink of an eye the penny dropped. He would tell his own story, his way.

"When I was just a boy," Mickey pounded frantically, "I met a girl named Mary. Romance was on the menu, love in the air. I would go all soft and doughy in her presence and before I knew it I had fallen head over heels in love with her. But love hurts and soon enough the tide had turned. I found her in the arms of another man. Oh, how blind love can be! Still, I was not going to throw in the towel. I would do or die. Hope sprang eternal. Once more I entered into the fray and gave her an offer she couldn't refuse: a ring of gold. We kissed and made up. Love conquered all, and set me free! We both lived happily ever after, of course."

Mickey gave a big sigh of relief and looked up.

Done and dusted.

Well, so far, so good, anyway.

But never again!

The End.